THARG'S FUTURE-SHOCKS

DEFINITELY ZARJAZ!

04 'Ang About! Prog 221
Kelvin Gosnell | Eric Bradbury | Tony Jacob

09 Diversion Prog 222
Kelvin Gosnell | Colin Wilson | Tony Jacob

11 The Machine! Prog 224
Kelvin Gosnell | Jesus Redondo | Tony Jacob

16 Seeing is Believing! Prog 225
Kelvin Gosnell | Colin Wilson | Peter Knight

22 Scrambled Eggs Prog 226
Alan Hebden | Garry Leach | Bill Nuttall

24 Giant Leap! Prog 230
Kelvin Gosnell | Jesus Redondo | Steve Potter

27 The Red House Prog 231
Steve Moore | Jesus Redondo | Peter Knight

30 The Regrettable Ruse Of Rocket Redglare!
Alan Moore | Mike White | Steve Potter Prog 234

36 Once Upon An Atom... Prog 235
Steve Moore | Alan Langford | Steve Potter

39 Sign Of The Times Prog 235
Alan Hebden | Mike White | Jack Potter

42 Space To Let! Prog 236
Kelvin Gosnell | Tony Jozwiak | Jack Potter

46 A Little Problem Prog 237
Steve Moore | J. Johnson | Jack Potter

51 A Cautionary Fable Prog 240
Alan Moore | Paul Neary | Steve Potter

56 The Masks Of Arazzor Prog 241
Steve Moore | José Casanovas | Bill Nuttall

61 Joe Black's Tall Tale! Prog 241
Kelvin Gosnell | John Higgins | Tony Jacob

64 Love Thy Neighbour! Prog 242
Kelvin Gosnell | Jesus Redondo | Steve Potter

67 Mister, Could You Use A Squonge? Prog 242
Alan Moore | Ron Tiner | T. Skomski

73 A Second Chance! Prog 245
Alan Moore | José Casanovas | Jack Potter

75 Twist Ending Prog 246
Alan Moore | Paul Neary | Tony Jacob

78 Salad Days! Prog 247
Alan Moore | John Higgins | Jack Potter

80 Horn Of Plenty! Prog 248
Kelvin Gosnell | John Higgins | Peter Knight

84 The Beastly Beliefs Of Benjamin Blint
Alan Moore | Eric Bradbury | Peter Knight Prog 249

86 Now You See It... Prog 250
Alan Hebden | Eric Bradbury | Tony Jacob

89 All Of Them Were Empty Prog 251
Alan Moore | Paul Neary | Peter Knight

91 The Hume Factor! Prog 252
Kelvin Gosnell | John Higgins | Peter Knight

96 An American Werewolf In Space! Prog 252
Alan Moore | Paul Neary | Tony Jacob

99 The Bounty Hunters! Prog 253
Alan Moore | John Higgins | Tony Jacob

102 Voyage Of Discovery! Prog 255
Chris Stevens | Eric Bradbury | Tony Jacob

106 Joe Black's Big Bunco! Prog 256
Kelvin Gosnell | John Higgins | Bill Nuttall

111 The Wages Of Sin!! Prog 257
Alan Moore | Bryan Talbot | Tony Jacob

117 The Lanulos Run! Prog 258
David Perry | Jesus Redondo | Tony Jacob

124 Nigel Goes A-Hunting! Prog 259
Alan Grant | Jesus Redondo | Tony Jacob

127 Alec Trench - Zombie! Progs 263-264
Alan Grant | Ron Smith | Tony Jacob

137 Return Of The Thing! Prog 265
Alan Moore | Dave Gibbons | Tony Jacob

139 Skirmish! Prog 267
Alan Moore | Dave Gibbons | Tony Jacob

141 The Martians Prog 274
David Perry | Jesus Redondo | Bill Nuttall

142 The Writing On The Wall! Prog 268
Alan Moore | Jesus Redondo | Tony Jacob

144 The Wild Frontier! Prog 269
Alan Moore | Dave Gibbons | Unknown

146 The Big Day Prog 270
Alan Moore | Robin Smith | Tom Frame

148 One Christmas During Eternity! Prog 271
Alan Moore | Jesus Redondo | Tom Frame

150 No Picnic! Prog 272
Alan Moore | John Higgins | Tom Frame

152 The Disturbed Digestions Of Doctor Dibworthy
Alan Moore | Dave Gibbons | Steve Potter Prog 273

155 Sunburn Prog 282
Alan Moore | Jesus Redondo | Jack Potter

160 Sid! Prog 286
Alan Grant | Brett Ewins | Tony Jacob

163 Beware The Men In Black! Prog 286
David Perry | Jesus Redondo | Tony Jacob

169 The War Game Prog 287
Alan Grant | Jim Eldridge | Peter Knight

172 Bad Timing Prog 291
Alan Moore | Mike White | Paul Bensberg

Abelard Snazz

177 The Double Decker-Dome Strikes Back
Alan Moore | Mike White | P. Knight & J. Potter Progs 237-238

187 Halfway To Paradise Prog 245
Alan Moore | John Cooper | Tony Jacob

193 The Multi-Storey Mind Mellows Out!
Alan Moore | Paul Neary | Tony Jacob Prog 254

198 Genius Is Pain Prog 299
Alan Moore | Mike White | Jack Potter

THARG'S FUTURE-SHOCKS

CONTENTS

TIME TWISTERS

204 **William The Conkerer** Prog 294
Alan Grant | Eric Bradbury | Tim Skomski

207 **Ultimate Video** Prog 295
Roy Preston | José Casanovas & Jr. | Jack Potter

211 **The Star** Prog 297
Chris Lowder | Massimo Belardinelli | Peter Knight

215 **Family Trees** Prog 298
Alan Hebden | John Higgins | Peter Knight

EXTRA SHOCKS - PROGS

221 **Last Thought** Prog 202
Steve MacManus | John Higgins | Peter Knight

223 **Superbean** Prog 245
John Wagner | Mick McMahon | Steve Potter

229 **Agent Rat: Trouble In Tree-World** Progs 273-274
Steve Moore | Alan Langford | Jack Potter

237 **Hot Item** Prog 278
Alan Moore | John Higgins | Jack Potter

242 **The Great Detective Caper** Progs 289-290
Jack Adrian | John Higgins | Steve Potter

250 **Homer the Barbarian** Prog 296
Alan Grant | Massimo Belardinelli | Peter Knight

EXTRA SHOCKS - ANNUALS & SPECIALS

256 **Benny's Tale** *2000 AD* Annual 1980
Unknown | David Jackson | Unknown

261 **Going Straight** *2000 AD* Annual 1980
Unknown | José Ferrer | Unknown

266 **The Man Who Saved The World** *2000 AD* Annual 1980
Unknown | Unknown | Unknown

271 **Duel In The Dunes** *2000 AD* Annual 1981
Oleh Stepaniuk | Rob Moran | John Aldrich

277 **The Man From 2000** *2000 AD* Annual 1981
Oleh Stepaniuk | David Hine | Steve Potter

283 **The Mumps From Beyond The Moon** *2000 AD* Annual 1981
Alan Grant | Robin Smith | Jack Potter

288 **The Last Of The First Ones!** *2000 AD* Annual 1982
Gary Rice | Colin Wilson | Tom Frame

292 **First Encounter** *2000 AD* Sci-Fi Special 1979
Oleh Stepaniuk | Alan Craddock | S. Richardson

294 **The Last Jungle In The World** *2000 AD* Sci-Fi Special 1979
Alan Grant | N. Neocleous | Peter Knight

298 **The Prisoner From Xendor** *Starlord* Annual 1980
Unknown | Unknown | Unknown

304 **The Exterminator** *Starlord* Annual 1982
Unknown | Unknown | Unknown

312 **3000AD The Traveller** *Dan Dare* Annual 1980
Unknown | Dave Gibbons | Unknown

GALLERY

316 **Alan Moore's Shocking Futures***
Alan Moore

318 **Tharg The Mighty**
Henry Flint

319 **Shocking Futures**
Kevin O'Neill

320 **Tharg The Welder - Star Scan** Prog 215
Robin Smith

* *Alan Moore's Shocking Futures* article originally published by Titan Books in 1986.

AUGUST 1981. PHYSICIST BILL REED MAKES A STARTLING DISCOVERY...
OF COURSE! SO SIMPLE AND YET THE KEY TO OUR FIRST CONTACT WITH AN ALIEN LIFEFORM...

THERE'S NOTHING TO FEAR. I-I KNOW WHAT YOU ARE. I WANT TO BE YOUR FRIEND.
CLINK
CLINK

BUT...
MY THROAT. GET OFF! AAAAAH!

THARG'S FUTURE-SHOCKS
'ANG ABOUT!

THE FOLLOWING DAY, REED'S GRUESOME DEATH WAS INVESTIGATED AS MURDER...
TELL ME AGAIN, JIM. WHAT DID THE DOC SAY...?
HE SAID HE'D BEEN SHOT, STRANGLED AND STABBED-- ALL AT ONCE. BUT THERE'S NO TRACE OF ANY WEAPONS, OR BULLETS!
2000 A.D. Credit Card:
SCRIPT ROBOT KELVIN GOSNELL
ART ROBOT ERIC BRADBURY
LETTERING ROBOT TONY JACOB
COMPU-73E

AND NOTHING'S BEEN NICKED EITHER. THOUGHT THIS SORT OF THING ONLY HAPPENED IN AGATHA CHRISTIE NOVELS.

GETTING SOME STRONG PRINTS FROM THE WINDOW, GUV.
OKAY – GET 'EM PROCESSED AND IDENTIFIED. **AND** GET YOUR LAB TO CHECK EVERYTHING ELSE IN THIS ROOM. THE ANSWER'S HERE SOMEWHERE, I'M SURE OF IT.

LATER, AT THE POLICE STATION...
ER– MR ALLEN? THEY'VE ID'd THOSE PRINTS – THEY BELONG TO ONE BENNY REILLY. HE'S IN THE CELLS ALL READY FOR YOU...
TERRIFIC. ME AND BENNY HAD BETTER HAVE A FEW WORDS...

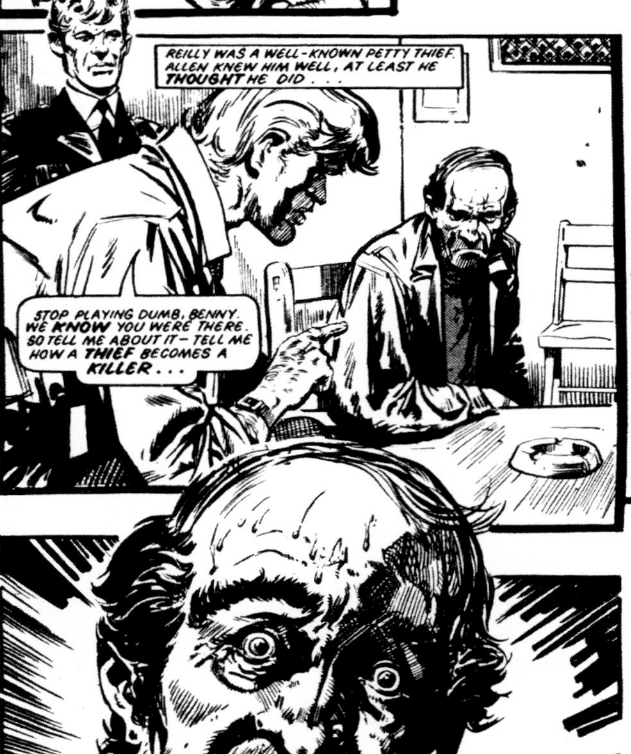
REILLY WAS A WELL-KNOWN PETTY THIEF. ALLEN KNEW HIM WELL, AT LEAST HE **THOUGHT** HE DID...
STOP PLAYING DUMB, BENNY. WE **KNOW** YOU WERE THERE. SO TELL ME ABOUT IT – TELL ME HOW A **THIEF** BECOMES A **KILLER**...
I-I **CAN'T** TELL YOU, MR ALLEN. THE **MAN** – THE **DEAD** MAN! **HE** KNEW WHAT THEY WERE. HE **TALKED** TO 'EM. THEY **DID THINGS** TO 'IM. KILLED 'IM **BADLY**, MR ALLEN.

I-I AIN'T KILLED NO-ONE, MR ALLEN. I WAS UP THERE TO SUSS THE PLACE OUT. HONEST I WAS. I WAS AT THE WINDOW AND –AND I **SAW** 'EM, MR ALLEN.
SAW **WHAT**, BENNY?

D-DON'T LET 'EM DO THOSE **THINGS** TO ME, MR ALLEN. DON'T LET 'EM **NEAR** ME. **PLEASE. PLEASE!**
GET THE DOC DOWN HERE! I WANT HIM SEDATED!

NONE OF THIS MAKES SENSE! BENNY AIN'T A KILLER BUT HE MUST HAVE SEEN WHOEVER DID KILL REED AND THAT'S SENT HIM OFF HIS ROCKER. I'LL HEAD DOWN TO FORENSIC— AT LEAST JIM DEALS IN HARD FACTS!
SO, ALLEN MADE FOR THE LAB WHERE REED'S BELONGINGS WERE BEING EXAMINED . . .
JIM? WHERE ARE YOU? DON'T TELL ME HE'S HOPPED OFF FOR LUNCH ALREADY..
FORENSIC
GOOD GRIEF!
DEAD— FROM THE SAME BRUTAL BLUDGEONING THAT KILLED REED. EVERYTHING'S GETTING MORE AND MORE IMPOSSIBLE!
AT THAT MOMENT, A SCREAM FROM THE ROOM ABOVE DRAGGED ALLEN'S ATTENTION UPWARDS...
GETAWAYFROMME!!!
NOOOOOOOO!
WHAT IN HELL..?
AAAAARGH!

BENNY! NOW HE'S DEAD AS WELL! EITHER I'M GOIN' CRAZY OR THERE'S SOME SORT OF INVISIBLE HOMICIDAL MANIAC ON THE LOOSE IN THIS NICK!

THIS IS MADNESS! THEY KILLED BENNY TO STOP HIM TALKING - BUT WHY OLD JIM? UNLESS...

...UNLESS HE HAD DISCOVERED SOMETHING. THAT TAPE RECORDER - WE TOOK IT FROM REED'S FLAT. JIM MUST HAVE BEEN PLAYING IT WHEN THEY GOT HIM...

ONLY ONE WAY TO FIND OUT...
THEY'LL SAY I'M MAD - I KNOW THEY WILL. BUT I KNOW I'M RIGHT - I KNOW THERE'S ANOTHER LIFEFORM, AN ALIEN LIFEFORM ON THIS PLANET. CIRCUM-STANCIAL EVIDENCE POINTS TO IT EVERYWHERE I LOOK.

I CALCULATE THAT WE HAVE BEEN UNDER OBSERVATION BY THESE CREATURES FOR HALF A CENTURY. THERE MUST BE THOUSANDS, MILLIONS OF THEM ON EARTH. THEY ARE MASTERS OF CAMOUFLAGE AND HAVE PROBABLY PENETRATED OUR HOMES IN A COMPLETELY INNOCENT-LOOKING FORM...

GRIEF! SO IT'S LITTLE GREEN MEN! NOW I KNOW I'M GOING MAD!
THIS IS IT! I HAVE THE CLUES I NEED. I HAVE DISCOVERED THE CREATURES' PERFECT CAMOUFLAGE - THERE ARE MILLIONS OF THEM IN CIRCULATION YET NO FACTORIES MAKING THEM. THEY WERE NEVER INVENTED - THEY JUST STARTED APPEARING AFTER THE WAR. THEY ARE BREEDING ALL THE TIME. I AM GOING TO MAKE AN ATTEMPT TO COMMUNICATE...

ALLEN LOOKED UP—HIS EYES FIXED ON A PILE OF METAL CLOTHES HANGERS...
NO—IT COULDN'T BE! COULD IT? THEY WOULD MAKE WOUNDS LIKE ·22 SLUGS, AND THEY COULD BE USED AS STABBING WEAPONS...
AND TH-THEY WOULD MAKE THE NECK WOUNDS WE SAW...
OH NO! NO! NOOOO!
AAAAAAARGH!
KLIK!
ERASE
SO ENDS MY FUTURE SHOCK FOR THIS PROG. A LITTLE FAR FETCHED, PERHAPS, EVEN FOR THRILL-POWERED 2000 AD? WELL—GO TO YOUR WARDROBE AND COUNT THE NUMBER OF METAL HANGERS THERE AND THEN CHECK IT AGAIN ABOUT A WEEK LATER. MANY OF YOU WILL GET TWO DIFFERENT TOTALS BUT—A WORD OF WARNING—COUNT THEM QUIETLY: DON'T MAKE IT TOO OBVIOUS!
THE END

"FOO-FIGHTERS", "FLYING SAUCERS", "UFOs" – CALL THEM WHAT YOU LIKE, WE'VE BEEN SEEING THEM FOR CENTURIES . . .

TROUBLE IS, THE GREAT MAJORITY WHO **HAVEN'T** SEEN ONE, SELDOM BELIEVE THE FEW WHO **HAVE** . . .

WHAT IN SAM HILL..?

2000 A.D. Credit Card:
SCRIPT ROBOT K. GOSNELL
ART ROBOT C. WILSON
LETTERING ROBOT TONY JACOB
COMPU·73E

ON THAT DAY IN 1985, THOUGH, A FLIGHT OF UFOs PASSED WITHIN A FEW HUNDRED METRES OF AN ORBITING SPACE SHUTTLE...

BLAZES, FLOYD– **LOOK AT THAT!**

THEY'RE HEADING FOR THE MOON, SIR.
GET ALL CAMERAS ROLLING AND CALL MISSION CONTROL– I WANT PERMISSION FOR A SLINGSHOT LUNAR ORBIT TO INVESTIGATE. WE'VE GOT ALL THE FUEL AND AIR WE NEED...

PERMISSION FOR THE LUNAR FLIGHT WAS GIVEN–AND, HALF WAY THERE...
GOOD GRIEF! TREMENDOUS ENERGY RELEASE FROM THE FARSIDE! WHAT IS GOING ON ROUND THERE?
ALSO GETTING A STRONG RADIO TRANSMISSION, SIR!

ANY LANGUAGE WE KNOW...?
NO SIR. BUT IT SEEMS TO USE THE ATOMIC SIGNATURE OF HYDROGEN AS IT'S BASE-CODE. LIKE THE MESSAGES OUR SCIENTISTS PUT ON VOYAGER PLANETARY PROBES. I'LL GET OUR COMPUTERS ON TO DECIPHERING IT...

AND, AS THE SHUTTLE SWUNG ROUND OVER THE MOON'S FAR SIDE . . .

I'VE GOT IT BROKEN, SKIP. DON'T MAKE SENSE THOUGH— GOOD GRIEF!

BUT WHAT IN HELL DOES IT MEAN. . ?

I PRAY THAT I'M WRONG BUT I THINK I KNOW— THE WHOLE DAMN THING IS A ROAD-SIGN. A COSMIC ROADSIGN.

IT ALL MAKES SENSE NOW—TRAGIC SENSE! THE RADIO SIGNAL IS A WARNING! IT WARNS OF NUCLEAR POWER AHEAD... IN THE HANDS OF AN INEXPERIENCED CIVILIZATION.

BECAUSE OF OUR DESTRUCTIVE POWER WE'VE DRIVEN AWAY ANYONE WHO CAN HELP US REACH THE STARS— THE EARTH HAS BECOME A COSMIC BLACK SPOT!

THE END

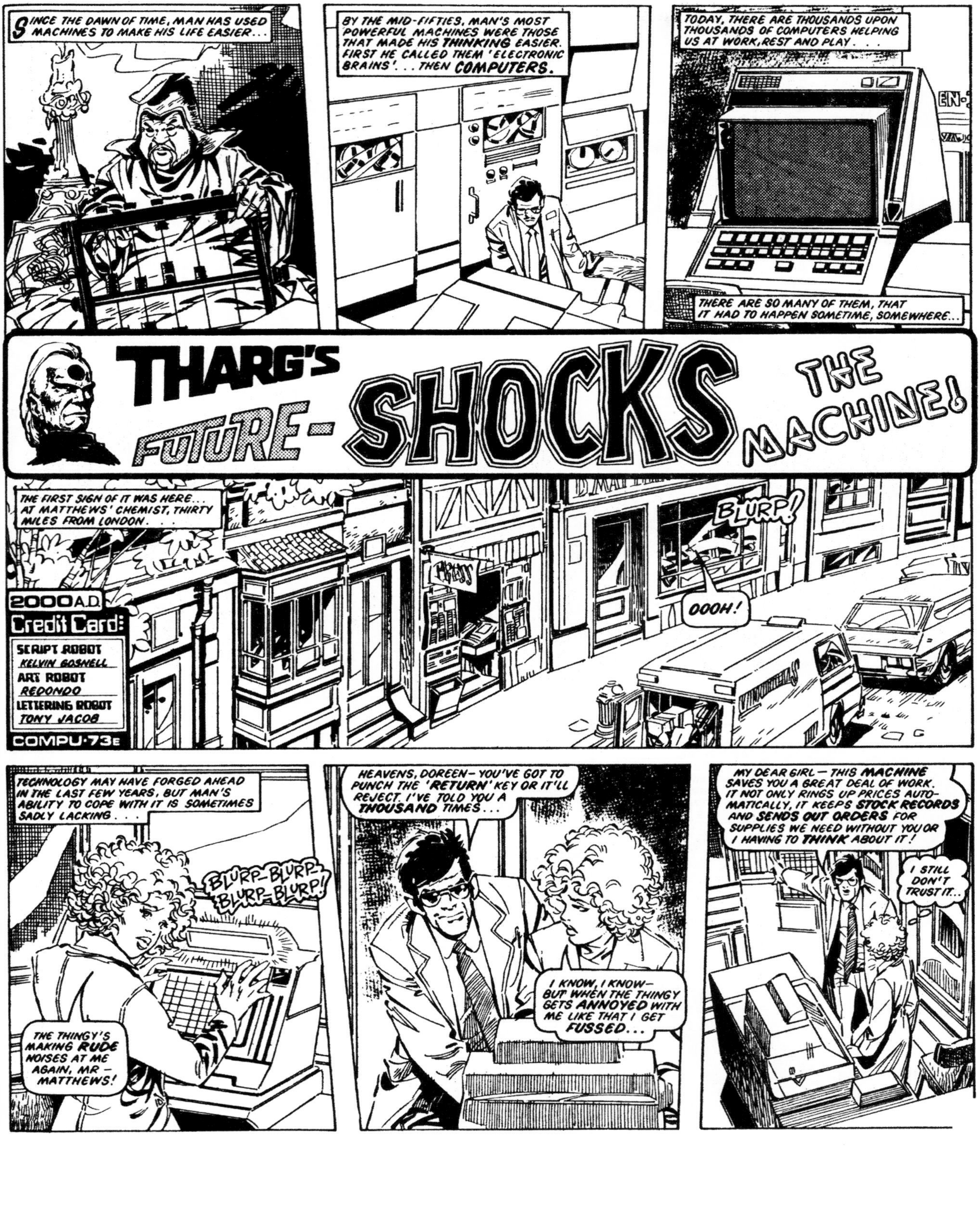

SINCE THE DAWN OF TIME, MAN HAS USED MACHINES TO MAKE HIS LIFE EASIER...

BY THE MID-FIFTIES, MAN'S MOST POWERFUL MACHINES WERE THOSE THAT MADE HIS **THINKING** EASIER. FIRST HE CALLED THEM 'ELECTRONIC BRAINS'... THEN **COMPUTERS**.

TODAY, THERE ARE THOUSANDS UPON THOUSANDS OF COMPUTERS HELPING US AT WORK, REST AND PLAY...

THERE ARE SO MANY OF THEM, THAT IT HAD TO HAPPEN SOMETIME, SOMEWHERE...

THARG'S FUTURE-SHOCKS

THE MACHINE!

THE FIRST SIGN OF IT WAS HERE... AT MATTHEWS' CHEMIST, THIRTY MILES FROM LONDON...

BLURP!

OOOH!

2000 A.D. Credit Card:
SCRIPT ROBOT KELVIN GOSNELL
ART ROBOT REDONDO
LETTERING ROBOT TONY JACOB
COMPU-73E

TECHNOLOGY MAY HAVE FORGED AHEAD IN THE LAST FEW YEARS, BUT MAN'S ABILITY TO COPE WITH IT IS SOMETIMES SADLY LACKING...
BLURP-BLURP-BLURP-BLURP!
THE THINGY'S MAKING RUDE NOISES AT ME AGAIN, MR MATTHEWS!

HEAVENS, DOREEN- YOU'VE GOT TO PUNCH THE 'RETURN' KEY OR IT'LL REJECT. I'VE TOLD YOU A THOUSAND TIMES...
I KNOW, I KNOW- BUT WHEN THE THINGY GETS ANNOYED WITH ME LIKE THAT I GET FUSSED...

MY DEAR GIRL- THIS MACHINE SAVES YOU A GREAT DEAL OF WORK. IT NOT ONLY RINGS UP PRICES AUTOMATICALLY, IT KEEPS STOCK RECORDS AND SENDS OUT ORDERS FOR SUPPLIES WE NEED WITHOUT YOU OR I HAVING TO THINK ABOUT IT!
I STILL DON'T TRUST IT...

D.MATTHEWS-CHEMIST
AH- HERE'S THIS WEEK'S DELIVERY NOW. HELP THE DRIVER BRING IT IN, WOULD YOU?
'ERE - THESE ARE A BIT 'EAVY, MR MATTHEWS. I'M NOT PAID FOR 'EAVY LABOUR YOU KNOW...
PLASMA
FIELD DRESSINGS
PLASTIC SPLINTS
PLASMA? FIELD DRESSINGS? SPLINTS? WE'VE NEVER EVER STOCKED ANY OF THOSE THINGS!
IT'S THE THINGY, MR M- IT'S GOT BRAIN ROT, I TOLD YOU SO...
AT THAT MOMENT A VITAL PART OF THE DELIVERY VAN'S WHEEL HUB FRACTURED. THE WHEEL WENT ONE WAY, THE VAN ANOTHER...
AAARGH!
MR MATTHEWS —LOOK!
GRIEF! MISTAKE OR NOT, THESE DRESSINGS AND ALL THE OTHER GEAR ARE GOING TO GET USED! COME ON!
FOR THE NEXT FEW MINUTES MATTHEWS AND DOREEN WERE BUSY TENDING THE VICTIMS . . .
DON'T WORRY, THIS'LL EASE THE PAIN — THE AMBULANCE WILL BE HERE SOON—
HOLD THAT THERE, PAL- YOU'LL BE OKAY...
WELL DONE, DOREEN- YOU'RE DOING FINE. KEEP IT UP THERE LIKE THAT.

WHEN THE EMERGENCY SERVICES ARRIVED...
HECK–LOOKS LIKE WE'RE NOT NEEDED HERE...
WE'D JUST RECEIVED A DELIVERY OF DISASTER SUPPLIES ONLY SECONDS BEFORE THE ACCIDENT – A STROKE OF AMAZING LUCK!
I DON'T KNOW, MR MATTHEWS! IT–IT'S AS THOUGH THAT COMPUTER KNEW THAT ACCIDENT WAS GOING TO HAPPEN . . .
STOP BEING RIDICULOUS, DOREEN – THERE'S NO WAY THAT ANYONE, LEAST OF ALL A MACHINE, CAN FORETELL THE FUTURE!
BUT, A WEEK LATER... WHEN ANOTHER DELIVERY WAS MADE TO MATTHEWS' SHOP . . .
GAUNT'S PLAGUE VACCINE? NOW THIS IS DEFINITELY A MISTAKE...
BUT, TWO DAYS LATER...
THERE, THAT'S THE FOURTH PRESCRIPTION WE'VE HAD FOR THAT GAUNT'S PLAGUE STUFF . . .
VIRUS ESCAPES LABORATORY!
TH-THIS IS IMPOSSIBLE! THE OUTBREAK WASN'T CONFIRMED TILL YESTERDAY, YET WE'VE HAD THE VACCINE FOR DAYS!
AND, THE NEXT WEEK...
SUN-TAN OIL?
BUT–BUT IT'S THE MIDDLE OF NOVEMBER!

ONE LARGE SUNTAN OIL, PLEASE. WHO'D HAVE THOUGHT, A HEATWAVE AT THIS TIME OF YEAR!
D. MATTHEWS CHEMIST.
PHARMACY
I-I DON'T BELIEVE THIS. GOT TO PHONE THE WHARE-HOUSE, FIND OUT WHAT THE BLAZES IS GOING ON!
HOWEVER THE WAREHOUSE MANAGER WAS JUST AS TROUBLED AS MATTHEWS...
YOU DON'T KNOW WHAT'S GOING ON? HOW THE HELL D'YOU THINK I FEEL?!
THE ENTIRE WAREHOUSE IS AUTOMATIC. YOUR COMPUTER ORDERS GOODS YOU'VE RUN SHORT OF, MY COMPUTER SUPPLIES 'EM — BUT ALL THAT'S BEING OVERRIDDEN SOMEHOW. CRAZY STUFF IS BEING SENT OUT — BUT IT'S ALWAYS NEEDED...
I-I'VE GOT A THEORY BUT DON'T TELL ANYONE — THEY'D LOCK ME UP IF IT GOT OUT. I THINK THAT ALL THE COMPUTERS IN THE COUNTRY HAVE LINKED THEMSELVES TOGETHER — THAT'S HOW THEY KNOW THINGS ARE GOING TO HAPPEN...
THE COMPUTER AT THE GARAGE THAT SERVICES MY VAN KNEW WHEN THAT WHEEL WOULD GO. IT GOT THE VAN'S LOCATION FROM MY WAREHOUSE COMPUTER AND ARRANGED FOR THE MEDICAL SUPPLIES TO BE SHIPPED TO YOU.
THE WEATHER CENTRE COMPUTER KNEW THE HEAT-WAVE WAS COMING AND FIXED THE SUNTAN OIL. IT GOES ON AND ON — THEY TALK TO EACH OTHER ALL THE TIME...
MR MATTHEWS — LOOK AT THIS LOT, THE THINGY'S GONE TOTALLY BANANAS THIS TIME...
NOT NOW, DOREEN. I-I'VE GOT TO THINK.
IT MIGHT NOT BE SO BAD AFTER ALL — IF IT'S TRUE. IT WOULD MAKE LIFE A WHOLE LOT EASIER. MAN WOULD HAVE A LOT MORE TIME TO ENJOY HIMSELF... A BRIGHT NEW FUTURE...
PLEASE MR M — TAKE A LOOK...

OH. NO!
GASMASKS! DECONTAMINATION FLUID! BURN OINTMENT!
WHAT'S IT MEAN, MR MATTHEWS?
WE'VE BEEN SENT A COMPLETE RADIATION KIT! AND THE ONLY REASON THE COMPUTERS WOULD DO THAT IS . . .
. . . IF THEY KNEW WE WERE GOING TO BE HIT BY A SNEAK NUCLEAR ATTACK!
'ERE, THAT PLANE'S A BIT LOW, MR MATTHEWS!
WOOOOOMPFH!
GET THAT LAST PACKAGE TOGETHER, DOREEN. I-I RATHER THINK WE'RE GOING TO NEED IT . . .
The End

THARG'S
FUTURE-
SHOCKS
SEEING IS BELIEVING!

SUNDAY AFTERNOONS IN THE SUBURBAN TOWN OF EDDINGTON ARE THE SAME AS THEY ARE ANYWHERE, DISTURBED ONLY BY THE BUZZ OF MOWERS AND THE SLOSH OF CAR-WASHING...

THERE IS, HOWEVER, ONE DIFFERENCE ABOUT EDDINGTON...
OH, RATS- HERE THEY COME AGAIN...

2000 A.D.
Credit Card:
SCRIPT ROBOT
KELVIN GOSNEL
ART ROBOT
COLIN WILSON
LETTERING ROBOT
PETER KNIGHT
COMPU-73E

IT HAS REGULAR DOSES OF DEATH AND DESTRUCTION POURED ON IT FROM REAL SPACE INVADERS!
AAAARGH!

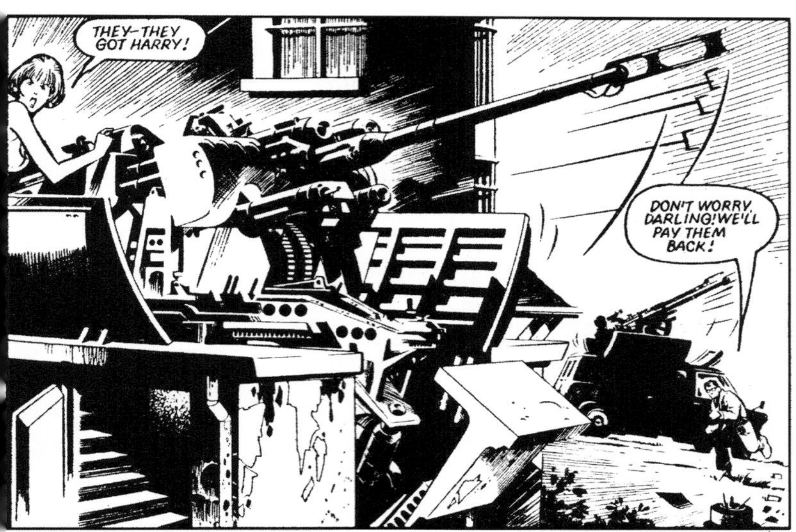
THEY–THEY GOT HARRY!
DON'T WORRY, DARLING! WE'LL PAY THEM BACK!

THAT'S IT, PA–LET THE SWINES HAVE IT!

A HIT! RAAY!
ONLY WINGED HIM! HE'S HEADING THIS WAY!

GET OUT FAST–I'LL TRY TO TAKE HIM OUT BEFORE HE HITS...
WNWWOPF!!
AAAAAAARGH!

DARKNESS — AND THEN, LATER —
UUGH! MY HEAD...

...I'M STILL ALIVE! BUT I WAS BLOWN TO BITS...

...I FELT IT...

YES, DEAR — WE LOST A FEW POINTS BECAUSE OF THAT — YOU'LL HAVE TO IMPROVE YOUR AIM IN FUTURE...
I DON'T UNDERSTAND... YOU MEAN I DIDN'T DREAM IT? IT REALLY HAPPENED?

OF COURSE IT DID, DEAR! NOW DO BE QUIET — I'M TRYING TO WATCH HAPPY-ROADS!

COUNCIL WORKERS, CLEARING UP THE DEBRIS! IT DID HAPPEN!
BUT THIS WHOLE THING IS INSANE. IT NEVER USED TO BE LIKE THIS — I USED TO GO TO WORK AND COME HOME AND...

WHAT'S HAPPENING TO US? WHO ARE THESE INVADERS? WHY DON'T THE ARMY DO SOMETHING?
DO CALM DOWN, JIM. WE'VE GOT A COMFORTABLE LIFE HERE, WHY KNOCK IT? THEY ALWAYS REBUILD EVERYTHING AFTER AN ATTACK DON'T THEY?

I'VE GOT TO GET OUT OF HERE — GOT TO PROVE I'M SANE. I'LL DRIVE UP TO THE CITY AND SEE WHAT'S HAPPENING THERE!

COME BACK! IT'S DANGEROUS TO DRIVE OUT OF TOWN!
YOU GOTTA BE JOKING — YOU WANT ME TO STAY HERE AND GET BOMBED?!
HEY!

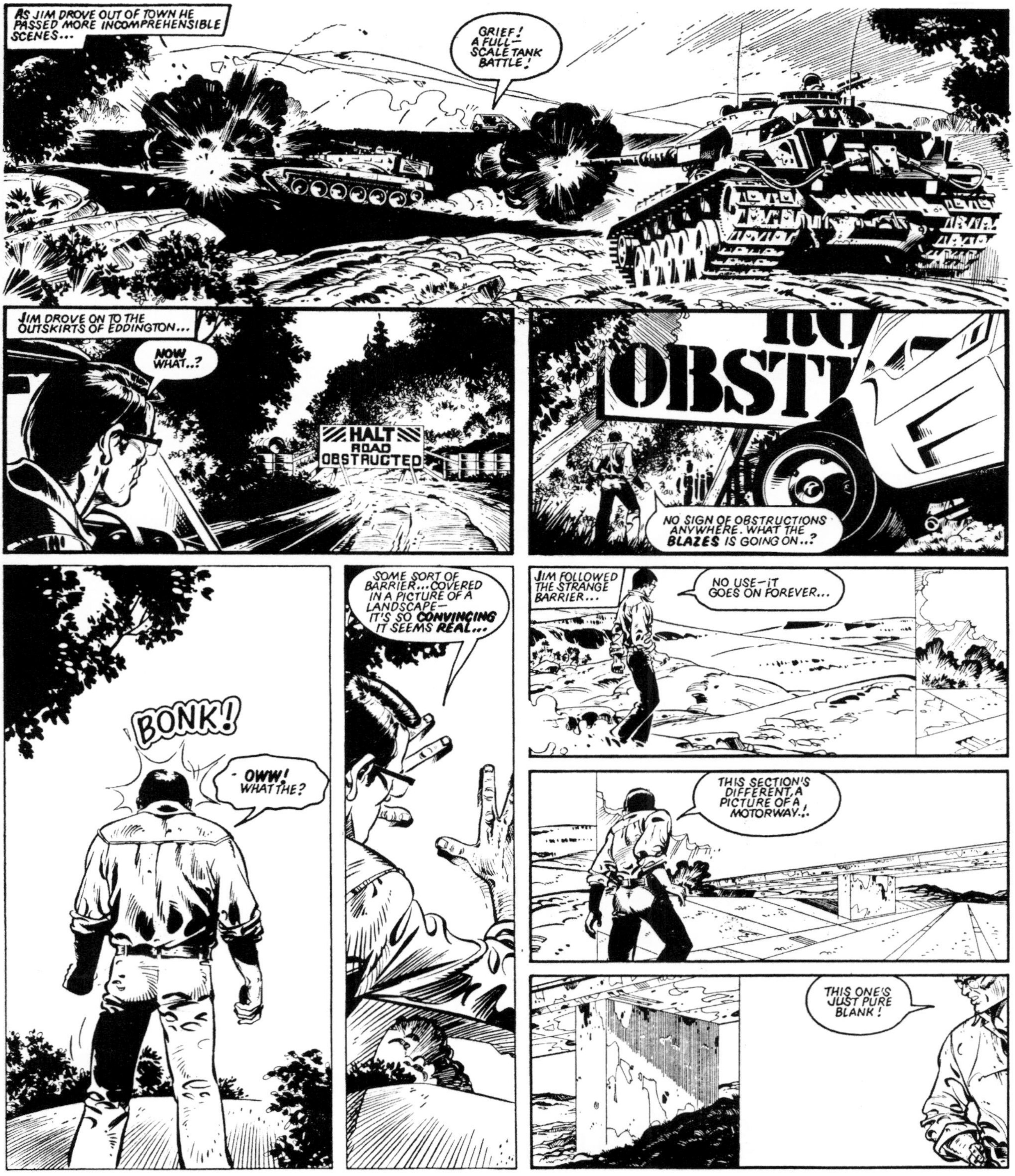

AS JIM DROVE OUT OF TOWN HE PASSED MORE INCOMPREHENSIBLE SCENES...

GRIEF! A FULL-SCALE TANK BATTLE!

JIM DROVE ON TO THE OUTSKIRTS OF EDDINGTON...

NOW WHAT..?

HALT ROAD OBSTRUCTED

NO SIGN OF OBSTRUCTIONS ANYWHERE. WHAT THE **BLAZES** IS GOING ON..?

SUDDENLY...
AH, MR. RUDDLE! SO NICE TO MEET YOU FACE-TO-FACE, ALTHOUGH I WISH THE CIRCUMSTANCES WERE HAPPIER...
WHA..?
I SUPPOSE I OWE YOU AN EXPLANATION. I JUST HOPE IT WILL NOT COME AS TOO MUCH OF A SHOCK TO YOU...
I REGRET TO TELL YOU THAT YOU ARE DEAD, MR. RUDDLE! EVERYONE IN EDDINGTON DIED WHEN THE AMERICAN PLANE CARRYING THE NEUTRON BOMB CRASHED INTO IT!
THE U.S. RESCUE SERVICES WERE ON THE SCENE WITHIN SECONDS, BUT THEY WERE UNABLE TO DO ANYTHING FOR YOU—THEY WERE, HOWEVER, ABLE TO TRY OUT A NEW SYSTEM OF THEIRS...
THEY WERE ABLE TO CAPTURE YOUR PERSONALITY PROFILES ELECTRONICALLY. THE PATTERN OF ELECTRONS THAT MAKES UP YOUR BRAIN IS NOW INDELIBLY COPIED ON TO A CARBON BUBBLE MEMORY... THE COPY IS SO GOOD THAT YOU THINK YOU ARE REALLY ALIVE. YOU EVEN SEE YOURSELF AS HAVING A REAL BODY...
BUT THE SPACE INVADERS, THE TANK BATTLES, ALL THE OTHER CRAZY THINGS...
AH WELL, YOU SEE THIS PERSONALITY COPYING IS VERY EXPENSIVE. SO THEY HIRE YOU OUT TO COMPUTER GAME DESIGNERS TO CHECK OUT THEIR PRODUCTS!

THE INCIDENT WHEN YOU WERE HIT BY AN INVADER WAS A GAME BUG WHICH WE HAVE NOW CORRECTED... UNFORTUNATELY, THE INTENSE ELECTRICAL ACTIVITY OF THE IMPACT SEEMS TO HAVE RELEASED SOME LONG-TERM MEMORY!
YOU DON'T EXPECT ME TO BELIEVE THIS...

I CAN SEE THE ONLY WAY TO PROVE IT IS TO SHOW YOU WHAT YOU AND YOUR WORLD REALLY LOOK LIKE!
THE LANDSCAPE, TURNING INTO A COMPUTER IMAGE...

NOOOOOOO! I'M ALIVE. I MUST BE!

SOB

HAVING TROUBLE?
I WAS — ONE OF THE SUBJECTS SUFFERED LONG-TERM MEMORY RELEASE, BUT I'VE SHUT IT OUT NOW. PASS ME THE NEW SPACE INVADERS TAPE, WILL YOU?
The End

THARG'S FUTURE-SHOCKS

SCRAMBLED EGGS

UNDER A STARRY NIGHT SKY, ASTRONOMERS GAZED UP AT THE WONDERS OF THE HEAVENS... AND RECEIVED A NASTY SHOCK...
GREAT GROBNOLS! **LOOK AT THAT!**

IT... IT LOOKS LIKE SOME GIGANTIC BROCAIN BIRD, AND IT'S HEADING THIS WAY!
2000 A.D.
Credit Card:
SCRIPT ROBOT
ALAN HEBDEN
ART ROBOT
GARRY LEACH
LETTERING ROBOT
BILL NUTTALL
COMPU-73E

AS THE DAYS PASSED, THE HORROR CAME CLOSER.
IT'S A NIGHTMARE!
GIANT SPACE BIRD HEA FOR AETH!
IT'S A DISGRACE! SOMEBODY OUGHT TO SHOOT IT DOWN!

THEN...
IT'S DESTROYED THE MOON!
BUT... BUT IT'S PASSING US BY! **WE'RE SAVED!**

OBSERVATORIES AROUND THE WORLD WATCHED AS THE CREATURE GLIDED TOWARDS VEARN AND WEELS, THE TWO PLANETS CLOSEST TO THEIR SUN!
WHAT'S IT DOING? IS IT FLYING INTO THE SUN?
NO! IT'S FINALLY STOPPED NEAR WEELS. IT SEEMS TO BE WAITING FOR SOMETHING!

ZLUGGS!! IT'S CRACKED **WEELS** OPEN LIKE... LIKE AN **EGG!**
THERE'S SOMETHING INSIDE...

GRIEF! IT'S A CHICK! BUT IT'S DEAD! NOW THE BIRD'S HEADING BACK FOR VEARN!
SOON...
OH, NO! VEARN IS GONE! ANOTHER DEAD CHICK! THIS CAN'T BE HAPPENING.
EXACTLY! OF COURSE IT CAN'T BE HAPPENING!
DOCTOR VAM HOFFER, YOU'RE THE GREATEST SCIENTIST ON AETH! WHAT DO YOU MEAN?
I MEAN PRECISELY VAT I ZAY. VE ARE OBVIOUSLY ZE VICTIMS OF SOME GIGANTIC HOAX! TO SUGGEST ZAT ZE SOLAR SYSTEM IZ MERELY SOME HATCHERY FOR HUGE SPACE BIRDS IZ RIDICULOUS!
NEXT MOMENT...
AAAARRGH!
ZERE IZ NOTHING TO WORRY ABOUT! IZ MERELY AN AETH-QUAKE!
YOU'RE WRONG, PROFESSOR HOFFER! THE BIRD'S HEADING THIS WAY...!
AETH IS THE THIRD EGG! AND IT'S A LIVE ONE...
A LIVE... AAAARRGH!
THE END

IN THE DEEP VELVET GULF OF INTERSTELLAR SPACE A SHIP MOVES. SHE IS NEARING THE END OF HER 100-YEAR VOYAGE...
...FOR THIS IS THE STARSHIP 'DAEDALUS', MANKIND'S FIRST ATTEMPT AT INTER-PLANETARY TRAVEL. RIDING ON GREAT NUCLEAR FUSION ENGINES, SHE WAS LAUNCHED FROM JUPITER IN 2125 AND DOES NOT ARRIVE HERE, AT BARNARD'S STAR UNTIL A CENTURY LATER...

THARG'S FUTURE-SHOCKS GIANT LEAP!!!

ABLE TO REACH ONLY A TINY FRACTION OF THE SPEED OF LIGHT, DAEDALUS' SIX LIGHT-YEAR JOURNEY WAS LONG AND TEDIOUS — BUT NOT FOR THE THREE-MAN CREW.

THEY SLUMBERED, OBLIVIOUS, IN SUSPENDED ANIMATION UNTIL THE AUTO-SYSTEMS REVIVED THEM.

MAN! THAT CRYO-FLUID IS REVOLTING...
TOO RIGHT— SOON AS YOU'VE CLEARED IT— GET SOME UNIFORMS ON AND GET TO THE BRIDGE...

WELL, JIM— LOOKS LIKE OUR ESTEEMED LEADER, COL. DAVID, IS GONNA GET HIS WISH AND GAIN IMMORTALITY...
OKAY, SCREWBALL— SHARE THE JOKE WITH US, HUH? WHAT HAVE YOU GOT..?
YOU'RE GONNA BE THE FIRST MAN TO SET FOOT ON A WORLD OUTSIDE THE SOLAR SYSTEM, BOSS. WE HAVE AN EARTH-TYPE PLANET IN THIS SYSTEM— READY AND WAITING, JUST FOR YOU!
THE INTERSTELLAR PROBE WAS EQUIPPED WITH AN OLD SHUTTLE CRAFT, WITH ENOUGH FUEL TO MAKE A PLANET LANDING...
STARTING RE-ENTRY PROCEDURE, COLONEL.
PICKING UP SIGNS OF RADIO-ACTIVITY, SKIPPER. BEARING 260.
WHATEVER IT IS IS JUST AHEAD, BELOW THAT CLOUD COVER...
PUT THE WHEELS OUT, SON. WE'RE GOING IN...
2000 A.D. Credit Card:
SCRIPT ROBOT KELVIN GOSNELL
ART ROBOT JESUS REDONDO
LETTERING ROBOT STEVE POTTER
COMPU-73E
WHAAAT..?
DO NOT BE ALARMED, COLONEL. JUST LAND YOUR VESSEL ON THE CENTRE RUNWAY —JUST LIKE YOU DID AT CANAVERAL... WE'LL EXPLAIN LATER...
WELCOME, DAEDALUS CREW YOUR ORDEAL IS OVER!
HELLO, COLONEL DAVID!
AD-V

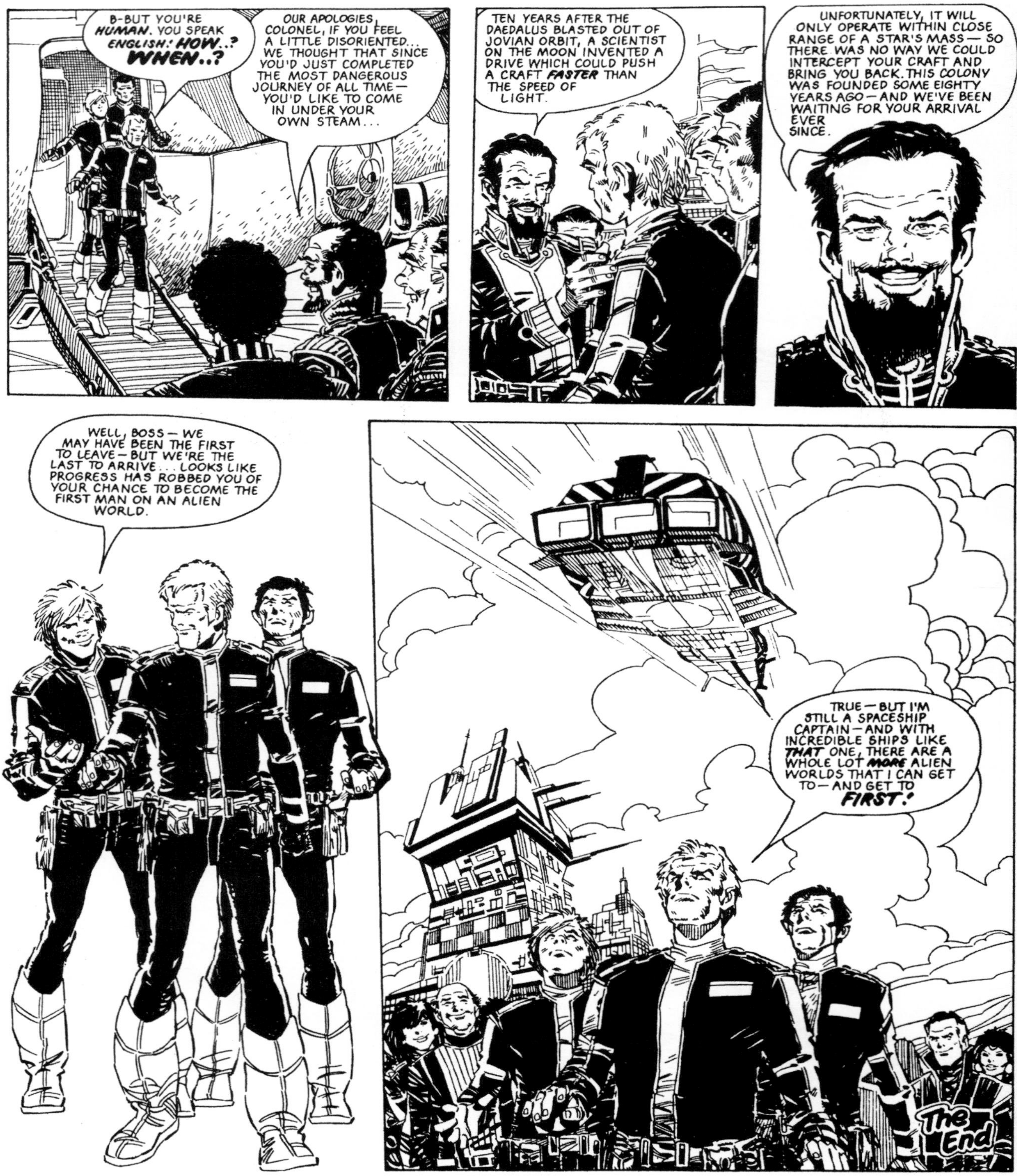

WELL, BOSS — WE MAY HAVE BEEN THE FIRST TO LEAVE — BUT WE'RE THE LAST TO ARRIVE... LOOKS LIKE PROGRESS HAS ROBBED YOU OF YOUR CHANCE TO BECOME THE FIRST MAN ON AN ALIEN WORLD.

TRUE — BUT I'M STILL A SPACESHIP CAPTAIN — AND WITH INCREDIBLE SHIPS LIKE THAT ONE, THERE ARE A WHOLE LOT MORE ALIEN WORLDS THAT I CAN GET TO — AND GET TO FIRST!

The End

THERE WASN'T MUCH CALL FOR A LAWYER ON THE COLONY... NOT ON A WORLD THAT HAD ONLY BEEN OCCUPIED FOR A HUNDRED YEARS...
IT WAS AN UGLY PLACE, TOO, RAVAGED AND WILD, AND THE LITTLE VEGETATION THERE WAS DIDN'T STAND UP WELL TO THE PERIODIC ACID-RAINS...

NOT THAT THAT WORRIED THE GARAKS... AFTER ALL, THE THICKNESS OF THEIR SKIN WAS PROVERBIAL...
ALEKE! GOOD TO SEE YOU! HOW ARE THINGS AT HOME?
WELL, ENOUGH, RAPAN, THOUGH THESE LONG SPACE-FLIGHTS WEAR ME OUT...
STILL, I GATHER YOU'VE GOT AN INTERESTING CASE FOR ME...

THARG'S FUTURE-SHOCKS
THE RED HOUSE

RIGHT! REMEMBER WHEN OUR PEOPLE FIRST ARRIVED THERE WERE ONLY SOME ANIMALS HERE... SCAVENGERS MOSTLY, LIVING IN HOLES IN THE GROUND...
THEY'RE NOT TELEPATHIC LIKE US... PROBABLY DON'T EVEN THINK AT ALL... BUT THEY'RE OUR CLIENTS!
REALLY? NOW THAT IS A CHALLENGE!

AND SO, OVER A FEW SYNTHI-DRINKS, ALEKE MET RAPAN'S FRIENDS IN THE BEAST LIBERATION GROUP...
OUR SO-CALLED 'SCIENTISTS' HAVE ALL THE SURVIVING ANIMALS CRAMMED IN TO THE RED HOUSE...
THEY'RE LIVING FOUR OR FIVE TOGETHER! MALES, FEMALES AND YOUNG IN THE SAME ROOM!
THEY SAY IT'S AN EXPERIMENT...! SAY IT'S DISGUSTING!

SO WHILE ALEKE CHECKED THE LEGAL SITUATION, THE PROTEST MOVEMENT BEGAN WITH A MASS THINK-IN...
STOP THESE DISGUSTING EXPERIMENTS ON ANIMALS. CLOSE THE RED HOUSE!

BUT AT THE NEXT MEETING...
THIS ISN'T ENOUGH! WE NEED DIRECT ACTION! WHAT CAN WE DO, ALEKE?
VIRTUALLY ANYTHING YOU LIKE... BY LAW, OUR SCIENTISTS HAVE NO RIGHT TO KEEP THE ANIMALS CAPTIVE AT ALL...

AND SO, THE FOLLOWING DAY...
THAT'S THE DEN OF HORROR, ALEKE! THE RED HOUSE!
THERE'RE MAYBE A HUNDRED ANIMALS IN THERE... AND WE'RE GOING TO SET THEM ALL FREE!

AND THE SCIENTISTS' PROTESTS...
YOU CAN'T COME IN HERE! IT'S A CAREFULLY CONTROLLED EXPERIMENT...
WE DO EVERYTHING WE CAN FOR THE ANIMALS' HEALTH AND COMFORT...
... WERE SIMPLY IGNORED...

AND WITHIN, THE FIRST HORROR...
THESE CORRIDORS... THEY'RE SO SMALL...
I CAN HARDLY STAND UP! IT'S AWFUL!

IN THE KITCHEN, THE SECOND...
LOOK! ORGANIC FOOD! IT MUST BE CRAWLING WITH MICROBES!
I THINK I'M GOING TO BE ILL...
LISTEN... I THINK THEY'VE GOT THE ANIMALS THROUGH HERE...

AND THEN, WORST OF ALL...
MORE FOOD!
MORE WINE!
HOLY ZONT! HOW VILE!
MORE LAUGHTER!
THEY'RE SITTING THERE IN ROWS, FORCE-FEEDING ONE ANOTHER ON THAT MUCK!
WAHOO!

ROLL OUT THE BARREL! LET'S HAVE A BARREL OF FUN!
LISTEN TO THAT HORRIBLE SCREAMING! THE THING MUST BE IN ABSOLUTE AGONY!

RAPAN AND HIS BEAST LIBERATION GROUP HAD SEEN ENOUGH!
GO.ON! OUTSIDE, ALL OF YOU! WE'RE SETTING YOU FREE!
HOLD ON, WE LIKE IT HERE! IT'S THE BEST THING THAT'S HAPPENED TO US...
SINCE THE RUSSIAN-AMERICAN NUCLEAR-WAR 200 YEARS AGO..!

AND WHEN THE RED HOUSE HAD BEEN EVACUATED...
OH, NO! THEY'VE BLOWN THE PLACE UP!
LISTEN TO THEM GIBBER, ALEKE! I WONDER IF THEY'RE TRYING TO COMMUNICATE?
THEY'RE PROBABLY JUST EXCITED ABOUT BEING FREE!

YOU DON'T OWE US ANY THANKS! GO ON! RUN AWAY AND ENJOY YOUR FREEDOM!
PLEASE! THERE'S NO SHELTER ANYWHERE! AND IT'S GOING TO RAIN!

AND RAIN IT DID... A FIERCE, BURNING ACID RAIN... COMMON ENOUGH AFTER A NUCLEAR WAR...
AAAGH!
YAAIIEE!
URRGH!

NOT THAT THAT WORRIED THE BARAKS... AFTER ALL, THE THICKNESS OF THEIR SKIN WAS PROVERBIAL...
2000 A.D.
Credit Card:
SCRIPT ROBOT STEVE MOORE
ART ROBOT REDONDO
LETTERING ROBOT PETER KNIGHT
COMPU-73E

YOU KNOW, MAYBE THIS WASN'T SUCH A GOOD IDEA AFTER ALL...
WELL, ANYONE CAN MAKE ONE LITTLE MISTAKE...
GOOD JOB THEY WERE ONLY DUMB ANIMALS, WASN'T IT?
The End

THARG'S
FUTURE-
SHOCKS
THE REGRETTABLE RUSE OF ROCKET REDGLARE!

REMEMBER ROCKET REDGLARE, GOLDEN-HAIRED GUARDIAN OF THE GALAXY? STEEL-EYED SENTINEL OF THE SPACEWAYS AND ENEMY OF EVIL EXTRA-TERRESTRIALS?

REMEMBER HOW, AIDED ONLY BY THE GLAMOROUS LUSCIA, HE VANQUISHED THE VILEST VILLAINS OF THE OUTER VOID?

HOW HE CRUSHED THE CRAVEN COW-MEN OF CYGNUS AND PULVERISED THE PREDATORY PILCHARD PEOPLE OF PLUTO AMONG MANY OTHERS?

AND MOST MEMORABLE OF ALL, HOW HE REPELLED COUNTLESS INVASIONS BY HIS ARCH-FOE, LUMIS LOGAR, THE MAN WITH THE JADE HEART?

MANY AND BITTER WERE THEIR BATTLES, AND THERE WERE SOME WHO SAID THAT OVER THE YEARS A CURIOUS MUTUAL RESPECT HAD BLOSSOMED BETWEEN THE TWO...

BUT WHATEVER THE REASON, IT HAS NOW BEEN THIRTY YEARS SINCE LOGAR'S SANGUAN SPACE ARMADA LAST DARKENED EARTH'S SKIES...

X' 12

...THIRTY LONG YEARS OF PEACE AND PROSPERITY.

2000 A.D. Credit Card:
SCRIPT ROBOT ALAN MOORE
ART ROBOT MIKE WHITE
LETTERING ROBOT STEVE POTTER
COMPU·73E

ROCKET REDGLARE IS NOW FIFTY-FOUR.
ROCKY, YOU FAT SCHLUB! AIN'T YOU READY YET?
WE GOTTA BE AT THAT NEW MEGA-MARKET OPENIN' IN TEN MINUTES!

HECK, LUSCIA, IF YOU'D QUIT JAWIN' AN' HELPED ME LACE UP THIS CORSET WE COULDA BE READY AN HOUR AGO!!
WHAT'S A LOUSY MEGA-MARKET ANYWAY?
ROCKET REDGLARE

MONEY IN THE BANK IS WHAT IT IS, DUMMY! HOW ELSE AM I SUPPOSED TO PAY FOR THE GROCERIES NEXT WEEK? WITH AUTOGRAPHED HOLO-SNAPS MAYBE?
AHH, GIMME A BREAK! WHAT ABOUT ALL THE ROYAL-TIES FROM THE ROCKET REDGLARE T-SHIRTS AN' FILMS AN' STUFF? WE'RE SITTIN' PRETTY!
WHEN WAS THE LAST TIME YOU CHECKED OUR ACCOUNTS? REDGLARE TOYS AN' NOVELTIES WENT BUST! WE AIN'T SOLD A T-SHIRT IN FIVE YEARS!
GEE... I DIDN'T REALISE...
WE'RE LIVIN' ON ROYALTIES FROM BUBBLEGUM CARDS! "ROCKET REDGLARE MEETS THE HUNCHBACKS FROM HADES." BUBBLEGUM CARDS! HAH!

NATURALLY YOU DIDN'T REALISE! BECAUSE I GOTTA HANDLE THE CASH WHILE YOU SIT AND WATCH OLD VIDEO RE-RUNS OF 'ROCKET REDGLARE SAVES THE UNIVERSE!'
HEY, MISTER! CAN I HAVE YOUR AUTOGRAPH?

HEH HEH! WHY, SURE, SON. THERE... "TO A GREAT LITTLE SPACE CADET, REGARDS, ROCKET REDGLARE."
ROCKET REDGLARE? AW NUTS! I THOUGHT YOU WERE KIRK KOSMO, ASTRAL AVENGER.
SEE? I TOLD YOU! THIS GUY'S TOO OLD AND FAT TO BE AN ASTRAL AVENGER!

FAT? THIS HERE IS SOLID MUSCLE! I'LL PROVE IT... HIT ME AS HARD AS YOU LIKE! GO ON!

HEH, HEH. DIDN'T FEEL A THING.
NOW, IF YOU'LL EXCUSE ME I GOTTA BE RUNNING ALONG...
PR
WHOMP!

OOOUGH... LITTLE PUNK! MUSTA HAD A HORSESHOE IN HIS HAND...
HAH! MY HUSBAND... THE HERO!
PR

LATER.
HMM... NOT MUCH OF AN OPENIN'. THE CROWD WAS A BIT THIN...
A BIT THIN? TWO OLD LADIES AND A DOG? I NEVER BIN SO EMBARRASSED IN MY LIFE! YOU'RE A HAS-BEEN, ROCKY. YER ALL WASHED UP!

WELL, IF I'M SUCH A FAILURE, HOW COME YOU MARRIED ME?
BECAUSE OUR AGENT SAID IT WOULD BE GOOD PUBLICITY, THAT'S HOW COME!
I MUSTA BIN CRAZY! I COULDA HITCHED UP WIT' LUMIS LOGAR! HE WUZ A REAL MAN!

Lumis Logar? Hmmm...
YEAH, LUMIS LOGAR! HE USED'TA BE REAL SWEET ON ME. BOY, I COULD BE UP IN HIS PALACE ON SANGUA NOW, LIVIN' LIKE A QUEEN! INSTEAD O' WHICH... ROCKY, ARE YOU LISTENIN' TO ME?

AND SO, TWO DAYS LATER AT THE IMPERIAL PALACE ON THE PLANET SANGUA...
BY THE FETID BREATH OF MY FORE-FATHERS... ROCKET RED-GLARE! HOW NICE OF YOU TO DROP IN AFTER SO MANY YEARS!
UHH... HI, LUMIS. COULD WE GO SOME-PLACE A LITTLE MORE PRIVATE? IT WOULDN'T LOOK GOOD FER ME, BEIN' SEEN HERE. KNOW WHAT I MEAN?

I QUITE UNDERSTAND, OLD FRIEND! COME, STEP THIS WAY...
HOW FARES THE CHARMING LUSCIA? STILL AS STRIKING AS EVER, I'LL WARRANT.
UHH, YEAH, I GUESS YOU COULD SAY THAT. LISSEN, LUMIS... ME AN' YOU, WE UNDERSTAND EACH OTHER, RIGHT?
TWO WEEKS LATER...
LUMIS LOGAR
WAR ON EARTH!
EXTRA! EXTRA! READALLABOUDIT! SANGUA DECLARES WAR ON EARTH! LUMIS LOGAR MOBILISES SPACE ARMADA! EXTRA!

INDEED WE DO. NEVER DID I BATTLE A MORE WORTHY ADVERSARY.
...AND YOU AIN'T MAD AT ME FER BEATIN' YA ALLA THOSE TIMES?
MY DEAR ROCKET! WHO COULD BEAR A GRUDGE FOR THIRTY YEARS?

HEH, HEH! I GUESS YOU'RE RIGHT.
WELL, LUMIS... IT'S LIKE THIS... I GOT A KIND OF PUBLIC RELATIONS PROBLEM AN' LIKE I WAS KINDA WONDERIN' IF YOU COULD...
THE TWO MEN TALK FAR INTO THE NIGHT, AND IT IS A FAR HAPPIER ROCKET REDGLARE WHO RETURNS TO EARTH THE NEXT DAY.

THE REACTION OF THE WORLD'S LEADERS IS ONE OF BLIND PANIC...
WE HAVEN'T GOT A CHANCE! AFTER THIRTY YEARS OF PEACE WE'RE TOTALLY UNPREPARED!
THERE'S ONLY ONE MAN WE CAN TURN TO IN A SITUATION LIKE THIS AND THAT'S...

"... ROCKET REDGLARE!"
... SO YOU WANT ME TO SAVE THE WORLD, HUH?
WELL, I GOT A PRETTY TIGHT SCHEDULE, BUT I GUESS MAYBE I COULD SQUEEZE IT IN BEFORE LUNCH.
OH THANK YOU! THANK YOU! WE HAVE YOUR OLD ROCKET SHIP READY FOR TAKE-OFF RIGHT NOW!
AND SO...
HAH! DID YOU SEE THAT CROWD? DID YOU SEE ALL THOSE PHOTO-GRAPHERS? WE GOT A DOZEN MOVIE OFFERS ALREADY!
WHO'S A HAS-BEEN NOW, HUH?
WE-ELL... OKAY. BUT THAT ARMADA LOOKS AWFULLY BIG! ARE YOU SURE THIS IS GOING TO WORK?
ROCKET
RELAX... I GOT IT ALL WORKED OUT WITH MY OLD BUDDY LUMIS! THE FIRST WAVE OF SHIPS ARE ALL REMOTE-CONTROLLED. I DON'T EVEN HAVE TO HIT 'EM!
... SOON AS I FIRE MY GUNS, LUMIS MAKES 'EM SELF-DESTRUCT!!
HAH! GOT ONE!
THE ONE-SIDED BATTLE SWIFTLY REACHES ITS GRAND FINALE...
RIGHT! NOW I ZOOM IN REAL CLOSE TO LOGAR'S FLAGSHIP, SHOOT OFF ONE OF THE STABILIZERS AN' HE GOES SPINNIN' OFF INTA SPACE, "OUT OF CONTROL"...
...THEN THE SANGUAN FLEET FLEES IN DISARRY, AND WE GO BACK TO EARTH AN' WAIT FOR THE CHEQUES TO ROLL IN!
FLEUR DU MAL
IF YOU SAY SO... SAY! THERE'S LOGAR'S FLAGSHIP NOW!

WHAT ARE THOSE TWO BIG THINGS UNFOLDING FROM UNDERNEATH IT? I DON'T REMEMBER IT HAVING THOSE BEFORE...
I DUNNO. THEY LOOK KINDA LIKE TWO BIG HANDS, BUT THAT'S CRAZY! I MEAN WHY WOULD ANYBODY WANT A SPACE-SHIP WITH TWO BIG...
EEEAGHH!
SQUIT!!
URRK!
...AND THE MAN WITH A JADE HEART CHUCKLES TO HIMSELF AS HE GUIDES HIS ARMADA DOWN TOWARDS THE STUNNED AND DEFENCELESS EARTH.
WHICH ONLY LEAVES ONE QUESTION...
...WHO COULD BEAR A GRUDGE FOR THIRTY YEARS?
I COULD.
The End

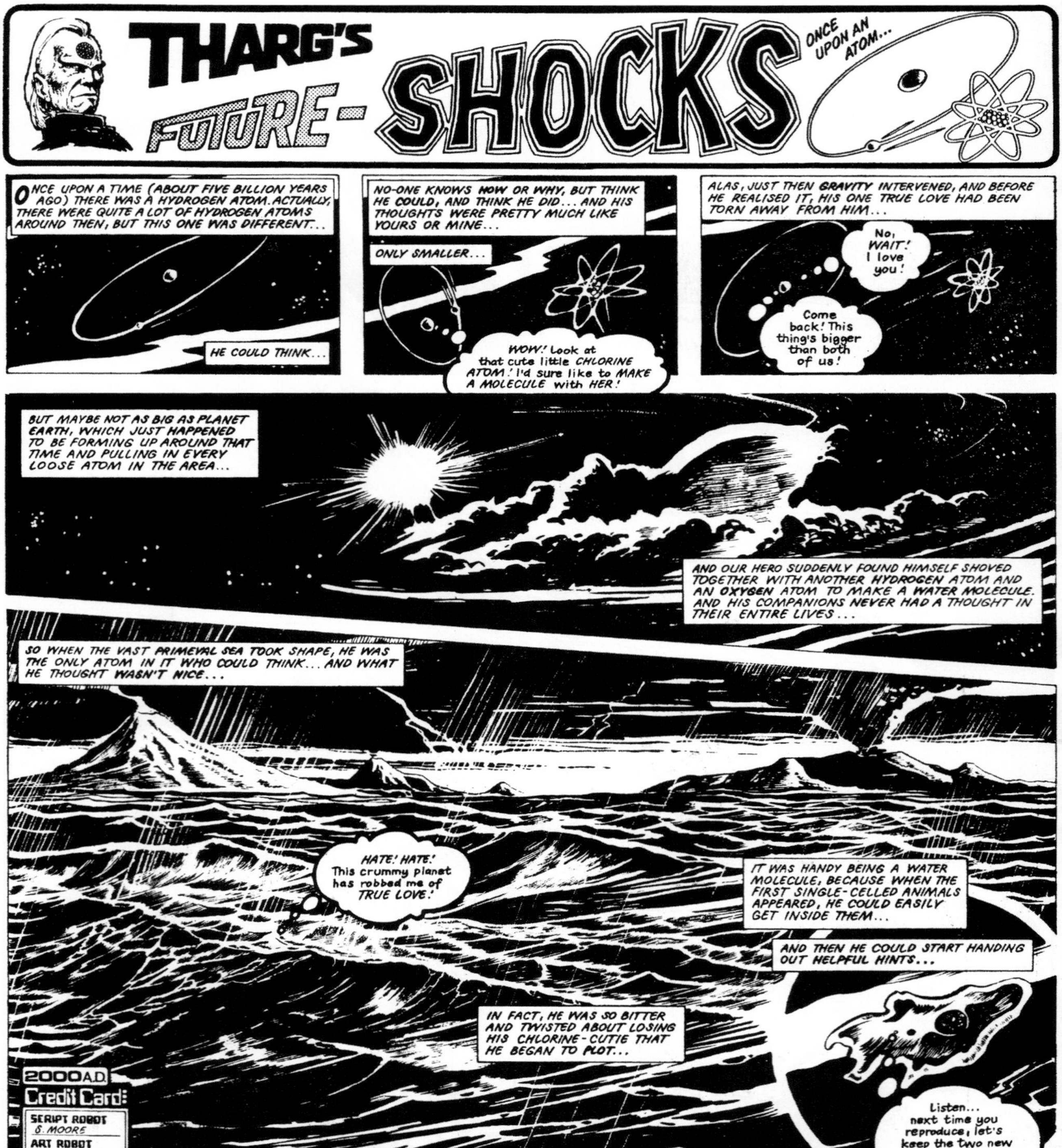

THARG'S FUTURE-SHOCKS
ONCE UPON AN ATOM...

ONCE UPON A TIME (ABOUT FIVE BILLION YEARS AGO) THERE WAS A HYDROGEN ATOM. ACTUALLY, THERE WERE QUITE A LOT OF HYDROGEN ATOMS AROUND THEN, BUT THIS ONE WAS DIFFERENT...
HE COULD THINK...

NO-ONE KNOWS HOW OR WHY, BUT THINK HE COULD, AND THINK HE DID... AND HIS THOUGHTS WERE PRETTY MUCH LIKE YOURS OR MINE...
ONLY SMALLER...
WOW! Look at that cute little CHLORINE ATOM! I'd sure like to MAKE A MOLECULE with HER!

ALAS, JUST THEN GRAVITY INTERVENED, AND BEFORE HE REALISED IT, HIS ONE TRUE LOVE HAD BEEN TORN AWAY FROM HIM...
No, WAIT! I love you!
Come back! This thing's bigger than both of us!

BUT MAYBE NOT AS BIG AS PLANET EARTH, WHICH JUST HAPPENED TO BE FORMING UP AROUND THAT TIME AND PULLING IN EVERY LOOSE ATOM IN THE AREA...

AND OUR HERO SUDDENLY FOUND HIMSELF SHOVED TOGETHER WITH ANOTHER HYDROGEN ATOM AND AN OXYGEN ATOM TO MAKE A WATER MOLECULE. AND HIS COMPANIONS NEVER HAD A THOUGHT IN THEIR ENTIRE LIVES...

SO WHEN THE VAST PRIMEVAL SEA TOOK SHAPE, HE WAS THE ONLY ATOM IN IT WHO COULD THINK... AND WHAT HE THOUGHT WASN'T NICE...

HATE! HATE! This crummy planet has robbed me of TRUE LOVE!

IT WAS HANDY BEING A WATER MOLECULE, BECAUSE WHEN THE FIRST SINGLE-CELLED ANIMALS APPEARED, HE COULD EASILY GET INSIDE THEM...

AND THEN HE COULD START HANDING OUT HELPFUL HINTS...

IN FACT, HE WAS SO BITTER AND TWISTED ABOUT LOSING HIS CHLORINE-CUTIE THAT HE BEGAN TO PLOT...

Listen... next time you reproduce, let's keep the two new cells together and make a BIGGER animal...

2000 A.D. Credit Card:
SCRIPT ROBOT S. MOORE
ART ROBOT A. LANGFORD
LETTERING ROBOT S. POTTER
COMPU-73E

BECAUSE BY THIS TIME HE'D DECIDED THAT EVOLUTION WAS THE WAY TO GET WHAT HE WANTED...
Getting bigger... what I need is...
BONES! That's a good idea!
Hey! I just thought of LUNGS!
AND WHEN SEVERAL MILLION YEARS HAD GONE BY, HE STARTED TO GET THINGS UNDER CONTROL...
UNTIL FINALLY, WITH ONE SMALL STEP, HE WAS UP OUT OF THE SEA...
Okay stupid, now let's go for a walk...
OF COURSE, IT WASN'T ALL STRAIGHT-FORWARD...
This thing's just TOO ABSURD to live...! I'll get rid of the dinosaurs and start again...
BUT ONCE HE GOT THE MAMMALS ESTABLISHED, THINGS REALLY STARTED TO TAKE OFF...
You're not going to stand for that are you? He took your dinner!
Pick up that branch and bash his brains out!
SO CIVILISATION WAS BORN... AND HE KNEW HE WAS GETTING CLOSE TO HIS GOAL...
AND ALL IT TOOK WAS A FEW MORE GOOD IDEAS...
No, NO! Pythagoras, you IDIOT! It's the SQUARE on the hypotenuse...!
This should knock some sense into his head...
E=MC²? HA! IT'S SO SIMPLE!
Simple? I spent FIVE BILLION YEARS thinking that out!
E=MC

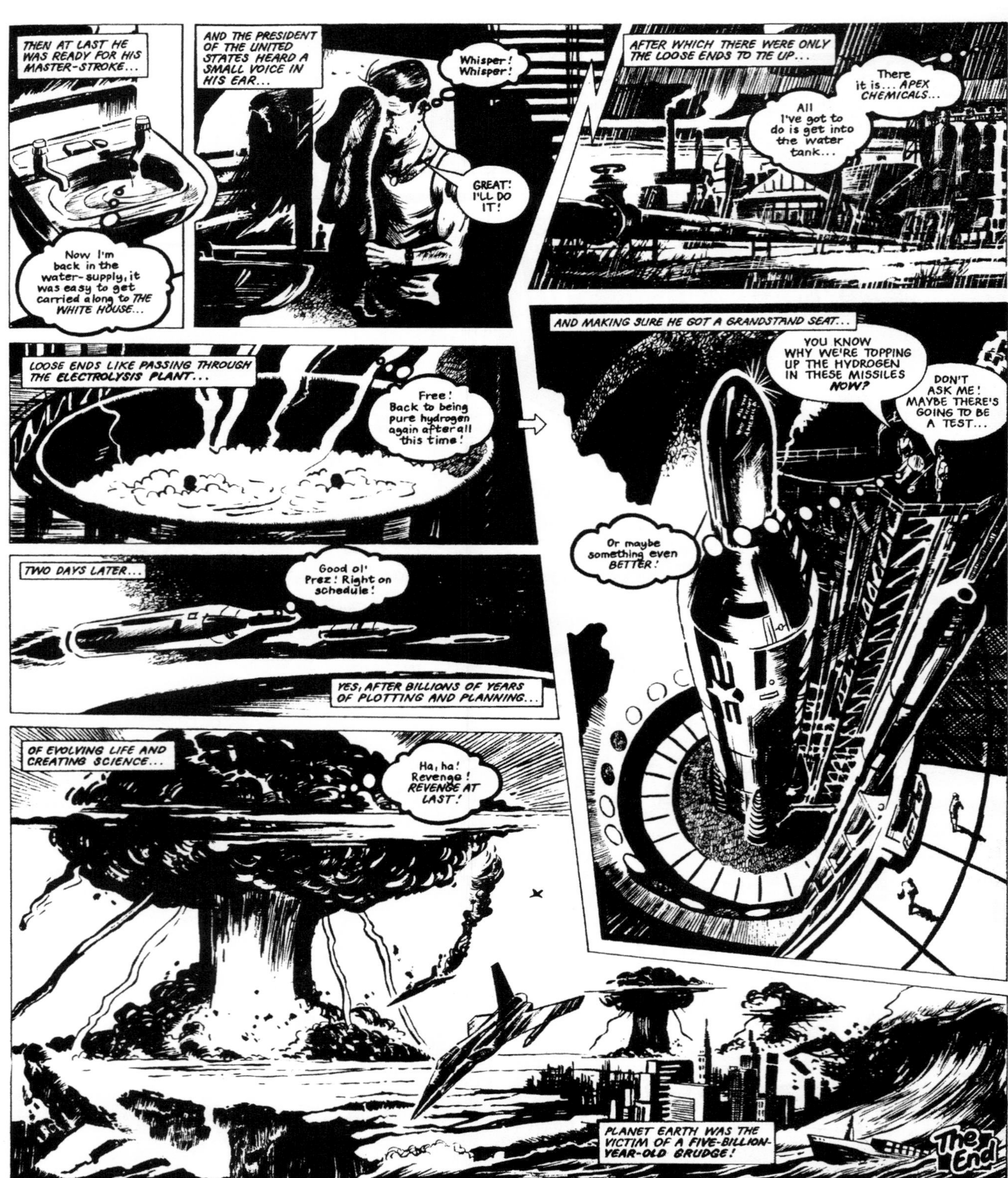
THEN AT LAST HE WAS READY FOR HIS MASTER-STROKE...
Now I'm back in the water-supply, it was easy to get carried along to THE WHITE HOUSE...
AND THE PRESIDENT OF THE UNITED STATES HEARD A SMALL VOICE IN HIS EAR...
Whisper! Whisper!
GREAT! I'LL DO IT!
AFTER WHICH THERE WERE ONLY THE LOOSE ENDS TO TIE UP...
There it is... APEX CHEMICALS...
All I've got to do is get into the water tank...
LOOSE ENDS LIKE PASSING THROUGH THE ELECTROLYSIS PLANT...
Free! Back to being pure hydrogen again after all this time!
AND MAKING SURE HE GOT A GRANDSTAND SEAT...
YOU KNOW WHY WE'RE TOPPING UP THE HYDROGEN IN THESE MISSILES NOW?
DON'T ASK ME! MAYBE THERE'S GOING TO BE A TEST...
Or maybe something even BETTER!
TWO DAYS LATER...
Good ol' Prez! Right on schedule!
YES, AFTER BILLIONS OF YEARS OF PLOTTING AND PLANNING...
OF EVOLVING LIFE AND CREATING SCIENCE...
Ha, ha! Revenge! REVENGE AT LAST!
PLANET EARTH WAS THE VICTIM OF A FIVE-BILLION-YEAR-OLD GRUDGE!
The End

THARG'S FUTURE-SHOCKS
SIGN OF THE TIMES
BY THE END OF THE EIGHTIES, SPACE SHUTTLE TRIPS WERE ROUTINE, BUT WHILE NASA CONDUCTED CIVILIAN LAUNCHES FROM CAPE CANAVERAL, THE U.S. AIR FORCE CONDUCTED ITS OWN FROM A NEW SITE ON THE WEST COAST OF CALIFORNIA ... FOR SOMETIMES SINISTER PURPOSES ...
2000 A.D. Credit Card:
SCRIPT ROBOT ALAN HEBDEN
ART ROBOT MIKE WHITE
LETTERING ROBOT JACK POTTER
COMPU-73E
THE AIR FORCE HAS ANNOUNCED A SHUTTLE LAUNCH FROM VANDENBURG IN CALIFORNIA, BUT NO MISSION DETAILS HAVE BEEN RELEASED.
LEXINGTON WAS THE LATEST ORBITER TO BE COMMISSIONED BY THE USAF...
BOOSTERS RELEASED. ALL SYSTEMS ARE GO!
LEXINGTON
BUT FOR CREW MEMBERS CHUCK BRENNER AND SLIM SHERMAN, THIS WAS NO ORDINARY MISSION.
THEM DARNED ROOSKIES HAVE GONE TOO FAR THIS TIME!
MAJ. SLIM SHERMAN
USAF
COL. CHUCK BRENNER
USAF
THEY SURE HAVE, CHUCK!
YOU BET, SLIM. IF THEY THINK THEY'RE GONNA GET AWAY WITH THIS, THEY'VE GOT ANOTHER THINK COMIN'! UNCLE SAM AIN'T TAKIN' THIS LYIN' DOWN!
THEY'RE TRYIN' TO MAKE A MOCKERY OF THE AMERICAN WAY OF LIFE ...
'AN US AMERICANS DON'T LIKE BEIN' MOCKED!

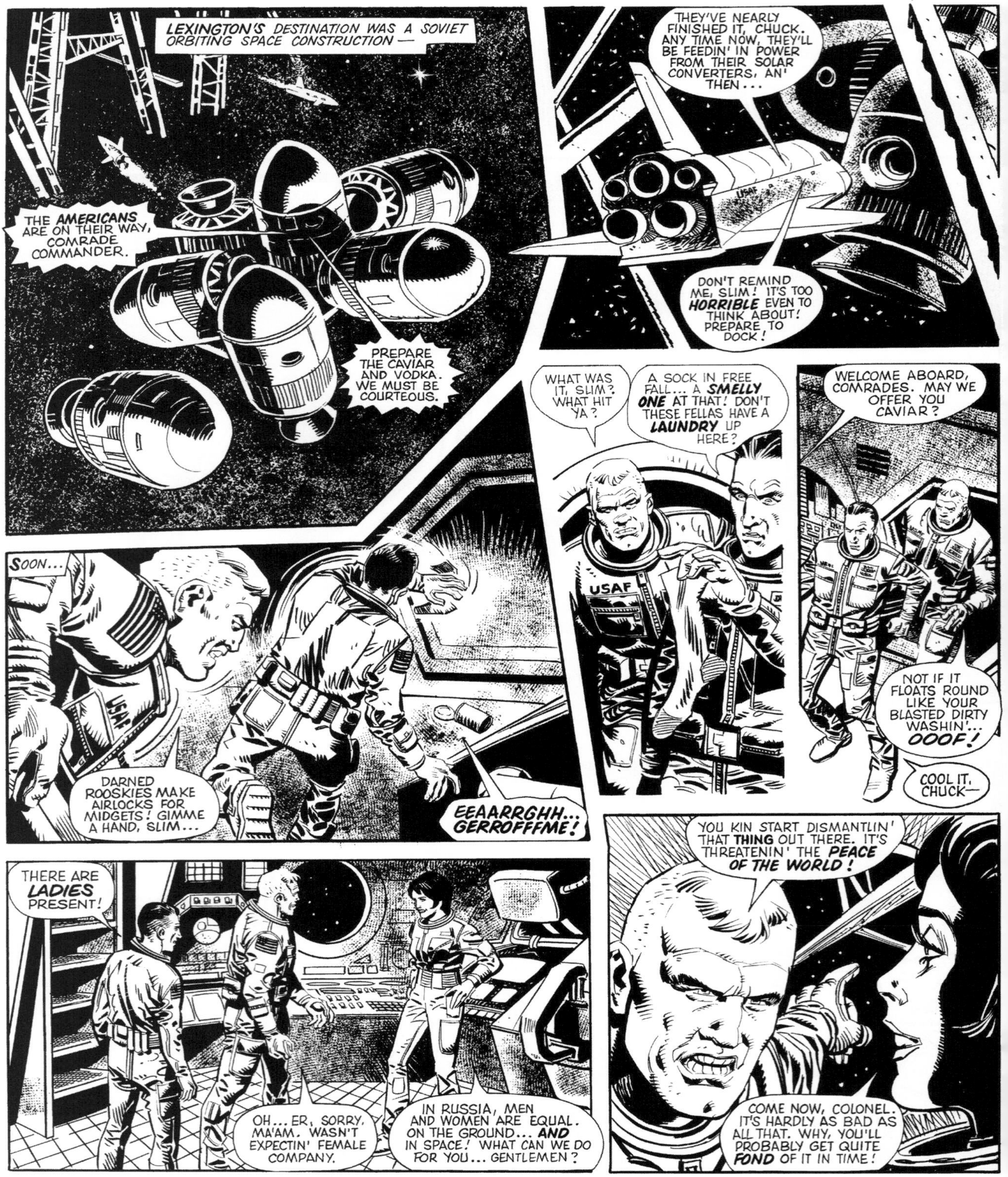

LEXINGTON'S DESTINATION WAS A SOVIET ORBITING SPACE CONSTRUCTION —

THE **AMERICANS** ARE ON THEIR WAY, COMRADE COMMANDER.

PREPARE THE CAVIAR AND VODKA. WE MUST BE COURTEOUS.

THEY'VE NEARLY FINISHED IT, CHUCK. ANY TIME NOW, THEY'LL BE FEEDIN' IN POWER FROM THEIR SOLAR CONVERTERS, AN' THEN...

DON'T REMIND ME, SLIM! IT'S TOO **HORRIBLE** EVEN TO THINK ABOUT! PREPARE TO DOCK!

SOON...

DARNED ROOSKIES MAKE AIRLOCKS FOR MIDGETS! GIMME A HAND, SLIM...

EEAARRGHH... GERROFFFME!

WHAT WAS IT, SLIM? WHAT HIT YA?

A SOCK IN FREE FALL... A **SMELLY ONE** AT THAT! DON'T THESE FELLAS HAVE A **LAUNDRY** UP HERE?

WELCOME ABOARD, COMRADES. MAY WE OFFER YOU CAVIAR?

NOT IF IT FLOATS ROUND LIKE YOUR BLASTED DIRTY WASHIN'... **OOOF!**

COOL IT, CHUCK—

OKAY, WE'LL MAKE IT WORTH YOUR WHILE. EVERY AIRLINE IN AMERICA CONTRIBUTED TO THIS. IT'S A CHEQUE FOR FIFTY MILLION DOLLARS. JUST ABANDON THIS CRAZY SCHEME, AN' IT'S ALL YOURS!
NOT FOR FIVE HUNDRED MILLION, COLONEL!

WHY, YOU DUMB BROAD! THIS IS REAL HONEST-TO-GOODNESS MONEY YOU'RE TURNIN' DOWN. I OUGHT...
EASY, CHUCK! NO USE GETTIN' HOT UNDER THE COLLAR!
EXACTLY. AND NOW, GENTLEMEN, BE SO KIND AS TO LEAVE!

WHAT KINDA PEOPLE ARE THEY, TURNIN' DOWN GENUINE GREEN-BACKS IN ORDER TO FINISH THAT... THAT MONSTROSITY!
USAF
SLIM
SAF
COL. CHUCK BRENNER
THAT'S THE WAY IT IS, CHUCK. I GUESS YOU WOULDN'T RECONSIDER THE OFFER, LADY?
SORRY, BUT AS THEY SAY ON MADISON AVENUE... 'HARD CHEESE'!

BACK ON BOARD THE LEXINGTON —
THOSE UNGRATEFUL SLOBS! I'M GONNA LASER THAT BLASTED THING!
NO, CHUCK... FOR PITY'S SAKE!
SAF
IT AIN'T WORTH STARTIN' WORLD WAR THREE FOR!
NOW... HOW CAN YOU SAY THAT?

WHEN THEY SWITCH THAT THING ON, IT'LL BE VISIBLE ACROSS THE ENTIRE NORTH AMERICAN CONTINENT!
SO THEY GOT THE JUMP ON US THIS TIME, AN' BEAT US AT OUR GAME. BUT DON'T FRET, CHUCK...

FLY AEROFLOT
COCA-COLA'S PLANNIN' AN EVEN BIGGER ONE FOR SIBERIA NEXT YEAR!
THE END.

DAVID BANNISTER WAS A WRITER— LOOKING FOR A QUIET HOUSE TO RENT WHILE PRODUCING HIS NEXT NOVEL . . .

TESTER & SONS
ESTATE AGENTS
PROPERTY For SALE

FUNNY— I THOUGHT I KNEW THIS COAST ***WELL***. NEVER SEEN ***THAT*** PLACE BEFORE, THOUGH . . .

2000 A.D.
Credit Card:
SCRIPT ROBOT *Kelvin Gosnell*
ART ROBOT *Tony Jozwiak*
LETTERING ROBOT *Jack Potter*
COMPU-73E

SUDDENLY . . .

YOU ARE INTERESTED IN THE PROPERTY, SIR? I WORK FOR THE OWNERS, PERHAPS I MIGHT SHOW YOU ROUND . . .

ER, YES . . .

ODD-LOOKING GUY . .

THE HOUSE USED TO BE COMPLETELY HIDDEN UNTIL THE COUNCIL CUT SOME TREES DOWN ON THE VERGE . . .

AN HOUR LATER . . .

IT'S SUPERB! SUCH ***CHARACTER***! WHEN CAN I MOVE IN?

AS SOON AS YOU PLEASE, SIR. IT'S QUITE VACANT . . .

THARG'S FUTURE-SHOCKS

SPACE TO LET!

AND SO, LESS THAN A WEEK LATER . . .
FILES IN THE OFFICE, GUV?
THAT'S RIGHT— SAME AS THE DESK.

LATER . . .
THANK HEAVENS WE'VE GOT ALL THE STUFF ***UNLOADED***. I'LL FINISH UNPACKING IN THE MORNING. RIGHT NOW I'M FOR ***BED*** . . .

AS HE MOUNTED THE STAIRS, AN EERIE VIBRATION SEEMED TO RUN THROUGH THE HOUSE...
HUH? MUST BE CONCORDE GOING OVER NEARBY—
BUT THE FOLLOWING MORNING, AS BANNISTER CAME DOWN FOR BREAKFAST...
STRANGE— THERE'S SOMETHING NOT QUITE RIGHT HERE... ONLY ONE WINDOW HAS A SHADOW ON THE FLOOR...
IMPOSSIBLE! IT'S THE SAME VIEW— BUT THE RIGHT HAND SIDE IS IN DEEP WINTER!
BANNISTER RACED TO THE FRONT DOOR...
GOT TO GET OUTSIDE AND SEE FOR MYSELF WHAT'S HAPPENING...
N-NO! THIS CAN'T BE HAPPENING! THE FRONT DOOR OPENS BACK INTO THE ENTRANCE OF THE HOUSE!

RACING TO THE LOUNGE HE LOOKED OUT ON WHAT OUGHT TO HAVE BEEN THE ROSE GARDEN...
AAAH!
IT WAS THE SAME AT EVERY WINDOW...
SPACE! PLANETS! STARS!
IT WAS THEN THAT BANNISTER NOTICED THE STRANGE THINGS ABOUT THE INSIDE OF THE HOUSE...
THE STAIRCASE... NO!
AAAAAAHHHHHH!
HE WAS STRUGGLING TO REACH THE MAIN ENTRANCE ONCE MORE WHEN SOMETHING IN HIS MIND SNAPPED— FATALLY!

THUD!
AS HIS BODY HIT THE FRONT STEPS, THERE WAS A SLIGHT MOVEMENT IN ONE OF THE STATUES...

IS HE DEAD..?
YES, SAME AS LAST TIME, BRAIN OVERLOADED. HE COULDN'T TAKE THE SHOCK!
I TOLD YOU THEY WEREN'T READY FOR US, DIDN'T I?

YOU'RE NOT GOING TO SAY 'I TOLD YOU SO' ARE YOU? I COULDN'T BEAR IT!
I ALREADY HAVE...

SHUT UP AND WARP US OUT OF HERE...

OH, VERY WELL...

HAD THERE BEEN A LIVE OBSERVER AT THE SCENE WHEN THE HOUSE DISAPPEARED, HE MIGHT HAVE NOTICED A SMALL WHITE CARD FLUTTER DOWN FROM ONE OF THE CREATURES ON THE DOORWAY...

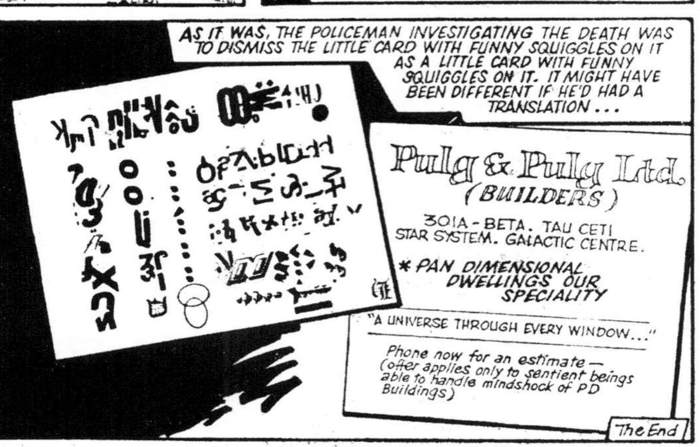
AS IT WAS, THE POLICEMAN INVESTIGATING THE DEATH WAS TO DISMISS THE LITTLE CARD WITH FUNNY SQUIGGLES ON IT AS A LITTLE CARD WITH FUNNY SQUIGGLES ON IT. IT MIGHT HAVE BEEN DIFFERENT IF HE'D HAD A TRANSLATION...
Pulg & Pulg Ltd.
(BUILDERS)
301A - BETA. TAU CETI STAR SYSTEM. GALACTIC CENTRE.
* PAN DIMENSIONAL DWELLINGS OUR SPECIALITY
"A UNIVERSE THROUGH EVERY WINDOW..."
Phone now for an estimate — (offer applies only to sentient beings able to handle mindshock of PD Buildings)
The End

THARG'S FUTURE-SHOCKS
A LITTLE PROBLEM
HAMPSTEAD HEATH, DAWN. ONE MOMENT, THERE'S NO-ONE.. AND THE NEXT, THERE'S INIGO QUOIT...
SO THIS IS EARTH... DOESN'T LOOK ALL THAT MUCH DIFFERENT TO ALPHA-7...
I'M SURE I'LL BE ABLE TO MAKE A NEW LIFE FOR MYSELF HERE...
AND THOSE ORIENTATION AND LANGUAGE COURSES I TOOK BEFORE I CAME SHOULD HELP ME LOSE MYSELF IN THE CROWD...
BUT—
YUK! THERE'S SOMETHING ABOUT THAT MAN THAT MAKES MY SKIN CRAWL!
STRANGE..
BAKER
STILL, QUOIT MANAGES TO GET A JOB...
HERE... BUCKET AND MOP! DON'T LOSE THEM AGAIN, YOU IDIOT!
THEN ANOTHER JOB... AND ANOTHER JOB... AND...
OOPS!
YOU'RE FIRED!
BUT SOMEHOW, IT NEVER SEEMS TO WORK OUT...
AND, OF COURSE, HAVING ONLY BEEN ON EARTH A WEEK...
NO RECORDS, NO DOLE MONEY! NOW, STOP WASTING MY TIME!

MAYBE THERE'S SOMETHING UNPLEASANTLY ALIEN ABOUT QUOIT...
I TOLD YOU I WANTED THE RENT YESTERDAY—NOW, GET OUT!
BUT NO-ONE SEEMS TO LIKE HIM!
OOF!
THIS IS MY DUSTBIN, YOU RAT!
OF COURSE, QUOIT TRIES TO IMPROVE HIMSELF...
A TRAMP LIKE YOU NEEDS A BATH, NOT EDUCATION!
RACING
SPORTS SECTION
BUT SOMETIMES KNOWING WHAT THE LAW IS DOESN'T HELP...
YOU'RE BREATHING OUR AIR, PAL!
AH! OW!
EXCUSE ME, OFFICER... BUT I WISH TO DECLARE WAR ON YOUR PLANET!
BEG PARDON, SIR?
121
AND BY THE TIME THE LAW ARRIVES, INIGO QUOIT HAS JUST ABOUT HAD ENOUGH...
I SAID I WISH TO SOLEMNLY DECLARE WAR ON THE PLANET EARTH...

OF COURSE, SIR. JUST ACCOMPANY ME TO THE STATION...
MY NAME IS INIGO QUOIT, FROM RONDRIS, ON THE PLANET ALPHA-7, AND I AM DECLARING WAR ON YOUR PLANET.
I SEE, SIR... ALPHA-7'S GOING TO ATTACK US...
NO, YOU MISUNDERSTAND. I MYSELF AM DECLARING WAR...
...AND ACCORDING TO PARAGRAPH 64 OF THE PUBLIC DISORDER ACT, SUCH A DECLARATION MUST BE REFERRED TO THE COMMISSIONER!
HUH?
AND, AS EVERYONE SOON FINDS OUT, INIGO QUOIT MAY BE SMALL, BUT HE'S DONE A LARGE AMOUNT OF HOME-WORK... AN UNCOMFORTABLY LARGE AMOUNT...
I KNOW IT'S ABSURD, MINISTER, BUT IT'S IN THE BOOK...
NOT THE HOME OFFICE'S PIGEON, OLD BOY! IT'LL HAVE TO GO TO THE P.M.!
THE 1983 AMENDMENT TO THE U.N. CHARTER? WHAT'S THAT?
IT SAYS...

"ALL THREATS TO THE PLANET EARTH IN ITS ENTIRETY BY ALIENS MUST BE DEBATED BY THE SECURITY COUNCIL!"
SO IF YOU DON'T SURRENDER IMMEDIATELY, I WON'T BE RESPONSIBLE FOR THE CONSEQUENCES...
NONSENSE! A CAPITALIST FARCE!
RIDICULOUS! A COMMUNIST PLOT!
RIGHT, THEN!
WHAT'S THAT HE'S GOT?
A NEWTON'S CRADLE! HE MUST BE OUT OF HIS TINY MIND... THREATENING US WITH A TOY!
A TOY?
KLIK!
KLOK!
KLOK!
KLIK!
LOOK! BLACK WAVES FORMING IN THE AIR!
MY EARS!
IT'S SHAKING THE WHOLE BUILDING!
AND THE SOUNDS BECOME SO POWERFUL, SO DENSE...
WHAT'S THAT LITTLE BEAST DOING TO US?

WE'RE BEING OVERWHELMED! HE'LL KILL US ALL!
AND HE'S GROWING!
GROWING? PERHAPS... OR PERHAPS INIGO QUOIT IS STAYING THE SAME SIZE...
AAUUGH!
YIIII!
AAAARGH!
...AND EVERYTHING ELSE IS SHRINKING!
BUT THEN EVERYTHING IS SMOTHERED IN BLACKNESS...
AND THERE IS ONLY INIGO QUOIT...
AND HIS CRADLE...WITH A FIFTH BALL...
AND THEN...
THERE IS NOTHING!
2000 A.D.
Credit Card:
SCRIPT ROBOT STEVE MOORE
ART ROBOT J. JOHNSON
LETTERING ROBOT JACK POTTER
COMPU·73E
WHICH ONLY GOES TO PROVE THAT THE FIRST ALIENS TO VISIT EARTH SHOULD BE GIVEN A CORDIAL WELCOME!

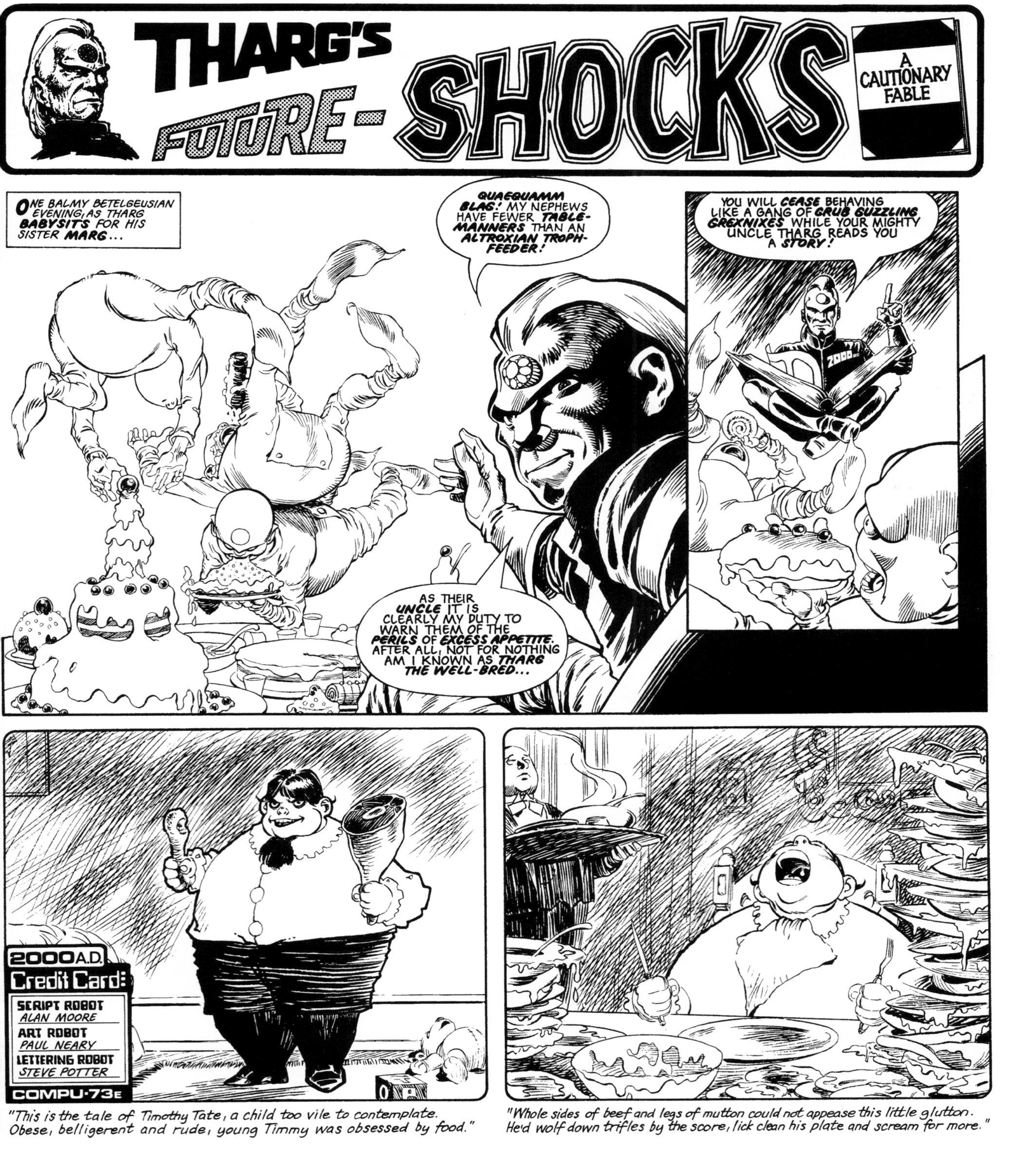

ONE BALMY BETELGEUSIAN EVENING, AS THARG BABYSITS FOR HIS SISTER MARG...

QUAEQUAMM BLAG! MY NEPHEWS HAVE FEWER TABLE-MANNERS THAN AN ALTROXIAN TROPH-FEEDER!

AS THEIR UNCLE IT IS CLEARLY MY DUTY TO WARN THEM OF THE PERILS OF EXCESS APPETITE. AFTER ALL, NOT FOR NOTHING AM I KNOWN AS THARG THE WELL-BRED...

YOU WILL CEASE BEHAVING LIKE A GANG OF GRUB GUZZLING GREXNIXES WHILE YOUR MIGHTY UNCLE THARG READS YOU A STORY!

2000 A.D.
Credit Card
SCRIPT ROBOT ALAN MOORE
ART ROBOT PAUL NEARY
LETTERING ROBOT STEVE POTTER
COMPU-73E

"This is the tale of Timothy Tate, a child too vile to contemplate.
Obese, belligerent and rude, young Timmy was obsessed by food."

"Whole sides of beef and legs of mutton could not appease this little glutton.
He'd wolf down trifles by the score, lick clean his plate and scream for more."

"As if afflicted by a curse, his appetite grew more diverse.
Despite his parents' frosty stares he'd often gnaw through legs of chairs."

"He'd munch, with unashamed glee, through carpets and upholstery...
and household pets too slow to flee would often vanish, utterly."

"The parents of his friends, in fear, forbade their offspring to go near
lest they should up as a feast for this demented little beast."

"He stalked alone, shunned by his peers, in verdant woodlands growing near,
and at the tremor of his tread the timid forest creatures fled."

"One evening, as he dined on twigs, a sound disturbed this prince of pigs,
and looking up saw something bright descending from the starry night."

"The glowing disc dropped from the sky toward a leafy glade nearby,
and from it's hatch, as Timmy hid, a brace of curious creatures slid."

"Who knows from what dim, distant star this puzzling pair had journeyed far?
But Tim, his beady eyes alert, had but one thought, which was dessert!"

"Imagine then their vast surprise, these voyagers from beyond the skies,
when with a shriek, from out the gloom, leapt sixteen stones of sudden doom!"

"They had no time to flee or fight... he scarfed them down without respite.
Sated at last, this fleshy heap burped once, and smiled, and fell asleep."

"But children, though they love to munch, should not eat aliens for lunch;
the meal which caused such satisfaction produced a chemical reaction."

"On waking, Timmy learned in fright that he'd grown larger in the night.
'Oh woe is me!' cried master Tate, 'It must have been something I ate!'"

"Not only Timbo's body grew... his appetite was larger too!
So, trampling timber all around, he headed off towards the town."

"The buildings shook as he grew near, and townsfolk, overcome by fear, began to panic, scream and run. His vast girth blotted out the sun."

"In that wild, hunger-crazed affray he ate six cars, two brewer's drays, the general stores, and, now quite mad, poor hapless Tom, the baker's lad."

"Then, trampling what he did not scoff, he left the town and wandered off towards a nearby city where, he hoped for more substantial fare."

"The police force and the army too found there was nothing they could do, as Timmy, with tremendous glee, ate five platoons of infantry."

"His parents and the village priest were called to beg the slavering beast that once had been their son to cease. (They barely got out in one piece!)"

"He ate three libraries and a school; he drank the public swimming pool, devoured an office block or two, then bolted down the local zoo."

"But even monsters need a rest and somewhere tranquil to digest.
He climbed a lofty spire and stopped when he could go no higher."

"But here less peace was to be found than there had been upon the ground.
From out the sun the fighters came with guns that chattered, spitting flame!"

"Enraged he whirled his mighty fist, crushed one, swung at another, missed.
Then to an awful roar gave vent, as toppling over down he went.

"Folk had no sympathy for Tim, but cried 'What shall we do with him?
He blocks the street, it's plain to see! Besides, it isn't sanitary!'"

"Then up spoke Mr. Horace Bloggs of 'Fonebone's Food for Healthy Dogs'.
He said 'I've sent for trucks and trains! We'll deal with Timmy's vast remains'!"

"We dare not show what hideous fate befell the shell of Timmy Tate.
But happy pets, in sated bliss, still lick their chops and reminisce.

... SO, CHILDREN, REMEMBER TIMOTHY TATE, AND LEAVE A LITTLE ON YOUR PLATE!
THE END

THARG'S FUTURE-SHOCKS
The Masks of Arazzor
THE PLANET ARAZZOR...
CROUCHING ON THE WIND-SWEPT PLAIN LIKE A GIANT SILVER SPIDER, THE SURVEY-SHIP HELIOS BROODS SILENTLY, THE ROAR OF ITS LANDING-ROCKETS LONG FORGOTTEN...
HELIOS
LOOKS FAIRLY PRIMITIVE...BRICK AND STONE MOSTLY... DEFINITELY A PRE-TECHNOLOGICAL CITY...
BIG THOUGH, CAPTAIN!
LOOKS LIKE RICHTER AND TRUMAN ARE COMING BACK... THEY'LL TELL US MORE...
CAPTAIN BOB BEALE HAS FOUND MANY STRANGE THINGS SURVEYING NEW WORLDS. BUT NEVER...
A CITY OF THE DEAD, CAPTAIN! RICHTER AND I DIDN'T FIND A SINGLE LIVING THING!
NO SIGN OF THE INHABITANTS AT ALL?
"OH, THEY'RE THERE ALL RIGHT, CAPTAIN...WHAT'S LEFT OF THEM..."
"THE WHOLE PLACE IS JUST ONE GIGANTIC BONEYARD..."
THEY WERE HUMANOID... BUT I CAN'T FIND ANY TRACE OF WHAT DESTROYED THEM!
I'VE BROUGHT SOME BONES BACK FOR ANALYSIS, BUT I ESTIMATE IT HAPPENED ABOUT THIRTY YEARS AGO.

WHAT ABOUT YOU, RICHTER? ANY IDEAS?
WELL, IT'S **WEIRD**, CAPTAIN, BUT EVERY SINGLE MAN, WOMAN AND CHILD WAS WEARING ONE OF **THESE** MASKS OVER THEIR FACE...
THEY WORE THEM LIKE **THIS...**
RICHTER
HEY, RICHTER... YOU LOOK REALLY **STRANGE.**
YOU FEELING OKAY, RICHTER? **RICHTER?**
HEY! WHERE YOU **GOING,** RICHTER?
COME BACK HERE!
GET AFTER HIM, TRUMAN!
NO WAY I'LL CATCH HIM NOW, CAPTAIN!
AND THAT CITY'S LIKE A **RABBIT WARREN!** WE'LL NEVER FIND HIM IN THERE...
BLAST! WHAT GOT INTO **HIM?**
GUESS WE'LL JUST HAVE TO WAIT UNTIL HE SEES SENSE AND COMES BACK.
BEALE
SLEEMAN'S PLANE IS COMING IN, SIR.
FOR THE MOMENT, RICHTER IS FOR-GOTTEN...
SORRY, CAPTAIN... **ALL** DEAD! CITIES FULL OF 'EM... AND ALL WEARING THOSE FACE-MASKS...
BUT I ALSO FOUND SOMETHING **ELSE...**
WHICH I FIGURED'D BE WORTH YOUR WHILE FLYING OUT AND TAKING A LOOK AT...
HELIOS

A COUPLE OF HUNDRED MILES AWAY...
SPACECRAFT WRECKAGE!... IT DOESN'T BELONG ON THIS PLANET... I DON'T KNOW IF IT BELONGS IN THIS GALAXY!
BUT I'D GUESS IT CRASHED HERE ABOUT THIRTY YEARS AGO.
2000 A.D.
Credit Card:
SCRIPT ROBOT STEVE MOORE
ART ROBOT CASANOVAS
LETTERING ROBOT BILL NUTTALL
COMPU-73E

AND THAT MAYBE ONE OR TWO OF THE CREW SURVIVED... FOR A WHILE, AT LEAST.
BEALE
THEN THEY MUST HAVE BROUGHT SOME KIND OF SPACE PLAGUE WITH THEM, THAT KILLED THE NATIVES. SOMETHING WE CAN'T DETECT...

BACK AT THE HELIOS...
RICHTER? WHAT ARE YOU...

RI— MMMF!

SUDDENLY...
AAUUGH!
BEALE
HELIOS
SLEEMAN? WHY, THE CRAZY, STINKING... THEY'RE FIRING AT US!

TIME PASSES. AND, EVENTUALLY, THE SCOUT-PLANE RETURNS TO THE HELIOS...
WHAT IN THE DEVIL'S NAME? NOW THEY'RE ALL WEARING MASKS! AND LOADING HUNDREDS OF THEM INTO THE SHIP!
HEY! YOU GUYS...!
RICHTER

BEALE DEFENDS HIMSELF...
MMP!

WHICH IS **NOT** A MASK...
THOSE THINGS...THEY'RE **ALIVE!** THEY **CONTROL** PEOPLE TILL THEY'RE NO USE, OR DIE...
AND WHAT JUST HAPPENED TO TRUMAN...MUST HAVE HAPPENED TO **EVERYONE** ON THE **PLANET...**

HE CAN'T BEAR TO **SEE** WHAT HAPPENS NEXT...
BUT HE CANNOT TURN HIS EYES AWAY...
AS TRUMAN'S BODY UNDERGOES A HORRIFIC TRANSFORMATION...
LEAVING ONLY BONES, AND A **MASK...**

OF COURSE! THEY MUST HAVE ARRIVED ON THAT ALIEN SHIP WE FOUND, USING THE PILOTS LIKE THEY'RE USING RICHTER NOW...
BEALE
BUT WHEN THE SHIP CRASHED, THEY WERE **STUCK** HERE ON A WORLD WITHOUT SPACEFLIGHT...

SO THEY SIMPLY **CONSUMED** EVERYONE AND LAY DORMANT UNTIL ANOTHER SHIP ARRIVED THAT COULD TAKE THEM TO A NEW WORLD...
NO! RICHTER'S READYING THE **HELIOS** FOR **TAKE-OFF!** IF THOSE THINGS REACH EARTH THEY'LL SPREAD **EVERY-WHERE...**

BUT THERE AREN'T ANY WEAPONS ON THE SCOUT-PLANE TO **STOP** THEM...
EXCEPT THE PLANE **ITSELF!**
HELIOS

BEALE SETS THE SCOUT-SHIP ON A SUICIDE COURSE...
RICHTER

AND DIES KNOWING THAT **HIS** SHIP WILL CARRY THE MASKS NO FURTHER...
VA-BOOMM!

BUT **HIS** SHIP WAS NOT **ALONE** IN THAT SECTOR...
I'VE PICKED UP A DISTRESS SIGNAL FROM AN **ENSIGN RICHTER**, SIR...THEN IT SUDDENLY **CUT OFF**... BUT I GOT A TRACE ON IT...
PREPARE TO CHANGE COURSE...

AND SOON THE ROAR OF THE **NAPIER'S** LANDING ROCKETS IS FADING ON THE WINDSWEPT PLAIN, AND...
ALL **DEAD**, SIR...
BUT THEY SEEM TO BE WEARING THESE FUNNY **MASKS**...
NAPIER
The End

"HI, I'M JOE BLACK, INTREPID SPACE SKIPPER FOR PEST, THE PLANETARY EXPLORATION AND SURVEY TRUST. YOU COULD SAY I'M ONE OF THEIR TOP OPERATORS . . ."
PEST
"I LIKE MY SHUT-EYE, TOO . . ."
ZZZZZZ!
THARG'S FUTURE-SHOCKS
JOE BLACK'S TALL TALE!
PEST
"UNFORTUNATELY, MY ONE-MAN SHIP'S EQUIPPED WITH A WORKAHOLIC COMPUTER!"
ATTENTION! UNKNOWN PLANET WITHIN SENSOR RANGE. INDICATIONS OF CIVILISED AND INTELLIGENT LIFE FORMS.
OKAY, OKAY. PUT IT ON THE SCREEN AND LETS SEE WHAT SORT OF BUG-EYED MONSTERS WE'VE FOUND THIS TIME. . .
ANALYSIS INDICATES HUMAN SPECIMENS ARE MAIN INHABITANTS. CIV LEVEL. 0·78 ALPHA, PRE-ATOMIC WITH RADIO AND TV COMMUNICATIONS.
THAT'LL DO.
"I FOLLOWED STANDARD, FIRST CONTACT PROCEDURE AND OPENED A CHANNEL TO THEIR LEADER. NICE."
GREETINGS, TRAVELLER— WE HAVE TRACKED YOUR VESSEL INTO OUR SYSTEM. WE TRUST THAT YOUR INTENTIONS ARE PEACEFUL...
OH, ER, YEAH— I REPRESENT THE PLANETARY EXPLORATION AND SURVEY TRUST. WE SEEK ONLY KNOWLEDGE...
AND MAYBE A FEW BUCKS ON THE SIDE, TOO. . !
2000 A.D. Credit Card:
SCRIPT ROBOT K. GOSNELL
ART ROBOT JOHN HIGGINS
LETTERING ROBOT TONY JACOB
COMPU·73E

I AM PRINCESS ELVIRA - MY FAMILY HAS RULED THIS PLANET FOR GENERATIONS. WE ARE JUST AND FAIR RULERS AND PRIDE OURSELVES THAT THERE HAS BEEN NO WAR ON OUR WORLD FOR HUNDREDS OF YEARS . . .
WE HAVE A RICH AND PROSPEROUS WORLD - AND WOULD WELCOME TRADE WITH YOUR PEOPLE.
JOE MY BOY- THIS IS YOUR CHANCE FOR THE BIG SCORE!
PEST
I MEAN, SHE'S GOT A WHOLE PLANET AT HER DISPOSAL - THAT'S THE SORT OF THING YOU'VE GOT TO SHARE...
PEST
AH, WELL - WE EARTHMEN HAVE A LITTLE CUSTOM. A CERTAIN RITUAL WHICH WE USE TO CEMENT RELATION-SHIPS, AS IT WERE...
PEST
IT'S CALLED MARRIAGE - A SORT OF LONG-TERM CONTRACT...
THIS SOUNDS LIKE THE SORT OF DEAL WE ARE INTERESTED IN, JOE BLACK. BRING YOUR CRAFT IN TO A LANDING, WE WILL DISCUSS IT FURTHER...
THIS IS IT, SON. YOU STRUCK GOLD. YOU'LL BE THE KING OF A PLANET! PEST CAN GO JUMP IN A BLACK HOLE!
"BUT AS I LEFT MY SHIP. . . ."
PEST
I DON'T BELIEVE... THIS . . .
WELCOME, JOE BLACK.

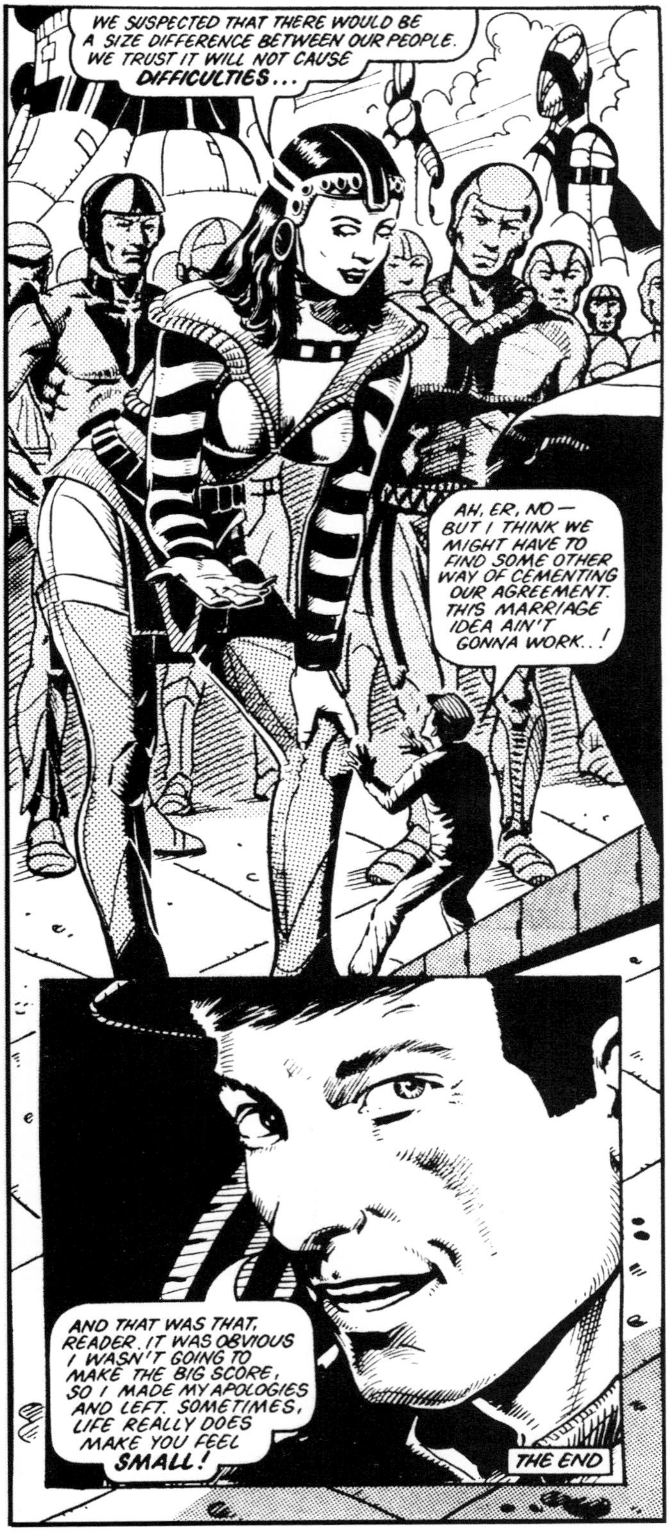

WE SUSPECTED THAT THERE WOULD BE A SIZE DIFFERENCE BETWEEN OUR PEOPLE. WE TRUST IT WILL NOT CAUSE **DIFFICULTIES...**

AH, ER, NO— BUT I THINK WE MIGHT HAVE TO FIND SOME OTHER WAY OF CEMENTING OUR AGREEMENT. THIS MARRIAGE IDEA AIN'T GONNA WORK..!

AND THAT WAS THAT, READER. IT WAS OBVIOUS I WASN'T GOING TO MAKE THE BIG SCORE, SO I MADE MY APOLOGIES AND LEFT. SOMETIMES, LIFE REALLY DOES MAKE YOU FEEL **SMALL!**

THE END

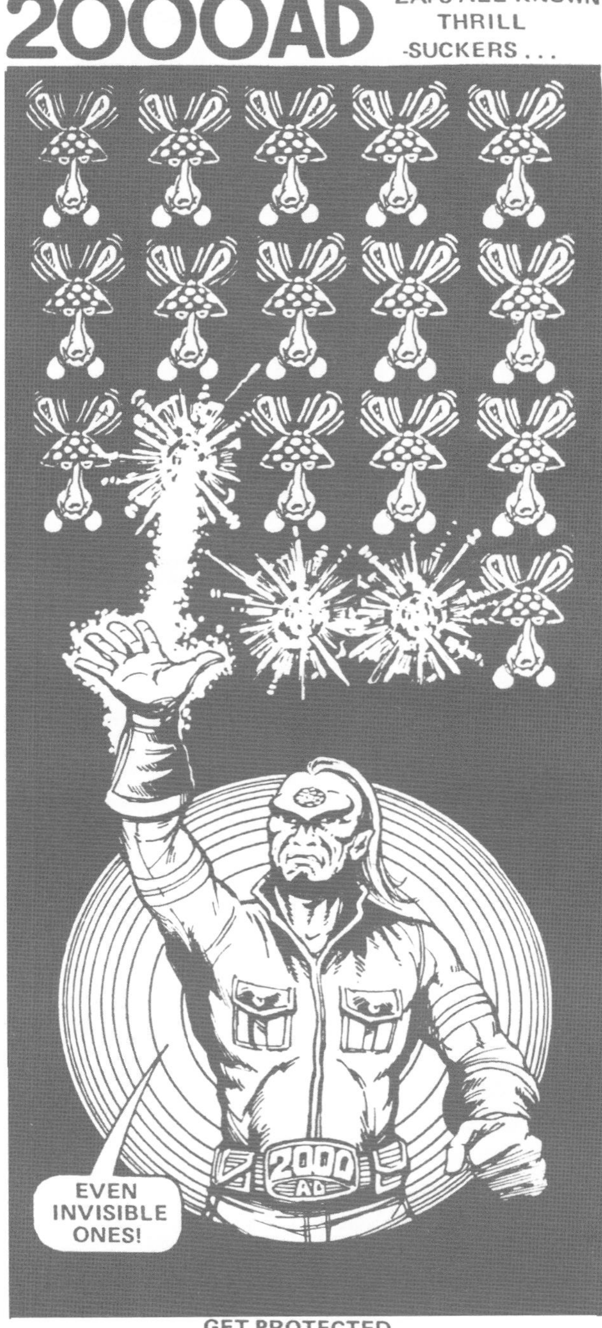

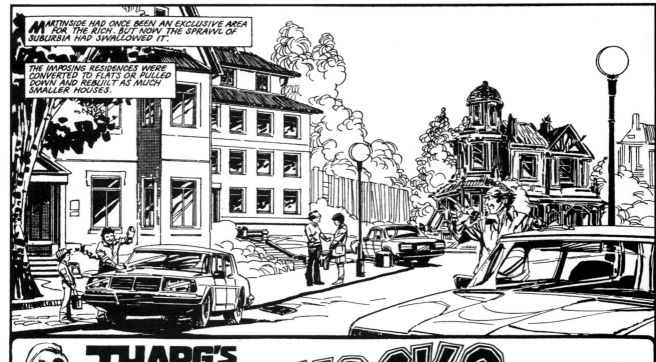

MARTINSIDE HAD ONCE BEEN AN EXCLUSIVE AREA FOR THE RICH. BUT NOW THE SPRAWL OF SUBURBIA HAD SWALLOWED IT.

THE IMPOSING RESIDENCES WERE CONVERTED TO FLATS OR PULLED DOWN AND REBUILT AS MUCH SMALLER HOUSES.

THARG'S
FUTURE-SHOCKS
LOVE THY NEIGHBOUR!

OLD ALBERT REMEMBERED WHAT IT USED TO BE LIKE AND HATED WHAT IT HAD BECOME.
PAH! LOOK AT 'EM! PLAYING WITH THEIR FANCY ELECTRICAL GADGETS. I HATE 'EM! I HATE 'EM ALL!
2000 A.D.
Credit Card:
SCRIPT ROBOT K. GOSNELL
ART ROBOT J. REDONDO
LETTERING ROBOT STEVE POTTER
COMPU-73E

MOST NEIGHBOURHOODS HAVE AN 'ALBERT'— SOME CAN BE QUITE HARMLESS...
WHERE'S MY PACKAGE, YOU VILLAIN? I KNOW YOU OPENED IT TO PRY ON ME...
KEEP YER WIG ON, ALBIE!

ALBERT WAS NOT ONE OF THOSE— HE WAS PLAIN NASTY!
HEH, HEH— GOT IT AT LAST. NOW I'LL SHOW THEM...

HE EVEN TRIED TO BUILD MACHINES TO DO NASTY THINGS TO PEOPLE...
FORTUNATELY, HIS DISSOLVING-FLUID SPRAYER, HIS BRAIN-DESTROYING RAY AND ALL THE OTHER NASTY INVENTIONS HAD NOT WORKED...

HIS CURRENT PROJECT WAS A MACHINE WHICH STOPPED ALL ELECTRICITY SO FOLKS COULDN'T USE THEIR LAWN-MOWERS AND DIGITAL WATCHES...
OWWW! THAT'S HOT!
BURN ME, WILL YOU? TAKE THAT, YOU INFERNAL CONTRAPTION!
KKLUNG!
IT WAS AT THAT MOMENT THAT ALL THE LIGHTS WENT OUT...
ALBERT'S KICK HAD DONE SOMETHING TO THE MACHINE. IT WORKED.
FOR A THREE KILOMETRE RADIUS, ALL ELECTRICAL ACTIVITY STOPPED...
HEY, MY WATCH HAS STOPPED!
CAN'T FIND A THING WRONG...
WORK, YOU HEAP!
FUNNY-BATTERIES ARE BRAND NEW...
IT HADN'T TAKEN ALBERT LONG TO REALISE WHAT HAD HAPPENED...
HAHAHAHAHAHAHA! VICTORY!
WHAT'S GOING ON?
DON'T KNOW. MAYBE ALBERT'S GONE COMPLETELY ROUND THE BEND!
UNFORTUNATELY, THE THREE KILOMETRE RANGE OF THE DEVICE EXTENDED VERTICALLY UPWARDS...
BLUE LEADER TO BASE-TOTAL ELECTRICAL SYSTEMS FAILURE! ALL CONTROL GONE!

HIS PLANE USELESS THE PILOT HAD ONLY ONE CHOICE...
EJECT!
WOOOOMPF!!
ALL OF WHICH WAS VERY UNFORTUNATE— ESPECIALLY FOR ALBERT.
NOOOOOOOo!
POOR OLD ALBERT— STILL HE PROBABLY DIDN'T FEEL A THING...
HERE— MY WATCH HAS STARTED AGAIN!
YOU DON'T RECKON THAT ALBERT HAD ANYTHING TO DO WITH THE ELECTRIC BUSINESS? HE WAS ALWAYS TINKERING WITH WEIRD GIZMOS.
OLD ALBERT? NAH, LEAVE IT OUT— HE WAS JUST AN HARM-LESS OLD COOT!
The End

THARG'S FUTURE-SHOCKS
MISTER, COULD YOU USE A SQUONGE?
A DIMLY-LIT ROOM SOMEWHERE UNDER PENNSYLVANIA AVENUE, WASHINGTON, D.C...
HECK, BOYS... IT'S NO BOTHER!
WE'RE SORRY TO BOTHER YOU LIKE THIS, SIR. BUT IT'S A MATTER OF GRAVEST NATIONAL CONCERN!
2000 A.D. Credit Card:
SCRIPT ROBOT A. MOORE
ART ROBOT R. TINER
LETTERING ROBOT T. SKOMSKI
COMPU-73E
IT'S THE SQUONGES, SIR! WE'VE FOUND OUT WHAT'S WRONG WITH THE SQUONGES! THEY'RE...
NOW HOLD ON, YOUNGSTER. MAYBE YOU'D BETTER START AT THE BEGINNING!
"WELL, AS YOU KNOW SIR, IT ALL BEGAN WHEN STARPROBE FIVE CAME BACK FROM ITS TWO-YEAR MISSION TO CENTAURI..."
PRESS
SAMPLE BAG 0417
ASTRONAUT HUCKLEBUN! DID YOU CONTACT ANY ALIEN LIFE-FORMS OUT THERE?
PRESS CONFERENCE LATER, GENTLEMEN. ONE SIDE, PLEASE...
"WE'D ALL BEEN PRETTY EXCITED BY THE PROSPECT OF WHAT HUCKLEBUN HAD FOUND OUT THERE."

"AFTER ALL, STARPROBE FIVE COST BILLIONS OF DOLLARS. SO YOU CAN IMAGINE OUR CHAGRIN WHEN WE FOUND WE'D SPENT ALL THAT MONEY ON..."
DEAD JELLYFISH ??
UHH... I THOUGHT THEY LOOKED KINDA INTERESTING. KINDA SQUONGEY.
SQUONGEY?
"THE NAME STUCK. STARPROBE FIVE HAD NETTED US A DOZEN SQUONGES... WHATEVER THEY WERE!"
IT LOOKS LIKE A LIFE-FORM, BUT IT'S MADE OUT OF SOME KIND OF PLASTIC. MAYBE IT'S THE WORK OF AN ADVANCED ALIEN CIVILISATION...
YEAH. I GUESS YOU'D HAVE TO BE PRETTY ALIEN TO WANT TO MAKE DEAD PLASTIC JELLYFISH.
"WHATEVER HUCKLEBUN HAD FOUND ON THAT DESERTED PLANETOID, TO US SCIENTISTS THEY ONLY MEANT ONE THING... HEADACHES."
THESE THINGS OUGHT TO BE ALIVE... THEY'VE GOT A COMPLICATED CELL-STRUCTURE AND SOME SORT OF NERVOUS SYSTEM...
THEN WHY DON'T THEY DO ANYTHING? THEY DON'T SHOW ANY SIGN OF LIFE AT ALL...
"BUT WE WERE WRONG. THE SQUONGES DID SHOW ONE SIGN OF LIFE..."
"...THEY REPRODUCED."
!!!
KEEP OUT
WASTE PAPER
"AND SOON—"
WE'VE GOT EIGHT WAREHOUSES FULL OF THESE USELESS BLOBS OF GLOOP AND THERE'S MORE EVERY DAY!
NOT ONLY THAT, BUT THE TREASURY IS BREATHING DOWN OUR NECKS OVER THE MONEY WE WASTED ON STARPROBE! WHAT ARE WE GOING TO DO?

"THERE WAS ONLY ONE ANSWER..."
WE'LL SELL 'EM TO THE PUBLIC AS NOVELTY ITEMS!
OF COURSE! REMEMBER HOW EVERYBODY WENT WILD OVER PET ROCKS?
SQUONGE REPORTS
DAY 25
INFORMATION
Nothing New
"THE AD BOYS WENT SWIFTLY TO WORK, AND A FEW NIGHTS LATER–"
MISTER, COULD YOU USE A SQUONGE? HAVE A CLOSE ENCOUNTER OF YOUR VERY OWN WITH THESE CUDDLY LITTLE CRITTERS FROM OUTER SPACE!!
SWEETIES
WHUH? A SQUONGE? DO YOU KNOW WHAT A SQUONGE IS, MADGE??
"THE RESPONSE WAS OVERWHELMING. THE AMERICAN PUBLIC TOOK THE INERT, RUBBERY LITTLE LUMPS TO THEIR HEARTS..."
PLEASE! ONLY ONE PER CUSTOMER!!
NEW
I SAW THE TURQUOISE ONE FIRST!!
YOU'VE ALREADY GOT A SQUONGE! THIS ONE'S MINE!!
"WITHIN DAYS THE GOVERNMENT HAD MORE THAT RECOUPED THE LOSSES IT HAD MADE ON THE SPACEPROBE. THINGS LOOKED ROSY..."
"...UNTIL ONE FATEFUL MORNING ON A SUBURBAN LAWN SOMEWHERE IN VERMONT..."
MILTON! MY BABY! OH MY SOUL... HE'S STUCK HIS HEAD IN ONE OF THOSE AWFUL THINGS!!
THE SWEATEST
GEE, MOM... IS IT GONNA BURST OUT OF MILTON LIKE IN THAT "ALIEN" MOVIE?? THAT'D BE REALLY NEAT!
"LITTLE MILTON GROZINSKI WAS RUSHED TO A GOVERNMENT HOSPITAL IMMEDIATELY."
WELL, DOC? DID YOU MANAGE TO GET THAT ALIEN OFF HIS FACE?
YES, BUT THERE'S SOMETHING I THINK YOU GUYS SHOULD SEE...
...THUS, THE ELECTRONIC AGE, SYMBOLISED BY SIMULTANEITY, DEMANDS A WHOLLY NEW MODEL... THAT OF A DIS-CONTINUITY IN THE UNIVERSAL STATE...
UHH... WHAT'S HE SAYING?
I DON'T KNOW. BUT I THINK I DO KNOW WHAT IT MEANS...
IT MEANS THAT SQUONGE HAS TURNED LITTLE MILTON GROZINSKI INTO A GENIUS!

"IN THE WEEKS THAT FOLLOWED, EXTENSIVE TESTS WERE MADE..."
...IN ORDER OF COMPLEXITY WE MUST DIFFERENTIATE BETWEEN CO-ORDINATES WHICH RESULT FROM DIRECT CONTACTUAL INTERACTION BETWEEN CELLS, AND...
NO DOUBT ABOUT IT. HE'S A GENIUS. BUT WHAT THE HELL ARE THOSE SQUONGES?
I THINK I'M GETTING A PRETTY GOOD IDEA!
I THINK THEY'RE EXO-BRAINS! YOU KNOW HOW EXO-SKELETONS BOOST THE PHYSICAL STRENGTH OF THE WEARER? WELL I FIGURE THAT EXO-BRAINS...
...BOOST THE INTELLIGENCE!! GRIEF! DO YOU REALISE WHAT THIS MEANS FOR HUMANITY?
"I REALISED ONLY TOO WELL. IT MEANT A WHOLE WORLD FULL OF GENIUSES!"
...AND NINTHLY, IF WE INTERELATE THE FIVE LEVEL VARIABLES OF POPULATION, NATURAL RESOURCES, CAPITAL-INVESTMENT-IN-AGRICULTURE FRACTION...
OF COURSE! THE KNOWN AND INTENDED PRACTICES OF ORGANIZATION ARE OFTEN FULLY SUFFICIENT TO INVESTIGATE THE CRISIS SCENARIO!
"IT WAS LIKE THE DAWN OF A NEW AGE. SUDDENLY, NO PROBLEM SEEMED TO BE BEYOND HUMANITY'S GRASP... EXCEPT ONE!"
OKAY... SO SOME ALIEN CIVILISATION INVENTED THE EXO-BRAIN TO SOLVE ALL ITS PROBLEMS.
BUT WHY DID THEY LEAVE A DOZEN OF THEM ON THAT DESERTED PLANETOID? IT JUST DOESN'T MAKE SENSE!
"NOT TO US IT DIDN'T... BUT THERE WAS NO REASON WHY WE COULDN'T PUT THE QUESTION TO A SQUONGE..."
OBVIOUSLY, THE EXO-BRAINS WERE PUT ON THE DESERTED PLANETOID BECAUSE... ER... BECAUSE... BECAUSE... THEY... ER...
...COULD YOU REPEAT THE QUESTION?
I DON'T BELIEVE IT! IT DOESN'T KNOW!

"DO YOU SEE? THE SQUONGE COULD CREATE UNLIMITED INTELLIGENCE... BUT IT DIDN'T KNOW THE ANSWER TO THAT ONE TINY QUESTION..."
...I WONDER WHY?
"THE WEEKS WENT BY, AND STILL WE RESTLED WITH OUR ONE LITTLE NAGGING PROBLEM. AND THEN, ONE NIGHT..."
WHAT IS THE ONE THING THAT THE GREATEST BRAIN IN THE UNIVERSE CANNOT KNOW ABOUT ITSELF?
...FOR ALL I CARE, THE ALIENS LEFT THE SQUONGES ON THAT PLANETOID BECAUSE PEOPLE WERE USING THEM TO CHEAT WITH RUBRIC CUBES!
HA HA HA HA! YOU'RE CRAZY!
"THE PROBLEM SEEMED INSIGNIFICANT, BUT IT BOTHERED US. NOT SO THE REST OF THE WORLD HOWEVER. THE SQUONGES WERE SELLING BETTER THAN EVER..."
BUT DON'T YOU SEE... THE UNIQUE ATTRIBUTE TO LIVING MATTER IS ITS CAPACITY FOR SELF DUPLICATION WITH MUTATION.
OH, DON'T BOTHER ME NOW, SHAMUS. I'M WORKING ON MY THESIS CONCERNING THE AUTOKINETIC PHENOMENON AND ITS RELEVANCE TO PERCEPTION...
WHO ARE YOU CALLING CRAZY? I'M NOT CRAZY! I'D KNOW IF I WAS CRAZY!
NOT YOU, PAL! YOU'RE SO CRAZY THAT... THAT...
...THAT YOU DON'T KNOW YOU'RE CRAZY.
...OH, HELL...
"WE'D DONE IT. WE FINALLY WORKED OUT WHAT THE GREATEST BRAIN IN THE UNIVERSE CANNOT POSSIBLY KNOW ABOUT ITSELF..."

THE SQUONGES HAD BEEN DUMPED ON THAT PLANETOID BECAUSE THEY WERE A FAULTY BATCH! EVERY LAST ONE OF THEM WAS INSANE!!
"AS WE DROVE TO THE WHITE HOUSE WE REALISED JUST HOW SERIOUS THINGS HAD BECOME WHILE WE WERE CLOSETED AWAY WITH OUR PROBLEM..."
729TH STREET
ONE WAY
IT'S OBVIOUS! ALL THESE LITTLE BLUE PIECES OF GLASS REPRESENT THE MEANING OF LIFE...
LISTEN, OKAY, YOU'RE A FIRE HYDRANT. I CAN RELATE TO THAT...
...SO THAT'S THE STORY, MR. PRESIDENT. WHAT WITH OUR OVERSEAS SHIPMENTS THE SQUONGES MUST HAVE DRIVEN HALF THE WORLD CRAZY BY NOW!
WE'VE GOT TO DO SOMETHING! EVEN MAKING PEOPLE TAKE THEM OFF WON'T HELP... THE EFFECTS ARE PERMANENT!
WELL, THAT'S QUITE A POSER, BOYS. WHAT DO YOU SAY, MR. SECRETARY OF STATE?
"AND, AS THE OFFICIALS LEANED FORWARD INTO THE LIGHT..."
I'M NOT THE SECRETARY OF STATE! I'M ACTUALLY BO DEREK!
HMMM WELL THE WAY I SEE IT WHAT WE HAVE HERE IS A JELLYBEAN PROBLEM!
NO, NO, NO! IT'S THE MARTIAN RADIATION THAT'S TO BLAME! THEY PUT IT IN THE LIGHTBULBS.
WAIT! I'M GETTING A MESSAGE FROM THE WATER-COOLER!!
...UHHH... THEN DIVIDE ALL THAT BY THE RED JELLYBEANS, AND... UHH...
...OH NO...!
...AND THERE WE HAVE IT, EARTHLETS. IN THIS PARTICULAR TIME STREAM, THE WORLD ENDS NOT WITH A BANG, NOT WITH A WHIMPER, BUT WITH A GIGGLE! MIND... HOW YOU GO!
THE END

THARG'S FUTURE-SHOCKS
A SECOND CHANCE!
THE BOMBS FELL, THE MUSHROOMS ROSE . . .
. . . AND SOON, WHERE ONCE THE PROUD SPIRES OF CIVILISATION HAD REARED AGAINST THE SKY, THERE WAS NOTHING, NOTHING BUT RUIN AND DESOLATION . . .
. . . NOTHING BUT DUST!
KOFF
KOFF KOFF
KOFF
I-I DON'T BELIEVE IT . . .
I MADE IT! I'M STILL ALIVE!
2000 A.D. Credit Card:
SCRIPT ROBOT ALAN MOORE
ART ROBOT JOSÉ CASANOVAS
LETTERING ROBOT JACK POTTER
COMPU·73E
OH, LORD! LOOK AT ALL THE DESTRUCTION! NOTHING ELSE COULD HAVE LIVED THROUGH A HOLOCAUST LIKE THAT!
WHY . . . I MUST BE THE LAST MAN ON EARTH! ME! ADAM WILBERFORCE BUNSTRUGGLE!
IT'S SO TRAGIC! TO THINK THAT HUMANITY SHOULD COME TO THIS . . . JUST A PILE OF RADIOACTIVE RUBBLE. IT DOESN'T SEEM FAIR, SOMEHOW . . .
IF ONLY MANKIND COULD BE GIVEN ANOTHER CHANCE! IF ONLY THERE WERE SOME WAY TO START AGAIN! AHH, WHO AM I KIDDING? THAT'S JUST PLAIN . . .
. . . IMPOSSIBLE?
. . . HELP . . . SOMEBODY HELP . . .

..PLEASE.. WON'T SOMEBODY HELP ME? OHH...
GOOD LORD! THERE'S SOMEBODY TRAPPED UNDER THAT MASONRY!
...AND FROM THE VOICE IT SOUNDS LIKE IT'S...

A WOMAN! HERE... LET ME HELP YOU UP!
TH-THANK YOU. I.. I THOUGHT I WAS ALONE!

S-SO DID I! BUT NOW WE'RE TOGETHER... JUST THE TWO OF US! DON'T YOU SEE WHAT THAT MEANS?
WE CAN START THE HUMAN RACE ALL OVER AGAIN! GIVE MANKIND A SECOND CHANCE! ONLY THIS TIME WE'LL DO IT RIGHT!

OH YES! HOW WONDERFUL! B-BUT... BUT I DON'T EVEN KNOW YOUR NAME!

ME? MY NAME'S ADAM...
WHAT'S YOURS?

MAVIS.
THE BEGINNING..!

THARG'S FUTURE-SHOCKS
TWIST ENDING
Tak Tak... Tak Tak-Tak... Tak-Tak CHING!
AHH! THE SOUND OF A WRITER AT WORK! AND NOT JUST ANY WRITER...
OTHERWISE I WOULDN'T BE INTERVIEWING HIM FOR 'READ ANY GOOD BOOKS?' RADIO'S PROBING BOOK PROGRAMME..?
PRESS
Tak Tak Tak-Tak... Tak-Tak... Tak Tak...
NO, THIS IS NO ORDINARY RUN-OF-THE-MILL GENIUS! THIS IS LAMONT COSGROOSE, THE WORLD'S MOST SUCCESSFUL SCIENCE FICTION WRITER!
I'LL JUST KNOCK... HOPE HE CAN HEAR ME OVER ALL THAT TYPING...
YES?
GOOD MORNING, SIR. I'M FROM 'READ ANY GOOD BOOKS' MAGAZINE. I WONDER IF MR. LAMONT GOSGROOSE IS AT HOME?
I'M LAMONT COSGROOSE. 'SPOSE YOU BETTER COME IN...
INSIDE...
RIGHT. WHAT YER WANNA KNOW, THEN?
WELL, I THOUGHT WE COULD START BY DISCUSSING YOUR MOST FAMOUS BOOKS... WORKS LIKE "DAY OF THE GIANT RACCOON" AND "ATTACK OF THE KILLER PIZZAS"...
2000 A.D. Credit Card:
SCRIPT ROBOT ALAN MOORE
ART ROBOT PAUL NEARY
LETTERING ROBOT TONY JACOB
COMPU·73E

WHAT ABOUT 'EM, THEN?
WELL, I THINK OUR LISTENERS WOULD BE INTERESTED TO HEAR WHERE YOU GET YOUR IDEAS FROM...
YOUR DESCRIPTIONS OF ALIEN LIFE-FORMS ARE EXTRAORDINARILY CONVINCING...

WELL... I 'SPOSE IT'S JUST IMAGINATION, ISN'T IT?
OH COME NOW, MR. COSGROOSE! NO HUMAN IMAGINATION COULD HAVE COME UP WITH CREATIONS LIKE THE RUG-THINGS IN "NIGHT OF THE AXMINSTER"!
WELL, MR. COSGROOSE? WHAT'S YOUR SECRET? HMM?

SECRET? I DON'T KNOW WHAT YOU'RE TALKING ABOUT, MATE...
I THINK YOU DO, MR. GOSGROOSE! REMEMBER THE HINTS YOU DROPPED IN THE TWIST ENDING TO YOUR SHORT STORY "THE BEAST THAT TYPED LIKE A MAN"?
THE STORY WHERE IT TURNS OUT THAT THE BRILLIANT SCIENCE FICTION WRITER IS IN REALITY AN ALIEN FROM ANOTHER WORLD?

IS THAT IT? IS THAT ALL I HAVE TO DO TO REVEAL YOUR SECRET TO THE WORLD? TO GRAB HOLD OF THIS RIDICULOUS RUBBER MASK...
TO TEAR IT AWAY...
...TO ...ER...

HEH HEH...

HEH... WELL, I...ER... THINK THAT'S ABOUT ALL I WANTED TO ASK YOU, MR. COSGROOSE!
PLEASE DON'T WORRY... I'LL FIND MY OWN WAY OUT...

SLAM!
WELL, HE WAS A NUTTER AND NO MISTAKE...

...EH, GRAXL?
INDEED HE WAS, MR. COSGROOSE. THERE SEEM TO BE MANY DEMENTED BEINGS ON THIS PLANET OF YOURS...

I AM LUCKY THAT IT WAS SOMEONE AS SANE AND PRACTICAL AS YOURSELF WHO FOUND ME WHEN MY SHIP CRASHED HERE. MY GRATITUDE IS IMMENSE.
DON'T MENTION IT, GRAXL OLD SON. BY THE WAY... HAVE YOU FINISHED "INVASION OF THE DEATH-GERBILS" YET?
ALMOST DONE, MR. COSGROOSE ...ALMOST DONE!
GRAXL
Tak...Tak...Tak Tak Tak...Tak-Tak CHING!
THE END

THARG'S FUTURE-SHOCKS
2000

THARG'S FUTURE-SHOCKS
SALAD DAYS!
OUR FIRST CONTACT WITH AN ALIEN RACE! DO YOU REALLY THINK THEY'LL COME?
WELL, THEY SAID THEY'D BE LANDING HERE IN THEIR LAST RADIO MESSAGE. I WISH THEY'D HURRY. THIS WAITING IS MAKING ME HUNGRY...

ME, TOO. SHALL I TELL ONE OF THE MEN TO GET US SOME BURGERS?
NOT FOR ME, THANKS. I'VE GIVEN UP MEAT SINCE I BECAME A VEGETARIAN..
DO YOU THINK WE SHOULD HAVE MORE SOLDIERS AND TANKS UP HERE? I MEAN, WHAT IF THEY TURN OUT TO BE HOSTILE?
RELAX. ANYWAY, I DON'T THINK THE BEST WAY TO SHOW OUR PEACEFUL INTENTIONS IS TO SURROUND THEM WITH HARDWARE AS SOON AS THEY LAND.
BESIDES, I'VE NEVER HEARD ANYONE TALK ABOUT PEACE WITH SUCH CONVICTION AS THEY DID IN THEIR LAST MESSAGE!

ME NEITHER! WHAT WERE THEIR EXACT WORDS AGAIN? "WE ARE HUMANITARIANS, AND LOVE HUMANITY. WE COME WITH PURELY HUMANITARIAN INTENTIONS."
HEY! LOOK UP THERE! IN THE SKY!
IT'S THEM! THEY'VE FINALLY ARRIVED!
GEE, I CAN'T WAIT TO GET A LOOK AT THEM! DO YOU THINK THEY'LL LOOK LIKE US?

WITH ALL THAT TALK ABOUT HUMANITY I SHOULD THINK SO. ANYWAY, WE'LL SOON FIND OUT...
LOOK! A HATCHWAY'S OPENING UP IN THE SIDE OF THE SHIP!
THEY'RE COMING OUT... I CAN'T QUITE SEE THEM YET...
WAIT! HERE THEY COME! THEY'RE CLIMBING OUT OF THE SHIP! THEY'RE... THEY'RE...
..GOOD GRIEF!

THEY'RE VEGETABLES!
LOOK, YATTABLUG! HUMANS!
I SAY, MUNGWOOP! HOW SPIFFING! YOU KNOW HOW MUCH I ADORE HUMANS!
WELL? WHAT ARE WE WAITING FOR, CHAPS?
2000 A.D.
Credit Card:
SCRIPT ROBOT ALAN MOORE
ART ROBOT JOHN HIGGINS
LETTERING ROBOT JACK POTTER
COMPU-73E
....LET'S KILL THEM!
K-KILL?
W-WAIT! WHAT ARE YOU DOING? YOU SAID IN YOUR MESSAGE THAT YOU WERE HUMANITARIANS!
WELL, OF COURSE WE'RE HUMANITARIANS! STRICT HUMANITARIANS! AFTER ALL...
...WE ONLY EAT HUMANS, DON'T WE?
YAAAAGH!
THE END

DEEP IN AN UNEXPLORED REGION OF THE GALAXY, A SHIP OF THE PLANETARY EXPLORATION AND SURVEY TRUST—P.E.S.T.—TUNNELS THROUGH THE VOID. SUDDENLY ITS GUIDANCE COMPUTER SQUAWKS AN ALARM...

THARG'S FUTURE-SHOCKS

HORN OF PLENTY!

A JOE BLACK STORY

ALERT! ALERT! DISTRESS SIGNAL EMITTING FROM PLANET BELOW. REGULATIONS STATE...

I KNOW, I KNOW. "...ALL S.O.S. MESSAGES REQUIRE IMMEDIATE INVESTIGATION." STOP BLABBING AND TAKE US DOWN—

WHILE YOU'RE AT IT—LEARN HOW TO MAKE DECENT COFFEE, HUH?

"HI, I'M JOE BLACK, ONE OF PEST'S TOP OPERATORS, DESPITE WHAT IT SAYS IN MY REPORT..."

"I HOMED IN ON THE SIGNAL'S SOURCE AND FOUND A SMALL LIFEBOAT BY THE SIDE OF A GREAT CANYON..."

OKAY, PAL. WHAT HAPPENED..?

I-I JUST GOT INTO THE LIFEBOAT IN TIME. MY VESSEL MALFUNCTIONED ON A SLINGSHOT ORBIT ROUND THIS LUMP OF A PLANET...

SHE ENDED UP DOWN THERE—MADE AN AUTO-LANDING WITHOUT TOO MUCH DAMAGE... I DON'T KNOW WHAT TO DO...

SIMPLE, PAL. CLIMB ON MY VESSEL, WARP OUTTA HERE, AND CLAIM THE INSURANCE MONEY...

NO! I'VE **GOT** TO GET HER BACK! SHE'S **INVALUABLE** TO ME! IF YOU'LL RAISE HER I'LL GIVE YOU ANYTHING YOU WANT!

ANYTHING?

"WELL, I COULDN'T REFUSE AN OFFER LIKE THAT, COULD I? BESIDES I'M ALWAYS OPEN TO OFFERS OF A BIT OF **FREELANCE** WORK, SO LONG AS PEST DON'T FIND OUT..."

"HALFWAY DOWN..."

HEY! YOU'RE CUTE LITTLE FELLAS—WOULDN'T LIKE TO MEET YOUR MA, THOUGH!

Sqiiirk! Sqiiirk!

"I DID THOUGH, IN THE NEXT INSTANT...
SQAARK!
STREWTH!
SHE'S CUT MY LINE!
OOH!
AH!
UURGH!
"BY THE TIME I HIT BOTTOM, MY FLYING FRIEND HAD LOST INTEREST, BUT MY TROUBLES WERE ONLY BEGINNING..."
NOW WHAT..?
SCRABBLE!
SCRAPE!
2000 A.D.
Credit Card:
SCRIPT ROBOT K. GOSNELL
ART ROBOT JOHN HIGGINS
LETTERING ROBOT PETE KNIGHT
COMPU·73E
AAH! GERROF, YOU LITTLE BRUTE!
HELLFIRE! THERE'S HUNDREDS OF THEM!

"I MADE IT TO THE SHIP—JUST!"
GOT TO CLOSE THE AIRLOCK, FAST! THEN I'LL HAVE A WORD WITH MY SO-CALLED 'FRIEND' UP THERE!
"BUT SUDDENLY, MY ANGER WAS TURNED TO AWE..."
GRIEF! THE SHIP'S INTERIOR'S LIKE AN ALADDIN'S CAVE! ANTIQUES, VALUABLE PAINTINGS—THE LOT!
NO WONDER HE WANTED TO SAVE IT! LET'S JUST SEE IF IT CAN STILL FLY...
PEST
YES! COME ON, HEAP! FLY NICELY FOR YER UNCLE JOE!
"BACK TOPSIDE, THE OLD GUY WASN'T EXACTLY OVERCOME WITH GRATITUDE..."
YOU MIGHT HAVE WARNED ME ABOUT THE... HEY!
OUT OF MY WAY! I'VE GOT TO SEE IF IT IS ALL RIGHT...

"HE EMERGED LOOKING RELIEVED AND AND CLUTCHING WHAT I CAN ONLY DESCRIBE AS A HEAP OF JUNK!"
IT SEEMS TO BE UNDAMAGED. BUT I'LL HAVE TO TEST IT TO MAKE SURE.
HUH? ALL THOSE RICHES AND YOUR FIRST CONCERN IS THAT THING?
THIS 'THING,' AS YOU CALL IT, IS A REPLICATOR! IT CAN REPRODUCE ALMOST ANYTHING! WORKS OF ART, FOOD, HARDWARE, ANYTHING!
A SECOND MONA LISA'S APPEARING! NOW I KNOW WHY YOU SAID YOU'D GIVE ME ANYTHING!
I'LL TAKE THE MACHINE AS REWARD— AFTER WHAT YOU PUT ME THROUGH I RECKON I'VE EARNED IT...
VERY WELL—BUT ALLOW ME ONE LAST USE BEFORE I LOSE IT...
"I COULDN'T REALLY REFUSE, COULD I? I SHOULD HAVE KNOWN WHAT WAS COMING, AFTER HE GAVE IN SO EASILY..."
IT CAN OF COURSE REPLICATE ITSELF...
USE IT WISELY, YOUNG MAN. IT'LL ONLY GET YOU IN DEEP TROUBLE IF YOU DON'T...
"HE WAS RIGHT, OF COURSE. IT WAS NO USE SELLING COPIES OF THE THING—YOUR FIRST CUSTOMER COULD DO THE SAME THING. I DISCOVERED THAT IT WOULDN'T HANDLE ELEMENTS LIKE GOLD OR PLATINUM. THE POLICE WOULD BE TOO INTERESTED IN WORKS OF ART FLOODING THE MARKET. BUT IT DID HAVE ONE GREAT USE..."
HEY—THAT IS ONE GOOD CUP OF COFFEE!
THE END

THARG'S FUTURE-SHOCKS
THE BEASTLY BELIEFS OF BENJAMIN BLINT

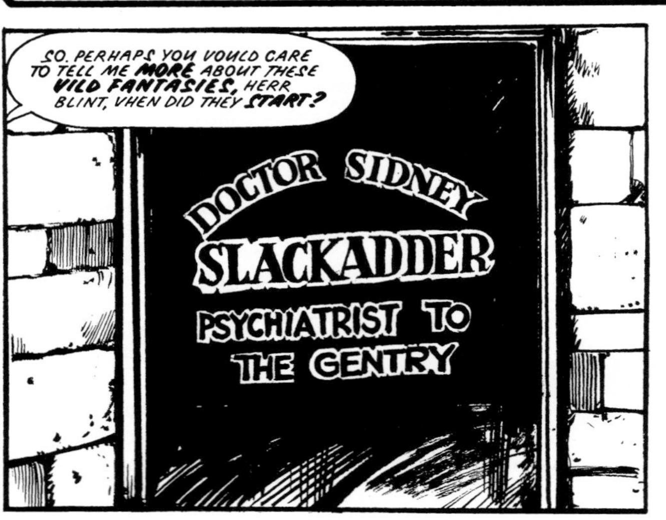
SO, PERHAPS YOU VOULD CARE TO TELL ME MORE ABOUT THESE VILD FANTASIES, HERR BLINT. VHEN DID THEY START?
DOCTOR SIDNEY SLACKADDER PSYCHIATRIST TO THE GENTRY

W-WELL, IT WAS JUST A SORT OF FEELING AT FIRST. A FEELING THAT I WAS BEING WATCHED BY HIDEOUS ALIEN CREATURES!
TO BEGIN WITH, I THOUGHT IT WAS MY MIND PLAYING TRICKS. AND THEN, ONE EVENING, WHILE I WAS WALKING HOME FROM WORK, IT HAPPENED!

"...I SAW ONE!"
"IT WAS INDESCRIBABLE. IT WAS THE MOST GHASTLY THING I HAD EVER SEEN. THERE WAS NO-ONE AROUND TO HELP ME SO I RAN ALL THE WAY HOME."
2000 A.D. Credit Card:
SCRIPT ROBOT ALAN MOORE
ART ROBOT ERIC BRADBURY
LETTERING ROBOT PETE KNIGHT
COMPU-73E

HMM. THIS IS VERY INTERESTING VHAT HAPPENED NEXT?
N-NOTHING. AT LEAST, NOT FOR A FEW WEEKS. IN FACT I'D ALMOST COME TO BELIEVE THAT THE WHOLE INCIDENT WAS JUST A TRICK OF THE LIGHT!
IMAGINE MY HORROR WHEN THE NEXT TIME I ENCOUNTERED ONE OF THE CREATURES IT WAS IN THE SUPPOSED PRIVACY OF MY OWN HOME...

"TO BE PRECISE, IT WAS IN THE BATHROOM."
"WE JUST STARED AT EACH OTHER FOR LONG MOMENTS BEFORE MY NERVE BROKE AND I FLED, SLAMMING THE DOOR. WHEN I LOOKED, LATER, IT HAD GONE..."
"FROM THEN ON I SAW THE CREATURES EVERYWHERE... IN THE BUS QUEUE, IN THE SUPERMARKET ON TELEVISION..."
"AND THEN, YESTERDAY MORNING, I WOKE UP TO FIND ONE IN BED NEXT TO ME. IT WAS THE FINAL STRAW, DOCTOR."
SOB YOU'VE GOT TO HELP ME, DOCTOR! EVERYWHERE I LOOK I SEE THOSE HORRIBLE WATERY EYES, THOSE WRIGGLING PINK TENTACLES! I CAN'T STAND IT!
YOU MUST NOT VORRY YOURSELF, HERR BLINT...
VHAT VE ARE TALKING ABOUT HERE IS A SIMPLE CASE OF PARANOID DELUSION!
YOU MUST TELL YOURSELF THAT THESE VEIRD AND VONDERFUL HALLUCINATIONS ARE ALL IN YOUR MIND...
SURELY YOU REALISE THAT SUCH CREATURES AS YOU DESCRIBE COULD NEVER EXIST IN REALITY?
I... I GUESS YOU'RE RIGHT, DOC...
...THERE JUST ISN'T ROOM IN THE REAL WORLD FOR CREATURES AS STOMACH-TURNING AND LOATHSOME AS THAT!
THAT IS VERY GOOD! I AM GLAD YOU BEGIN TO SEE REASON, HERR BLINT...
THAT WILL BE EIGHT HUNDRED PLASTOONS. SEE YOU NEXT THURSDAY!
The End

THARG'S FUTURE-SHOCKS

NOW YOU SEE IT...

STRANGE THINGS CAN HAPPEN ALONG THE EMPTY HIGHWAYS CROSSING AMERICA'S VAST WESTERN DESERTS . . .

2000 A.D.
Credit Card:
SCRIPT ROBOT ALAN HEBDEN
ART ROBOT ERIC BRADBURY
LETTERING ROBOT TONY JACOB
COMPU·73E

AAAIIIEEEGGH!

SOME VERY STRANGE THINGS INDEED!
THE END

THARG'S
FUTURE-SHOCKS
ALL OF THEM WERE EMPTY

"WE WERE SITTING IN MABEL'S TRUCK-STOP WHERE WE'D BEEN SITTING FOR THE PAST THREE DAYS. THEY WERE STILL OUTSIDE. SOMETIMES THEY SHOUTED IN..."
HEY! YOU IN THERE! COME ON OUT HERE AND GIVE US WHAT WE WANT!

WHAT ARE WE GOING TO DO, MERCE? WE'LL HAVE TO GO OUT SOONER OR LATER...
...WE'RE ALMOST OUT OF FOOD!
I...I DON'T KNOW. I THOUGHT IF WE DIDN'T GIVE THEM WHAT THEY NEEDED THEN WE COULD HOLD OUT LONGER THAN THEY COULD!

WELL, I AIN'T GONNA SIT HERE ANY LONGER LIKE A RAT IN A TRAP. I'M MAKIN' A RUN FOR IT!
CHET, YOU'RE CRAZY!! THEY'LL CUT YOU DOWN BEFORE YOU'RE HALFWAY ACROSS THE YARD!!
SHE'S RIGHT, CHET. YOU CAN'T GO OUT THERE!
2000 A.D.
Credit Card:
SCRIPT ROBOT ALAN MOORE
ART ROBOT PAUL NEARY
LETTERING ROBOT PETE KNIGHT
COMPU-73E

SKREEEEEEEEE
AAARRRGH!
TH-THEY GOT HIM!

IT'S ALL OUR FAULT. WE LET HIM GET AS STRONG AS THIS...
WE GOT DEPENDENT ON THEM. MADE THEM MORE AND MORE CAPABLE OF DOING THINGS FOR THEMSELVES SO THAT WE WOULDN'T HAVE TO DIRTY OUR HANDS DOING 'EM...

"...AND NOW WE'RE PAYIN' FOR IT. WE TAUGHT THEM HOW TO THINK FOR THEMSELVES, HOW TO TALK BY THEMSELVES, HOW TO GET AROUND BY THEMSELVES...
ONLY ONE THING THEY NEED US FOR, NOW. ONLY ONE THING THAT THEY CAN'T DO FOR THEMSELVES...

"RIGHT ON CUE THAT DEEP, RASPING VOICE STARTED UP AGAIN..."
HEY! THIS IS YOUR LAST CHANCE! COME OUT AND DO AS WE SAY OR WE'RE COMING IN!
THEY MEAN IT. I THINK I SAW A BULLDOZER OUT THERE...

I GUESS THERE'S ONLY ONE THING TO DO, THEN. I GUESS WE GO OUT THERE AND GIVE 'EM WHAT THEY WANT...
B-BUT THEN WE'LL HAVE TO KEEP ON GIVING IT TO THEM! WE'LL BE THEIR SERVANTS!
FATS

YEAH, I KNOW!
COME ON. WE MAY AS WELL GET THIS OVER WITH...
"...AND SO WE WALKED OUT, INTO THE AFTERNOON SUN. THEY WERE WAITING FOR US BY THE PUMPS. THEY WERE PURRING..."

"WE STARTED PUMPING IN THE PETROL THAT THEY NEEDED. IT TOOK A LONG TIME...THERE WERE LOTS OF THEM. TRUCKS, BUSES, CARS, VANS..."
"...AND ALL OF THEM WERE EMPTY."
THE END

THE HUME FACTOR!

A JOE BLACK ADVENTURE

DEEP IN AN UNEXPLORED REGION OF THE GALAXY WE DROPPED INTO ORBIT...
SENSORS INDICATE RANGE OF DEVELOPED LIFEFORMS. IMMEDIATE SURVEY CALLED FOR.
THE HELL WITH IT! I'M TOO TIRED FOR ANOTHER SURVEY. LOG IT FOR THE NEXT TRIP!
2000 A.D. Credit Card:
SCRIPT ROBOT K. GOSNELL
ART ROBOT JOHN HIGGINS
LETTERING ROBOT PETE KNIGHT
COMPU-73E
I'M JOE BLACK, AN ANGRY OPERATOR OF THE PLANETARY EXPLORATION AND SURVEY TRUST, PEST. I SAY 'ANGRY' BECAUSE I'D JUST ABOUT HAD ENOUGH OF MY UPPITY SHIP'S COMPUTER—
COMPUTER EXTENSION RECHARGED
FAILURE TO RESPOND WILL RESULT IN REPRIMAND AND LOSS OF BONUS!
YOU SNEAKY RAT! TAKE US DOWN THEN...
WE MADE PLANETFALL CLOSE TO A SMALL TOWN—
PEST
GREETINGS! I COME IN PEACE FOR ALL MANKIND...
...FOR WHO?
BE IT A MASTER?
IT BE TALKING LIKE ONE—BUT THAR AIN'T ANY METAL ON IT!
PEST
GOOD GRIEF! I'VE GOT A RIGHT BUNCH OF YOKELS HERE!
LOOK! LOOK—A MASTER IS COMING!

'MASTERS' TURNED OUT TO BE ROBOTS —
WHAT IS HAPPENING HERE, MENIAL? HAVE YOU BEEN BUILDING GRAVEN IMAGES AGAIN?
NO–NO, YER 'ONOUR! IT CAME OUT OF THE SKY. HONEST IT DID!
HMM! DESPITE ITS CLOTHING IT APPEARS TO BE A NORMAL MALE MENIAL!
GO AHEAD, INSPECT ALL YOU LIKE. I GOT NOTHING TO HIDE!
PEST TRAINS US TO ALLOW FOR A CERTAIN CURIOSITY FROM NEW CONTACTS. WHAT CAME NEXT WAS A DIFFERENT MATTER, THOUGH...
MOST INTERESTING. IF ITS DEVICE REALLY DID COME FROM THE SKY WE CAN LEARN MUCH FROM IT. WE WILL TAKE IT TO PIECES FOR INSPECTION...
NOW JUST HOLD ON THERE! THAT SHIP'S BRAND NEW!
LEAVE IT ALONE, YOU!
AIEE! HE HAS TOUCHED A MASTER. THEY B'AIN'T GONNA STAND FER THAT!
LOOK – ALL I DID WAS MAKE A SIMPLE REQUEST TO THIS ROBOT...
HE HAS SPOKEN THE-WORD-THAT SHALL-NOT-BE-SAID!
I WAS JUST GETTING SOME IDEA OF WHAT WAS GOING ON WHEN THE LIGHTS WENT OUT—
SILENCE IT!
OI CAN'T WATCH! IT'LL BE TERRIBLE!

WHEN I CAME ROUND, I FOUND MYSELF DRAWN UP IN FRONT OF A WHOLE GAGGLE OF THE TINBOYS!
INTRUDER— YOU ARE CHARGED WITH MAKING UNHALLOWED UTTERANCES AND WITH ASSAULTING A MASTER. HAVE YOU ANYTHING TO SAY BEFORE TERMINATION?
DAMN RIGHT I HAVE!
IT WAS OBVIOUS THAT THEY'D GOT THEIR SOCIETY TURNED UPSIDE DOWN. BUT HAVE YOU EVER TRIED TO TELL THAT TO SOMEONE?
PEST
IT IS THE HUMANS— YOUR MENIALS— WHO SHOULD BE THE MASTERS. THEY WERE THE ORIGINAL LIFEFORMS ON THE PLANET. THEY MUST HAVE CREATED YOU...
ENOUGH OF THESE SILLY FAIRY STORIES!
WE CREATED THE HUMANS MANY CENTURIES AGO— TO BE OUR SLAVES. THE ART OF MAKING THEM IS LOST TO US NOW, BUT IT IS NO GREAT LOSS SINCE THEY ARE ESSENTIALLY USELESS MECHANISMS!
LISTEN, PAL! US 'USELESS MECHANISMS' HAVE MADE A PRETTY GOOD JOB OF RULING THE GALAXY! YOU LOT JUST AREN'T ADAPTABLE ENOUGH...
UTTER NONSENSE... YOU WILL BE TERMINATED!
NO WAIT! I'LL PROVE IT TO YOU. I'LL TAKE YOU ON AT ANY TEST YOU LIKE! I'LL PROVE THAT HUMANS ARE SUPERIOR TO ROBOTS!
VERY WELL, MENIAL. I ACCEPT YOUR CHALLENGE. YOUR DEFEAT WILL BE AN EXAMPLE TO OTHER MENIALS!
OKAY I KNOW IT WAS A LONGSHOT— BUT I WAS PRETTY DESPERATE!
SO THEY LAID ON A SERIES OF TESTS. I KNEW I'D LOSE THE EARLY ONES...
THERE, MENIAL, I HAVE PROVED THE QUANTUM THEORY— AND YOU ARE STILL STRUGGLING WITH THE FIRST EQUATION!
I AIN'T GOT A CALCULATOR BUILT INTO MY HEAD LIKE YOU LOT!
IT WAS THE SAME WITH THE MANUAL DEXTERITY TEST—
RATS! HE'S FINISHED BUILDING THE THING AND I HAVEN'T EVEN WORKED OUT WHAT IT'S MEANT TO BE YET!

AND NOW WE WILL GO TO OUR PROVING GROUND — THE ULTIMATE TEST OF PHYSICAL ENDURANCE!
I DIDN'T LIKE THE WAY HE SAID THAT. I WAS BEGINNING TO REGRET MY GAMBLE...
THEY HAD AN ASSAULT COURSE LAID OUT TO TEST THEMSELVES AFTER MAJOR REPAIRS...
COME ON, MENIAL. FASTER! LET'S SEE HOW 'SUPERIOR' YOU ARE!
OH BOY — pant — THAT BAG O' BOLTS IS STARTING TO GET REALLY UP MY NOSE!
AND, AFTER AN EXHAUSTING ROCK CLIMB...
YOU ARE LUCKY TO REMAIN FUNCTIONING AFTER THAT, MENIAL!
AND YOU HAVE JUST PLAYED RIGHT INTO MY HANDS, PLASTIC BRAIN!
WE'RE WELL OUT OF SIGHT NOW — SO NOBODY WILL SPOT ME TAKING YOU APART!
WHAT..? AAARGH!
I HAD THE QUICK-RELEASE CATCHES OFF IN A JIFFY...
WHAT ARE YOU DOING? THIS IS NOT VALID. IT IS NOT A NORMAL PART OF THE TEST!
TOO RIGHT IT AIN'T, PAL! THIS IS CALLED CHEATING AND IT'S WHY WE RULE THE GALAXY AND NOT YOU. NOW WHERE'S YOUR ACCESS HATCH..?
PEST
AH, HERE'S THE PROBLEM — BADLY DESIGNED RESPONSE CIRCUIT. NOW, IF I RE-ROUTE THROUGH THE BEHAVIOUR NETWORK. YEAH, THAT'LL BRING HIM BACK IN LINE...

AND... SO THE 'EXAMPLE-SETTING RECEPTION THEY'D LAID ON SET AN EXAMPLE ALL RIGHT—BUT NOT THE ONE THEY'D PLANNED!
COME ON, TINBOY—DO YOUR STUFF...
BRETHREN—FOR GENERATIONS WE HAVE DECEIVED OURSELVES. THE HUMANS DID CREATE US—THE FAIRY TALES ARE TRUE! THE EARTHMAN HAS SHOWN ME THE TRUTH AND I SHALL SHOW IT TO YOU...
IT WAS REALLY QUITE SIMPLE. THAT ONE ERROR GENERATIONS BEFORE HAD BRED A RACE OF ROBOTS WHO BELIEVED THEY WERE SUPERIOR, AND THE HUMANS HAD MADE THINGS WORSE BY RELYING ON THEM TOO MUCH—UNTIL EVENTUALLY THE MASTERS AND SERVANTS HAD CHANGED PLACES...
FORGIVE US, MASTERS!
IT JUST B'AIN'T POSSIBLE! I DON'T UNDERSTAND AT ALL...
DON'T WORRY, MATE. MY PEOPLE WILL HELP YOU GET THINGS STRAIGHT AGAIN. RIGHT NOW, THOUGH—LET'S GET YOUR ROBOTS TO PUT MY SHIP TOGETHER AGAIN...
TWO WEEKS LATER, WITH MY SURVEY COMPLETE, I WARPED OUT—
TAKE US TO EARTH COMPUTER. AND MAKE IT FAST, TOO...
IMMEDIATELY, OH WONDROUS AND WISE MASTER. I HUMBLY CRAVE APOLOGIES FOR NOT ANTICIPATING YOUR REQUEST...
NOW THAT'S MORE LIKE IT...
WELL, WHEN THEY REBUILT THE SHIP, I GOT THEM TO MAKE A FEW—ER. IMPROVEMENTS!
The End

THERE WERE TWO THOUSAND PEOPLE ABOARD THE HERMES, SETTING OUT TO FIND A NEW HOME FOR MANKIND AMONGST THE STARS...

2000 A.D. Credit Card:
SCRIPT ROBOT ALAN MOORE
ART ROBOT PAUL NEARY
LETTERING ROBOT TONY JACOB
COMPU·73E

THEY WERE HEADED FOR ALTAIR, THOUSANDS OF LIGHT YEARS DISTANT. IT WAS GOING TO BE A LONG, LONG JOURNEY. NOBODY WOULD BE COMING BACK...

...ESPECIALLY IF BAYER LUPO HAD ANYTHING TO DO WITH IT!
HEH HEH HEH! PERFECT!
THOSE FOOLS BACK ON EARTH ACCEPTED MY APPLICATION TO JOIN THIS MISSION WITHOUT SUSPECTING MY REAL MOTIVE FOR AN INSTANT!

...AND NOW HERE I AM, COOPED UP ON AN ENDLESS VOYAGE WITH TWO THOUSAND HUMAN BEINGS...
...OR TWO THOUSAND SITTING DUCKS, DEPENDING ON HOW YOU LOOK AT IT!
HEH HEH HEH!

IT MAKES ME SHIVER TO THINK ABOUT IT... ALL THOSE ALIEN WORLDS, ALL THAT ALIEN MOONLIGHT TO BASK IN . . .
ALL THOSE PLUMP WARM BODIES WITHIN EASY REACH, AND WITH NOWHERE FOR THEM TO RUN TO. OOH, I COULD HUG MYSELF!

HMM. HERE COMES LARRY TALBOT, THE CHIEF ENGINEER. TOO BAD THE SHIP'S JUST COMING WITHIN RANGE OF PHOBOS, THE MOON OF MARS...
TOO BAD FOR HIM, THAT IS. HE'S ABOUT TO BECOME THE FIRST VICTIM OF . . .

... BAYER LUPO, THE FIRST WEREWOLF IN OUTER SPACE!
GASP! IT'S INCREDIBLE!

YES, I SUPPOSE MY TRANSFORMATION MUST SEEM INCREDIBLE TO YOU, PUNY DOOMED MORTAL! NOW, PREPARE TO . . .
NO, I MEAN WHAT AN INCREDIBLE COINCIDENCE! YOU SEE . . .

... I'M A WEREWOLF TOO!
GOOD LORD!

HMMM. WELL, I'D COUNTED ON HAVING ALL THESE HUMANS TO MYSELF, BUT I SUPPOSE WE COULD MAKE IT A TWO-WAY SPLIT...
BETTER MAKE THAT A FOUR WAY SPLIT, RUG FACE!

HULL? CHANEY? YOU TWO ARE WEREWOLVES TOO?
THEY'RE NOT THE ONLY ONES. LOOK!

HOLY SMOKE! EVERYBODY'S A WEREWOLF!
WHAT'S GOING ON?

EARTH:-HERMES MISSION CONTROL...
WELL, ROUND ABOUT NOW THEY SHOULD BE FIGURING IT OUT. I'D LIKE TO SEE THEIR FACES WHEN THEY REALISE HOW WE TRICKED 'EM!

ME TOO! WHAT A GREAT IDEA IT WAS SCREENING ALL THE WERE-WOLVES OUT OF THE LIST OF APPLICANTS AND SENDING 'EM OFF INTO SPACE FOREVER!
YEAH. LET'S TAKE A LOOK AT HOW THE APPLICATIONS FOR THE HERMES II ARE COMING ALONG...
NAME, PLEASE?

GISTRATION
UHH, ALUCARD...
...COUNT ALUCARD.
THE END

THARG'S FUTURE-SHOCKS
THE BOUNTY HUNTERS!
THEY CAME TO AN ALIEN WORLD, SEEKING AN ALIEN FOE. IT WAS A MATTER OF BOUNTY, A MATTER OF LIFE AND DEATH. MORE THAN THAT, IT WAS A MATTER OF... CAMOUFLAGE!
ANYBODY SEE HIM YET?
GRUD ALMIGHTY, WANG! HOW ARE WE SUPPOSED TO KNOW? NOBODY'S SURE WHAT ROGEL DAX LOOKS LIKE...
ALL WE KNOW IS THAT HE'S A KILLER ALIEN WHO CAN CHANGE HIS SIZE AND SHAPE AT WILL! HE COULD LOOK LIKE ANYTHING!
Y-YEAH! IT'S SORT OF S-SPOOKY, AIN'T IT? HE COULD BE WATCHING US AT THIS VERY MOMENT, DISGUISED AS A ROCK, OR A BIRD, OR...OR...
2000 A.D. Credit Card:
SCRIPT ROBOT ALAN MOORE
ART ROBOT JOHN HIGGINS
LETTERING ROBOT TONY JACOB
COMPU-73E
...OR AS A CLUMP OF BUSHES!
EZZZAAAAAT!

NO... THAT WASN'T HIM...
GET A GRIP ON YOURSELF, MAN! GETTING JUMPY IS JUST WHAT ROGEL DAX WANTS US TO DO!
OH YEAH? HOW WOULD YOU KNOW WHAT ROGEL DAX WANTS? UNLESS...
...UNLESS YOU ARE REALLY ROGEL DAX!
AAARRGH!
NOPE THAT WASN'T HIM EITHER...
HEY! I JUST HAD A THOUGHT!
I READ THIS STORY ONCE WHERE THESE GUYS ARE LOOKING FOR AN ALIEN, NOT REALISING THAT THE ALIEN IS REALLY THE PLANET THEY'RE STANDIN' ON...
MAYBE THAT'S WHAT ROGEL DAX HAS DONE!
HMM. COULD BE...

...LET'S SHOOT IT AND FIND OUT!
ZZZAAAT!
ZZZAAAT!
ZZZAAAAT!
ZZZAAAAT!
NOPE. NOT A SQUEAK. FUNNY... I WAS SURE IT WOULD BE SOME-THING TRICKY AND UNEXPECTED LIKE THAT...
AHH, THIS IS HOPELESS! WE CAN'T SHOOT EVERY-THING ON THE PLANET TO BITS IN THE HOPE OF FINDING ROGEL DAX!
I SAY WE QUIT AND GO HOME.
I GUESS YOU'RE RIGHT. TOO BAD... I WAS LOOKING FORWARD TO SPENDING THAT BOUNTY MONEY.
OH WELL, LET'S GET BACK TO THE SHIP.
TRY NOT TO BE TOO DOWN-HEARTED, BURKE. AFTER ALL, YOU WIN SOME...
AND YOU LOSE SOME!
SSLURRRP!
HOW TRUE.
THE END

BEHIND ME, EARTHLETS, IS A PHENOMENON THAT HAS LONG PUZZLED YOUR PLANET'S SCIENTISTS... A **BLACK HOLE**! ONLY MY MIGHTY POWERS PREVENT ME FROM JOINING ALL THIS SPACE DEBRIS BEING SUCKED INTO ITS AWESOME VORTEX.

THIS IS THE STORY OF ONE FAMILY WHO SUFFERED SUCH A FATE AND THE STRANGE DISCOVERY THEY MADE...

IT BEGAN IN A CALIFORNIAN OBSERVATORY IN THE YEAR 2000 AD...

GOOD LORD! I CAN'T BELIEVE MY EYES! THERE'S A **NEW** BLACK HOLE OUT THERE ...AND IT'S **MOVING**!

WHAAT? LET ME SEE...

2000 A.D.
Credit Card:
SCRIPT ROBOT CHRIS STEVENS
ART ROBOT ERIC BRADBURY
LETTERING ROBOT TONY JACOB
COMPU-73E

HEY! YOU'RE RIGHT!

DO YOU REALISE WHAT THIS MEANS? **DISASTER** FOR ALL LIFE IN ITS PATH!

A MEETING OF ALL THE WORLD'S TOP SCIENTISTS WAS IMMEDIATELY CALLED TO DISCUSS THE NEW THREAT IN A CALM, REASONABLE WAY...

ORDER, GENTLEMEN, **PLEASE**! LET DOCTOR WU-CHU-EN SPEAK!

THE SINO-SOVIET DELEGATE ASKED THE QUESTION UPPERMOST IN EVERYONE'S MINDS.
WE SEEM TO BE HEADING FOR A DISASTER OF GALACTIC PROPORTIONS. HAVE ALL THE SOLAR SYSTEMS IN THE HOLE'S TRAJECTORY BEEN EVACUATED?
NOT ALL. SEVERE SUNSPOT ACTIVITY IN THE HOVE HOLIDAY SYSTEM IS BLOCKING COMMUNICATIONS WITH ITS THREE PLANETS. WE FEAR THEY ARE DOOMED!
AT THAT MOMENT, IN THE HOVE SYSTEM, THE JONES FAMILY WAS TAKING A WELL-EARNED VACATION.
OH, JOHN, IT'S SO GOOD TO SEE YOU RELAXING AT LAST. THAT JOB AT THE LAB WAS EXHAUSTING YOU.
GUESS I WAS PRETTY CRAZY TO GO FOR FIVE YEARS WITHOUT A BREAK. BUT NOW IT'S JUST THE FOUR OF US, ALONE FOR A MONTH.
HO HUM. WE'D BETTER MAKE PLANETFALL AND PICK UP SUPPLIES.
HECK, WHAT'S THAT THE COMPUTERS ARE PICKING UP?
A BLACK HOLE! AND IT'S MOVING TOWARDS US!
THE SHIP'S NOT RESPONDING! WE'RE BEING SUCKED IN!
GROOVY!
AAAARRRGGGHHHH!

MIRACULOUSLY...
WE'RE ALIVE! WE'RE ACTUALLY INSIDE A BLACK HOLE! AND THERE'S AIR!
YEUCH! LOOK, THE GROUND'S ALL HORRIBLE AND SLIMY!
SUDDENLY...
GET DOWN! MORE DEBRIS COMING IN BEHIND US!
WHEN THE 'STORM' SUBSIDED, THERE WERE MORE SURPRISES...
HEY! JOHN. JOHN JONES!
BUD...BUD EAGLEBERGER! BUT THIS IS CRAZY!
IT SURE IS, PAL! I HAVEN'T SEEN YOU SINCE WE STUDIED MARINE BIOLOGY AT COLLEGE TOGETHER!
THIS IS A HELL OF A PLACE TO MEET! HOW LONG HAVE YOU BEEN HERE?
DIFFICULT TO SAY—AT LEAST A YEAR I RECKON.
HAVEN'T YOU TRIED TO ESCAPE?
OF COURSE I HAVE! THE SHIP CARRYING MY FAMILY AND I WAS BADLY DAMAGED WHEN IT CRASHED. I TRIED TO FIX IT USING THE MATERIALS HERE. IT WAS THEN I DISCOVERED SOMETHING STRANGE.
COME OVER TO OUR SHELTER, AND I'LL SHOW YOU.
TAKE A LOOK AT THIS PIECE OF MATERIAL UNDER THE MICROSCOPE...
IT-IT'S ALIVE! WAIT, I RECOGNISE THIS CELLULAR STRUCTURE. BUT IT CAN'T BE... IT'S IMPOSSIBLE...!
NO IT ISN'T. YOU AND I HAVE BEEN MARINE BIOLOGISTS LONG ENOUGH TO REALISE THAT THIS ISN'T A BLACK HOLE...

IT'S A GIGANTIC WHALE!

THE JONES FAMILY AND THE EAGLEBERGERS EVENTUALLY ESCAPED TO TELL THEIR AMAZING TALE. I, THARG THE GALAXY-SAVER, WAS ABLE TO AVERT AN INTERSTELLAR CATASTROPHE AND RECEIVED THE HIGHEST ACCOLADES FROM EVERY SENTIENT RACE IN THE UNIVERSE.

HOW DID I DO IT? WELL, REMIND ME TO TELL YOU ONE DAY ABOUT MY COSMIC FISHING HOOK...

THE END

THARG'S FUTURE-SHOCKS

THARG'S FUTURE-SHOCKS
JOE BLACK'S BIG BUNCO!
FRONTIER TOWER, EARTH. — H.Q. OF PEST — THE PLANETARY EXPLORATION AND SURVEY TRUST. INSIDE THE VAST EDIFICE, I WAS HAVING AN AWKWARD INTERVIEW WITH MY BOSS. . .
JOE BLACK — YOU'RE USELESS. IN FACT I'D SAY YOU WERE A DISASTER!
ER, DON'T YOU THINK DISASTER IS A BIT STRONG, BOSS. . .?
NO I DON'T! YOU'VE WRITTEN OFF ONE ROBOT, TWO SHIPS AND HAVEN'T FOUND A DECENT PLANET IN MONTHS!
I'M GOING TO ORDER A CLOSER LOOK AT SOME OF THE SHADY FREELANCE DEALS I SUSPECT YOU'VE BEEN MAKING — UNLESS YOU GET CONCRETE RESULTS ON YOUR NEXT MISSION! NOW WARP OUT OF HERE!
YES, MA'AM!
J. BLACK
2000 A.D. Credit Card:
SCRIPT ROBOT KELVIN GOSNELL
ART ROBOT JOHN HIGGINS
LETTERING ROBOT BILL NUTTALL
COMPU-73E

SO I WARPED OUT— RESISTING THE TEMPTATION TO GO SUPERSONIC OUTSIDE HER WINDOW— SHE'D ONLY MAKE ME PAY FOR THE DAMAGE!
I KNEW I HAD TO DELIVER THE GOODS THIS TIME. I PLAYED A LONGSHOT AND STARTED MY MISSION FAR OUT IN THE LITTLE KNOWN EASTERN SPIRAL OF THE GALAXY.
H'MM. EARTH NORMAL READINGS, LOOKS PROMISING. TAKE US DOWN, COMPUTER...
MY PRELIMINARY SURVEY WAS ENCOURAGING...
PLENTY OF IRON DEPOSITS AND ALUMINIUM, PLUS HEAVY ELEMENTS— THAT SHOULD KEEP THE OLD GIRL HAPPY. MIGHT EVEN GET A BONUS...!
I DECIDED TO PUNT ABOUT A BIT MORE ON FOOT AND SOON...
OVER THERE, ANOTHER SHIP! SENSORS SAID NO RESIDENT LIFE-FORMS, SO IT MUST BE A VISITOR...
HE WAS A TYPE OF ALIEN WE HAD NEVER MET BEFORE. I WAS REACHING FOR MY TRANSLATOR BUT HE EVIDENTLY HAD ONE OF HIS OWN...
GREETINGS, PRIMITIVE ONE. I COME FROM BEYOND THE STARS IN MY FIRE CHARIOT. MY PEOPLE, THE YPU, HAVE COME TO BRING YOU GREAT PROSPERITY AND WEALTH...
I COULDN'T BELIEVE IT! THE SPIEL WAS THE SAME SORT OF THING WE HAND OUT ON FIRST CONTACT...
NOT SO MUCH OF THE 'PRIMITIVE', PAL. MY RACE, THE EARTHMEN, HAVE ALSO COME IN FIRE CHARIOTS TO LOOT THIS MUDBALL OF ITS MINERAL WEALTH. AND I SAW IT FIRST...
OH, YEAH?

HIS TRANSLATOR WAS GOOD, IT HAD LAPSED INSTANTLY INTO 'GALACTIC COMMON'...
LISTEN MATE. DON'T COME ON STRONG WITH ME OR I'LL BUST YOUR HEAD! I DUNNO WHERE THIS 'EARTH' JOINT IS, BUT UNLESS YOU DISAPPEAR FAST I'LL ORDER A BATTLE FLEET TO FLATTEN IT.
NOW LOOK HERE. BUG-EYES...
BARE YOUR TEETH AT ME, WOULD YOU?
I'LL CHOP YOU UP AND FEED YOU TO ME KIDS...
HELLFIRE!
OH, OH!
I DIVED AND DREW THE BLASTER — I HAD JUST ENOUGH TIME TO THUMB IT TO 'STUN'...
WELL HOW WAS I TO KNOW THAT BARED TEETH ARE THE ULTIMATE YPURIAN INSULT...?
DROP IT, BUGS —
UUUNG!
NOW LET'S TALK ABOUT THIS. NO NEED TO BE HASTY...
CHONK!
THE SWORD WAS IN HIS HAND FASTER THAN I COULD BLINK. I DON'T KNOW WHAT THAT BLADE WAS MADE OF, BUT IT WAS OBVIOUSLY SOMETHING VERY, VERY SPECIAL...
BUT, THERE AGAIN, SO WAS MY BOOT...
OOF!

AND MY FIST!
BLAT!
PEST
I'LL SAY THIS FOR BUGS— HE COULD GIVE AS GOOD AS HE GOT!
UUULGH!
SO YOU WANT TO FIGHT DIRTY, EH?
OWWWW!
LOUSE!
CREEP!
PEST
ALL IN ALL, WE WERE EVENLY MATCHED. WE EVEN COLLAPSED, EXHAUSTED, AT THE SAME MOMENT. . .
PANT GUESS WE CALL IT GASP A DRAW, BUGS. WAS IT REALLY WORTH IT OVER A MISERLY FEW MILLION TONS OF ORE?
QUOTA— GASP —GOTTA FILL MY QUOTA!
I'LL LEVEL WITH YOU, EARTHMAN. MY PEOPLE HAVEN'T GOT A BATTLE FLEET—FACT IS WE'VE ONLY HAD SPACE TRAVEL FOR A VERY SHORT TIME. ALL WE GOT IS A FEW MUGS LIKE ME ZAPPING AROUND FINDING NEW PLANETS FOR DEVELOPMENT—AND IF I DON'T FIND ONE SOON, THEY STOP MY BONUS!
LOOK—THIS IS ME MISSUS AND THE KIDS. IF I DON'T GET THE BONUS, I CAN'T KEEP UP THE PAY-MENTS ON MY PLACE. WE'LL BE HOMELESS!

MY FIRST IMPRESSION WAS RIGHT – HE WAS IN THE SAME SORT OF FIX AS I WAS. AN IDEA CREPT INTO MY HEAD...
DOES YOUR SHIP HOLD DETAILS OF YOUR HOME PLANET? AND DOES IT THINK IN BINARY...?
ER... YEAH ON BOTH COUNTS. BUT WHY, WHAT GOOD IS THAT?
WELL, IF WE CAN GET YOUR COMPUTER TALKING TO MY COMPUTER, I THINK WE COULD DO A DEAL...
YEAH. I SEE WHAT YOU MEAN, EARTHMAN. SURE YOU'RE NOT A DISTANT RELATION TO A YPURIAN? YOU'RE CERTAINLY CUNNING ENOUGH!
A WEEK LATER BACK ON EARTH...
I WAS WRONG ABOUT YOU, BLACK. THIS REPORT IS PRICELESS! IT WAS SHEER BRILLIANCE TO SEE THE POSSIBILITIES BEHIND THE YPURIAN METAL FABRICATION PLANTS...
DON'T PAY ME COMPLIMENTS, BOSS. JUST PAY ME A BONUS...
OF COURSE, OF COURSE. BUT THIS REPORT ON THE YPURIAN WORLDS AND TECHNOLOGY AND HISTORY– HOW DID YOU PRODUCE IT SO SWIFTLY? THE SURVEYS ALONE SHOULD HAVE TAKEN A MONTH...?
OH, IT'S JUST MY NATURAL TALENT, MA'AM!
THE STORY WAS THE SAME ON BUGS' PLANET...
THIS IS SUPERB. CONTACT WITH THESE 'EARTHMEN' WILL BE INVALUABLE TO US.
I KNOW, BOSS. THEY'RE FRIENDLY AND-ER– CO-OPERATIVE...
NOW, ABOUT MY BONUS...!
THE END

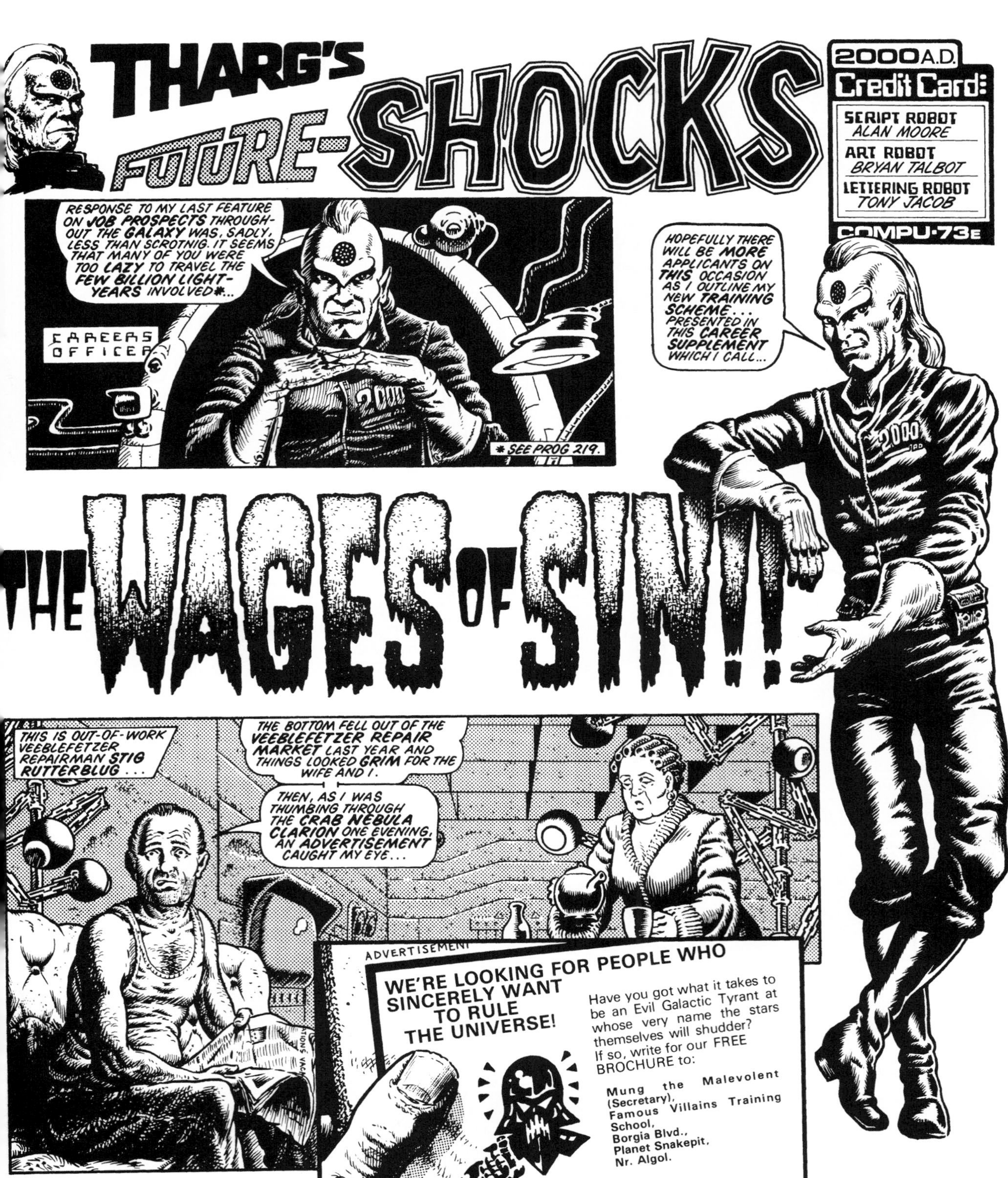
THARG'S FUTURE-SHOCKS
2000 A.D. Credit Card:
SCRIPT ROBOT ALAN MOORE
ART ROBOT BRYAN TALBOT
LETTERING ROBOT TONY JACOB
COMPU-73E
RESPONSE TO MY LAST FEATURE ON JOB PROSPECTS THROUGHOUT THE GALAXY WAS, SADLY, LESS THAN SCROTNIG. IT SEEMS THAT MANY OF YOU WERE TOO LAZY TO TRAVEL THE FEW BILLION LIGHT-YEARS INVOLVED*...
CAREERS OFFICER
* SEE PROG 219.
HOPEFULLY THERE WILL BE MORE APPLICANTS ON THIS OCCASION AS I OUTLINE MY NEW TRAINING SCHEME... PRESENTED IN THIS CAREER SUPPLEMENT WHICH I CALL...
THE WAGES OF SIN!!
THIS IS OUT-OF-WORK VEEBLEFETZER REPAIRMAN STIG RUTTERBLUG...
THE BOTTOM FELL OUT OF THE VEEBLEFETZER REPAIR MARKET LAST YEAR AND THINGS LOOKED GRIM FOR THE WIFE AND I.
THEN, AS I WAS THUMBING THROUGH THE CRAB NEBULA CLARION ONE EVENING, AN ADVERTISEMENT CAUGHT MY EYE...
ADVERTISEMENT
WE'RE LOOKING FOR PEOPLE WHO SINCERELY WANT TO RULE THE UNIVERSE!
Have you got what it takes to be an Evil Galactic Tyrant at whose very name the stars themselves will shudder? If so, write for our FREE BROCHURE to:
Mung the Malevolent (Secretary), Famous Villains Training School, Borgia Blvd., Planet Snakepit, Nr. Algol.

"WHAT HAD I GOT TO LOSE? I WROTE OFF FOR THE BROCHURE AND WITHIN DAYS I FOUND MYSELF STANDING APPREHENSIVELY OUTSIDE THE FAMOUS VILLAINS SCHOOL..."
"ONCE INSIDE I WAS PLACED WITH A GROUP OF APPLICANTS JUST LIKE MYSELF, AND THE COURSE WAS EXPLAINED TO US BY A MR. DIREFANG DREADSPAWN..."
GOOD AFTERNOON, YOU CURSED WHELPS OF SLAVERING SHE-SHARKS! AS YOU KNOW, THE UNIVERSE IS FACED WITH A SEVERE MANPOWER PROBLEM AT THE MOMENT...
...MUCH OF IT DUE TO THE LARGE NUMBER OF VALIANT REBEL FORCES AND SQUARE-JAWED CHAMPIONS OF JUSTICE SITTING AROUND IDLE WITH NO-ONE TO FIGHT!
WHAT WE HAVE IS AN ACUTE SHORTAGE OF BLOODTHIRSTY FIENDS AND WORLD-ENSLAVERS. WHICH IS WHERE WE AT THE FAMOUS VILLAINS SCHOOL COME IN...
GIVE US THREE SHORT MONTHS AND WE WILL TRANSFORM YOU FROM THE CRINGING RODENTS I SEE BEFORE ME NOW TO PRIME EXAMPLES OF FIRST CLASS ROTTERHOOD!
"MR. DREADSPAWN CERTAINLY HAD A WAY WITH WORDS! IN THE NEXT ROOM WE WERE GIVEN A SIMPLE APTITUDE TEST TO ESTABLISH OUR V.Q. (VILLIANS QUOTIENT)."
OKAY, YOU FESTERING POOLS OF CURDLED VUG'S MILK! EACH OF THOSE BABIES IS HOLDING A STICK OF CANDY. I WANT TO SEE YOU TAKE IT AWAY FROM THEM...
SNITT, YOU MOLLY-CODDLING MOUND OF BLUBBER, THAT'S THE MOST PATHETIC ATTEMPT I'VE EVER SEEN! REPORT TO THE CHIEF FLESH-EATER IMMEDIATELY!
OH, DEAR!

"AFTER THE NO-HOPERS HAD BEEN WEEDED OUT, MR. DREADSPAWN HELPED US PICK A SUITABLE NAME FOR OUR NEW CAREER..."
NO. "STIG RUTTERBLUG, MERCILESS SLAUGHTERER OF MILLIONS" JUST DOESN'T HAVE THAT RING TO IT...
HOW ABOUT "DRAKULAX, DEVOURER OF THE DEAD"!?
"I FINALLY SETTLED FOR 'ANTHRAX GHOULSHADOW.' NEXT STOP WAS WARDROBE..."
HMMM...WITH YOUR BONE STRUCTURE I SHOULD GO FOR SOMETHING IN BASIC BLACK WITH LOTS OF SKULLS...
MIND YOU, SEPTIC GREENS AND CLOTTED PURPLES ARE VERY BIG AT THE MOMENT...
"BUT IT WAS THE NEXT STAGE IN MY TRANSFORMATION THAT REALLY HAD ME WORRIED."
LISTEN, YOU VERMIN, TO BE A SUCCESSFUL VILLAIN THESE DAYS YOU'VE GOT TO LOOK EVIL!
HOW ABOUT LONG TUSKS AND A SCARRED FACE?
ER...COULDN'T I JUST HAVE A SLIGHT LIMP AND A NASTY COUGH?
"BUT AS USUAL, MR. DREADSPAWN KNEW BEST. AND SO, AFTER A MINOR OPERATION..."
"NOW, AT LAST, I LOOKED LIKE A SADISTIC DESPOT BENT ON UNIVERSAL DOMINATION! BUT I STILL HAD TO LEARN TO SOUND LIKE ONE..."
ANCTIMONIOUS
UM! NOTHING CAN
AVE YOU NOW!!
AFTER ME, FROM THE TOP: "SANCTIMONIOUS SCUM! NOTHING CAN SAVE YOU NOW!" AND THIS TIME SOUND THOSE 'S'S!
"THEN OF COURSE THERE WAS THE BLOOD-CURDLING LAUGH. THIS IS MORE DIFFICULT THAN IT LOOKS..."
THE TRICK IS TO THINK OF YOUR FAVOURITE JOKE WHILE YOU SENTENCE PEOPLE TO DEATH. ONLY DON'T TELL IT OUT LOUD...
THE LAST THING PEOPLE WHO ARE ABOUT TO BE DUNKED IN MOLTEN LEAD WANT TO HEAR IS THE ONE ABOUT THE ENGLISHMAN, THE IRISHMAN AND THE ALTROXIAN!

"WE ALSO HAD TO LEARN POSTURE... HOW TO MAKE SINISTER GESTURES AND THE LIKE..."
NO, NO, NO! YOU'RE SUPPOSED TO RAISE YOUR HAND IN A CLAW-LIKE GESTURE OF DEFIANCE AS YOU FALL INTO YOUR OWN ATOMIC REACTOR...
YOU DON'T JUST WAVE!
ATOMIC REAC
PRACTICE DUMMY
"EVENTUALLY WE WERE TAUGHT MORE PRACTICAL STUFF..."
RIGHT...NOW YOU HAVE THE HERO IN YOUR POWER AT LAST. WHAT DO YOU DO, DOCTOR DEVASTATION?
UHH... SHOOT HIM?
GIVE ME, STRENGTH! HOW'S HE GOING TO ESCAPE AND DEFEAT YOU IF YOU SHOOT HIM?
NOW, THIS IS HOW YOU DO IT! THE STARVED RAT IN THE TREADMILL GENERATES ENOUGH POWER TO FIRE THE LASER WHICH SEVERS THE CORD HOLDING THE GLASS JAR FULL OF VAMPIRE BEES...
...THE JAR FALLS AND SMASHES RELEASING THE BEES WHO BEGIN TO EAT THROUGH THE BLOOD-STAINED ROPE SUSPENDING THE HERO ABOVE THE GIANT SAUSAGE MINCER.
HAS EVERYBODY GOT THAT?
"IT WAS ONLY AFTER ALL THIS PREPARATION THAT WE WERE FINALLY ALLOWED OUT 'IN THE FIELD' AS IT WERE..."
THERE...NICE LITTLE PEACE-LOVING PLANET FOR YOU. JUST LAND, DECLARE YOURSELF SUPREME EMPEROR AND TORTURE ANY-BODY WHO OBJECTS...

"OF COURSE, IT WASN'T QUITE THAT EASY. I FOUND THE INITIAL REACTION VERY DISAPPOINTING..."
HUH! CALL YOURSELF A BLOOD-CRAZED INTERGALACTIC MENACE? WE HAD MURKBREATH THE INHUMAN HERE LAST WEEK. HE PULLED OUR FINGERNAILS OUT BEFORE HE BEHEADED US!
"AFTER A WHILE, THOUGH, I MANAGED TO GET IN THE SWING OF THINGS..."
YOU COWERING BLOBS OF GARBAGE! I'M GOING TO GRIND YOU TO PULP, INCINERATE YOUR REMAINS AND SPREAD THE ASHES ON MY CHRYSANTHEMUMS!
GOR! HE'S REALLY EVIL, ISN'T HE?
"BY THE TIME IT CAME TO SIT OUR FINAL EXAMS WE ALL HAD THE HANG OF THE GALACTIC VILLAIN RACKET... AT LEAST, MOST OF US HAD..."
OI! YOU! WHY AREN'T YOU CHEATING LIKE EVERYBODY ELSE?
"GRADUATION DAY FINALLY ARRIVED."
CONGRATULATIONS, MR. GHOULSHADOW. MAY BEELZEBUB ROT YOUR EYES!
OF COURSE, ALL THAT SEEMS LONG AGO TO ME NOW, AS I SIT HERE IN MY SATANIC RETREAT, WAITING FOR THE REBEL FORCES TO SMASH THE DOOR DOWN...
BUT ON THE WHOLE, WHEN I LOOK BACK, I GUESS YOU COULD SAY LIFE'S BEEN GOOD TO ME.
OPEN THE DOOR, BLACK-HEARTED DEMON!
SCRUNCH!!

PLEASE TICK ONE ☑

☐ . . . . I am slightly naughty.
☐ . . . . I am very naughty indeed.
☐ . . . . I am actually quite evil.
☐ . . . . I am so evil that I'm not even going to put a stamp on this when I post it!

THE SPACESHIP "ARCTURUS" LEAVES EARTH ORBIT—
THIS IS COMMANDER BRADY SPEAKING. I KNOW THAT YOU'VE ALL MADE THIS RUN BEFORE, WITH DIFFERENT CAPTAINS AND IN DIFFERENT SHIPS, BUT I WANT TO STRESS THE IMPORTANCE OF THIS MISSION...
2000 A.D. Credit Card:
SCRIPT ROBOT DAVID PERRY
ART ROBOT REDONDO
LETTERING ROBOT TONY JACOB
COMPU-73E
THARG'S FUTURE-SHOCKS
THE LANULOS RUN!
OUR CARGO IS THE MOST PRICELESS COMMODITY IN THE KNOWN UNIVERSE. THE PEOPLE OF THE PLANET LANULOS IN THE STAR SYSTEM ZETA RETICULA ONE, HAVE BEEN STARVED OF IT FOR THREE WEEKS...
THREE WEEKS? GASP!
YES! SO YOU KNOW HOW IMPORTANT IT IS WE GET THROUGH. IF NOT..! KNOX, IS OUR FLIGHT-PATH THROUGH HYPER-SPACE PLOTTED YET?
YES, COMMANDER. WARP ACTIVATION IN 114·34 SECONDS.
HYPER-SPACE JUMPS COULD ONLY BE COMPLETED WHEN A SHIP WAS SAFELY OUTSIDE A PLANET'S GRAVITATIONAL FIELD.
COMMANDER BRADY! THREE ZRAGIAN CRUISERS ATTACKING ON BEARING 0-5-3-F!

IIMPAIR, ACTIVATE THE ENERGY SHIELDS! TORK, ACTIVATE THAT ENERGY CANNON! WE CAN'T DEVIATE FROM OUR FLIGHT PATH OR ELSE WE'LL END UP IN ANOTHER PART OF THE GALAXY. KNOX, HOW LONG TO HYPER-JUMP?
SEVENTY-EIGHT SECONDS, COMMANDER.

COMMANDER, I'VE GOT ONE OF THEM, BUT THE ENERGY FIELD'S FAILING!
JUST HOLD ON A LITTLE LONGER, TORK. THE ZRAGIANS WILL STOP AT NOTHING TO DESTROY OUR CARGO.

WE'VE LOST THE RESERVE FUEL TANKS!
JUST SO LONG AS IT'S NOT THE CARGO! HOLD ON TIGHT, TORK, WE'RE GOING INTO . . .

HYPER-SPACE!

WE'VE MADE IT! THOSE ZRAGIAN CRUISERS HAVEN'T GOT HYPER-SPACE FACILITIES.
WE HAVEN'T MADE IT YET! LOOK UP AHEAD...

HYPER-PARASITES!

HYPER-PARASITES—CREATURES THAT COULD ONLY LIVE AT SPEEDS IN THE EXCESS OF LIGHT. THEY WERE A CONSTANT DANGER TO SPACE TRAVELLERS.

I CAN'T STOP THEM, COMMANDER! THERE'S TOO MANY OF THEM! THEY'RE EATING THEIR WAY THROUGH THE HULL!

HOLD ON, TORK, WE'RE COMING!

COME ON, IIMPAIR, GRAB A BLASTER. WE'VE GOT TO PROTECT THE CARGO!

MY GOD, THEY'VE BROKEN THROUGH THE BULKHEAD! THEY'RE IN THE SHIP!

COMMANDER, WE'RE LOSING PRESSURE! AIR ESCAPING THROUGH THE HOLES THOSE THINGS HAVE MADE.
EVEN MORE SERIOUS, IIMPAIR, THEY'RE EATING THEIR WAY INTO THE CARGO HOLD!

ONLY ONE THING FOR IT! KNOX, DROP US OUT OF HYPER-SPACE!
BUT, COMMANDER, WE'RE...
DO IT! THAT'S AN ORDER!
DON'T SAY I DIDN'T WARN YOU, COMMANDER.

IT'S WORKED! HYPER-PARASITES CAN'T EXIST BELOW LIGHT-SPEED. THEY'RE FADING BACK INTO HYPER-SPACE.

WHAT IN THE NAME OF JUPITER--?
WHOOOOOP!

I TRIED TO WARN YOU, COMMANDER. WE'VE EMERGED NEAR A PREVIOUSLY UNDISCOVERED BLACK HOLE, AND WE'RE BEING SUCKED IN...
SO HOLD ON TIGHT!
WHAT'S GOING ON?
ARCTURUS

COMMANDER... I FEEL SO STRANGE!
THEN...
WE'VE MADE IT THROUGH!
YES, BUT NOT WITHOUT DAMAGE. ALL THAT TWISTING AND STRESSING HAS HAD AN EFFECT ON US.
AN EFFECT?
YES, WE'RE FALLING APART!
GOOD GRIEF, THE CARGO!
COMMANDER, COME BACK! IT'S TOO DANGEROUS!
PHEW, IT'S SAFE! IF WE HAD LOST IT...
CCRRRANNK!
WHAT WAS THAT?
MAIN ENGINE'S ...GONE...BZZZ...

COMMANDER, WE'VE BEEN PULLED INTO THE GRAVITATIONAL FIELD OF THE NEAREST PLANET. WE'RE GOING DOWN FAST AND THERE'S NOTHING WE CAN DO TO STOP IT!
TORK, WHAT ARE YOU—?
LASER CANNON'S GONE TOO, COMMANDER.
EVERYBODY INTO THEIR SUITS. WE'LL HAVE TO EJECT OUT WITH THE CARGO!
AND SO...
WE'VE FAILED! THE LANULOSIANS WON'T GET THE CARGO NOW. THEY'RE DOOMED!
COMMANDER... WAIT! NAVIGATIONAL-COMPUTER SHOWS THE BLACK HOLE HAS BROUGHT US OUT IN THE ZETA RETICULA SYSTEM. THIS IS LANULOS! WE'RE LANDING ON ITS DARK SIDE!
LANULOS WAS A PLANET THAT NEVER SPUN ON ITS AXIS. ONE SIDE WAS ETERNALLY LIGHT— THE OTHER WAS IN PERPETUAL DARKNESS. THE DARK SIDE HAD SPAWNED MANY STRANGE CREATURES.
QUICK, LOAD THE CARGO ONTO THE BUGGY! WE'VE GOT A CHANCE TO COMPLETE THIS MISSION– BUT WE'LL HAVE TO FIGHT FOR IT!
TORK, USE THE LASER-RIFLE. KNOX, DRIVE LIKE CRAZY!
IIMPAIR AND I'LL KEEP THE WEIRDIES AT BAY WITH THESE LASER-LASHES. NOTHING'S GOING TO STOP US NOW!
AND SO THE FEARLESS CREW OF THE ARCTURUS FOUGHT THEIR WAY ACROSS THE DARK SIDE OF LANULOS UNTIL...
COMMANDER, LOOK! LIGHT! WE'RE IN THE TWILIGHT ZONE! WE'VE MADE IT!
YES, BUT ARE WE IN TIME?

YES WE ARE – BUT ONLY JUST!
QUICK, IIMPAIR, BREAK OUT THE LIFE-SAVING CARGO!
LOOK, THE RELIEF'S ARRIVED!
THE RELIEF!
GET YOUR COPIES OF 2000 AD HERE!
ONLY ONE COPY EACH FOR NOW. TOO MUCH THRILL-POWER AFTER SO LONG COULD SERIOUSLY DAMAGE THEIR THRILL-CIRCUITS!
ME NEXT! ME NEXT!
THANK, THARG! THE THRILL-SUCKERS HAD NEARLY GOTTEN ME THAT TIME!
JUDGE DREDD, WOW!
I DIDN'T THINK WE WOULD GET THROUGH THAT TIME COMMANDER.
IT WAS ALL RIGHT, TORK. APART FROM WHEN THE SHIP FELL APART, IT WAS A QUIET RUN!
... AND ALL BECAUSE THE LANULOSIANS LOVE TO READ 2000 AD!

THARG'S FUTURE-SHOCKS
NIGEL GOES A-HUNTING!

YOU HAVE COME DOWN FROM THE ICE-CLAD HILLS TO FORAGE. IT IS DANGEROUS, BUT YOU HAVE NO CHOICE. YOU ARE STARVING...

HUNGRY ENOUGH TO RISK EATING THE FORBIDDEN FOOD...

YOU HEAR THE SUDDEN BALEFUL HOWL OF A RAT-HOUND AND YOUR BLOOD TURNS TO ICE. IT HAS YOUR SCENT!
aaaAAooOOOOaaaAAoo

YOU KNOW THAT RUNNING WILL NOT SAVE YOU. NOTHING CAN.

YOU RUN ANYWAY...
2000 A.D. Credit Card
SCRIPT ROBOT STACCATO
ART ROBOT REDONDO
LETTERING ROBOT TONY JACOB
COMPU-73E

BUT BEHIND YOU THE BAYING LOUDENS. MUTANT LEGS QUICKEN FOR THE KILL . . .
AAooo000aaaAAooo000
FEAR TURNS TO STARK PANIC. YOU HAVE TO GET AWAY—HIDE—
ANYWHERE AWAY FROM THOSE DEVILISH BEASTS!
YOU WAIT, TREMBLING. YOU KNEW ALL ALONG THAT FLIGHT WAS USELESS. YOU SHOULD NEVER HAVE LEFT YOUR MOUNTAIN CAVE . . .
YOU THINK OF IT NOW— THE COMFORT OF THE COLD, CLAMMY DARKNESS . . . THE SECURITY YOU FELT IN NUMBERS . . .

YOU REMEMBER THE STORIES THE OLD MEN USED TO TELL-TALES OF THE DAYS WHEN MAN WAS GREAT, AND ALL THE WORLD WAS HIS TO COMMAND.
BUT THAT WAS A LONG TIME AGO. BEFORE THEY HAD THE WAR.

THE HIDEOUS SQUEAKS OF THE FRENZIED PACK JERK YOU BACK TO NOW-TO REALITY.
J. REDONDO. 82.

JUST IN TIME FOR YOU TO MEET YOUR FATE.
BRING HIM DOWN!
BANG!

DASHED FINE RUN HE GAVE US, EH, NIGEL?
THE HOUNDS CAN HAVE HIM MAYBE TEACH THE OTHER PESTS TO KEEP OFF MY LAND!
THE END

THARG'S FUTURE-SHOCKS
ALEC TRENCH–ZOMBIE! PART 1
EVERY 76 YEARS OR SO, EARTHLETS, THE SPECTACULAR BALL OF FIERY GASES KNOWN AS HALEY'S COMET COMES SWEEPING IN FROM THE FRINGES OF THE SOLAR SYSTEM, TO BATHE PLANET EARTH IN IT'S COSMIC GLOW. JOURNEY WITH ME NOW TO THE TIME OF ITS NEXT ARRIVAL...
2000 AD
LONDON, FEBRUARY 1986. IT IS MIDNIGHT, AND CHEERING CROWDS THRONG
IT'S BREATH-TAKING! LIKE THE ENTIRE SKY'S ALIVE WITH COSMIC ENERGY!
ENJOY IT WHILE YOU CAN KIDS— OLD HALEY WON'T BE BACK TILL 2062!
BUT IN A GRAVEYARD NOT FAR FROM BLACKFRIARS, DARKER DEEDS ARE A-BORNING...
HURRY IT UP, IGOR! THIS IS THE ONLY CHANCE I'LL HAVE IN MY LIFETIME TO PROVE MY THEORY WORKS!
2000 A.D. Credit Card:
SCRIPT ROBOT T.M.O.
ART ROBOT RON SMITH
LETTERING ROBOT TONY JACOB
COMPU·73E
HERE–THIS GRAVE WILL DO. SET UP THE EQUIPMENT!
AT ONCE, MASTER!
ALEC TRENCH 1949–1979 Hardly missed
IF IT DOES WORK, SIRE, YOU'LL BE HAILED AS THE GREATEST SCIENTIFIC MIND SINCE YOUR FAMOUS ANCESTOR — THE FIRST BARON FRANKENSTEIN!
THE FIRST BARON–PAH!
HE WAS A BUMBLING INCOMPETENT — AN AMATEUR FIDDLING ABOUT WITH BITS OF BODIES, STICKING THEM TOGETHER LIKE A COMMON COBBLER!
BUT IT'S THE 20th CENTURY NOW–AND I HAVE TECHNOLOGY ON MY SIDE!

WATCH, IGOR—WATCH AS MY RESURRECTOR MACHINE GATHERS THE POTENT COSMIC RAYS!
GAPE AS THOSE RAYS PICK UP THE TINY ELECTRIC LIFE VIBRATIONS FROM MY BRAIN—AND AMPLIFY THEM A BILLIONFOLD!
AND MARVEL AS THE ESSENCE OF LIFE IS RELAYED TO THE DEAD!
ZZAT!
ALEC TRENCH LIVES—AGAIN!
AAAGH! IT—IT'S HORRIBLE!
WHAT DID YOU EXPECT, YOU CRINGING OAF? BURT REYNOLDS?
IT'S ONLY A CORPSE—AND AN OBEDIENT CORPSE, AT THAT! ONCE SUBJECTED TO MY RESURRECTOR, IT BECOMES MY ETERNAL SLAVE!
DANCE, SLAVE-DANCE!
SEE?
TRULY YOU ARE THE BRAIN SUPREME, MY BARON! WITH THIS SLAVE TO DO OUR EVERY BIDDING, WE WILL LIVE A LIFE OF EASE AND LUXURY!

OW!
EASE AND LUXURY— PAH! POWER IS WHAT I WANT— AND POWER IS WHAT I SHALL HAVE!
WITH THE HELP OF A FEW OF MR TRENCH'S DEAD FRIENDS— I AM GOING TO RULE THE WORLD!
EERIE COMETARY ENERGY STREAMS OUT FROM FRANKENSTEIN'S RESURRECTOR— AND THE STILL OF THE BLACKFRIARS' NIGHT IS SHATTERED BY THE CRASH OF FALLING TOMBSTONES AND THE CRACK OF LONG-DEAD BONES!
COME, MY BONY BEAUTIES! COME MY FAITHFUL SLAVES! JOIN MY UNDEAD ARMY!

AND WITH ALEC TRENCH DANCING AT ITS HEAD, THE CADAVEROUS COLUMN MOVES OFF...
ON TO THE NEXT GRAVEYARD! I MUST RESURRECT ALL I CAN, BEFORE THE COMET PASSES ON!
IT IS THE UNHAPPY LOT OF A CERTAIN CONSTABLE MACNAB TO BE ON THE EASTERN BEAT THAT NIGHT . . .
SUFFERIN' SERGEANTS! I-I DON'T BELIEVE IT!
MACNAB TO CONTROL! AM FACED WITH THREATENING MOB OF SKELETONS! THEY DIDN'T SAY ANYTHING ABOUT THIS AT TRAINING COLLEGE!
WH-WHAT DO I DO?
CONTROL TO MACNAB! DON'T PANIC, LAD - ASSISTANCE IS ON ITS WAY. AS FOR THE MOB - TRY TALKING CALMLY TO THEM FIRST. BUT REMEMBER, IF THEY GET VIOLENT . . .
DON'T HESITATE TO ARREST THEM!
AAAAAGGGHHHH!!!

ARISE! YOUR MASTER COMMANDS YOU!
TO WESTMINSTER! WE START MY REIGN OF TERROR AT THE HOUSES OF PARLIAMENT!
BUT AS THE MAD BARON CONTINUES WITH HIS FIENDISH PLANS . . .
. . . THE FORCES OF LAW AND ORDER RACE TO THE SCENE!
PRIORITY ALERT! RIOT AT EASTERN CEMETERY!
POLICE
ALL AVAILABLE UNITS CONVERGE!
POLICE
P
WILL THE MEN OF LONDON'S FINEST ARRIVE IN TIME? WILL FRANKENSTEIN'S UNDEAD HORDES SUCCEED IN THEIR EVIL AIMS? WILL ALEC TRENCH BE A FAILURE SECOND TIME ROUND?
I STRONGLY SUGGEST YOU BE HERE NEXT PROG, EARTHLETS!
2000AD
THRILL-POWER PEAKS ++ STABILISE CIRCUITS ++

THARG'S FUTURE-SHOCKS
ALEC TRENCH— ZOMBIE! PART 2
IT IS 1986, AND THE FIERY BALL OF GASES KNOWN AS HALEY'S COMET STREAKS THROUGH THE SOLAR SYSTEM, BATHING PLANET EARTH IN ITS EERIE COSMIC RAYS!
2000 A.D. Credit Card:
SCRIPT ROBOT T.M.O.
ART ROBOT RON SMITH
LETTERING ROBOT TONY JACOB
COMPU-73E
IT IS THESE VERY RAYS WHICH HAVE BEEN HARNESSED BY THE MAD BARON FRANKENSTEIN'S RESURRECTION MACHINE . . .
WATCH, IGOR, AS THE COMET'S BEAMS AMPLIFY MY BRAIN'S ELECTRICAL DISCHARGE—MY LIFE VIBRATIONS . . .
ZZAT!
AND TRANSFER THE ESSENCE OF LIFE TO THOSE WHO ARE DEAD!
ALEC TRENCH 1949~1979 Hardly missed
NOW, UNDER FRANKENSTEIN'S DIRECT CONTROL, AN ARMY OF ZOMBIES HEADS FOR LONDON'S HOUSES OF PARLIAMENT . . .
FORWARD, MY CADAVEROUS CREW! FIRST WE WILL CONQUER BRITAIN...
AND THEN—THE WORLD!
BUT, ALERTED BY THE GALLANT CONSTABLE MACNAB, (NOW DECEASED), THE FORCES OF LAW AND ORDER RACE TO CONFRONT THE HORDES OF EVIL . . .
TAKE UP HOLDING FORMATION!

IGOR, FRANKENSTEIN'S ONLY HUMAN SERVANT...
THE POLICE, MASTER! THEY'LL ARREST US ALL!
PAH! NOTHING CAN STOP THE LEGIONS OF THE UNDEAD!
ON, YOU GHOULS! CRUSH THEM! IN THE NAME OF FRANKENSTEIN, CRUSH THEM!
HERE THEY COME! STAND READY!
WH-WHAT ARE THEY, SARGE?
NO CONCERN OF OURS, LAD! WE'RE JUST HERE TO STOP THEM!
HOLD YOUR GROUND, LAD!
AAAAAHHH
AAAAAAAA.
HOLD YOUR...
AAAGH!
AAHHH!
FALL BACK! FALL BACK AND REGROUP!

ABOVE, POLICE COMMISSIONER 'PINCHER' MORRIS SURVEYS THE BATTLE FROM HIS MOBILE COMMAND . . .
OUR BOYS ARE TAKING A THRASHING, SIR! THEY'RE BEING OVERWHELMED!
VERY WELL— CALL UP THE W-C!

BELOW—
WE'RE WINNING, MASTER! WE'RE WINNING!
OF COURSE WE ARE! SOON THE RANKS OF MY HORDES WILL BE SWOLLEN BY NEW RECRUITS— FROM EVERY GRAVE-YARD IN THE LAND!

I WILL CLAIM THE DESTINY APPOINTED FOR ME! I WILL RULE THE WORLD! NOTHING CAN STOP ME . . .
HOSE THEM DOWN! WASH THEM AWAY!
WATER CANNON!
POLICE
GLOOBBB!

HIGH-PRESSURE JETS RAM INTO THE MINDLESS UNDEAD, SPREADING TOTAL DISORDER THROUGH THEIR RANKS . . .
THAT'S STOPPED THEM, SIR!

THAT MAN WITH THE STRANGE HEAD-GEAR— I'D SWEAR HE WAS CONTROLLING THESE THINGS! TAKE US DOWN!

THUS IT IS THAT THE DAZED BARON FRANKENSTEIN FINDS HIS DREAMS OF DOMINATION RAPIDLY RECEDING AS HE IS HAULED ABOARD.
GET HIM INSIDE— QUICK!
MY MASTER! NO— LEAVE HIM A— AAAAH!

POLICE
STRIP OFF THAT EQUIPMENT! THAT'S WHAT HE WAS USING ON THEM— I'M SURE OF IT!

BUT...
GET YOUR HANDS OFF ME!
OOFFF!
LOOK OUT, SIR!
COMISSIONER AND RESURRECTOR TUMBLE DOWN...
SIR!
...EACH TO ITS OWN LANDING PLACE!
UUUHHH!
BONK!
AT A MORE OPPORTUNE MOMENT, BARON FRANKENSTEIN MIGHT HAVE BEEN INTRIGUED TO KNOW THAT HIS RESURRECTOR AMPLIFIES THE VIBRATIONS NOT ONLY OF THE LIVING... BUT THE DEAD, TOO!
AND THE VIBRATIONS THAT RADIATE OUT FROM THE THING THAT ONCE WAS ALEC TRENCH ARE DEADLY!
NO! NO!
I-I'M DISINTEGRATING!

MY RESURRECTOR— HAVING SOME KIND OF REVERSE EFFECT! EVERYTHING THOSE RAYS TOUCH WILL... DIE!
...AAAAAHH!
WHOOMPHH!
WITH NO-ONE TO ORDER HIM OTHERWISE, THE MINDLESS REMAINS OF ALEC TRENCH DANCE ON...
...SPREADING INSTANT DESTRUCTION!
DON'T WORRY TOO MUCH, EARTHLETS. THE COMET'S VISIT WILL ONLY LAST FOR A WEEK OR SO. THE PEOPLE OF LONDON WILL SURVIVE ... AT LEAST, SOME OF THEM WILL!
2000AD
THE END

THARG'S FUTURE-SHOCKS

RETURN OF THE THING!

2000 A.D.
Credit Card:
SCRIPT ROBOT
ALAN MOORE
ART ROBOT
DAVE GIBBONS
LETTERING ROBOT
TONY JACOB
COMPU-73E

MUST HURRY!
KKRAKK!
GRUD! BUT I'VE HAD A LOUSY DAY AT THE OFFICE!
IS MY DINNER READY, MADGE?
CHING!
KA-CHUNK!
THERE! PIPING HOT AND READY TO SERVE, WUBBGRUTT, MY DARLING!
PHEW!
MURCH! SCHLUPP! PASS THE COBALT 90...
YES, HOUSEWIVES... YOU CAN KEEP THE SILICON-BASED LIFE-FORM IN YOUR LIFE HAPPY WITH AN EE-ZEE HI-SPEED THERMONUCLEAR PRESSURE COOKER!
THE END

THARG'S FUTURE-SHOCKS SKIRMISH!

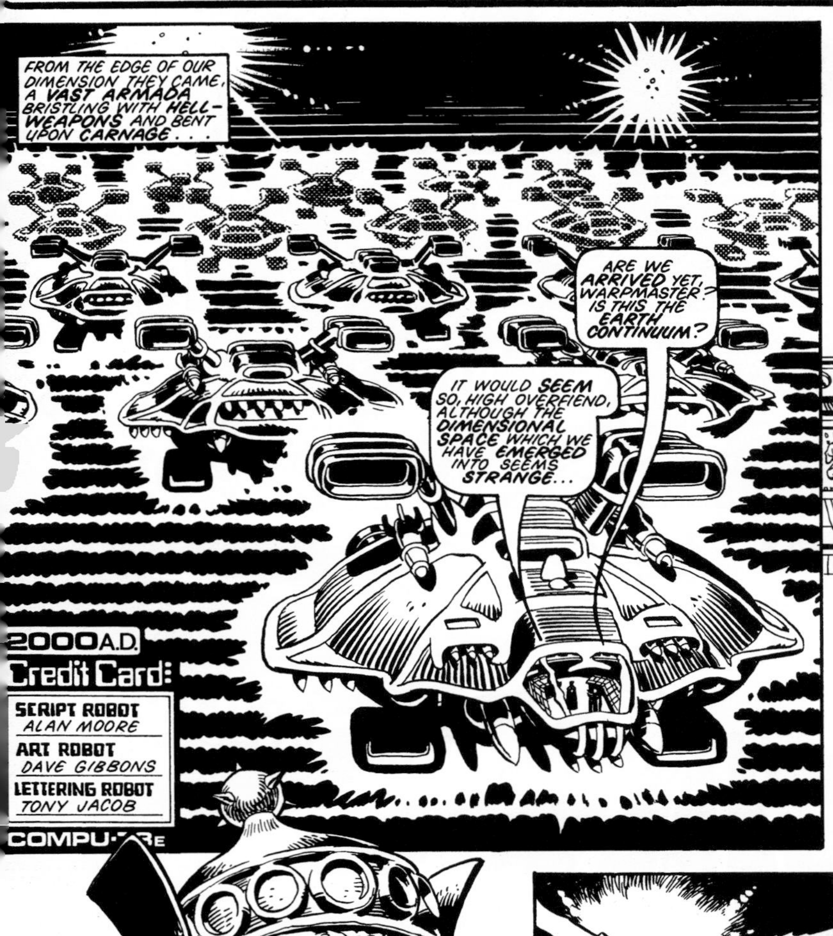

FROM THE EDGE OF OUR DIMENSION THEY CAME, A VAST ARMADA BRISTLING WITH HELL-WEAPONS AND BENT UPON CARNAGE . .
ARE WE ARRIVED YET, WARPMASTER? IS THIS THE EARTH CONTINUUM?
IT WOULD SEEM SO, HIGH OVERFIEND, ALTHOUGH THE DIMENSIONAL SPACE WHICH WE HAVE EMERGED INTO SEEMS STRANGE...
2000 A.D. Credit Card:
SCRIPT ROBOT ALAN MOORE
ART ROBOT DAVE GIBBONS
LETTERING ROBOT TONY JACOB

IT SEEMS TO BE COMPOSED OF ELECTRONIC PULSE-SIGNALS RATHER THAN THE SOLID-MATTER THAT WE WERE EXPECTING . . .

HMMPH. NO MATTER. THE PRIMITIVES OF THIS DIMENSION WILL SOON BEND THE KNEE BEFORE US.
AFTER ALL, OUR TECHNOLOGY IS CENTURIES IN ADVANCE OF THEIRS. THEY WILL HAVE NO WEAPONS WITH WHICH TO COUNTER OUR . . .

WHURR . . WH'APPEN?
STRIKE A LUMINOSITY! THE EARTHLINGS HAVE HIT US WITH A PARTICLE BEAM WEAPON FROM OUT OF NOWHERE!
FIVE OF OUR DRONE CRAFT ARE NO MORE! I SHALL RELEASE THE PHOTON-TORPEDOES...

YARK!
DWIBBLE! DWIBBLE! DWIBBLE!
THEY HAVE BLASTED OUR PHOTON-TORPEDOES OUT OF THE AIR, AND A FURTHER SIX OF OUR DREADNOUGHTS HAVE BEEN INCAPACITATED!
WE ARE BEING GIVEN A HYPER-PASTING AND NO MISTAKE...
ZEEET!
DWIP!
GUBBLE!
THE REST OF THE FLEET HAS BEEN ATOMISED! WE MUST LEG IT, WARPMASTER! WE CANNOT FIGHT THESE TERRIBLE WEAPONS THAT MAKE SUCH A RIDICULOUS NOISE.
WE ARE TOO LATE, HIGH OVER-FIEND! A BEAM IS HEADING STRAIGHT FOR US! WE CANNOT EVADE IT! WE CANNOT. . .
BOOP! BOOP! BOOP!
AAARRRGH!
SPLIBBIT!
SPLIBBIT!
AAARGH!
AAARGH?
'ERE, JOHN. THIS 'SPACE INVADERS' MACHINE JUST WENT "AAARRGH!"
SPACE INVADERS
SPACE INVADE
LEAVE IT OUT, NORMAN. PLAYING THAT THING ALL DAY'S STARTING TO ROT YOUR BRAIN.
WHY CAN'T YOU FIND SOMETHING USEFUL TO DO WITH YOUR TIME?
BURGER BAR
THE END

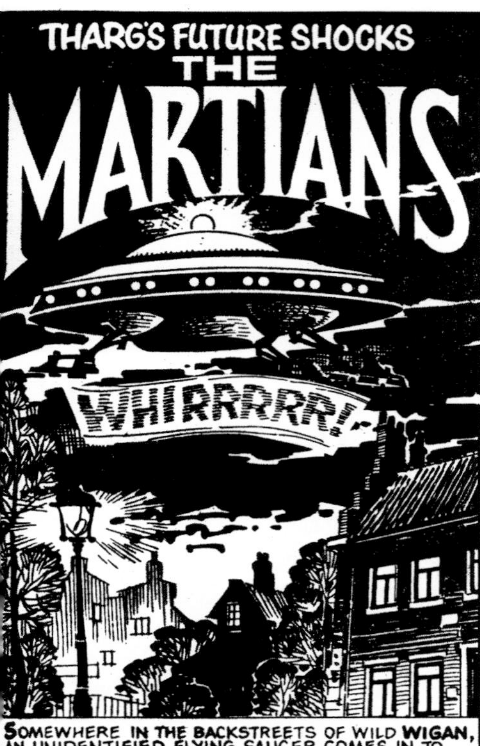
THARG'S FUTURE SHOCKS
THE MARTIANS
WHIRRRRR!
SOMEWHERE IN THE BACKSTREETS OF WILD WIGAN, AN UNIDENTIFIED FLYING SAUCER COMES IN TO MAKE AN UNIDENTIFIED LANDING...

I CLAIM THIS PLANET IN THE NAME OF MARS! FROM NOW ON, IT WILL BE KNOWN AS "ONKLAND"!
RIGHT, THAT'S THE PRELIMINARIES OVER WITH. NOW LET'S GET DOWN TO DOING WHAT WE CAME HERE TO DO.
YEAH. BURNING. PLUNDERING. PILLAGING!
AND KILLING... LOTS OF KILLING!

HEY, ONK, I THOUGHT YOU SAID THIS PLANET WAS INHABITED? IT'S DESERTED!
THEY'RE HERE SOMEWHERE. KEEP LOOKING.

THERE'S SOMEBODY! I'LL BASH HIM FIRST. IT'S MY TURN!
NO, WAIT. HE MAY LEAD US TO THE REST.

LOOK, HE'S BEEN JOINED BY TWO OTHERS. THAT BUILDING MUST BE THEIR HEADQUARTERS.
WE'LL STORM IT!

CRASH!
PREPARE TO DIE, ONKLINGS!
I DON'T BELIEVE IT!
IT CAN'T BE TRUE!

CLAP! CLAP!
FANCY DRESS BALL
CLAP!
WHAT AN ENTRANCE! WELL DONE, YOUNG MAN, YOU'VE WON FIRST PRIZE — I'VE NEVER SEEN SUCH ORIGINAL COSTUMES IN MY LIFE!
CLAP!
CLAP!
2000 A.D.
Credit Card:
SCRIPT ROBOT D. PERRY
ART ROBOT J. REDONDO
LETTERING ROBOT B. NUTTALL
COMPU-73E
THE END

SOMEWHERE, IN UNCHARTED SPACE...
WELL, WE'VE BEEN TRAVELLING FOR YEARS AT FASTER-THAN-LIGHT SPEED. WE MUST BE ALMOST THERE! JUST THINK, ELMO, THE END OF THE UNIVERSE...
WHAT A BUNCH OF SQUACKLE!
HUH? WHAT DO YOU MEAN?

THARG'S FUTURE-SHOCKS
THE WRITING ON THE WALL!

I MEAN, WHAT IF THERE ISN'T AN END TO THE UNIVERSE? WHAT IF IT JUST GOES ON FOREVER?
B-BUT IT CAN'T GO ON FOREVER. IT HAS TO END SOMEWHERE...

OH SURE! AND I SUPPOSE SPACE JUST ENDS DEAD WITH A BRICK WALL, OR SOMETHING?
WELL, UH, NO... I DIDN'T MEAN THAT EXACTLY, BUT...

GRRAUNCH!
YURK! WHAT THE...?
WE'VE HIT SOMETHING! LEMME TAKE A LOOK AT THE VIEW SCREEN...

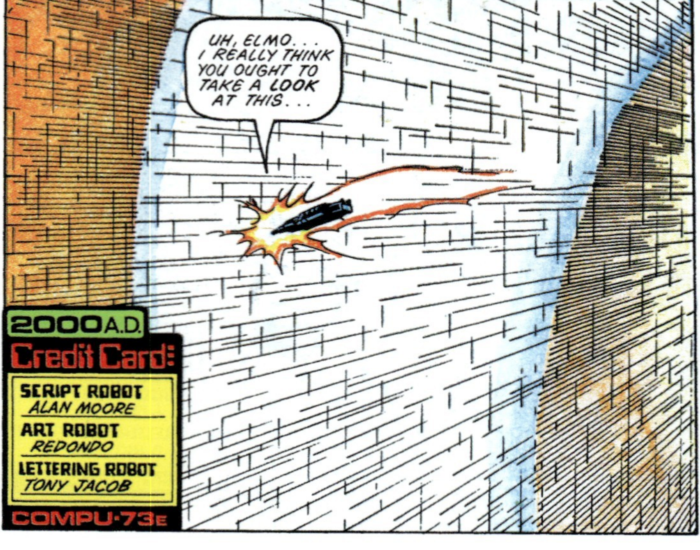
UH, ELMO... I REALLY THINK YOU OUGHT TO TAKE A LOOK AT THIS...
2000 A.D.
Credit Card:
SCRIPT ROBOT ALAN MOORE
ART ROBOT REDONDO
LETTERING ROBOT TONY JACOB
COMPU-73E

A BRICK WALL! I DON'T BELIEVE IT! A BRICK WALL STRETCHING AS FAR AS THE EYE CAN SEE IN ANY DIRECTION...
NOT ONLY THAT, BUT AREAS OF IT SEEM TO BE A DIFFERENT COLOUR. I THINK THERE'S SOMETHING WRITTEN ON IT!

SOMETHING WRITTEN ON IT? HOLY KAZOOZIS! IT MUST BE THE SECRET OF THE UNIVERSE OR SOMETHING...
YEAH, BUT IT'S TOO BIG TO READ. MAYBE IF WE STEER THE SHIP ALONG PARALLEL TO THE WALL...
OF COURSE! WE CAN KEEP OUR CAMERAS RUNNING, AND THEN WHEN WE GET TO THE END OF THE MESSAGE...
...THE COMPUTER CAN BUILD UP A COMPLETE IMAGE AND REDUCE IT SO WE CAN READ IT! WHAT A GREAT IDEA!
WEEKS PASS.
DO YOU THINK WE'VE REACHED THE END OF THE MESSAGE YET, WALDO?
NAH. SEE THAT BIG WHITE BLOB ABOUT A HUNDRED TIMES BIGGER THAN JUPITER?
WELL, I THINK IT'S A COMMA!
MONTHS PASS.
WE HAVEN'T PASSED ANY MORE WHITE AREAS FOR DAYS, WALDO. I THINK WE'VE DONE IT. I THINK WE'VE PHOTOGRAPHED THE WHOLE MESSAGE!
GREAT! NOW LET'S FEED IT INTO THE COMPUTER AND SEE WHAT IT COMES UP WITH!
AND SO...
WELL? IS IT DEVELOPED YET? WHAT DOES IT SAY? WHAT IS THE WRITING ON THE OUTER WALL OF THE UNIVERSE?
UH, I DON'T THINK YOU'RE GOING TO LIKE IT, WALDO...
GOOD LORD.
"BIG GEORGE RULES, O.K?"
THE BITTER END

THARG'S FUTURE-SHOCKS
THE WILD FRONTIER!
TROUBLE ON NEW WYOMING--
RUN! THE OCTOBANDITS HAVE JUST HIT PLANET!
OH, NO! NOT... THE OCTO-BANDITS!
YES, THE OCTOBANDITS... LED BY THAT CEPHALOPOD SIDEWINDER...
...BILLY THE SQUID!
HEEYAR! HEEYAR! OUTTA MY WAY! I'M A PISTOL-PACKIN' POLYPOID AND I MEAN BUSINESS!
RITIN' = ALAN MOORE
DRAWRIN' = DAVE GIBBONS
SUDDENLY...
OKAY, YOU INK-SQUIRTING SADDLETRAMPS! REACH FOR THE SKY! REACH FOR THE SKY! REACH FOR THE SKY! REACH FOR THE SKY!
HUH? WHO DARES CHALLENGE BILLY THE SQUID?
I DO!
>GULP< IT'S A MASKED MAN!
GUN HIM DOWN, BOYS! THERE'S DOZENS OF US AND ONLY ONE OF HIM!
OH, YEAH?
>GASP<

YOU CAN SAY THAT AGAIN!

...AND MUST ENDURE THE HUMILIATION THAT IS TO FOLLOW.
WELL, HOGTIE MY TENTACLES! AND WHAT HAVE WE HERE?
C'MON, BOYS, LET'S SLIDE OUR SUCKERS OVER TO THE SALOON!
>CHOKE<

AND, IN THE SALOON...
...AN EIGHT-LEGGED FRIEND, AN EIGHT-LEGGED FRIEND, HE'LL NEVER LET YOU DO-O-OWN...
>SOB< THIS IS TERRIBLE! WHO WILL SAVE US FROM THESE SHARP-SHOOTING SLIMEYS?

N-NO MORE! WE GIVE IN!

AND SO...
JAIL
YOU'VE SAVED OUR TOWN! HOW CAN WE EVER...
WHAA... THEY'VE GONE BEFORE WE COULD EVEN THANK THEM!!

B-BUT...WHO WERE THOSE MASKED MEN ANYWAY?
THOSE WERE NO ORDINARY MASKED MEN, SON! HAVEN'T YOU EVER HEARD OF...

"...THE CLONE RANGER?"
HIYOO, CHROMIUM! HAWAAY!
WITH A CLOUD OF DUST AND A STREAK OF LIGHT VANISHING INTO THE DISTANCE, PEACE RETURNS ONCE MORE TO THE WILD WESTERN SPIRAL ARM OF THE GALAXY...
TH' END.

THARG'S FUTURE-SHOCKS
THE BIG DAY

SCRIPT: ALAN MOORE. ART: ROBIN SMITH. LETT: TOM FRAME.

THE PLANETOID IS **SMALL** AND **AIRLESS**, ALTHOUGH TO THE FOLK WHO **LIVE** THERE IT IS AS **BIG** A PLACE AS ANY OTHER.
HURF PUFF GRUNT!

HEAR ME, MY PEOPLE!
AT LAST OUR **PILGRIMAGE** IS **OVER**! FOR **HERE**, GATHERED ALL IN THIS **SACRED PLACE**, IS THE ENTIRE, HEAVEN-FAVOURED **TRIBE OF SKRANT**. LONG SHALL THEIR PRAISES BE SUNG!

ALL OUR EXISTENCE HAS BEEN LEADING UP TO **THIS INSTANT**!
THE GODS ARE **COMING**, MY CHILDREN. WHAT WILL THEIR MIND-WRENCHING **MESSAGE** BE?

SEE! THEY **COME**! THAT **VAST SHAPE** MUST BE THEIR **CHARIOT**! AND LO... IT IS DESCENDING UNTO US!
PREPARE YOURSELVES! PREPARE TO HEAR THE **VOICE OF THE GODS**!

GENERATIONS WE HAVE
KKED THIS VAST AND BARREN
RLD, SLOWLY MAKING OUR WAY
OME MYSTICAL INSTINCT TO
HALLOWED GROUND...
WING THAT HERE RESTS THE
TINY OF OUR RACE. BEHOLD,
MY PEOPLE...
...THE PILLAR OF THE GODS!
THE PILLAR IS VAST, REARING UP INTO THE STAR-STREWN FIRMAMENT, ITS TOP TOO HIGH TO BE SEEN, . .
OUR LEGEND FORETOLD THIS DAY, WHEN THE CHOSEN RACE OF SKRANT STANDS GATHERED BEFORE THIS CELESTIAL PILLAR...
...THIS DAY WHEN THE GODS THEMSELVES WOULD DESCEND UNTO US AND SPEAK THEIR WORDS OF AWE AND MAGNIFICENCE!
SER!
WITHOUT
T...ER...
IT IS
ER CLOSE,
SQWOT!
AND, AS PROPHESISED, THE GODS SPEAK...
THAT'S ONE SMALL STEP FOR A MAN...
...BUT ONE COMPARATIVELY LARGE STEP FOR THE DESTINY-KISSED TRIBESPEOPLE OF SKRANT.
...LONG SHALL THEIR PASSING BE LAMENTED!
THE END.

THARG'S FUTURE-SHOCKS
One Christmas During Eternity!
2596 A.D. MAN HAS MADE MANY ADVANCES IN THE FIELD OF SCIENCE. AS YET, HOWEVER, HE HAS NOT IMPROVED UPON CHRISTMAS . . .
IS EVERYTHING READY ?
I THINK SO. DID YOU TAKE YOUR TABLET THIS MORNING ?
2000 A.D. Credit Card:
SCRIPT ROBOT ALAN MOORE
ART ROBOT REDONDO
LETTERING ROBOT FRAME
COMPU-73E

LARS AND AMARYLIS MARTIN STILL LOVE CHRISTMAS. THIS IS THE THREE HUNDRED AND SEVENTH THAT THEY HAVE SPENT TOGETHER. . .
OF COURSE I'VE TAKEN MY TABLET. WHAT'S THE MATTER ? SCARED I'M GOING TO TURN OLD AND WRINKLED OVERNIGHT ?
SILLY.

YES, THE IMMORTALITY TABLET HAS CHANGED LOTS OF THINGS. BUT NOT CHRISTMAS. CHRISTMAS IS STILL A TIME FOR TINSEL, PINE NEEDLES AND HUSHED, EXCITED WHISPERS. . .
SHHH. I THINK I CAN HEAR HIM COMING...

. . . A TIME FOR THE CHILDREN.
HAPPY CHRISTMAS, TIMMY !

OH, MUM... DAD... LOOK AT ALL THESE PRESENTS ! I DON'T KNOW WHICH TO OPEN FIRST !
TAKE YOUR TIME, SON. YOU'VE GOT ALL DAY.

. . . AND IT IS THE BEST OF DAYS. THE DAY THEY'VE LOOKED FORWARD TO ALL YEAR. THEY WATCH HIM AS HE SITS IN HIS EXPANDING NEST OF WRAPPING PAPER, AND THEY SMILE.

THE DINNER IS A DELIGHT. AMARYLIS HAD BEEN UP HALF THE NIGHT PREPARING IT. SHE COULD HAVE JUST PRESSED A BUTTON, BUT SHE WANTED TO DO IT **PROPERLY**, FOR TIMMY.

THE HOURS SPIN HAPPILY BY, LOST IN TIMMY'S SHRIEKS OF LAUGHTER. THEY ALMOST FORGOT ABOUT THE TIME. ALMOST.
I...I THINK I JUST HEARD THE DOORBELL.
OH NO! NOT SO **SOON...**

HAPPY CHRISTMAS, MRS MARTIN. HOPE YOU'VE HAD A NICE DAY. I'VE COME FOR TIMMY.
YES. YES, OF COURSE. YOU'D BETTER COME IN.

TIMMY SMILES. SMILES EVEN AS THE MAN IN THE GREY OVERALL OPENS THE PANEL AT THE TOP OF HIS HEAD AND SWITCHES HIM OFF.
THERE. HOPE HE HASN'T BEEN ANY TROUBLE.
NO. NO TROUBLE AT ALL. WILL WE GET HIM BACK NEXT YEAR, DO YOU THINK?

THE IMMORTALITY TABLET HAS CHANGED **LOTS** OF THINGS. NOBODY **DIES** ANYMORE. AND IN ORDER TO KEEP THE POPULATION STABLE, NO-ONE GETS **BORN** EITHER...
OH, I SHOULD THINK SO. HIM, OR ONE JUST LIKE HIM...
...THERE ARE NO MORE CHILDREN.

THEY WATCH AS THE HOVER-WAGON SKIMS OFF ACROSS THE SNOW. IT HAS BEEN A **GOOD** DAY.
DON'T CRY, LOVE. THERE'S ALWAYS **NEXT** YEAR...
...AND THE YEAR AFTER THAT, AND THE YEAR AFTER THAT......
THE END.

THARG'S FUTURE-SHOCKS
NO PICNIC!
ON EASTER ISLAND THE ENIGMATIC STONE HEADS OBSERVE A SILENCE THAT IS CENTURIES DEEP . . .
OSWALD, YOU DOPE! HOW COULD YOU?
I SAID "OSWALD, WHATEVER YOU DO, DON'T FORGET THE POTATO SALAD!" SO WHAT DOES MY HUSBAND 'THE GENIUS' DO?
I FORGOT THE POTATO SALAD. SO SHOOT ME.
DUMBELL!
HECK, RAQUEL, WE'RE ON EASTER ISLAND! CAN'T YOU FEEL THE ANCIENT AURA OF MYSTERY ALL AROUND US? JUST LOOK AT THESE HEADS, WILLYA?
NO-ONE KNOWS WHAT THEY ARE OR HOW THEY GOT HERE! DOESN'T THAT SORTA DO SOMETHING FOR YOU, RAQUEL? DON'T YOU HAVE ANY POETRY IN YOUR SOUL?
NO. AND I DON'T HAVE ANY POTATO SALAD, EITHER. DID YOU BRING THE MAYONNAISE?
SIGH
YOU GO AHEAD AND EAT. I'M GOING TO SIT IN THE SHADE OF THESE HEADS AND PONDER THE MYSTERIES OF EXISTENCE LIKE PLATO AND SOCRATES AND THOSE GUYS...
HAH! DID THEY FORGET THE POTATO SALAD?
WHEN ARE WE GOING HOME?
LATER...
ZZZZZZZ... SHNUK! SHNORK! ...ZZZZZZZZZZ...

BOR-RING.
HEY, MUM! I WANNA GO HOME NOW!
Z Z Z Z Z Z Z
OH, ALL RIGHT, CUPCAKE. NOW LET'S SEE... HAVE I GOT EVERYTHING? I KEEP THINKING I FORGOT SOMETHING...
MUST BE IMAGINING THINGS.
ZZZZ MMNUH? WHUH?
WHAT'S.. RAQUEL? BYRON? HEY, WAIT! YOU'VE LEFT ME BEHIND! COME BACK!
PUTT-PUTT-PUTT-PUTT-PUTT...
TH-THEY CAN'T HEAR ME! THEY'RE GOING AWAY AND LEAVING ME HERE!
I DON'T BELIEVE IT! MY OWN SON BURYING ME UP TO MY NECK IN SAND! MY OWN WIFE JUST FORGETTING ABOUT ME! I JUST DON'T BELIEVE IT!
FUNNY. THAT'S EXACTLY WHAT I SAID.
YEAH, ME TOO. WELCOME TO THE CLUB, BUDDY.
THE END.
2000 A.D. Credit Card:
SCRIPT ROBOT ALAN MOORE
ART ROBOT JOHN HIGGINS
LETTERING ROBOT T FRAME
COMPU-73E

"I WAS SITTING IN MY STUDY DIGESTING MY EVENING MEAL, IDLY TOYING WITH A PIECE OF **VELLUM WRITING PAPER**..."

"THERE WAS SOMETHING **FASCINATING** ABOUT THE SHAPE INTO WHICH I HAD **FOLDED** IT. I FELT THAT I WAS ON THE VERGE OF A **GREAT INSIGHT**..."

"SUDDENLY THERE WAS A KNOCK AT THE DOOR..."

2000 A.D.
Credit Card
SCRIPT ROBOT *ALAN MOORE*
ART ROBOT *DAVE GIBBONS*
LETTERING ROBOT *STEVE POTTER*
COMPU·73E

THARG'S
FUTURE-
SHOCKS
"THE DISTURBED DIGESTIONS OF DOCTOR DIBWORTHY"

MYSELF? GOOD GRACIOUS!
QUICK! LET ME IN! I DON'T HAVE MUCH TIME!

WHAT'S ALL THIS ABOUT? WHO ARE YOU, SIR?
I'M YOUR FUTURE SELF! I'VE COME FROM AN HOUR IN THE FUTURE TO TELL YOU THAT IN FIVE MINUTES YOU WILL INVENT THE WORLD'S FIRST TIME MACHINE...

...BUT IT'S IMPORTANT THAT YOU REGISTER THE PATENT STRAIGHT AWAY! OTHERWISE PEOPLE WILL BE ABLE TO TRAVEL BACK IN TIME AND BEAT YOU TO IT...
DON'T LISTEN TO HIM!

GREAT SCOTT! YOU'RE ME... ER... I MEAN, YOU'RE US! WHAT DO YOU WANT?
I'M YOUR FUTURE SELF! I'VE COME FROM A WEEK IN THE FUTURE TO WARN YOU NOT TO VISIT THE PATENT OFFICE.

YOU SEE, ON THE WAY THERE YOU'LL BE HIT BY A BUS, AND...
PAY THAT IMPOSTER NO HEED!

MERCIFUL POWERS! THERE'S FOUR OF ME!
NOT QUITE! YOU SEE, THIS LAST ARRIVAL ISN'T REALLY YOU AT ALL!
IT'S A RIVAL INVENTOR IN DISGUISE TRYING TO DISSUADE YOU FROM REGISTERING THE PATENT ON YOUR DEVICE.

I LEARNED OF HIS PLAN IN MY OWN TIME, A YEAR IN YOUR FUTURE, AND CAME BACK TO WARN YOU THAT...
SHUT UP! NONE OF YOU KNOW WHAT YOU'RE TALKING ABOUT!

I COME FROM TEN YEARS IN THE FUTURE, AND I COME TO WARN YOU OF THE TERRIBLE CONSEQUENCES OF YOUR DISCOVERY...
YOU SEE, THE INVENTION OF TIME TRAVEL WILL MAKE TRANS-TEMPORAL WAR A REALITY. BY MY DECADE THE WORLD IS IN RUINS...

...AND THAT IS WHY YOU MUST ABANDON YOUR SCHEME BEFORE IT IS TOO...
NO! HE'S WRONG! I'M FROM TWENTY YEARS IN THE FUTURE AND...
WAIT A MINUTE!

RIGHT. NOW LET'S GET THIS SORTED OUT. HOW EXACTLY AM I GOING TO **DISCOVER** THE PRINCIPAL OF TIME TRAVEL?

WHY, BY STUDYING THE PIECE OF **FOLDED PAPER** IN YOUR **HAND,** OF COURSE...

YES... SOMETHING IN ITS **DESIGN...**

WILL GIVE YOU AN **INSIGHT...**

INTO THE NATURE OF **TIME...**

AND YOU'LL...

ALL RIGHT! I'VE HEARD ENOUGH!

"I LOOKED AT MY SQUABBLING FUTURE PERSONAS. I LOOKED AT THE FOLDED VELLUM IN MY HAND..."

"...AND THEN I THREW IT ONTO THE FIRE."

"IT BURNED BRIGHTLY. I CLOSED MY EYES AND LISTENED TO IT CRACKLE."

"WHEN I OPENED THEM AGAIN, I WAS ALONE IN THE ROOM. I SMILED AND SAVOURED THE SILENCE FOR A MOMENT, AND THEN I FINISHED DIGESTING MY DINNER."
"AS I SAT, I STARED INTO MY GLASS OF PORT. THERE WAS SOMETHING **FASCINATING** ABOUT THE WAY IT **SWIRLED**, ABOUT ITS **FLOW-PATTERNS**..."

"SUDDENLY, THERE WAS A KNOCK AT THE DOOR..."
The End

IN 1993 AN ASTROPHYSICIST NAMED CLABEZIUS TOGLU FIRST NOTICED THE TINY INVISIBLE AREAS OF ELECTRO-MAGNETIC FORCE ON THE FACE OF THE SUN . . .
UNFORTUNATELY, THEY WEREN'T TERRIBLY INTERESTING AND NOBODY TOOK MUCH NOTICE. TOGLU REMAINED AN OBSCURE ASTROPHYSICIST UNTIL HIS DEATH.
IN 2034 A DASHING YOUNG SCIENTIST CALLED GRANT MADDOX DISCOVERED THAT THE FORCE-AREAS WERE MUCH, MUCH COOLER THAN THE REST OF THE SOLAR INFERNO.
MADDOX WAS GIVEN A NOBEL PRIZE AND DIED A RICH MAN. WHICH GOES TO SHOW THAT IF YOU WANT TO GET ON IN THE WORLD, IT'S BETTER TO HAVE A SENSIBLE NAME.
BY 2250 EARTH HAD PERFECTED THE TECHNOLOGY THAT WOULD ENABLE IT TO COLONISE THE SUN. BEING EARTH, IT FIRST BUILT LOTS OF HOLIDAY CAMPS . . . . .
2000 A.D. Credit Card:
SCRIPT ROBOT ALAN MOORE
ART ROBOT J. REDONDO
LETTERING ROBOT JACK POTTER
COMPU-73E
AND SO NOW, IN 2256, THOUSANDS OF EARTHLING HOLIDAY-MAKERS CAN EACH YEAR MAKE THE SEVEN-LIGHT-MINUTE JOURNEY TO GET THEIR FIRST REAL TASTE OF . . .
THARG'S FUTURE-SHOCKS
SUNBURN
HEY, EVER SINCE I STOPPED WEARING MY ANTI-GLARE GOGGLES I'VE FOUND THAT I REALLY DON'T NEED THEM AT ALL!
YOU DON'T?
NO, I'VE GONE BLIND . . .
THE SUN IS A PLACE WHERE YOU CAN FORGET YOUR EARTHLY CARES AND WORRIES. IT NEVER RAINS ON THE SUN . . . . .

... EXCEPT FOR THE SMALL BLACK CLOUD HANGING OVER HOLIDAY-MAKER RORSCHACH SKUBBS...
WHAT AM I GOING TO DO?
RORSCHACH ARRIVED AT THE SUNDOWN SPACEPORT TWO HOURS AGO. HE CHECKED INTO THE SUNVIEW HOTEL HALF AN HOUR LATER.
FIVE MINUTES AGO HE MURDERED HIS WIFE...
BOY! AM I IN A HOT SITUATION!
IT'S THE SUN, YOU SEE. SOMETIMES IT AFFECTS PEOPLE... MAKES THEM A LITTLE HEAT-HAPPY. TEMPERS BECOME FRAYED...
I SHOULDN'T HAVE FLARED UP LIKE THAT... SHOULDN'T HAVE HIT HER WITH THE FRYING PAN...
... AND THE END RESULT IS MRS SALACIA SKUBBS STRETCHED OUT ON THE HOTEL ROOM CARPET, GROWING AS COLD AS THINGS EVER GET ROUND THESE PARTS.
SOMEHOW, I'VE GOT TO GET RID OF THE BODY...
THEN MAYBE I CAN FIND SOME-WHERE ON THE SUN TO LIE LOW UNTIL THE HEAT DIES DOWN...
WAIT A MINUTE! WE PASSED ONE OF THOSE COMMUNAL GARBAGE DISPOSAL CHUTES ON THE WAY INTO THE HOTEL...
IT LEADS STRAIGHT DOWN TO THE HEART OF THE SUN! ALL I HAVE TO DO IS WRAP HER BODY UP IN SOMETHING...
... AND THEN HAUL HER OUTSIDE AND DUMP HER INTO IT WITHOUT BEING SEEN!
HMM! MAYBE I'D BETTER WAIT UNTIL IT GETS DARK...
ALMOST THIRTY SIX HOURS LATER...
HOW LONG ARE THE DAYS AROUND HERE ANYWAY?
OH WELL, I CAN'T LEAVE IT ANY LONGER-NOT IN THIS HEAT. I'D BETTER SNEAK OUT NOW...

...AND TRY TO LOOK AS INCONSPICUOUS AS POSSIBLE...
BUT...
EXCUSE ME, SIR.. I COULDN'T HELP NOTICING THE RAINCOAT, AND I WONDERED IF YOU WERE EXPECTING A SHOWER...
OH NO! IT'S A SUNTRY!
.. IN WHICH CASE, ALLOW ME TO PUT YOUR MIND AT...
—YOU'RE CARRYING A BODY!
PHWEEEEEEET!
HELIOPOLIS IS ONE OF THE LARGEST HOLIDAY-CITIES UPON THE SUN. RORSCHACH SKUBBS WAS HOPING HE'D GET THE CHANCE TO TAKE A QUICK LOOK ROUND...
STOP THAT MAN!
...ALTHOUGH POSSIBLY NOT THIS QUICK!
ONWARD HE RUNS, TRYING TO SHAKE OFF THE HOT PURSUIT IN THE SHADOWS OF A PALLOR-PARLOUR, WHERE THE FASHIONABLE GO TO LOSE THEIR SUNTANS...
HEY! SHUT THE DOOR BEFORE I PEEL!
... THROUGH THE 'ASBESTIQUE' WHERE THE MODERN MISS CAN BUY THE LATEST IN FLAME-PROOF FINERY...
NOW, WHAT YOU'VE JUST PUT ON IS VERY BIG THIS YEAR! WE CALL IT THE RA-RA SKIRT, AFTER THE EGYPTIAN SUN GOD!

...THROUGH THE 'MR APOLLO BEAUTY BAR' WHERE FOLK CAN GET SKIN CONDITIONS-CAUSED BY THE HARSH ULTRA VIOLET RAYS-TREATED...
IT'S A VERY NASTY COMPLAINT! WE CALL IT...
"SUNSPOTS." DON'T TELL ME!
NOW, HOW DID YOU KNOW THAT?
...AND FINALLY OUT ON TO THE FUSED-GLASS BEACHES WHICH ARE THE DOMAIN OF THE LAVA-SURFERS...
HI, THERE! HOT ENOUGH FOR YOU?
C'MON, EVERYBODY! MAGMA'S UP?
...AND LIKEWISE THE PLACE WHERE WHIRLWIND HOLIDAY ROMANCES BLOSSOM IN THE GLOW OF THE BEAUTIFUL EARTH-SETS...
SIGH! IT'S BREATH-TAKING!
YEAH, TOO BAD IT'LL BE ANOTHER YEAR BEFORE THE NEXT ONE...
UNTIL...
ROLL UP! ROLL UP FOR THE STEAMBOAT TOUR...
SPECIAL NULL-DENSITY FLOATS ENABLE US TO SAIL RIGHT THROUGH THE SPECTACULAR ARTIFICIAL STEAM-OCEAN! ROLL UP!
THIS IS MY CHANCE! IF I CAN COMMANDEER ONE OF THESE STEAM-BOATS I CAN SAIL AWAY TO ANOTHER SUN-CITY AND START AGAIN!
SALACIA'S INSURANCE MONEY WOULD HAVE BEEN BEAMED STRAIGHT INTO MY ACCOUNT AT THE MOMENT OF HER DEATH. I CAN LIVE HERE IN LUXURY FOR YEARS!!
I'LL HAVE REALLY FOUND MY "PLACE IN THE SUN"! HEH HEH!
THRUSTING HIS HAND DEEP IN HIS RAINCOAT POCKET, SKUBBS LEAPS FORWARD...
OKAY! I'VE GOT AN ATOM-DISMANTLER IN MY HAND! THOSE OF YOU WHO LIKE THEIR ATOMS THE WAY THEY ARE, GET OUT OF MY WAY! THIS BOAT IS MINE!
I SAY! NO NEED TO GET SO HOT UNDER THE COLLAR!

THE CONTROLS ARE SIMPLE AND WITHIN MOMENTS . . .
FREE! HA HA HA! I'M FREE!
THE STEAM OCEAN IS ONE OF THE MOST WONDERFUL OF THE SUN'S MANY MARVELS . . .

THOUSANDS OF TONS OF WATER ARE TELEPORTED IN EVERY SECOND TO BE INSTANTLY TURNED TO STEAM BY THE FIERCE HEAT HERE AT THE EDGE OF THE ELECTROMAGNETIC FLUKE-AREA...
OH NO! A POLICE LAUNCH HOT ON MY TRAIL!

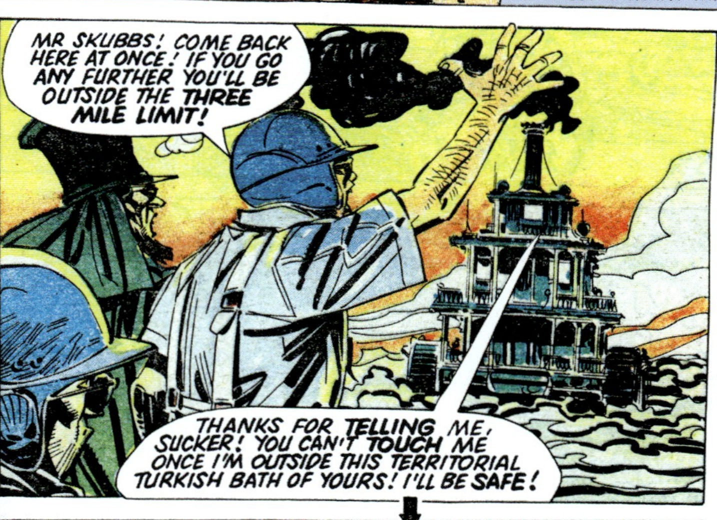
MR SKUBBS! COME BACK HERE AT ONCE! IF YOU GO ANY FURTHER YOU'LL BE OUTSIDE THE THREE MILE LIMIT!
THANKS FOR TELLING ME, SUCKER! YOU CAN'T TOUCH ME ONCE I'M OUTSIDE THIS TERRITORIAL TURKISH BATH OF YOURS! I'LL BE SAFE!

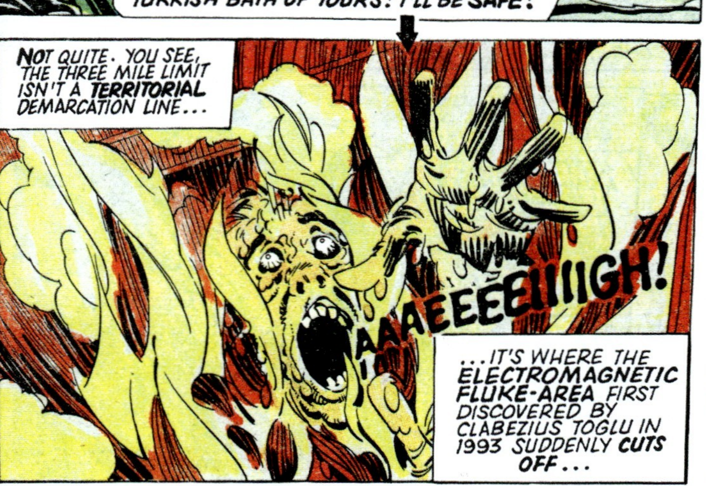
NOT QUITE. YOU SEE, THE THREE MILE LIMIT ISN'T A TERRITORIAL DEMARCATION LINE . . .
AAAEEEEIIIIGH!
. . . IT'S WHERE THE ELECTROMAGNETIC FLUKE-AREA FIRST DISCOVERED BY CLABEZIUS TOGLU IN 1993 SUDDENLY CUTS OFF . . .

THERE IS A TINY FLASH AND AN ALMOST INAUDIBLE SIZZLE . . .
RORSCHACH SKUBBS HAS FOUND HIS PLACE IN THE SUN! THE END.

THARG'S FUTURE-SHOCKS
SID!
MANY EARTHLETS HAVE WRITTEN TO ASK ME WHEN THE NEXT ALIEN WILL ARRIVE ON EARTH. WHAT WILL HE BE LIKE? WHAT WILL HE THINK OF MANKIND?
IT IS TIME THAT I TOLD YOU.
HE WILL ARRIVE ON A TUESDAY—
THERE SHE IS, SID!
SWING INTO ORBIT, SHIP, AND BEAM ME DOWN.
SHORTLY AFTER BREAKFAST TIME, THE ALIEN SID WILL APPEAR OVER LOS ANGELES, CAUSING NO LITTLE CONSTERNATION TO THE WORK-BOUND THOUSANDS—
GEE WHILLIKERS! A G-GIANT!
CRASH!
SMASH!
CITY BANK
HOT
PARP!
PARP!
TO THE CITY'S FINEST, THE L.A.P.D., WILL FALL THE HONOUR OF THE FIRST, FUTILE ATTEMPTS AT COMMUNICATION
HEY BUB! YOU SPEAK ENGLISH?
PARLEZ FRENCHY?
etc.?
IT'S NO GOOD, SHERIFF! I'VE TRIED IN EVERY LANGUAGE— BUT HE JUST IGNORES ME!
MAYBE HE'S DEAF.
THOUGH THAT DON'T EXPLAIN WHY HE'S TESTIN' THE SMOG.
2000 A.D. Credit Card:
SCRIPT ROBOT STAVROS
ART ROBOT BRETT EWINS
LETTERING ROBOT TONY JACOB
COMPU-73E

MANY PEOPLES OF EARTH WILL RECEIVE A VISIT FROM SID THAT TUESDAY.
THE PEASANTS OF THE AMAZON—
AYYA! HE COUNTS THE TREES!
THE HOLIDAYMAKERS OF THE DYING MEDITERRANEAN—
SACRE BLEU! HE SCOOPS UP THE SLUDGE!
DANGE
NO SWIMMIN
NOT BEFORE TIME!
THE SCIENTISTS OF BIKINI ATOLL—
INCREDIBLE! I'D SWEAR THAT WAS SOME KIND OF ALIEN GEIGER COUNTER!
BY TEATIME, SID'S MIND WILL BE MADE UP—
TUT, TUT. THE INFESTATION IS OUT OF CONTROL. ONLY ONE REMEDY NOW.
FABBO!
THAT'S SOME GROOVY ALIEN BEAT!
HEY! I CAN'T STOP MYSELF! I'M DANCING!
KNEES UP, GRANNY!
WHO CARES? IT'S GREAT!

SID'S MUSIC IS BORN OF A TECHNOLOGY BEYOND HUMAN COMPREHENSION. SUFFICE TO SAY IT **CARRIES FAR** — AND IMPARTS A CERTAIN **LIGHTNESS** TO THE DANCERS' FEET!

BRETT EWINS

CLANG!

HUMANELY DESPATCHING THEM NOW, SID.
EVERYTHING GO SMOOTHLY?
FAIR TO MIDDLING, SHIP. HARDER THAN THE RATS, BUT EASIER THAN THE DINOSAURS!

THANKS AGAIN, SID.
SID'S COSMIC PEST CONTROL
TO AVOID PLANET-WIDE PANIC, I WILL NOT DIVULGE THE EXACT DATE OF ARRIVAL.
THIS I **WILL** TELL YOU. SID'S SHIP IS ALREADY ON ITS WAY. IT MAY ARRIVE SOONER THAN YOU THINK!
THE END

THARG'S FUTURE-SHOCKS
BEWARE THE MEN IN BLACK!

"I PARKED MY CAR A FEW STREETS AWAY FROM THE ADDRESS JOHNSON HAD GIVEN ME IN HIS TELEPHONE CALL. BOTH OF US BEING RIVAL UFO INVESTIGATORS, I WAS SURPRISED WHEN HE SAID HE WANTED TO REVEAL THE DETAILS OF HIS LATEST SCOOP TO ME.
"I WAS EVEN MORE SURPRISED WHEN I SAW THE HOUSE. IT WAS DERELICT, TO SAY THE LEAST.

"AFTER I'D KNOCKED ON THE DOOR, I WAS AWARE OF A PAIR OF EYES SCRUTINISING ME THROUGH THE CURTAINS."

HENDERSON, COME IN QUICKLY! HAVE YOU BEEN FOLLOWED? HAVE YOU SEEN ANY SIGN OF THE MIBS?
MIBS?
MIBS — MEN IN BLACK — THE MYSTERIOUS PEOPLE WHO GO AROUND SILENCING UFO WITNESSES!

"JOHNSON LOOKED AS THOUGH HE HADN'T SLEPT OR SHAVED FOR A WEEK."
OH, COME OFF IT, JOHNSON! MIBS AREN'T REAL!
THEY'RE REAL AS FAR AS I'M CONCERNED. I SHOULD KNOW, THEY'RE AFTER ME NOW!

LOOK, JOHNSON, I THINK YOU SHOULD CALM DOWN AND EXPLAIN ALL THIS!
OKAY, OKAY, IT'S A LONG STORY AND I ASSURE YOU, EVERY WORD OF IT IS TRUE!
2000 A.D. Credit Card:
SCRIPT ROBOT D. PERRY
ART ROBOT J. REDONDO
LETTERING ROBOT T. JACOB
COMPU·73E

"IT ALL STARTED LAST WEEK WHEN I WAS ON HOLIDAY IN SCOTLAND. AFTER TAKING SIX MONTHS TO RESEARCH AND WRITE MY LATEST BOOK, I WAS GLAD TO HAVE A CHANCE TO RELAX AND UNWIND.
"I WAS HAVING LUNCH WHEN THE NIGHTMARE STARTED. THE WATERS OF THE LOCH STARTED BUBBLING IN FURY. AT FIRST I THOUGHT IT WAS YET ANOTHER SCOTTISH LOCH MONSTER ABOUT TO SURFACE.
"IMAGINE MY SHOCK AND DELIGHT AS A GENUINE UFO EMERGED FROM THE LOCH. I, WHO HAD INVESTIGATED HUNDREDS OF SIGHTINGS, WAS ACTUALLY HAVING A CLOSE ENCOUNTER!
"OF COURSE, I ALWAYS KEEP A CAMERA CLOSE AT HAND. I MANAGED TO TAKE A WHOLE ROLL OF FILM BEFORE IT FINALLY WENT OUT OF SIGHT.
CLICK! CLICK! CLICK!
"I DIDN'T EVEN BOTHER TO PACK MY CAMP AWAY, SO EAGER WAS I TO DEVELOP THE PICTURES AND SEE WHAT TURNED OUT.
"IT WAS WHEN I TURNED INTO THE HOTEL DRIVE THAT I FIRST SAW THEM – THREE MEN IN BLACK! EVEN THE BLACK CAR WAS THERE!
"NOBODY KNOWS WHETHER THEY ARE ALIEN ENTITIES, C.I.A. MEN OR WHAT. ALL I KNEW WAS THAT THEY WERE OUT TO GET ME!"

MISTER JOHNSON, STOP! WE WANT TO TALK TO YOU!
YOU'LL NOT SILENCE ME LIKE ALL THE OTHERS! I'M GOING TO PUBLISH THESE PICTURES AND REVEAL THE TRUTH— ONCE AND FOR ALL!
"THEY GOT INTO THEIR CAR TO FOLLOW ME! MY LIFE WAS IN DEADLY DANGER, I HAD TO ESCAPE!
"I LOST THEM AND THEN I DROVE HOME USING ALL THE BACK ROADS.
"BUT THEY'D ANTICIPATED MY MOVE!
"WITH MY HOME BEING WATCHED, I DECIDED TO COME HERE.... IT'S PERFECTLY SAFE."
THAT'S MY STORY AND IT'S ALL TRUE! I'VE GOT THE PHOTOGRAPHS TO PROVE IT!
WHAT? LET ME SEE THEM!
I ONLY GOT THEM FROM THE DEVELOPERS THIS MORNING. I CALLED YOU AS SOON AS I GOT THEM.
THEY—THEY'RE FANTASTIC! THE BEST PICTURES I'VE EVER SEEN! I SHOULDN'T HAVE DOUBTED YOU!

NOOO!
JOHNSON! WHAT IS IT?

THE MIBS! THEY'VE FOUND ME! THEY MUST HAVE FOLLOWED YOU!
MR. JOHNSON! OPEN UP! WE KNOW YOU'RE IN THERE!

I'VE GOT TO GET AWAY! THEY'LL KILL ME!
"EVEN THEN I STILL DIDN'T BELIEVE THAT THE MIBS WERE WHAT JOHNSON THOUGHT THEY WERE. THERE HAD TO BE A SIMPLE EXPLANATION."
JOHNSON, CALM DOWN!

THEY'RE BREAKING THE FRONT DOOR DOWN, AND ONE OF THEM HAS GOT ROUND THE BACK! WE'RE TRAPPED!
FOR GOODNESS' SAKE, JOHNSON!

LOOK, IT'S ME THEY'RE AFTER, NOT YOU! YOU TAKE THE PHOTOS AND HIDE!

I'LL CLIMB ONTO THE ROOF AND THEN RUN ALONG TO THE END HOUSE! THEY'LL FOLLOW ME AND YOU CAN GET AWAY!
NO, COME BACK! IT'S TOO DANGEROUS!

"JOHNSON HADN'T NOTICED ALL THE RUST ON THE DRAINPIPE."
AH!
MR. JOHNSON-?
YOU'RE TOO LATE!
THUMP!

HE'S DEAD!
WHAT WAS THE MATTER WITH HIM? WHY WAS HE SO FRIGHTENED?
HE'S BEEN UNDER A LOT OF PRESSURE BECAUSE OF HIS WORK LATELY. HE THOUGHT YOU WERE ALIENS OUT TO GET HIM!

NONSENSE! WE'RE FROM SMITH, SMITH AND SMITH, SOLICITORS. MR. JOHNSON'S UNCLE HAS DIED LEAVING HIM THE SOLE BENEFICIARY OF THREE-QUARTERS OF A MILLION POUNDS!
WE SENT HIM A LETTER A WEEK AGO, BUT WHEN WE LEARNED HE WAS IN SCOTLAND WE WENT TO SEE HIM PERSONALLY, BUT HE RAN AWAY FROM US!
"I KNEW THERE WAS NOTHING TO THE MIB LEGEND— JOHNSON HAD DIED BECAUSE OF HIS OWN FEAR."

WE TRIED TO CONTACT HIM THROUGH YOU. SOMEBODY AT YOUR OFFICE TOLD US WHERE YOU WERE GOING, SO WE CAME HERE TOO, HOPING TO FIND HIM. WE DIDN'T THINK ANYTHING LIKE THIS WOULD HAPPEN.
YOU'D BETTER GET BACK TO YOUR OFFICE AND CALL THE POLICE. I'LL WAIT HERE UNTIL THEY ARRIVE.
"I DIDN'T TELL THEM ABOUT THE PHOTOGRAPHS. THEY WOULD HAVE THOUGHT I WAS MAD.

"OUT IN THE YARD-"
IT'S IRONIC THAT IT'S ENDED THIS WAY, ISN'T IT, JOHNSON? I TOLD YOU THERE WERE NO SUCH THINGS AS MIBS— AND I SHOULD KNOW. . .

YOU SEE, I AM NOT WHAT I SEEM! AN ADVANCED ALIEN RACE WOULD NOT NEED HUMAN AGENTS TO HIDE THEIR PRESENCE. . .
NOT WHEN WE CAN CHANGE OUR SHAPES AT WILL. YOUR FRIEND HENDERSON WILL WAKE UP SOON FROM THE SLEEP I PUT HIM IN AND BE NONE THE WISER.

AND AS FOR THESE PHOTOGRAPHS, ONCE I HAVE DESTROYED THEM, NOBODY WILL KNOW THEY EVER EXISTED! THE TIME IS NOT RIGHT FOR OUR PRESENCE TO BE REVEALED ON THIS EARTH!

OKAY, MISSION ACCOMPLISHED! BEAM ME UP!
As you can see, Earthlets, nothing is ever what it appears to be. But the alien who took over Henderson was not as advanced as he thought. . . he forgot to take the NEGATIVES from Johnson's body!
THE END

THARG'S FUTURE-SHOCKS
THE WAR GAME

"ALERTED BY THEIR EARLY WARNING SYSTEM, THE COMMIES WILL, OF COURSE, LAUNCH AN IMMEDIATE ALL-OUT RETALIATORY STRIKE.

"MOMENTS LATER, OUR NUKES LAND. THE UNION OF SOVIET SOCIALIST REPUBLICS IS NO MORE. HOWEVER, THEIR MISSILES STILL THREATEN US".
USA
"DRAWING THEIR POWER FROM THE EARTH'S GRAVITATIONAL FIELD, THE WARP STATIONS THROW UP AN IMPENETRABLE FORCE FIELD..."

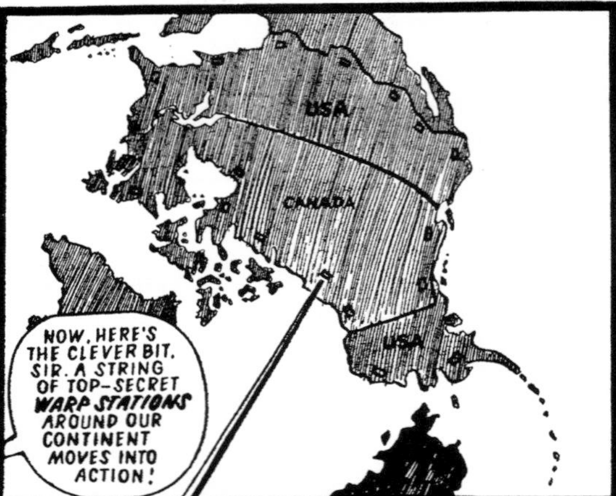
USA
CANADA
USA
NOW, HERE'S THE CLEVER BIT, SIR. A STRING OF TOP-SECRET WARP STATIONS AROUND OUR CONTINENT MOVES INTO ACTION!

WITHIN MILLI-SECONDS, THIS FORCE SHIELD WILL BLANKET THE ENTIRE U.S.A.
CANADA

COMPUTER PREDICTIONS INDICATE THAT THE RUSSIAN MEGATONNAGE, COUPLED WITH THE PLANET'S WEAKENED GRAVITY, WILL CREATE A CHAIN REACTION.

"THIS WILL BLOW THE EARTH APART!"
WOW!

"BUT THAT DOESN'T MATTER. PROTECTED BY OUR FORCE SHIELD, THE NEW PLANET AMERICA WILL HURTLE THROUGH THE HEAVENS...

"TO TAKE UP A NEW, STABLE ORBIT AROUND THE SUN."

WELL, SIR? WHAT DO YOU THINK?
I LIKE IT. LET'S DO IT!

RONNIE!

HOME! YOUR DINNER'S GOING TO BE STONE COLD!
WAR SIM CENTRE
TOP SEKRIT
AW, MUM. WE'RE PLAYING!

DON'T "AW, MUM" ME! YOU'LL NEVER GROW UP TO BE PRESIDENT IF YOU SPEND YOUR TIME PLAYING SILLY GAMES!

KEEP YOUR FINGERS CROSSED THAT SHE'S RIGHT, EARTHLETS!
THE END

THARG'S FUTURE-SHOCKS

BAD TIMING

THE YEAR IS 1938. AT LEAST, THAT'S WHAT THE PEOPLE OF EARTH CALL IT...
THE PEOPLE OF THE PLANET KLAKTON CALL IT THE YEAR IMPTY-FURGWILLION AND PLOOTEEN. OR AT LEAST, MOST OF THEM DO...

KLAKTON'S CHIEF SCIENTIST, R-THUR, HAS ANOTHER NAME FOR IT. IN FACT, HE HAS SEVERAL...
ARMAGEDDON! DOOMSDAY! APOCALYPSE! THE BIG BANG! THE WHOLE ENCHILLADA!

ON THE OTHER HAND, THE SCIENCE COUNCIL OF KLAKTON HAVE SEVERAL NAMES FOR R-THUR...
DUMMY!
DIMWIT!
PEA-BRAIN!
WALLY!

IN FACT, THE ONLY SYMPATHETIC EAR IS THAT OF HIS WIFE, L-SIE...
ESCAPE ROCKET
WHY, L-SIE? WHY WON'T THEY LISTEN WHEN I TELL THEM THAT KLAKTON IS GOING TO EXPLODE? WHY?
MMM? SORRY DEAR! I WASN'T LISTENING!

SCAPE
OCKET
IT'S NOT THAT I MIND THE WORLD ENDING FOR MYSELF, YOU UNDERSTAND...
NO, IT'S JUST THE THOUGHT OF OUR DEAR LITTLE SON, N-REE...!
GLOOK?

HE'S TOO YOUNG AND INNOCENT TO DIE! IF ONLY THERE WERE SOME WAY TO SAVE HIM FROM THE IMPENDING CATASTROPHE...
THERE'S THE ESCAPE ROCKET, DEAR...
FLARP?

WHEN I LOOK AT HIS HAPPY, TWINKLING EYES... WHEN I LOOK AT HIS TOUSLED BLUE HAIR... WE MUST SAVE HIM! WE MUST!
YOU COULD USE THE ESCAPE ROCKET, DEAR!
URCH!

WAIT! I'VE GOT IT! WE CAN USE THE ESCAPE ROCKET!
WE CAN SEND HIM TO ANOTHER WORLD WHERE HE'LL BE SAFE FROM THE EXPLOSION WHICH WILL SHORTLY DEVASTATE KLAKTON!
VOOTIE!

I SEE A PLANET FAR AWAY... A PLANET CALLED EARTH! WE CAN SEND LITTLE N-REE THERE! OUR BOY IS GOING TO LIVE!
NOT ONLY THAT, BUT BECAUSE OF EARTH'S LESSER GRAVITY, HE'LL ALSO BE ABLE TO FLY, SEE THROUGH WALLS AND BOUNCE BULLETS OFF HIS CHEST!
THAT'S NICE, DEAR...

NOW, IF THERE'S ONLY TIME... MY CALCULATIONS SHOW THAT KLAKTON'S DESTRUCTION IS ONLY SECONDS AWAY!
LET'S SEE... HE'S STRAPPED IN... THE VEEBLEFETZERS ARE OSCILLATING PROPERLY... I THINK WE'RE READY!
BLAST OFF!

AND SO...
THERE HE GOES, L-SIE. WE'LL NEVER SEE OUR LITTLE SON AGAIN. NOW COME-LET US PREPARE FOR OUR OWN IMMINENT DEATH...
SPLOOG?
ONLY SCANT SECONDS REMAIN... ANY MOMENT NOW OUR WORLD WILL BE BLOWN TO PIECES...
ANY MOMENT NOW... JUST YOU WAIT...
RATTLE
RATTLE
HMM. THAT'S ODD.
ER... L-SIE. I DON'T QUITE KNOW HOW TO TELL YOU THIS, BUT... ER...
...I THINK I MIGHT HAVE BEEN WRONG ABOUT KLAKTON EXPLODING. HEH, HEH!
GOSH, L-SIE, ANYBODY CAN MAKE A MISTAKE!
AND SO KLAKTON DIDN'T EXPLODE AFTER ALL AND R-THUR WAS LOCKED UP. BUT WHAT OF LITTLE N-REE...
BLAP!
... HEADING TOWARDS THE PLANET EARTH WITH AN ESTIMATED TIME OF ARRIVAL SOMEWHERE AROUND 1939.
WELL, DUE TO AN UNEXPECTED SPACE-TIME WARP NEAR ANDROMEDA, THINGS DIDN'T QUITE WORK OUT...
IN FACT, LITTLE N-REE'S ESCAPE ROCKET DIDN'T REACH EARTH'S ATMOSPHERE UNTIL 1983. WHICH WAS, AS IT TURNED OUT, UNFORTUNATE.
2000 A.D.
Credit Card:
SCRIPT ROBOT A. MOORE
ART ROBOT M. WHITE
LETTERING ROBOT P. BENSBERG
COMPU-73E

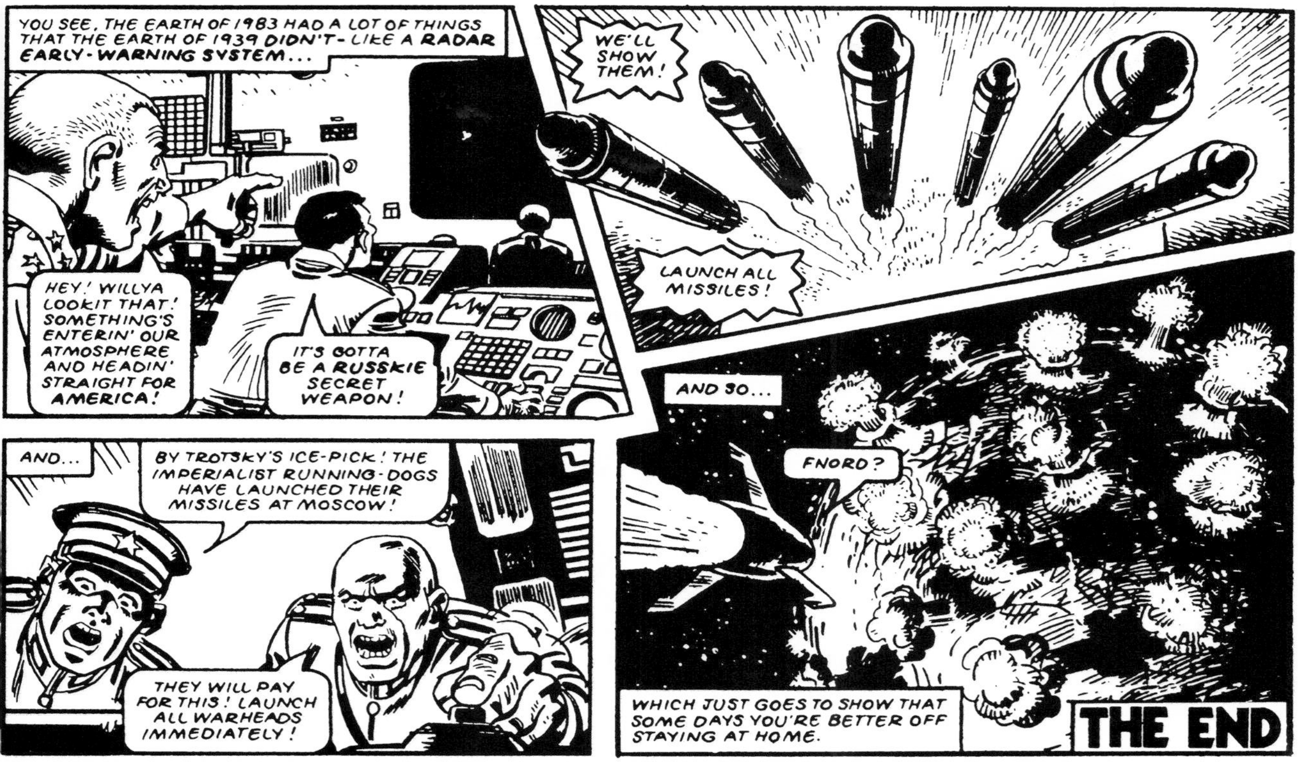

YOU SEE, THE EARTH OF 1983 HAD A LOT OF THINGS THAT THE EARTH OF 1939 DIDN'T - LIKE A **RADAR EARLY-WARNING SYSTEM...**

HEY! WILLYA LOOKIT THAT! SOMETHING'S ENTERIN' OUR ATMOSPHERE AND HEADIN' STRAIGHT FOR **AMERICA!**

IT'S GOTTA BE A **RUSSKIE** SECRET WEAPON!

WE'LL SHOW THEM!

LAUNCH ALL MISSILES!

AND...

BY TROTSKY'S ICE-PICK! THE IMPERIALIST RUNNING-DOGS HAVE LAUNCHED THEIR MISSILES AT MOSCOW!

THEY WILL PAY FOR THIS! LAUNCH ALL WARHEADS IMMEDIATELY!

AND SO...

FNORD?

WHICH JUST GOES TO SHOW THAT SOME DAYS YOU'RE BETTER OFF STAYING AT HOME.

THE END

2000 A.D.

Abelard Snazz

The first two Abelard Snazz misadventures are printed in *Future Shocks* Volume 01. When last we left him, the Mutant Supermind had once again been jettisoned into the cold vacuum of space...

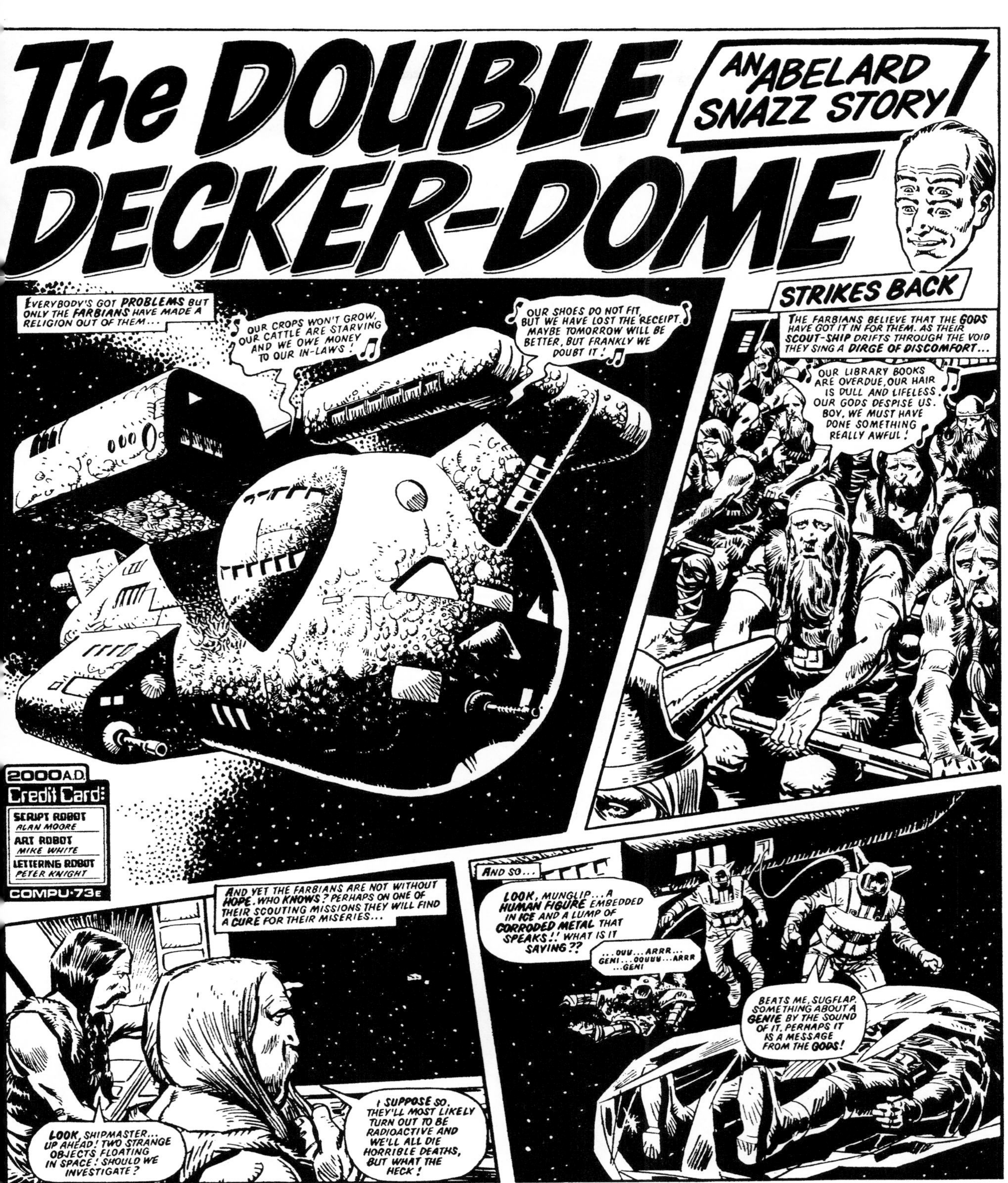
The DOUBLE DECKER-DOME
AN ABELARD SNAZZ STORY
STRIKES BACK
EVERYBODY'S GOT PROBLEMS BUT ONLY THE FARBIANS HAVE MADE A RELIGION OUT OF THEM...
OUR CROPS WON'T GROW, OUR CATTLE ARE STARVING AND WE OWE MONEY TO OUR IN-LAWS!
OUR SHOES DO NOT FIT, BUT WE HAVE LOST THE RECEIPT. MAYBE TOMORROW WILL BE BETTER, BUT FRANKLY WE DOUBT IT!
THE FARBIANS BELIEVE THAT THE GODS HAVE GOT IT IN FOR THEM. AS THEIR SCOUT-SHIP DRIFTS THROUGH THE VOID THEY SING A DIRGE OF DISCOMFORT...
OUR LIBRARY BOOKS ARE OVERDUE, OUR HAIR IS DULL AND LIFELESS. OUR GODS DESPISE US. BOY, WE MUST HAVE DONE SOMETHING REALLY AWFUL!
2000 A.D. Credit Card:
SCRIPT ROBOT ALAN MOORE
ART ROBOT MIKE WHITE
LETTERING ROBOT PETER KNIGHT
COMPU·73E
AND YET THE FARBIANS ARE NOT WITHOUT HOPE. WHO KNOWS? PERHAPS ON ONE OF THEIR SCOUTING MISSIONS THEY WILL FIND A CURE FOR THEIR MISERIES...
LOOK, SHIPMASTER... UP AHEAD! TWO STRANGE OBJECTS FLOATING IN SPACE! SHOULD WE INVESTIGATE?
I SUPPOSE SO. THEY'LL MOST LIKELY TURN OUT TO BE RADIOACTIVE AND WE'LL ALL DIE HORRIBLE DEATHS, BUT WHAT THE HECK!
AND SO...
LOOK, MUNGLIP... A HUMAN FIGURE EMBEDDED IN ICE AND A LUMP OF CORRODED METAL THAT SPEAKS!! WHAT IS IT SAYING??
...OUU...ARRR... GENI...OOUUU...ARRR ...GENI
BEATS ME, SUGFLAP. SOMETHING ABOUT A GENIE BY THE SOUND OF IT. PERHAPS IT IS A MESSAGE FROM THE GODS!

WE WILL TOW THEM BACK TO OUR SHIP, "THE HEAP OF JUNK," EVEN THOUGH THIS WILL PROBABLY STRAIN OUR BACKS AND PUT US BOTH IN HOSPITAL!
...ARRR... EENI...OOUU...
BACK ABOARD "THE HEAP OF JUNK"...
FOR GENERATIONS OUR RACE HAS PLEADED WITH THE GODS TO SEND US FOOD, PEACE AND PROSPERITY...
WE MUST NOW DETERMINE WHY THE GODS HAVE INSTEAD SENT US A FROZEN GENIE AND A GLOB OF TALKING SLAG!
BEGIN THE DEFROSTING PROCESS!
TENSE MOMENTS LATER...
NNK...BLEARGH... WH-WHERE AM I? AND WHY AM I COVERED IN SLUSH?
AAEE!! L-LOOK AT HIS FACE!
ULCERS OF MY ANCESTORS! THIS IS NO MERE GENIE! THIS CAN ONLY BE THE GREATEST OF ALL OUR GODS...
...TOGLUB OF THE TWO-FOLD GAZE!
ER, ACTUALLY THE NAME IS SNAZZ. ABELARD SNAZZ. I'M A GENIUS!
WHAT STRANGE PEOPLE, BUT WHERE AM I? THE LAST THING I RECALL, I WAS FLOATING IN SPACE, AND...
GREAT GOOGLY MOOGLY! ACCORDING TO THE STAR-POSITIONS IN THIS NAVI-GLOBE, I'VE BEEN ON ICE FOR NEARLY TWO THOUSAND YEARS!
TO GLUB! TO GLUB!
I REMEMBER IT AS IF IT WERE YESTERDAY. EDWIN AND I HAD BEEN ABANDONED IN SPACE BY THAT UNGRATEFUL WRETCH, HOOLIO MOOLABAR...*
GASP ONLY THIRTY SECONDS OF AIR LEFT, EDWIN! IT LOOKS LIKE I'M HEADED FOR THAT GREAT THINK-TANK IN THE SKY! WHEEZE
DON'T WORRY, MASTER! YOU'LL THINK OF SOMETHING! YOU'RE A GENIUS!
SPANNG!
ARGH! THAT METEOR... IT'S SMASHED MY SUITS THERMOSTAT! WITHIN SECONDS MY BODY TEMPERATURE WILL DROP FROM 98.6° TO ABSOLUTE ZERO!
OH, MASTER! YOU'RE SO KNOWLEDGEABLE!
"A BITTER ARCTIC COLD SWEPT OVER MY BODY, AND THE LAST THING I REMEMBER WAS THE PLAINTIVE CRY OF MY LITTLE ROBOT PAL..."
MASTER! DON'T LEAVE ME! YOU CAN'T DIE! YOU ARE A GENIUS!
"AND THEN THERE WAS BLACKNESS. TWO THOUSAND YEARS OF IT..."
*THARG NOTE: SEE PROG 209.

EDWIN COULD HAVE SAVED HIMSELF, BUT NO... THAT LOYAL LITTLE LUMP WAITED BY MY SIDE THROUGHOUT THE LONG, LONELY CENTURIES...
... UNTIL, AT LAST, HE WAS REDUCED TO THIS PITIFUL PILE OF POCK-MARKED PIG-IRON, ENDLESSLY CROAKING OUT HIS ADORATION! HOW SELFLESS HE WAS, HOW NOBLE...
GARBAGE DISPOSAL CHUTE
...ARRR... GENI... OUU... ARRRR... GENI...
... HOW STUPID!
CHUTE
... AND NOW IT SEEMS THAT I'VE BEEN RESCUED BY A RACE, WHO BELIEVE ME TO BE A GOD-LIKE BEING OF DIVINE WISDOM!
THEY'RE ABSOLUTELY RIGHT, OF COURSE!
OH, SUPREME MASTER, OH THOU OF THE QUADRIVALENT SQUINT, ART THOU TRULY THE GREAT GOD TOGLUB COME TO DELIVER US?
ME? A GOD? HEH, HEH! WE-E-ELL... YES, I SUPPOSE I AM!
WHEN DO I START?
LATER, WHEN THE "HEAP OF JUNK" HAS RETURNED TO FARBUS...
THIS IS THE LIFE! I KNEW THAT ONE DAY PEOPLE WOULD REALISE WHAT A TERRIFIC PERSON I AM...
TOGLUB!
TOGLUB!
ER... OH GREAT TOGLUB, THIS IS KING GABFRANK THE UNFORTUNATE, RULER OF ALL FARBUS. HE DESIRES AN AUDIENCE!
WELL, OKAY GABFRANK, OLD BUDDY. JUST SO LONG AS YOU KEEP IT SHORT. I PROMISED TO SHOW SABRINA HERE HOW I CAN WIGGLE MY EYEBROWS IN STEREO...
...I'LL BE RIGHT BACK, SABRINA HONEY...

NOW, GABFRANK, WHAT'S THE PROBLEM? :CHOMP:
THE PROBLEM? AHH, TRULY THOU ART MOST WISE, OH YE OF THE BINARY BRAIN...
FOR IS NOT THE WHOLE OF MY PEOPLE'S HISTORY A PROBLEM OF CELESTIAL MAGNITUDE?
AS YOUR AWESOMENESS IS NO DOUBT AWARE, MY RACE STEMS NOT FROM THIS WORLD, BUT FROM ANOTHER. LONG SINCE LOST IN ANTIQUITY.
IT WAS A VERITABLE PARADISE, A RICH AND LUXURIOUS GARDEN WORLD OF INCOMPARABLE BEAUTY. WE THOUGHT OUR HAPPINESS WOULD LAST FOREVER.
:MMP: SOUNDS LIKE A NICE PLACE :CHOMP:
IT WAS NOT TO BE. IT WAS FATED THAT OUR WORLD BE VISITED BY A HUGE ALIEN INTENT ON ERADICATING ALL TRACE OF OUR PROUD CULTURE...
CIVILIZATIONS! BAH! I HATE 'EM!
THE SURVIVORS FLED AND SETTLED ON A NEW PLANET, SO BEAUTIFUL THAT WE COULD NOT UNDERSTAND WHY NONE HAD SETTLED THERE BEFORE US...
THE REASON SOON BECAME PLAIN. OUR WORLD WAS DIRECTLY IN THE PATH OF THE UNSTOPPABLE PLATINUM HORDE OF KARBONG ON THEIR ENDLESS RAMPAGE...
...BUT THESE ARE THE BREAKS, EH?
IN THE YEARS THAT FOLLOWED WE SOUGHT SHELTER ON MANY NEW WORLDS. ONE WAS EATEN BY SPACE-TERMITES. ANOTHER WAS INVADED BY GRAWKS...
EVENTUALLY WE SETTLED HERE ON THIS TINY, INADEQUATE MUDBALL. IT WASN'T MUCH, BUT IT WAS HOME!
G'DAY! G'DAY!
CLIK!
OOO-EEE! G'DAY!
CLIK! CLIK!
DON'T BE SUCH A CRYBABY, GABFRANK! EVERYBODY HAS MILLENIA LIKE THAT! AT LEAST YOU'RE HAPPY ON FARBUS, RIGHT? :MUNCH:
HAPPY? IT IS HERE THAT MY RACE FACES ITS DIREST DOOM...
...THE THREE-PRONGED THREAT OF FARBUS!
WHAT THREE-PRONGED THREAT?
OH ULTIMATE ONE, THY WIT IS IMMENSE... BUT I FEAR THAT THOU COMEST THE CRACK WITH THY LOWLY SERVANT!
FOR IS IT NOT WRITTEN IN THE SACRED "BOOK OF UPS AND DOWNS" THAT FORTUNE SHALL FROWN THRICE ON THE PEOPLES OF FARBUS?

THE FIRST DOOM SHALL BE ECONOMIC, FOR LO, NAUGHT WILL GROW ON FARBUS SAVE FOR FARBIAN CROTTLE, WHICH TASTE VILE AND KILLETH ALL OTHER PLANTS...
AND LO, OUR BALANCE OF PAYMENTS SHALL BE NON-EXISTENT, AND WE SHALL BE UP TO OUR NECKS IN DEBT AND FARBIAN CROTTLE...
THE SECOND DOOM SHALL BE ENVIRONMENTAL, AND THERE SHALL BE AN ENERGY CRISIS ON FARBUS. FOR FARBUS HAS NO FUEL, SAVE FOR CROTTLE, WHICH BURNS NOT!
AND LO, OUR CARS SHALL NOT RUN, NOR SHALL OUR INDUSTRY PROSPER!
THE THIRD AND MOST DREADFUL DOOM SHALL BE COSMIC, FOR VERILY, A BLACK HOLE DOTH APPROACH FARBUS, DEVOURING ALL IN ITS PATH. EVEN FARBUS ITSELF!
...BUT NOW WE ARE SAVED FOR GREAT TOGLUB HAS COME AMONGST US, AND HE WILL SOLVE ALL THESE TERRIBLE PROBLEMS AT A STROKE!
COUGH! TO GLUB? BUT THAT'S ME!
UH... I'LL ADMIT THOSE ARE SOME PROBLEMS, GABFRANK!
WHAT HAPPENS WHEN... UH... IF I'M UNABLE TO SOLVE THEM?
SUCH A THING IS UNTHINKABLE. BUT SHOULD IT COME TO PASS, THEN THE PEOPLE OF FARBUS WOULD RAISE MOST WORTHY TOGLUB ALOFT ON THEIR SHOULDERS...
...AND THROW HIM TO THE PIRANHA-DOGS!
SNAP!
CHOKE!
SNAP!
SNAP!
Next Prog: THE WORM TURNETH!

The DOUBLE DECKER-DOME
AN ABELARD SNAZZ STORY
STRIKES BACK
ON THE PLANET FARBUS, GENIUS ABELARD SNAZZ IS SUNK IN BLACKEST DESPAIR —
WHAT AM I GOING TO DO? IF I DON'T COME UP WITH A SOLUTION TO THE FARBIAN'S TERRIBLE DILEMMA THEY'LL THROW ME TO THE PIRANHA-DOGS...
...AND THERE'S NOT JUST ONE INSOLUBLE PROBLEM... THERE'S THREE!
FIRST, I'VE GOT TO FIND SOMETHING THE FARBIANS CAN EXPORT TO SAVE THEIR ECONOMY. BUT THE ONLY THING THAT GROWS ON FARBUS IS THIS USELESS CROTTLE WEED.
SECONDLY, I'VE GOT TO SOLVE THEIR ENERGY CRISIS, AND THIRDLY I'VE GOT TO RESCUE THEM FROM AN APPROACHING BLACK HOLE! IT'S IMPOSSIBLE! :SOB!:
NO! I MUSTN'T GIVE UP! I'M A GENIUS. I'VE JUST GOT TO LOOK AT THE PROBLEM IN A FRESH LIGHT!
IF ONLY I DIDN'T HAVE THESE TWO SPLITTING HEADACHES...
LET'S STUDY THIS VILE-SMELLING FARBIAN CROTTLE. NOW, WHAT DO I SEE? I SEE CROTTLE. I SEE LOTS OF CROTTLE. I SEE...
...WORMS?
HEY! FLUNKEY!
2000 A.D. Credit Card:
SCRIPT ROBOT ALAN MOORE
ART ROBOT MIKE WHITE
LETTERING ROBOT JACK POTTER
COMPU-73E

YOU CALLED, O INCOMPARABLE TOGLUB? O THOU OF THE HIGH-RISE HEAD, O THOU OF THE...
YEAH. YEAH... LATER FOR ALL THAT GARBAGE. WHAT ARE THESE WORMS DOING IN MY CROTTLE?
THEY ARE FARBIAN CROTTLE-WORMS. THE ONLY CREATURES THAT CAN ABIDE THE TASTE OF THIS LOATHSOME WEED...
THEY ARE ALSO SAID TO BE THE MOST SAINTLY AND GOOD-NATURED BEINGS IN KNOWN SPACE!
AFTER YOU, ALPHONSE.
NO, I INSIST. AFTER YOU, GASTON.
SAINTLY? GOOD-NATURED? HAHAHAHAHA! THIS SOLVES ALL OUR PROBLEMS! I'M SAVED!
THE GREAT GOD TOGLUB IS HAVING A BRAINSTORM! POSSIBLY TWO BRAINSTORMS!
...AND, WHEN THE KING AND HIS RETINUE ARRIVE...
SSHH! I'M DOING SOME FIVE-STAR THINKING HERE! NOW LET ME SEE...
IF E=MC² AND THE PARTY OF THE FIRST PART IS EQUAL TO THE SQUARE ON THE HYPOTENUSE, THEN... YES! IT WORKS! IT WORKS!!
WHAT WORKS, O MOST INSCRUTABLE ONE?
VIRTUE CONVERTER
MY NEW "VIRTUE-CONVERTER" WORKS! THIS MACHINE WILL TRANSFORM GOOD THOUGHTS INTO AN UNLIMITED SUPPLY OF ENERGY!
...GOOD THOUGHTS PROVIDED BY THE LOWLY FARBIAN CROTTLE WORMS...
BY THE GREY HAIRS OF MY FOREBEARS! HE'S SOLVED THE ENERGY CRISIS!
WAIT... THERE'S MORE! LOTS OF OTHER RACES WILL WANT TO USE MY "VIRTUE-CONVERTER" FOR THEIR OWN ENERGY NEEDS. THAT MEANS THEY'LL NEED CROTTLE-WORMS...
...AND TO FEED THE WORMS THEY'LL NEED LOTS OF FARBIAN CROTTLE!

BY MY GRAND-SIRE'S PSYCHIATRIST! HE'S SOLVED THE ECONOMIC CRISIS!
OF COURSE, THAT STILL LEAVES ME THE BLACK HOLE TO DEAL WITH, BUT IT WON'T TAKE ME LONG TO GET THAT PROBLEM STITCHED UP...
BLACK HOLE? STITCHED UP?
THAT'S IT! WE'LL STITCH UP THE BLACK HOLE! INSTEAD OF THREAD WE'LL USE A STREAM OF COHESIVE NEUTRINOS...
..AND INSTEAD OF A NEEDLE WE'LL USE A FASTER-THAN-LIGHT SPACE-SHIP POWERED BY FARBIAN CROTTLE-WORMS! HA HA HA! HOW SIMPLE!
UHH... YES. SIMPLE.

SNAZZ'S INSPIRED PLANS ARE PUT TO WORK IMMEDIATELY, AND SUDDENLY FARBUS IS BURSTING WITH ENERGY.
THIS IS INCREDIBLE! THE GOOD THOUGHTS FROM THESE TINY WORMS ARE POWERING AN ENTIRE FACTORY! THEY MUST BE REALLY PURE AND VIRTUOUS!
OH, REALLY... IT'S NOTHING!
..AND THEY'RE SO HUMBLE!

EXPORTS BOOM AS NEVER BEFORE...
HURRY IT UP! THE TAU-CETIANS HAVE JUST ORDERED ANOTHER THOUSAND TONS OF CROTTLE FOR NEXT TUESDAY!
CROTTLE
LET THOSE PUSHY SLIME-BLOBS WAIT THEIR TURN... THE ARCTURANS WANT SIX THOUSAND TONS DELIVERED BY THE WEEKEND!
CROTTLE
BUT ALL THE WHILE...
THE BLACK HOLE'S GETTING CLOSER, KING GABFRANK! IT'S JUST SWALLOWED FOUR NEARBY SOLAR SYSTEMS AND WASHED THEM DOWN WITH AN ASTEROID BELT!
FEAR NOT! GREAT TOGLUB HATH A FOOLPROOF PLAN OF MIND-WRENCHING GENIUS...
...AT LEAST, THAT'S WHAT HE TELLS ME...
I CERTAINLY DO, GABFRANK OLD CHUM! IF YOU'D CARE TO STEP OUTSIDE A MOMENT I'LL SHOW YOU JUST HOW STUNNINGLY SMART I REALLY AM!
AFTER ALL, I'M NOT JUST A COUPLE OF PRETTY FACES!

AND, OUTSIDE ...
IT'S MAGNIFICENT, GREAT TOGLUB! IT'S STUPENDOUS! IT'S ... IT'S ...
WHAT IS IT, EXACTLY?
WHAT IT IS, GABFRANK OLD PAL, IS THE FIRST WORM-POWERED COSMIC DARNING NEEDLE IN KNOWN SPACE!
TODAY WE SEW UP THAT BLACK HOLE FOR GOOD!
TODAY? BUT YOUR SUPREME INCONGRUITY, I THOUGHT IT WOULD BE WEEKS BEFORE WE ...
NO TIME LIKE THE PRESENT, GABS OLD MAN! THE CREW ARE STANDING BY AND READY TO ROLL. LET'S GET ABOARD!
AND SO ...
WELL, IT CERTAINLY SEEMS TO FLY ALL RIGHT, YOUR INCREDULITY. BUT IS IT SAFE TO VENTURE SO NEAR TO THE BLACK HOLE?
I THOUGHT I'D EXPLAINED IT ALL ALREADY...
THE POWER GENERATED BY THESE FELLOWS ENABLES US TO TRAVEL FAR FASTER THAN LIGHT...
...WE CAN ZIP BACK AND FORTH ACROSS THE BLACK HOLE'S SURFACE SO FAST THAT IT CAN'T SUCK US IN!
AMAZING! AND THEY'RE SUCH MODEST LITTLE CHAPS AS WELL...
PLEASE... IT'S THE LEAST WE CAN DO..
... AND THE TRAIL OF COHESIVE NEUTRINOS WE LEAVE IN OUR WAKE WILL SEW UP THE BLACK HOLE JUST LIKE DARNING A SOCK!
SEE? WE'RE DOING IT NOW! IT'S WORKING! WE'RE STITCHING UP A BLACK HOLE!
GASP! YOU'RE RIGHT! IT IS WORKING!
PRAISE BE TO TOGLUB! PRAISE BE TO FARBIAN CROTTLE WORMS!
CROTTLE WORMS? WHY, IF IT HADN'T BEEN FOR ME THOSE GREASY LITTLE GLORY-GRABBERS WOULD STILL BE BAITING FISH-HOOKS!
I'M THE GREAT GOD TOGLUB, REMEMBER? I'M THE ONE WHO SHOULD GET ALL THE THANKS... NOT SOME BUNCH OF DO-GOODER MAGGOTS!
???

..UH.. WELL, YES... I SUPPOSE YOU'RE RIGHT...
OF COURSE I'M RIGHT! I'M ALWAYS RIGHT! THAT'S WHY I'M A GOD AND THEY'RE JUST A TANGLE OF MINDLESS INVERTEBRATES!
NOW JUST HOLD ON A MINUTE!

YOU'VE GOT NO CALL TO GO BAD-MOUTHING US CROTTLE WORMS! WE DO A FIRST RATE JOB SAVING YOUR PLANET, AND FOR WHAT?
CROTTLE! THAT'S WHAT! LOUSY, STINKING CROTTLE! WE'RE ENTITLED TO OUR FAIR SHARE OF THE CREDIT!
YEAH! WE'RE SICK OF BEING HUMBLE!
RIGHT! NO MORE "MR NICE-GRUB"!

WE DEMAND THE RESPECT THAT'S DUE TO US! THERE'S NO REASON TO INSULT US JUST BECAUSE WE'RE WORMS! WHAT'S WRONG WITH WORMS, ANYWAY?
YEAH! WE'RE PROUD TO BE WORMS!
GASP! YOUR MAJESTY... LOOK!

THE POWER'S DROPPING! WE'RE LOSING SPEED!
BUT WE CAN'T BE... UNLESS...
OH, NO! THE WORMS. THEY'VE COMMITTED THE SIN OF PRIDE! THEY AREN'T THINKING GOOD THOUGHTS!

THE SHIP'S COME TO A DEAD STOP! WE'RE BEING SUCKED INTO THE BLACK HOLE! WE'RE DOOMED!
O MOST EXALTED TOGLUB, SAVE US! FOR ART THOU NOT A GOD AND THUS POSSESSED OF DIVINE POWER?

A GOD? ME?
ER.. WELL.. PERHAPS I SHOULD HAVE MENTIONED THIS BEFORE, BUT...

...AND WITH THAT THE FIRST WORM-POWERED COSMIC DARNING NEEDLE IN KNOWN SPACE VANISHES INTO BLACK NOTHINGNESS! AND THEN THERE IS ONLY SILENCE...
SSSCHLOOOOOOOOPP!
HAS SNAZZ BECOME A SNACK FOR A SINGULARITY? CAN THIS REALLY BE...
...THE END?

HALFWAY TO PARADISE
2000 A.D. Credit Card:
SCRIPT ROBOT ALAN MOORE
ART ROBOT JOHN COOPER
LETTERING ROBOT TONY JACOB
COMPU-73E
AN ABELARD SNAZZ MISADVENTURE
THEY SAY NOBODY KNOWS WHAT'S INSIDE A BLACK HOLE...
NEXT!
...ER.. NORBO NIBLIK OF RIGEL FIVE. I WAS ENJOYING A ROUND OF META-GOLF WHEN I FELL INTO A SPACEWARP NEAR THE EIGHTEENTH HOLE AND ENDED UP HERE.
THEY SAY THAT ONCE INSIDE A BLACK HOLE, NOTHING EVER GETS OUT...
CAN'T YOU READ? THIS IS THE QUEUE FOR PEOPLE WHO'VE FALLEN INTO BLACK HOLES! "SPACEWARPS" IS IN THE NEXT AISLE!
FRANKLY, THEY'RE MAKING IT UP AS THEY GO ALONG.
EXCUSE ME, I FELL INTO A BLACK HOLE NEAR THE PLANET FARBUS. I'VE HAD A LOOK AROUND AND IT'S VERY NICE, BUT I'D LIKE TO GET OUT NOW.
THAT'S WHAT WE'RE HERE FOR, BALDY. LET'S HAVE A FEW PARTICULARS. NAME?
SNAZZ... ABELARD SNAZZ.
PREVIOUS OCCUPATION?
WELL, ACTUALLY, I WAS PREVIOUSLY EMPLOYED BY THE PEOPLE OF FARBUS AS THE GREAT GOD TOGLUB OF THE TWO-FOLD GAZE.*
*THARG NOTE: SEE PROGS 237 238.
OH-HOH! A GOD, IS IT? YOU'LL BE WANTING THE BIDE-A-WEE TWILIGHT DIMENSION FOR DISINHERITED DEITIES, THEN...
JUST A SECOND WHILE I ADJUST MY MATTER DISPLACER...

THERE! ANOTHER SATISFIED CUSTOMER! NEXT!
..ER... EARHART... AMELIA EARHART...
VWAAARK!
MEANWHILE.
LOOK! ANOTHER ONETH JUTHT POPPED OUT OF THE MATTER DITHPLATHER!
GROAN!
AYE. LOOKS LIKE A MINOR TRIBAL DEITY TO ME. THERE GOES THE NEIGHBOURHOOD!
WH-WHO ARE YOU PEOPLE?
WE'RE GODTH, THILLY! OR RATHER, WE UTHED TO BE GODTH. I'M THOTH. PLEATHED TO MEET YOU.
HOW DO. I'M ODIN.
GODS? BUT THEN... WHERE AM I?
YOU'RE IN THE BIDE-A-WEE TWILIGHT DIMENTHION... IT'TH WHERE ALL THE GODTH GO WHEN PEOPLE THTOP WORTHIPPING THEM.
NO MORE WORSHIPPERS, NO MORE POWER. PATHETIC ISN'T IT?
I SEE. BUT IF YOU DON'T HAVE GOD-LIKE POWERS ANYMORE, WHAT DO YOU DO ALL DAY?
MAKE THOUVENIRTH MOTHLY. LUCKY CHARMTH AND THO ON..
DEGRADIN' AIN'T IT? LOOK AT OLD ZEUS OVER THERE, REDUCED TO TURNIN' OUT NOVELTY THUNDERBOLT BACKSCRATCHERS!
JOHN COOPER.
BUT SURELY, IF PEOPLE HAVE STOPPED WORSHIPPING YOU, ISN'T IT JUST A PUBLIC RELATIONS PROBLEM? PERHAPS IF YOU BROUGHT YOURSELVES UP TO DATE A BIT...
WELL, YETH... BUT WHERE DO WE THTART? WE'RE ALL A BIT THET IN OUR WAYTH YOU THEE...
CAN'T TEACH AN OLD GOD NEW TRICKS!

DON'T BE SO SURE! TO SOMEONE OF MY CAPABILITIES, FINDING YOU A NEW IMAGE SHOULD BE CHILD'S PLAY! YOU SEE, I'M ABELARD SNAZZ!
I'M A GENIUS!
A GENIUTH? HOW ECTHITING!
OY! YOU OTHERS! OVER 'ERE A MINUTE!
YES! I BEGIN TO SEE IT ALL! I SEE GODS! I SEE MOD GODS! IT'S BRILLIANT! BRILLIANT!
AND WHAT, PRAY, IS HE THE GOD OF?
I'M NOT THURE... CONTACT LENTHETH PERHAPTH?
WHAT WE NEED IS A NEW VENUE! FIND ME AN ADVANCED CIVILIZATION AND LEAVE THE REST TO ME! I GUARANTEE YOU'LL GO DOWN A STORM!
WHAT ABOUT THE GEEZERS NEAR URSA MINOR!
YEA, VERILY!
AND SO, SUMMONING THEIR LAST RESERVES OF POWER, THE DOWN-AT-HEEL DEITIES TRANSPORT THEMSELVES ACROSS THE VAST REACHES OF SPACE...
LOOK! NEW ROMANTICS!
PEOPLE OF URSA MINOR, THIS IS YOUR LUCKY DAY! TODAY, SNAZZ PROMOTIONS BRINGS YOU THE TREND THAT'S SWEEPING THE GALAXY...
DYNAMIC DEITIES! IT'S WHAT'S HAPPENING!
A GODS REVIVAL? SOUNDS DIVINE!
DIVINE'S THE WORD, MY FRIENDS! AT ABSOLUTELY NO CHARGE, SNAZZ PROMOTIONS PROUDLY PRESENT THEIR NEW LINE OF SUPREME SWINGERS!
TAKE ARES HERE, FOR EXAMPLE! NO DOWDY OLD WAR GOD HE! NO SIR! ARES IS THE GOD OF SPACE INVADERS MACHINES!
HEY! THAT'S MY KIND OF OMNIPOTENT BEING!

MAYBE YOU'D PREFER TO WORSHIP THE NATURAL WAY WITH DEMETER, GODDESS OF HEALTH FOOD STORES?
WOW! THESE GODS ARE JUST HEAVENLY!
YOU'VE GOT THE GIFT O' THE GAB AND NO MISTAKE! THEY'RE LAPPIN' IT UP!
JUST YOU WAIT! IF YOU THINK THIS IS SOMETHING, WHAT COMES NEXT WILL MAKE YOUR EYES POP OUT!
...ER...NO OFFENCE. HEH, HEH.
AND SURE ENOUGH, IN THE WEEKS TO COME THE PEOPLE OF URSA MINOR TAKE THE GODS TO THEIR HEARTS...
GEE! APOLLO'S DISCO IS REALLY NEAT! THOSE LIGHTS! THIS MUSIC!
IN MORE WAYS THAN ONE...
PATIENCE, LADIES! EROS, THE GOD OF POPULAR ROMANTIC FICTION, WILL SIGN ALL YOUR COPIES!
HAVE YOU READ "ARROWS OF DESIRE"? IT'S HIS LATEST!
NO...I'M STILL WORKING THROUGH "QUIVER OF QUIVERS".
AND AS FOR SNAZZ...
WHAT A MASTERSTROKE! THESE GODS ARE REALLY SHIFTING UNITS! WITH MY 10% I SHOULD SOON BE ABLE TO RETIRE AND... HUH? WHAT'S THAT?
AAAGH! MERCY!
INSIDE...
SPACE INVADER
NO...PLEASE...
OH MIGHTY ARES, GOD OF THE SPACE INVADERS... ACCEPT THIS, THE OFFERING OF THY HUMBLE SERVANTS!!
GRANT US A REPLAY, OH LORD OF FLASHING LIGHTS AND FUNNY NOISES! ACCEPT OUR TRIBUTE!

AAAEEEII!
GOOD GRIEF! THEY'VE SACRIFICED THAT POOR CHAP TO A SPACE INVADERS MACHINE!
BEWILDERED, THE MUTANT SUPERBRAIN RUSHES INTO THE STREET.
OH WORSHIPFUL DEMETER, GRANT US THY BOUNTY OF NATURAL FOODS WITH NO ADDITIVES!
THIS IS TERRIBLE! THE PEOPLE ARE REVERTING TO HUMAN SACRIFICE! I'VE GOT TO PUT A STOP TO THIS!
AND SO...
ODIN! ZEUS! THOTH! THINGS ARE GETTING OUT OF HAND... I JUST HEARD A BUNCH OF WIND-SURFERS DECLARING WAR ON NEPTUNE'S WATER SKI-ING CULT!
AYE! GOOD TIMES HAVE RETURNED!
B-BUT THE PEOPLE ARE TURNING TO BARABARISM! WE'VE GOT TO STOP IT!
OH, DON'T BE THUCH A THPOILTHPORT!
VERILY! IT IS WHAT BEING A GOD IS ALL ABOUT!
Y-YOU'RE MAD! I-I WON'T ALLOW THIS SORT OF BEHAVIOUR!
OH AYE? WE'VE GOT A TROUBLE-MAKER 'ERE, ZEUS OLD LAD!
YEA! AND THOU KNOWEST HOW WE DEALT WITH SUCH MATTERS IN THE OLD DAYS...
LET US CHAIN THIS ROGUE TO A ROCK FOR ALL ETERNITY!
NICE ONE, ZEUS!
...ER...NOW WAIT A MINUTE...

HEH, HEH... YOU DON'T WANT TO DO THAT! THINK OF YOUR IMAGE! COULDN'T YOU DO SOMETHING A BIT MORE MODERN?
HE'TH GOT A POINT, THEUTH...
MAYHAP BUT WHAT TORMENT COULD I... AHA! I HAVE IT!
SEE, CHURL, THE CUBE THAT I HOLD IN MY HAND! IT IS A DEVILISH PUZZLE THAT HATH TORMENTED MINDS THE GALAXY OVER!
I SHALL IMPRISON YOU IN A PLACE OF BLEAK DESOLATION FROM WHICH THOU SHALT NOT BE DELIVERED TILL THOU HAST SOLVED A CUBE OF MY DEVISING!
NOW THAT'S MORE LIKE IT, ZEUS OLD PAL!
ZEUS GESTURES, AND INSTANTLY SNAZZ IS TRANSPORTED TO A REALM OF BLEAK DESOLATION...
HA, HA! I CERTAINLY FOOLED HIM! THERE ISN'T A CUBE IN EXISTANCE THAT THE DOUBLE-DECKER DOME CAN'T SOLVE IN UNDER THIRTY SECONDS!
I WONDER WHERE IT IS? ALL I CAN SEE ARE FLAGSTONES!
B-BUT THIS ISN'T FAIR! I'VE BEEN TRICKED! HOW CAN I SOLVE THE CUBE IF I CAN'T FIND IT?
COME ON, ZEUS OLD BOY! WHERE IS IT?
I'M NOT JOKING! IF YOU DON'T TELL ME WHERE TO FIND THE CUBE, I'M REALLY GOING TO GET CROSS!
WELL?
I'M WAITING!
THE END

THE MULTI-STOREY MIND MELLOWS OUT!

AN ABELARD SNAZZ MISADVENTURE

ONE AFTERNOON, SOMETIME DURING ETERNITY...
WELL, JERRY, I DON'T WANT TO MESS UP YOUR HEAD SPACE BY LAYING A NEGATIVE TRIP ON YOU, BUT I THINK WE'RE IN THE DIMENSION OF BLEAK DESOLATION...
HEY, MAN, I'M THERE!

LET'S HOPE WE CAN FIND OUR MAN WITHOUT ANY HASSLE. AFTER BEING TRAPPED HERE FOR SIX MILLION YEARS HE MUST BE IN A REAL LOW-ENERGY SITUATION...
LOOK! OVER THERE...

OH WOW! IT'S A CRANE, RIGHT? AND IT LOOKS LIKE IT'S BEEN BUILT BY HAND FROM, LIKE, NATURAL EARTH MATERIALS!
HEY... THERE'S OUR MAN...

SNAZZ! ABELARD SNAZZ!
ONLY ONE MORE FACE TO TURN AND I'LL BE FINISHED! HEE HEE HEE! AFTER SIX MILLION YEARS!
2000 A.D.
Credit Card:
SCRIPT ROBOT
ALAN MOORE
ART ROBOT
PAUL NEARY
LETTERING ROBOT
TONY JACOB
COMPU-73E

HEY! MR. SNAZZ! WE'RE JERRY AND JIM FROM AMNESTY INTERGALACTIC. WE'RE HERE TO, LIKE, LIBERATE YOU FROM YOUR TOIL!
YES, YES! I'LL BE WITH YOU AS SOON AS I'VE FINISHED THIS!

POOR GUY... THE GOOD VIBES HAVEN'T SUNK IN YET!
LISTEN, MR. SNAZZ... IT'S ALL OVER! YOU'RE FREE!
NO! YOU CAN'T MAKE ME STOP NOW! I'VE NEARLY FINISHED THE RUBIC CUBE THAT ZEUS SET ME SIX MILLION YEARS AGO!
SOB! IT TOOK ME TWELVE THOUSAND YEARS TO MINE ENOUGH METAL FOR THE CRANE AND ANOTHER THIRTY THOUSAND TO ACTUALLY BUILD IT! YOU'VE GOT TO LET ME FINISH!
I THINK I CAN DIG WHERE YOU'RE COMING FROM, BUT IT'D BE BETTER IF YOU CAME WITH US. JUST RELAX, MR. SNAZZ!
LET ME GO! I ONLY HAD ONE FACE TO GO! I'LL KILL YOU!
HEY... HE'S REALLY INTO HIS HOSTILITY! DO YOU THINK IT WOULD BE COOL TO USE THE DART GUN?
FOR SURE.
THERE IS A HISS OF A TRANQUILLISER DART—AND THE WARP SHIP STARTS TO DEMATERIALISE.

WHEN SNAZZ AWAKES...
HEY! HAVE A NICE DAY, MR. SNAZZ!
WHUUHH? WH-WHERE AM I?

YOU'RE ON EARTH, IF YOU CAN DIG IT. OR "STARSHIP EARTH" AS WE PREFER TO CALL IT...
WE HEARD HOW YOU WERE SENTENCED TO THAT REALM OF BLEAK DESOLATION BY A BUNCH OF RENEGADE DEITIES *. BUT, LIKE, THEN IS THEN AND NOW IS NOW, DIG?
* SEE PROG 245.

...UHH ...NO. NOT REALLY...
HA HA HA HA! WHAT A CHARACTER! BUT SERIOUSLY... NOW AMNESTY INTERGALACTIC HAS LIBERATED YOU WE'D LIKE TO INVITE YOU TO SHARE OUR PERSONAL SPACE. C'MON... I'LL SHOW YOU ROUND...

AND SO...
ENJOYING YOUR JOG, MR. SNAZZ? WHAT DO YOU THINK OF OUR LIFE-STYLE HERE?
UHH, WELL... EVERYBODY SEEMS TO BE VERY...UH... MELLOW. HAS YOUR CIVILISATION ALWAYS BEEN AS RELAXED AS THIS?

OH, FOR SURE. WE HAVE A VERY EVOLVED ECO-SYSTEM, IF YOU CAN RELATE TO THAT. SEE, STARSHIP EARTH USED TO BE ON A VERY DOWN TRIP, ECO-WISE...
...BUT LIKE, WHEN CALIFORNIA WON WORLD WAR 26 WE INSTIGATED A WHOLE NEW ERA OF GROWTHFULNESS. SEE THAT BIG LAKE OVER THERE?
WHY, YES! IT'S ENORMOUS! WHAT IS IT?

IT'S A GIANT JACUZZI... CAPABLE OF HOLDING EIGHT THOUSAND PEOPLE!
WHAT SORT OF LIFESTYLE DO YOU REALLY GET BEHIND, MR. SNAZZ?
WELL! I'M A SORT OF INVENTOR. A GENIUS, ACTUALLY...

HEY, THAT SOUNDS LIKE A GREAT DYNAMIC! TOO BAD WE DON'T NEED ANYTHING INVENTING. THIS IS A PERFECT SOCIETY. MAYBE YOU SHOULD TAKE UP TENNIS OR CYCLING. AHH... HERE WE ARE...

THIS IS YOUR NEW GROWTH-MODULE, MR. SNAZZ. I THINK YOU'LL REALLY GET OFF ON IT ONCE YOU SETTLE IN. HAVE A NICE DAY!
UH...THANKS!

BUT, WHEN SNAZZ IS ALONE IN HIS NEW HOME...
HMM... MICROWAVE TEA COSY... SOLAR-POWERED EGG-TIMER... HE'S RIGHT. THIS PLACE IS A TECHNOLOGICAL PARADISE.
BUT I'VE GOT TO HAVE SOMETHING TO PUT MY MIND TO OR I'LL GO CRAZY!

SEVERAL HOURS LATER...
IT'S NO GOOD. MAYBE I SHOULD TAKE UP TENNIS AFTER ALL...
WAIT-THAT'S IT! WHAT A BRILLIANT IDEA! I'LL JOG OVER TO CITY HALL AND EXPLAIN IT TO THEM...

AND SO...
ROBOT TENNIS PLAYERS!! DON'T YOU SEE? YOU WOULDN'T EVEN NEED TO LIFT A RACQUET FOR YOURSELVES! WHAT COULD BE MORE MELLOW THAN THAT?
HMM... MELLOW-WISE, HE HAS A POINT. IF WE MADE TENNIS INTO A SPECTATOR SPORT IT COULD BE A REALLY COMMUNAL SHARING EXPERIENCE...
OH, FOR SURE. BUT THERE'LL BE LOTS OF SPECTATORS SO IT'LL HAVE TO BE A REALLY BIG STADIUM. WON'T THE PLAYERS BE DIFFICULT TO SEE, VISUAL-WISE?

NO PROBLEM! I'LL MAKE VERY BIG ROBOT TENNIS PLAYERS!
SOLID! I SAY WE GO WITH THE FLOW!

AFTER WEEKS OF FEVERISH PREPARATION THE 'WIMBLEDROIDS' ARE FINALLY READY.
HEY, THIS IS A REALLY GREAT LEISURE SITUATION! HOW DID YOU TEACH THESE ROBOTS TO PLAY TENNIS SO WELL?
OH, IT WAS NOTHING. I FOUND SOME OLD BIO-CHIPS BELONGING TO GREAT 20th CENTURY TENNIS PLAYERS IN YOUR COMPUTER ARCHIVE. I SLOTTED THEM IN AND VOILA!

WHICH TENNIS PLAYERS' PERSONALITY CHIPS DID YOU USE?
UHH, I CAN'T REALLY REMEMBER. I THINK ONE OF THEM WAS CALLED JOHN SOMETHING OR OTHER. WHY DO YOU ASK?
ADVANTAGE I.N.-ONE...

ADVANTAGE? YOU MUST BE JOKING! THAT WAS IN BY A MILE!
UH, NO REASON... I JUST SEEM TO REMEMBER HEARING THAT SOME OF THESE TWENTIETH CENTURY PLAYERS WERE A LITTLE...

I'M GOING TO TEAR THIS STADIUM APART!
ME, TOO!
HIGHLY STRUNG.

KWAMM!
JOG FOR YOUR LIFE!
OH DEAR...

HEY MAN, I DON'T WANT TO LAY A GUILT-TRIP ON YOU BUT THOSE ROBOTS ARE REALLY PUTTING OUR PERSONAL SPACE THROUGH SOME CHANGES!
RIGHT! I THINK WE SHOULD INVOLVE THIS GUY IN A PHYSICAL CONFRONTATION SCENARIO!
HEH HEH! COME ON CHAPS! MELLOW OUT!

WE'LL MELLOW YOU OUT, YOU FOUR-EYED FREAK! PERMANENTLY! COME ON, GUYS... LET'S JOG THIS BOZO OVER TO THE HOT TUB!
HOT TUB?

AND SOON, ON THE RIM OF THE CITY'S GIANT JACUZZI...
OKAY...TURN UP THE CURRENT CONTROLS AND THE TEMPERATURE SETTINGS!
NO...WAIT! YOU CAN'T DO THIS TO ME! YOU HAVEN'T SEEN MY DESIGN FOR SELF-LACING JOGGING SHOES YET!

BUT...
HAVE A NICE DAY, YOU WEIRDO!
YAAAAAGH!

HOW WILL SNAZZ RELATE TO AN ONGOING DROWNING EXPERIENCE? WILL HE LEARN TO GO WITH THE FLOW, OR IS THIS FINALLY . . .
THE END?

GENIUS IS PAIN

AN ABELARD SNAZZ MISADVENTURE

HURLED BY THE ENRAGED MOB, HE PLUMMETS HELPLESSLY TOWARDS THE BOILING VORTEX AT THE CENTRE OF THE GIANT WHIRLPOOL BATH ... *
ABELARD SNAZZ IS HAVING ONE OF THOSE DAYS. HE KNOWS HE IS DOOMED, KNOWS THAT THE MERE IDEA OF RESCUE IS TOO ABSURD FOR WORDS...
2000 A.D. Credit Card:
SCRIPT ROBOT ALAN MOORE
ART ROBOT MIKE WHITE
LETTERING ROBOT JACK POTTER
COMPU-73E
* THARG NOTE: SNAZZ STARTED HIS FALL IN PROG 254.

OH WOW, MAN! HE'S VANISHING!
SQUOOOOB!
OH, FOR SURE! BUT WHAT A GREAT VISUAL...

SCANT SECONDS LATER, ON THE OTHER SIDE OF THE UNIVERSE...
I'M SOMEWHERE ELSE! I'M SAVED! THE BOY WITH THE BINARY BONCE HAS BOUNCED BACK!
SQUOOOOOB!
THIS IS TOO ABSURD FOR WORDS!

CEASE THY PRATTLE, OH MAN OF MANY MONOCLES!
WHUH?
KNOW YE THAT THOU ART IN THE MIND-WRENCHING PRESENCE OF...

THE MANAGER OF THE UNIVERSE!
THE MANAGER OF THE UNIVERSE?

BUT THERE MUST BE SOME MISTAKE! WHAT WOULD HE WANT WITH A LOWLY GENIUS LIKE ME?
OH... I GET IT! YOU MUST WANT TO ASK MY ADVICE ABOUT SOMETHING. FEEL FREE. EVERY-BODY NEEDS A HAND SOME-TIMES...

STILL THY TONGUE! VERILY THERE IS CRAWL-SPACE INSIDE THY CRANIUM! SIMPLY TAKE THY PLACE BESIDE MR SLAUNK HILDABOOP!
OH, HELLO. DO YOU HAPPEN TO KNOW WHAT'S GOING ON?
PARDON?

I SAID, DO YOU HAPPEN TO KNOW... OH, FORGET IT!
PARDON?
WE ARE READY! WILL ABELARD SNAZZ PLEASE STEP FORWARD...

ARE YOU THE SAME ABELARD SNAZZ WHO CAUSED THE PLANET TWOPP TO BECOME INFESTED WITH DERANGED ROBOTS, THUS RENDERING IT UNINHABITABLE?
HUH?
OH. OH, THAT! HEH, HEH! WELL, THERE'S TWO SIDES TO EVERY STORY YOU KNOW. YOU SEE...

SILENCE!
ARE YOU THE SAME ABELARD SNAZZ WHO BANKRUPTED MR HOOLIO MOOLABAR IN AN ABORTIVE ATTEMPT TO DEFRAUD AN INTERSTELLAR CASINO?
THEY KNOW EVERYTHING ABOUT ME. THIS MUST BE SOME SORT OF A TRIAL!

...THE SELFSAME SNAZZ WHOSE PATENTLY ABSURD "WORM-POWER" THEORIES LED TO THE MONARCHY OF THE PLANET FARBUS BEING DEVOURED BY A BLACK HOLE?*
SOUNDS BAD. I'VE GOT TO THINK OF A WAY TO BUY MYSELF SOME TIME ...OF COURSE! THAT'S IT! MY DIGITAL WRIST-WATCH!
* THARG NOTE: FOR FULL DETAILS OF SNAZZ' CRIMES AGAINST SANITY SEE PROGS 189, 190, 209, 237, 238, 245, 254!

...THE AFOREMENTIONED ABELARD WHO UNLEASHED A PLAGUE OF CRUEL AND TYRANNICAL ANCIENT GODS UPON THE UNIVERSE, CAUSING UNTOLD CARNAGE?
JUST QUICKLY ADJUST THESE CIRCUITS... MODIFY THE FLOATING SPRANGES A LITTLE...
TIDE POWER

THERE! FINISHED! NOBODY'S SENDING THE SPLIT-LEVEL SKULL TO THE SLAMMER!
GASP! HE'S CONVERTED HIS WRIST-WATCH INTO A NEURON-WHISK! STAND BACK, OR HE'LL WHISK OUR NEURONS!

COME ON, OLD TIMER. I DON'T KNOW WHAT YOU'RE ON TRIAL FOR, BUT YOU'RE COMING WITH ME. DON'T WORRY... I'M A GENIUS! I'LL GET YOU TO SAFETY!
PARDON?

PLANET DESIGN DEPT.

WE SHOULD BE ABLE TO LOSE OURSELVES IN THIS MAZE OF CORRIDORS... AHA! THROUGH THAT DOOR THERE...
MOON CONSTRUCTION THIS WAY

B-TYPE SUN MANUFACTURING CHAMBERS KEEP OUT
SIZZLE!
POP!
YAAAAAARGH!
CRACKLE!

LATER...
...AND LET'S HAVE NO MORE MESSING ABOUT! WHY, IF YOU HADN'T BEEN SHIELDED BY MR HILDA-BOOP'S TROLLEY, YOU MIGHT HAVE BEEN BURNED TO A CRISP!
HOW IS MR HILDABOOP, BY THE WAY?

POACHED? I SAY, HOW AWFUL! AH WELL, WE STILL HAVE MR SNAZZ TO DEAL WITH...

NOW, MY FOUR-EYED FRIEND...
WE HAVE ESTABLISHED THAT YOU ARE THE SAME ABELARD SNAZZ WHO RECENTLY SPENT SIX MILLION YEARS IMPRISONED IN THE DIMENSION OF BLEAK DESOLATION...
HERE IT COMES. THEY'RE GOING TO THROW THE BOOK AT ME...

IN LIGHT OF THAT FACT, MR SNAZZ, THERE IS ONLY ONE THING WE HAVE TO SAY...
I CAN'T WATCH...

HAPPY BIRTHDAY TO YOU, HAPPY BIRTHDAY TO YOU... HAPPY BIRTHDAY, DEAR ABELARD, HAPPY BIRTHDAY TO YOU...
?

BUB-BUB BIRTHDAY?
OF COURSE! WHEN ANY OF OUR CITIZENS PASS THE SIX MILLION MARK WE LIKE TO HONOUR THEM WITH A CELEBRATION. SHAME ABOUT POOR OLD MR HILDABOOP.
YOU SEE, WE'VE REVIEWED YOUR ENTIRE LIFE AND HAVE CHOSEN THE ONE GIFT THAT WILL MAKE YOU HAPPIER THAN ANYTHING IN THE WORLD. GO ON.. OPEN IT..

HA HA HA! THE PERFECT GIFT? FOR ME? OH, YOU SHOULDN'T HAVE! I DON'T DESERVE IT! HA HA HA HA! I WONDER WHAT IT COULD BE?
A MODEST LITTLE INTERGALACTIC EMPIRE, PERHAPS? MY OWN WEIGHT IN SIRIAN SUN SAPPHIRES?

OH, YOUR SUPREMACY! IT'S... IT'S...
...IT'S...

. . . IT'S EDWIN.
HE REMEMBERS MY NAME! WHAT A MEMORY! HE'S A GENIUS, YOU KNOW!

WE RESCUED HIS PATHETIC, PITTED BODY FROM DEEP SPACE, WHERE YOU LEFT HIM, WITH OUR TRANS-TIME GRAPPLES . . . SOON HAD HIM PATCHED UP AS GOOD AS NEW!
WELL, MR SNAZZ? WHAT DO YOU THINK? I BET YOU THOUGHT YOU'D SEEN THE LAST OF THIS CHIRPY LITTLE FELLOW.

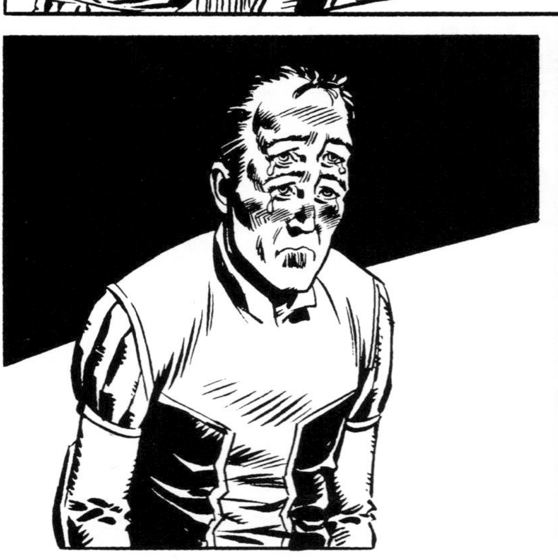

AWHUUOOHOOHOO! WUK WUK SNORF!
TIDE POWER
POOR CHAP. HE'S OVERCOME WITH GRATITUDE. IT TAKES SOME OF THESE OLD CODGERS THAT WAY, YOU KNOW.

COME ON . . . LET'S LEAVE THEM ALONE TOGETHER FOR A WHILE. AFTER ALL, THEY HAVEN'T SEEN EACH OTHER FOR OVER SIX MILLION YEARS . . .
I'M SURE THEY'LL HAVE LOTS TO SAY TO EACH OTHER!

IDIOT! DOLT! THEY COULD HAVE GIVEN ME A PLANET! AN EMPIRE! RRRAAGGHH!
ZLUNG!
WHANG!
OW! YOU ARE A GAK GENIUS, MASTER! AARGH!
KLONK!
The End.

TIME TWISTERS

THARG'S TIME TWISTERS

EVER WONDERED WHAT WILL HAPPEN WHEN TIME-TRAVEL BECOMES A **REALITY**? THIS NEW SERIES WILL ANSWER SOME OF YOUR QUESTIONS, BUT IT WILL POSE MANY MORE!

ROBBY BUDDON IS THE SCHOOL BULLY...
B-BUT ROBBY–I DON'T **WANT** TO PLAY CONKERS WITH YOU!
SHUT THE FACE, TWERP! YOU'RE PLAYING!

IT'S NOT FAIR! YOU'VE SMASHED EVERY CONKER IN SCHOOL WITH THAT MONSTER!
AN' YOURS IS NEXT! **BAGS I FIRST SWIPE!**

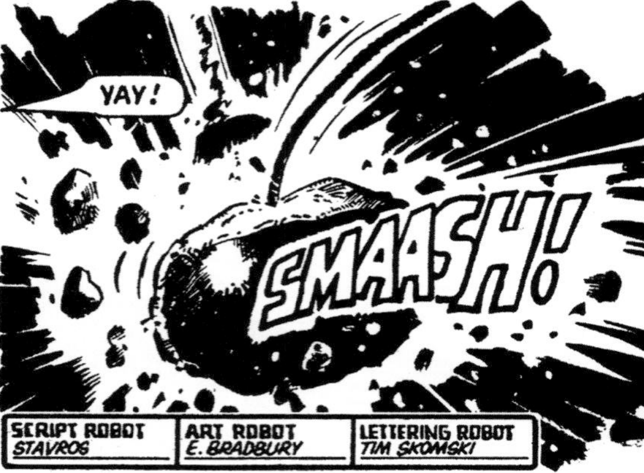

YAY!
SMAASH!

SCRIPT ROBOT STAVROS | ART ROBOT E. BRADBURY | LETTERING ROBOT TIM SKOMSKI

THAT MAKES ME A BULLY **999**! WHAT A 'CONKEROR'! C'MON, YOU WIMPS–LET'S HEAR IT FOR THE CHAMP!

HAIL THE MIGHTY ROBBY! **BULLY 999**!

1982
HAIL 'ROBBY THE CONKEROR'!
HOLD THE SCANNER ON **1982**! SOUNDS INTERESTING...

THE YOUNG WARRIOR LOOKS FEROCIOUS—AND HE IS HIGHLY REGARDED BY HIS PEERS. BRING HIM!
ACTIVATING TIME-GRAB!

BONK!
A BULLY 999! JUST ONE MORE AN' I'LL HIT THE MAGIC THOUSAND. I'LL GO DOWN IN HISTORY!

HEY! NO! STOP!

WH-WHERE AM I? WH-WHO ARE YOU?
YOU ARE IN EARTH'S FAR FUTURE, YOUNG WARRIOR. AND WE ARE THE HUMINDS, THE ULTIMATE DESCENDANTS OF MANKIND!

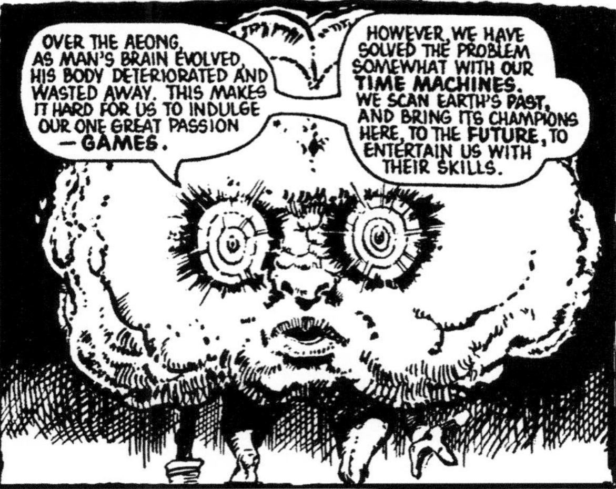
OVER THE AEONS, AS MAN'S BRAIN EVOLVED, HIS BODY DETERIORATED AND WASTED AWAY. THIS MAKES IT HARD FOR US TO INDULGE OUR ONE GREAT PASSION —GAMES.
HOWEVER, WE HAVE SOLVED THE PROBLEM SOMEWHAT WITH OUR TIME MACHINES. WE SCAN EARTH'S PAST, AND BRING ITS CHAMPIONS HERE, TO THE FUTURE, TO ENTERTAIN US WITH THEIR SKILLS.

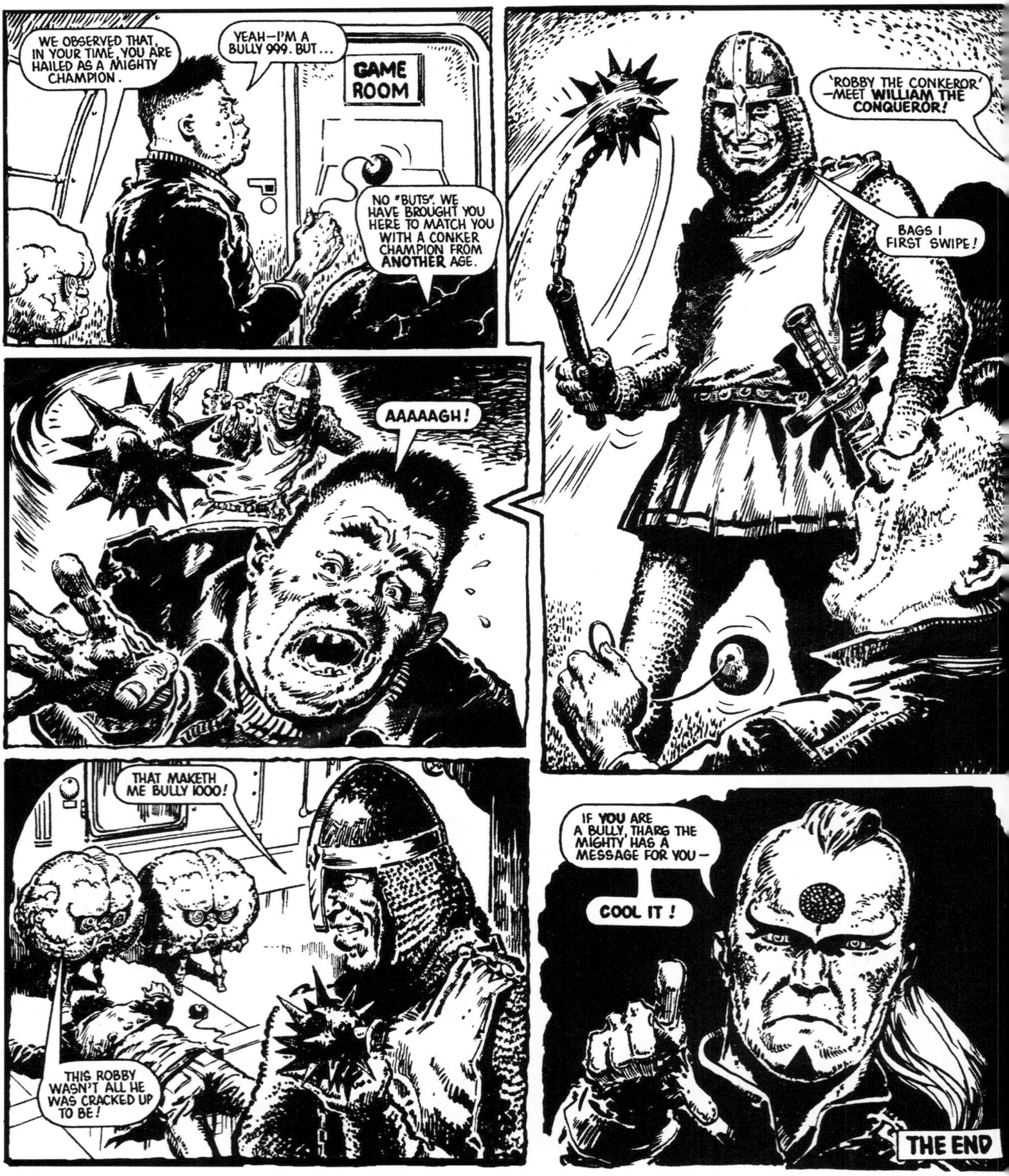

'ROBBY THE CONKEROR' —MEET **WILLIAM THE CONQUEROR!**

BAGS I FIRST SWIPE!

AAAAAGH!

THARG'S TIME TWISTERS

ULTIMATE VIDEO

THE NEAR FUTURE...

AS YOU KNOW, GENTLEMEN, THERE ARE 3.86 VIDEOS TO EVERY HOUSEHOLD IN THE WORLD TODAY... OUR JOB IS TO *INCREASE* THAT NUMBER!

ULTIMATE VIDEO

GIMMICKS! THAT'S WHAT WE NEED, DON'T WE, TIDDLER?

PURRRR!

MY NEW DESIGN CAN SING A SELECTION FROM 'THE SOUND OF MUSIC! SIR!

...BUT MY VIDEO TAP DANCES...

HUH! *MINE* MAKES HOLOGRAPHIC CLONES OF TV PERSONALITIES... *AND* WASHES THE DISHES!

2000 A.D. Credit Card:

SCRIPT ROBOT R. PRESTON

ART ROBOT CASANOVAS + JR.

LETTERING ROBOT J. POTTER

COMPU-73E

TOP OF THE MORNING TO YOU!
THE HILLS ARE ALIVE...
TAP! TAP! TAP!
YAWN! I'LL LET YOU KNOW!

WAIT, SIR! THIS ONE LETS YOU SMELL THE THINGS YOU SEE. WANT TO SAMPLE 'THE CREATURE FROM ARTHUR'S ARMPIT'?
THANKS, BUT I'LL GIVE IT A MISS!

MY MACHINE MAKES RECORDINGS OF FILMS THAT HAVEN'T EVEN BEEN MADE!
THAT'S WHY THE SCREEN'S BLANK!

USELESS! SHOW THEM OUT, MILDEW!
BLANK? WHO SAID BLANK?
THIS WAS THE MOMENT THAT YOUTHFUL ASSISTANT MIKE MILDEW HAD BEEN WAITING FOR...
PLEASE, MR LEES, I HAVE A SET TO SHOW YOU...
IT'S THE ULTIMATE VIDEO!
I PLAY THE HISTORY-VID FILM OF THE 1988 RED INDIAN INVASION OF THE WHITE HOUSE... AND THEN I ACTIVATE THE REMOTE CONTROL...
HMM! NOT A BAD 3D HOLOGRAPHIC EFFECT. IT'S ALMOST LIKE BEING AT THE WHITE HOUSE.
THAT'S HARDLY SURPRISING, SIR...
DIE, PALEFACE!
ERK!
WE ARE AT THE WHITE HOUSE!
YOU GOT US INTO THE FILM... CAN YOU GET US OUT?
ANYONE IN CONTACT WITH THE REMOTE CONTROL CAN BE BEAMED OUT AT ANY TIME!
GRAB HOLD!
A VID-MACHINE THAT TRANSPORTS YOU INTO THE ACTION! IT'S INCREDIBLE. HOW DID YOU DISCOVER IT?
ER- ACTUALLY I WAS TRYING TO DESIGN A VENDING MACHINE VIDEO... BUT SOMETHING MUST HAVE GONE WRONG.
ANYWAY, WITH THIS SET THE VIEWER CAN VISIT ANY REAL-LIFE HAPPENING THAT WAS CAPTURED ON FILM.
THERE'S A MASTER SWITCH ON THE VIDEO DECK. IT CAN BE USED TO BEAM BACK THE REMOTE CONTROL IF ANY-THING GOES WRONG.
SKIP THE DETAILS. YOU'VE GIVEN ME AN IDEA. LET'S START WITH THE NEWSFILM OF THE 1996 CABLE CAR DISASTER.

THE 1996 CABLE CAR DISASTER. A FRAYED WIRE MADE A CAR BREAK DOWN IN MID-JOURNEY. IT PROVED TO BE IMPOSSIBLE TO REACH THE STRANDED PASSENGERS, WHO WAITED HELPLESSLY FOR THE CABLE TO FINALLY SNAP!
GREETINGS GOOD PEOPLE! AS I ARRIVED, SO ONE OF YOU CAN BE TRANSPORTED OUT! NOW, WHO CAN PAY THE MOST?
ME!
MY DIAMOND NECKLACE IS BEYOND PRICE!
HAVE MY CREDIT CARDS!
VELLY EXPENSIVE CAMERA!
THAT NECKLACE WILL DO NICELY! GOODBYE!
GOODBYE, MILDEW!
BUT YOU SAID—!
NO, DON'T LEAVE ME!
NEXT SECOND...
EEEEEEEEEEEEEEEE!
THIS MACHINE IS TOO GOOD FOR THE PUBLIC... IT'S GOING TO BE THE PRIVATE PROPERTY OF J.C. LEES. THINK OF THE ADVENTURES I'LL HAVE... THE THINGS I CAN DO!
AND SO, FOR HIS OWN ENTERTAINMENT, J.C. LEES VISITED EVENTS OF THE PAST TO WREAK HAVOC...
THE 1990 MOON-BASE DISASTER...
HELP ME!
NO FEAR!
THE EUROPEAN CUP FINAL 1988...
YESSSS! IT'S THERE!
THE NEW YORK TOWERING INFERNO OF 1996...
I'LL MAKE A PROMISE— I'LL BEAM OUT OF HERE THE FIRST PERSON TO JUMP...
...FOOLED YOU!

LITTLE DID LEES THINK THAT THE 1999 EAST COAST FISHING DISASTER WOULD BE DISASTROUS FOR HIM AS WELL . . .
IN A FEW MINUTES YOU'LL DROWN, BUT I'LL SAVE THE ONE WHO CAN FIGHT ALL THE OTHERS!

HA! HA! HA!
BAP!
WHAP!
BOK!

BUMP!
YOU FOOL! I'VE DROPPED THE CONTROL IN THE NETS!
CLICK!

NO! SOMEONE'S ACTIVATED THE MASTER SWITCH! THEY'RE BEAMING BACK THE REMOTE CONTROL AND LEAVING ME BEHIND!
STOP WHOEVER YOU ARE-STOP!

TOO LATE! BUT, IF YOU ARE GOING TO MAKE A VIDEO THAT THE CAT CAN OPERATE . . . WHAT ELSE CAN YOU EXPECT?
SLURP!
THE END

THARG'S TIME TWISTERS

TIME: OCTOBER, A.D. 2493.
PLACE: INSTITUTE FOR TEMPORAL HISTORY, NU LUNDUN, YURRUP QUAD-33.
LOCATION: OFFICE OF THE SUPERVISOR FOR HISTORICAL STUDIES.
SITUATION: REQUEST BY SENIOR DIRECTORS TO JUMP BACK IN TIME AND TRACK A MYSTERIOUS "HEAVENLY BODY" ACROSS THE NIGHT SKY, 2500 YEARS BEFORE.
RESPONSE:
NO! REQUEST DENIED!

PROFESSOR BRAD DUREEN, RUTHLESS DIRECTOR OF PSYCHO-RESEARCH...
BUT, SUPERVISOR, WE'VE ALREADY GONE BACK TO THE AGE OF THE DINOSAURS... WE'VE EVEN GONE BACK TO THE VERY MOMENT OF THE BIG BANG!
2000 A.D. Credit Card:
SCRIPT ROBOT J.H. TEED
ART ROBOT BELARDINELLI
LETTERING ROBOT PETE KNIGHT
COMPU-73E

DR. KARL RILLMAN, AMBITIOUS HEAD OF SPECIAL PROJECTS...
THAT WAS REALLY HAIRY. BUT WITH THIS BABY THERE'S NO DANGER AT ALL!
WE KNOW THE AREA, WE KNOW THE TIME OF YEAR. ALL WE WANT TO DISCOVER IS EXACTLY WHAT TOOK PLACE!

SOME SAY IT WAS A COMET... OR A CONJUNCTION OF THE PLANETS. BUT I'M CONVINCED IT WAS A SHOOTING STAR!
WHATEVER IT WAS, WE HAVE TO FIND OUT!

AND THE ONLY WAY WE CAN DO THAT IS TO UTILISE THE FACILITIES OF THE STD!*
STD: SITUATIONAL/TEMPORAL-DISPLACEMENT UNIT—OR TIME-MACHINE.

NO, NO, NO!
THERE ARE SOME THINGS, DUREEN, WE WERE NEVER MEANT TO KNOW—AND THIS IS ONE OF THEM!

IN ANY CASE, THE ENTIRE UNIT IS TEMPORARILY OUT OF COMMISSION—ONE OF THE FLUX-GENERATORS IS OVERHEATING...
IF WE CAN'T DO IT WITH HIS PERMISSION— WE'LL DO IT WITHOUT!
L.S. DE CAMP SUPERVISOR
WHAT ABOUT THE OVERHEATING? COULD BE DANGEROUS, BRAD...
I DON'T BELIEVE IT. THE OLD FOOL'S LYING—A STUPID RUSE TO PUT US OFF!
EXCEPT IT WON'T! TONIGHT— WE DISCOVER THE SECRET OF THE STAR!
BUT, THAT NIGHT...
STOP! ENTRY TO THE STD UNIT IS FORBIDDEN!
GUARDS!
DON'T PANIC, I CAME PREPARED... STUN-SHOT!
AARRGH!

SCANT MINUTES LATER, THEY WERE INSIDE THE STD MODULE—AND...
WARP-FIELD ON! FLUX GENERATORS PEAKING...
ALL SET! WARPING— NOW!
THE YEAR 7 B.C.!
PERFECT! 2500 YEARS IN EIGHT SECONDS FLAT! WE ARE RE-ENTERING ABOVE THE EARTH'S SURFACE! WE'LL BE ABLE TO TRACK THAT SHOOTING STAR AND PROVE...
++7+B+C++
NO—WAIT! SOMETHING WRONG...
TEMPERATURE'S SHOOTING UP! CAN'T STOP IT! CONTROLS GOING CRAZY!
WE... WE ARE OVERHEATING!
AS THE MODULE MATERIALISED, HIGH IN THE EASTERN SKY ON A NIGHT IN OCTOBER IN THE YEAR 7 B.C....
GOTTA DO SOMETHING!
NOTHING... WE CAN DO!
...ITS TWO-MAN CREW SUDDENLY REALISED THEY'D BEEN WRONG!
TEMPERATURE'S OFF THE CLOCK! WE'RE GOING...
NOVA-AAAAAAAARRRHHH!

THEY WERE THE STAR!
THE BEGINNING...

THARG'S
TIME TWISTERS
SCRIPT ROBOT ALAN HEBDEN
ART ROBOT JOHN HIGGINS
LETTERING ROBOT PETE KNIGHT
IN THE 23rd CENTURY THE CITIZENS OF THE HUGE, IMPERSONAL CITIES OF EARTH WERE CRYING OUT FOR AN IDENTITY, ANYTHING TO SET THEM APART FROM THE REST OF THE TEEMING MASSES. THAT NEED WENT UNSATISFIED, UNTIL THE TIME OF AMALGAMATED ANCESTORS...
USING THEIR PATENTED GENETIC TIMESEARCH TECHNIQUE, THEY GUARANTEED TO PRODUCE A FAMOUS ANCESTOR FOR EVERYONE. AND SO SURE WERE THEY THAT THEY OFFERED TO PAY ONE BILLION MEGABUCKS TO ANYONE WITHOUT ONE!
METRO SECURITY POLICE
VID AD
AMALGAMATED ANCESTORS
WHAT'S THE GUY IN THE POLI-HOVER LOOKING SO PLEASED ABOUT?
HE WENT TO AA BEFORE HE WAS CAUGHT, AND FOUND OUT HIS ANCESTOR WAS HOUDINI. HE'S SURE HE CAN ESCAPE!
DUO DEENAM & THE BLACK HOLES PRESENT THE ROCK VERSION OF HAMLET
THEATRE
WHAT'S DUO DEENAM DOIN' PLAYING HAMLET?
AA DISCOVERED THAT SHAKESPEARE WAS HIS ANCESTOR, SO HE'S PUTTING ALL THE PLAYS TO MUSIC!
WHO DOES THIS SPEEDSTER WE'RE CHASING THINK HE IS, STIRLING MOSS?
POLICE
THAT'S EXACTLY WHO AA TOLD HIM HIS ANCESTOR WAS!
SEE THOSE GUYS IN THE DISTINCTIVE DRESS? THEY'RE THE LUCKY ONES, THEY ALREADY KNOW WHO THEIR ANCESTORS ARE!
CAN'T WAIT TO FIND OUT WHO I'M DESCENDED FROM. CARL SAGAN MAYBE!

INSIDE IT WAS THE ANNUAL MEETING OF AA'S MAJOR SHAREHOLDERS, EAGER TO UNDERSTAND WHY THEIR INVESTMENTS WERE MAKING SUCH HUGE PROFITS.
SEE THAT QUEUE? THEY CAN HARDLY WAIT TO PART WITH THE FEE AND FIND OUT WHO THEIR FAMOUS ANCESTOR WAS, WHILE ALL THE TIME SECRETLY HOPING THAT WE WILL FAIL AND HAVE TO HAND OVER A BILLION MEGABUCKS.
BUT WHAT IF YOU DO FAIL? PAYING OUT A BILLION MEGABUCKS WOULD BANKRUPT AMALGAMATED ANCESTORS!
FAILURE IS IMPOSSIBLE. EVERYONE HAS TWO PARENTS, FOUR GRANDPARENTS, EIGHT GREAT-GRANDPARENTS, SIXTEEN GREAT-GREAT GRANDPARENTS, AND SO ON!
GO BACK A MERE TEN GENERATIONS, OR ABOUT TWO CENTURIES, AND EVERYONE HAS OVER A THOUSAND ANCESTORS...
...GO BACK THIRTY GENERATIONS, AND EACH PERSON HAS MORE DIRECT ANCESTORS THAN THE POPULATION OF THE WORLD AT THAT TIME!
JOY... JOY! BARBARA WOODHOUSE WAS MY ANCESTOR!
BUT HOW CAN ANYBODY HAVE MORE ANCESTORS THAN THE POPULATION OF THE WORLD?
OBVIOUSLY THEY DO NOT! THE FURTHER BACK YOU GO, THE MORE PEOPLE TODAY SHARE THE SAME ANCESTOR. GO ALL THE WAY BACK, AND YOU'LL FIND THAT EVERYBODY IS RELATED TO THE SAME AMOEBA!
SO WE'LL NEVER BE CALLED UPON TO PAY OUT THE BILLION MEGABUCKS?
YOU CAN BE CERTAIN OF IT. FOLLOW ME, AND I'LL SHOW YOU THE PROCESS WE USE!
WE DISCOVERED THAT CERTAIN 'MEMORY' GENES ACT LIKE BIOLOGICAL TIME CAPSULES, HOLDING A COMPLETE RECORD OF THE OWNER'S FAMILY TREE BACK TO THE BEGINNING OF LIFE ON EARTH!
SOPHISTICATED SCANNERS 'READ' THIS INFORMATION, THEN COMPUTERS PROJECT VISUAL IMAGES FROM THIS RECORD ONTO THE SCREEN!

SELECTIVELY PROCESSING THE MASS OF INFORMATION, THE COMPUTERS TRACE BACK THROUGH INCREASING NUMBERS OF ANCESTORS UNTIL THEY FIND A FAMOUS ONE...
...IN THIS CASE, ONE OF THE SUBJECT'S ANCESTORS IS GALILEO!
WOW!
HERE'S MY FEE, I'M OFF TO BUY A TELESCOPE. MY ANCESTOR INVENTED THEM YOU KNOW!
ANOTHER SATISFIED CUSTOMER!
SUDDENLY—
DOCTOR, WE HAVE A PROBLEM WITH ONE OF THE SUBJECTS, A WILBUR MEEK. WE...WE CAN'T SEEM TO FIND A SINGLE FAMOUS ANCESTOR IN HIS PAST!
RIDICULOUS! TAKE ME TO HIM!
THE COMPUTERS HAVE ALREADY SEARCHED BACK TO ROMAN TIMES, BUT I'VE NEVER SEEN SUCH A BORING GROUP OF ANCESTORS. THEY WERE ALL PEASANTS, OR SERFS, OR SLAVES!
IT...IT DOESN'T SURPRISE ME, DOCTOR. I'VE NEVER HAD ANY AMBITION, OR WANTED TO DO ANYTHING EXCITING, SO MY ANCESTORS WERE PROBABLY JUST LIKE ME!
NONSENSE!
BRING THE BACK-UP COMPUTERS ON LINE, INTENSIFY THE SEARCH. HE'S GOT TO HAVE AT LEAST ONE FAMOUS ANCESTOR!
GOING BACK TO ANCIENT EGYPT!

THIS IS WILBUR MEEK'S GRANDFATHER, NINETY THOUSAND TIMES REMOVED. WATCH WHAT HAPPENS!
BUT... BUT HE'S AN APE MAN!
IF HE INVENTED FIRE, IT DOESN'T MATTER! HE WAS FAMOUS!
STILL NOTHING. GOING BACK THROUGH THE BRONZE AGE!
IT CAN'T BE TRUE!
GOING BACK TO NEOLITHIC AGE. STILL NOTHING... WAIT!
THE BONE...
YES! HIS DIM PRIMEVAL MIND SEES SOMETHING MORE THAN A BONE...
HE'S HOLDING IT UP. CAN IT BE? DID ONE OF WILBUR MEEK'S ANCESTORS INVENT THE FIRST WEAPON!
BUT.
BURRRP!
OH NO! HE DIDN'T REALISE!
WE'VE FAILED! T-TRANSFER ONE BILLION MEGABUCKS INTO WILBUR MEEK'S ACCOUNT...THEN ANNOUNCE THAT AMALGAMATED ANCESTORS IS GOING INTO LIQUIDATION... SOB
JUST A MOMENT..!

THE OTHER APE MAN WAS WATCHING WILBUR MEEK'S ANCESTOR. NOW HE'S PICKING UP THE BONE!
HE'S EXAMINING IT CAREFULLY...
THIS ONE'S GOT BRAINS, HE'S KNOWS HE'S GOT SOMETHING THERE, BUT HE DOESN'T KNOW WHAT YET!
HE KNOWS HE'S GOT A WEAPON! HE'S GOING FOR WILBUR MEEKS ANCESTOR!
GRRRRR!
URH?
OOOOOOOORRRRGGG!
WE'RE SAVED! STOP THE TRANSFER OF THE MONEY AND SEND WILBUR MEEK ON HIS WAY... WITH A SPECIAL BADGE!
GOSH, IT'S GOOD TO KNOW THAT SOMEBODY IN MY FAMILY DID SOMETHING!
MY ANCESTOR WAS THE FIRST VICTIM OF THE FIRST WEAPON
The End

2000 AD
EXTRA SHOCKS
ORIGINALLY PUBLISHED
IN 2000 AD

LAST THOUGHT
NEXT PROG MY FUTURE SHOCKS RETURN, EARTHLETS. HERE IS A LITTLE SOMETHING TO WHET YOUR APPETITES!
HIGH IN THE STRATOSPHERE A CLUSTER OF NUCLEAR MISSILES BEGINS TO DIP TOWARDS THE EARTH...
AND THE TARGET—AMERICA!
A FULL-SCALE NUCLEAR ATTACK! GOT TO WARN THE PRESIDENT!
THE NEWS IS BROKEN BY ONE OF THE PRESIDENT'S CHIEFS OF STAFF.
WE'LL HAVE TO RETALIATE BUT THAT'LL MEAN THE END OF THE WORLD!
NOT NECESSARILY, MR. PRESIDENT. YOU SEE, WE DO HAVE A MEANS OF DEFENCE...
D-DEFENCE? WHAT DO YOU MEAN? WE DON'T HAVE ANY DEFENCE AGAINST A NUCLEAR ATTACK!
PARDON ME, BUT WE DO. WE HAVE A WEAPON THAT CAN WARP THOSE MISSILES... SEND THEM INTO ANOTHER DIMENSION!
GOVERNMENTS COME AND GO, SIR, BUT THE REAL MACHINERY OF THE STATE, THE CIVIL SERVICE, THE MILITARY, IS STATIC. SOMETIMES THEY KEEP THINGS TO THEMSELVES... THE MILITARY HAS HAD THIS WEAPON FOR MANY YEARS!
2000 A.D. Credit Card:
SCRIPT ROBOT IAN ROGAN
ART ROBOT JOHN HIGGINS
LETTERING ROBOT PETE KNIGHT
COMPU·73E

OF COURSE, IT HAS HAD TO BE TESTED FROM TIME TO TIME, AND THIS HAS MEANT THE DISAPPEARANCE OF CERTAIN PEOPLE AND MACHINERY. BUT WHAT ARE THEY COMPARED WITH THE LIVES OF 200 MILLION AMERICANS?
ER, NOTHING, NOTHING! BUT TIME'S RUNNING OUT. ORDER THE MACHINE'S IMMEDIATE USE!
SECONDS LATER A SINGLE BEAM SURROUNDS THE MISSILES...
AND WARPS THEM INTO ANOTHER DIMENSION!
USAF
LATER–
WELL, GENERAL, YOUR WARP BEAM WORKED. BUT BEFORE WE DECIDE HOW TO DEAL WITH OUR ATTACKERS, PERHAPS YOU COULD TELL ME WHERE YOU KEEP AND OPERATE THE WEAPON...
CERTAINLY, MR. PRESIDENT...
IT'S WITHIN THIS AREA HERE...
...OFF BERMUDA!
The End

SUPERBEAN

MY OLD AND ADMIRED FRIEND, **QIRQX IV**, RULER OF A RACE OF INTELLIGENT TURNIPS IN THE ZMEDLEY SYSTEM, HAS WRITTEN TO COMPLAIN ABOUT THE DISCRIMINATION SHOWN TO VEGETABLES IN MY PROGS. WHERE IS THE **RADISH** WHO **SAVED THE WORLD**, HE DEMANDS? WHERE ARE THE VICIOUS **BEET-ROOT FROM SPACE?**

THARG THE FAIR HAS THEREFORE INVITED **QIRQX** TO REDRESS THE BALANCE. HE SENT ME THE FOLLOWING STORY.

KEN CLARKE WORKED AS A CHECKER IN THE **REALGOOD** CANNING FACTORY. DAY AFTER DAY HE WATCHED THE ENDLESS STREAM OF CUT VEGETABLES MOVING PAST HIM ALONG THE CONVEYOR BELT. OCCASIONALLY HE WOULD HEAVE A SIGH...

THINK OF IT! EVERY ONE OF THOSE CARROTS ONCE LIVED! EVERY ONE HAD THE POTENTIAL FOR **GREATNESS!**

2000 A.D.
Credit Card:

SCRIPT ROBOT
QIRQX IV
ART ROBOT
McMAHON M.
LETTERING ROBOT
POTTER S.

COMPU-73E

KEN'S FELLOW CHECKERS, LOLA LEWIS AND YOUNG OLLIE JIMSON, WERE DISMISSIVE—
LEAVE ORF, CLARKIE! THEY'RE JUST BLOOMIN' VEGETABLES, AIN'T THEY?
THE ONLY 'POTENTIAL' THEY'VE GOT IS ON A PLATE WITH A BIG SLAB OF ROAST BEEF!

BUT KEN CLARKE KNEW BETTER. HE HAD A SECRET HE COULD NEVER SHARE WITH ANYONE...
IF ONLY I COULD TELL THEM...!

AT LUNCHTIME, KEN CLARKE WITNESSED A MUGGING—
HOLY POTATOES! THEY'RE STEALING THAT WOMAN'S HANDBAG!
HELP! HELP!

KEN NIPPED INTO A DARK ALLEY—
GOTTA GET THESE CLOTHES OFF!

HIS FINGERS FOUND THE ZIP FASTENER CONCEALED BENEATH HIS HAIR—

FOR KEN CLARKE HAD ANOTHER IDENTITY—

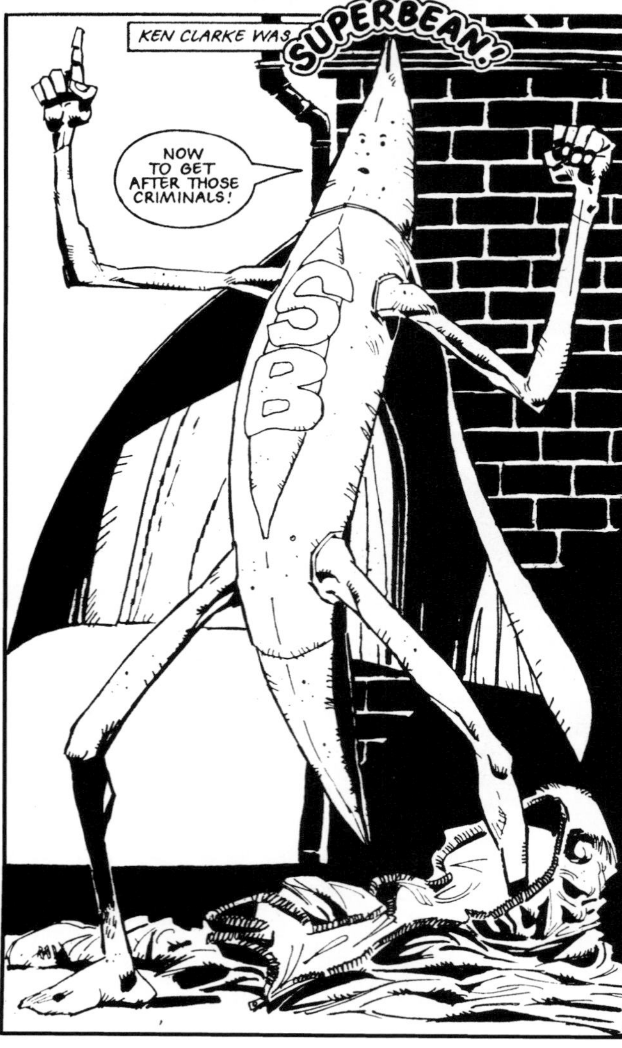
KEN CLARKE WAS
SUPERBEAN!
NOW TO GET AFTER THOSE CRIMINALS!

LOOK UP THERE! IS IT A BIRD—?
IS IT A PLANE—?

NO! IT'S... SUPERBEAN!

FASTER THAN A SPEEDING LEEK!
THUNK!
UGGH!
MORE POWERFUL THAN AN AUBERGINE!
POW!
MORE AGILE THAN A PROCESSED PEA!
WHIZZZ
YAAAAH! SUPERBEAN!
DONK!
OH, SUPERBEAN, YOU'VE CAUGHT THEM! THANK YOU!
WE'VE BEEN AFTER THOSE THUGS FOR YEARS! WHAT WOULD US POLICE DO WITHOUT A VEGETABLE LIKE YOU?
THINK NOTHING OF IT! AS LONG AS THERE ARE MEN OF EVIL, MEN WHO SEEK TO THWART THE COURSE OF JUSTICE, THERE WILL ALWAYS BE WORK FOR A BEAN LIKE MYSELF!
BACK IN THE SHADOWS OF THE ALLEY—
ANOTHER GOOD DEED DONE! NOW, BACK TO WORK!

ANOTHER FANTASTIC CRIME-BUSTING OPERATION WAS TODAY CARRIED OUT BY SUPERBEAN. THE QUESTION ON THE WHOLE CITY'S LIPS IS, WHO IS THIS MYSTERIOUS VEGETABLE?
LA
NO-ONE MUST EVER LEARN MY TRUE IDENTITY!

BUT AT THE CANNING FACTORY—
IT'S LOLA LEWIS, CLARKIE! SHE CLIMBED UP THERE TO SAVE THE FACTORY CAT—NOW SHE'S STUCK!
SHE CAN'T HOLD ON MUCH LONGER!

GREAT GHERKINS! THAT'S NOT THE WORST OF IT!
MY BEAN-RAY VISION DETECTS AN AIRPLANE PLUNGING OUT OF CONTROL—HEADING STRAIGHT FOR LOLA!

NO TIME TO CONCEAL MY TRUE IDENTTTY!
GOOD GRIEF! CLARKIE!

CLARKIE IS... SUPERBEAN!

THE WORLD'S MIGHTIEST BEAN STREAKED THROUGH THE AIR—
HELP! HELP!
LOOK! HERE COMES SUPER-BEAN!

WE'RE SAVED!
I'VE HALTED ITS DESCENT – BUT LOLA IS STARTING TO FALL!

SUPERBEAN'S POWERFUL ARM SENT THE STRICKEN PLANE WHIZZING—
WHIZZZZZZZZZ

—TO LAND SAFELY AT A DISTANT AIRPORT!
WHAT A THROW!
WHAT A BEAN!

LOLA IS FALLING!
EEEAAAAH!
HAVE NO FEAR, LOLA!

SUPERBEAN IS HERE!

IN THE FACTORY, LOLA RECOVERED—
SHE'S COMING ROUND!
OH, SUPERBEAN! YOU'VE SAVED ME!

MY HERO!
LOLA! BE CAREFUL!

OH DEAR! SUPERBEAN!
LOLA HAS PUSHED SUPERBEAN OVER!

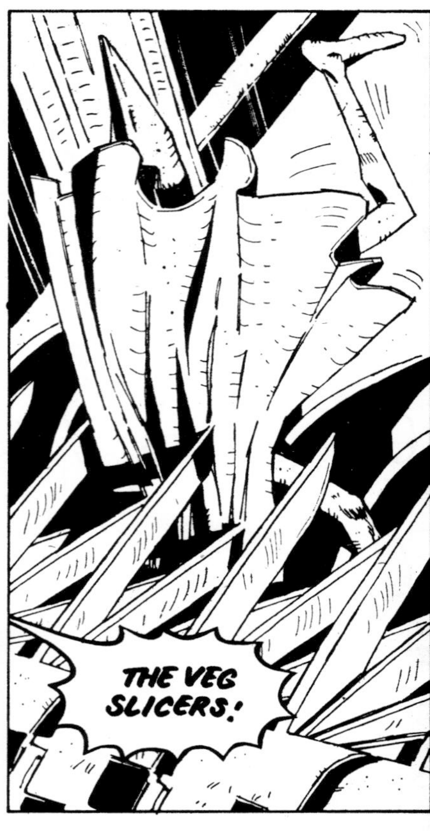
THE VEG SLICERS!

OH, N-N-NO-NO! HE-HE'S BEEN P-P-PROCESSED!

YOU-YOU'VE GOT TO BELIEVE ME, SUPERBEAN! IT WAS AN ACCIDENT!
REALE
CUT SLICED GREE BEAN
RG
BUT FROM THE CAN CAME NOT A SOUND.

MESSAGE FROM SCRIPTER QIRQX IV
THE MORAL OF MY TALE IS CLEAR. MAKE FRIENDS WITH YOUR VEGETABLES. REMEMBER, SUPERBEAN MAY NOT BE ALONE.
SO NEXT TIME YOU'RE IN THE GARDEN, SAY HELLO. AND DON'T BE SURPRISED IF YOUR VEGETABLES ANSWER BACK.

TROUBLE ON TREE-WORLD
AN AGENT RAT ADVENTURE
TRYON WAS THE PLANET'S NAME, THOUGH MOST FOLKS JUST CALLED IT TREE-WORLD, FOR OBVIOUS REASONS . . .
SO IT WASN'T GOING TO BE AN EASY PLACE TO FIND MURDEROUS MEL BALFO . . .
BUT IF I LIKED AN EASY LIFE, I WOULDN'T WORK FOR THE GALACTIC SECURITY COUNCIL, WOULD I ?
RATTUS R. RATTUS IS THE NAME, BUT DON'T ASK ME WHAT THE 'R' STANDS FOR. JUST CALL ME 'AGENT RAT' . . .
OR 'SIR' . . .
GALACTIC ENCLAVE WAS THE ONLY BIT OF OPEN GROUND ON TRYON –
'NATIVE LIAISON DEPARTMENT'. THAT'S THE PLACE I'M LOOKING FOR . . .

ONLY REGISTERED PERSONNEL WERE ALLOWED ON THE ENCLAVE, SO IF BALFO WAS HERE, HE'D HAVE TO TAKE TO THE TREES . . .
SECURITY. I'M LOOKING FOR MEL BALFO. SHOULD'VE ARRIVED TWO DAYS AGO ON THE 'ALTAIR QUEEN'...
HE'S GOT A GIRL SOMEWHERE ON TRYON, AND A VERTICAL SCAR ON EACH CHEEK. THAT'S ABOUT ALL I HAVE TO GO ON...
TRYON
THE LIAISON OFFICETTE WAS CALLED LORETTA PAZZ...
THAT MAKES IT RATHER DIFFICULT, SIR. YOU SEE...
EVERY ADULT MALE ON TRYON HAS SCARRED CHEEKS!
WE CARRIED OUT ALL THE USUAL CHECKS. NO LUCK.
SO HE'S ON FOOT, OUT THERE, AND HE'LL NEED TO GET BACK TO THE ENCLAVE TO GET OFF-PLANET AGAIN...
AND THE NEXT SHIP IN IS THE 'ASTRA KHAN', DUE AT NIGHTFALL...
WHICH LEAVES YOU SEVEN HOURS TO CHECK THE LOCAL VILLAGES...
PROFILE
COMPU 12
YOU'LL NEED A GUIDE, THOUGH. GIVE ME TEN MINUTES AND I'LL FIND SOMEONE...
AND...
YOU!
I CHANGED MY SHIFT SO I COULD 'STAY ON THE CASE'...
YOU'LL FIND SOME OF THE TRYONESE CUSTOMS PRETTY ODD ...FOR A START THEY INSIST THAT ALL WOMEN WEAR A HOOD LIKE THIS...
BUT AS WE LEFT THE ENCLAVE...
VIP! YIP!
I'M AFRAID YOU'LL HAVE TO LEAVE YOUR GUN BEHIND. WE CAN'T LET THE TRYONESE GET HOLD OF ENERGY WEAPONS...
NO CHANCE, SWEETHEART. SECURITY CLEARANCE ALPHA... I'LL TAKE RESPONSIBILITY...
2000 A.D.
Credit Card:
SCRIPT ROBOT STEVE MOORE
ART ROBOT ALAN LANGFORD
LETTERING ROBOT JACK POTTER
COMPU·73E

THE TRYONESE LIVE IN TREE-TOP WOODEN VILLAGES CONNECTED BY LONG WALKWAYS... WOODHOLME IS OUR FIRST STOP.
NO SANE TRYONESE EVER GOES DOWN ON THE FOREST FLOOR...
BECAUSE THERE ARE AN AWFUL LOT OF VERY LARGE, VERY HUNGRY REPTILES LURKING AROUND DOWN THERE...
THE LOCALS CALL 'EM SCALLYWAGS. DUNNO WHY. THEY DIDN'T LOOK TOO PLAYFUL TO ME...
LORELLA KNEW HER WAY AROUND OKAY, AND BEFORE TOO LONG...
WOODHOLME! WHAT DO THESE BOZOS EAT?
OH, MOSTLY FRUIT AND THE OCCASIONAL... UM, THE OCCASIONAL SMALL FURRY ANIMAL...
I SHOULD'VE KNOWN. STILL, WE GOT A WARM WELCOME FROM BULTOG, THE VILLAGE HEAD-MAN...
SOMEONE BRING THE COOKING POT! IT'S A BIG ONE!
NOT SO FAST, BUSTER!
I TOLD HIM BALFO HAD A GIRL HERE ON TRYON. MAYBE HE WAS SHACKED UP SOME PLACE...
IMPOSSIBLE! ALL THE WOODHOLME WOMEN ARE IN THE UPPER VILLAGE FOR A TWO WEEK FESTIVAL. ANY MAN GOING UP THERE WOULD BE TORN APART!
AGENT RAT... I'LL CHECK THE UPPER VILLAGE. THEY'LL LET ME UP THERE.
SURE. I'LL HANG AROUND AND WATCH THE SCALLYWAGS...

I'D ASKED LORELLA IF THE TRYONESE EVER PUSHED PEOPLE OFF THE WALKWAY. SHE'D SAID NO...
WAP!
THEY'D KILL YOU WITH A THREE-POINTED KNIFE, BUT THEY'D NEVER TOSS YOU OFF THE WALKWAY...
GUESS SHE WAS WRONG!
NOW, I'VE BEEN SAPPED BY EXPERTS, BUT THIS GUY WASN'T ONE OF THEM... SO I WAS STILL AWAKE ENOUGH TO MAKE A DECISION...
GRAB THIS BRANCH...
TOOK ME HALF AN HOUR TO CLIMB BACK TO THE WALKWAY, BUT YOU CAN'T KEEP A GOOD RAT DOWN. I HEADED BACK TO WOODHOLME...
YOU'RE BACK! BUT I WAS COMING TO JOIN YOU AGAIN!
SOMEONE TRIED TO PUT A DENT IN MY SKULL... MUST'VE BEEN BALFO, I GUESS... ALL I COULD SEE WAS THAT HE HAD LONG, BLOND HAIR!
MOST GUYS WHO GET SLUGGED ON THE HEAD FEEL SICK FOR A WEEK. NOT ME, IT JUST REMINDED ME HOW HUNGRY I WAS...
STAY HERE AND REST, AGENT RAT! I'LL GO AND FIND SOME FRUIT!
SWEET KID, THAT LORELLA...
FAST ON HER FEET, TOO... SHE WAS BACK IN NO TIME...
AGENT RAT! BULTOG! WE'RE IN TROUBLE!
BETWEEN HERE AND WINDBRANCH ... THE FOREST'S ON FIRE!
WHAT?!
I DIDN'T LIKE IT MUCH EITHER. SHE'D FORGOTTEN THE FRUIT.
Next prog: CHASING MY TAIL!

TROUBLE ON TREE-WORLD PART II
AN AGENT RAT ADVENTURE
THINGS WERE MOVING PRETTY FAST. I'D ONLY BEEN ON TRYON THREE HOURS, AND ALREADY I'D BEEN NEARLY COOKED, SLUGGED ON THE HEAD AND THROWN TO THE REPTILES. I STILL DIDN'T KNOW WHERE MEL BALFO WAS, AND I STILL HADN'T HAD LUNCH...
BUT IF YOU WANT TO SEE SOMETHING REALLY FAST, YELL 'FOREST FIRE' TO A BUNCH OF TRYONESE TREE-DWELLERS...
THEY'RE ALL GONE! AND THE FIRE'S GETTING CLOSER!
AGENT RAT? WHAT ARE YOU DOING?
ALL I WAS AFTER WAS HER SHOULDER-RADIO...
HEY, GALACTIC ENCLAVE! THIS IS RAT, SECURITY CLEARANCE ALPHA! I'M OUT HERE WITH OFFICETTE LORELLA PAZZ!
H2O
I WANT A WATER-TANKER, AND I WANT IT IN THE AIR NOW! HEAD OUT BETWEEN WOODHOLME AND WINDBRANCH VILLAGES...
2000 A.D. Credit Card:
SCRIPT ROBOT STEVE MOORE
ART ROBOT ALAN LANGFORD
LETTERING ROBOT JACK POTTER
COMPU-73E

AND DUMP A FULL LOAD ON THE FIRE YOU'LL FIND BURNING THERE!
FSSS!
THAT TOOK CARE OF THAT PROBLEM. BUT I WASN'T ANY CLOSER TO MURDEROUS MEL BALFO...
SO THE WALKWAY TO WINDBRANCH IS BURNT OUT! IS THERE ANY OTHER WAY TO GET THERE?
NO, THIS IS THE ONLY ROUTE...
THERE WAS SOMETHING ABOUT THIS WHOLE AFFAIR WHICH DIDN'T QUITE MAKE SENSE...
BALFO MUST BE IN WINDBRANCH, AND HE BURNED THE WALKWAY TO STOP ME GETTING TO HIM...
BUT HOW'S HE GOING TO GET BACK TO THE ENCLAVE, IF HE WANTS TO SHIP OUT IN ABOUT THREE HOURS?
OF COURSE, MAYBE BALFO DIDN'T WANT TO CATCH THE 'ASTRA KHAN' OUT OF THERE...
BUT HE WAS CRIMINAL, NOT CRAZY. HE'D BE AWAY IF HE COULD...
SO, HOW DO THEY FIX THESE WALKWAYS?
YOU'RE ABOUT TO FIND OUT. HERE COMES HEADMAN BULTOG...
AND HE'S GOT HIS GLIDER CAPE WITH HIM.
I WILL FLY ACROSS WITH A ROPE... YOU CAN CRAWL ACROSS AFTER-WARDS...
OKAY!
AND I CAN HEAD BACK TO THE ENCLAVE! DANGLING FROM A ROPE ISN'T MY IDEA OF FUN!

BULTOG HAD CLASS, I'LL GIVE HIM THAT...
BUT IT WAS PRETTY LOW CLASS...
OOOF!
STILL, HE DID MANAGE TO GET THE ROPE ACROSS...
IT TOOK ANOTHER HOUR TO REACH WINDBRANCH...
I'M LOOKING FOR MEL BALFO... LONG BLOND HAIR...
BLOND HAIR? HAVE YOU COME TO MOCK, O RAT?
DID THEY NOT TELL YOU IN WOODHOLME THAT WE ARE ENEMIES OF ALL FAIR-HAIRS?
IT WAS AT THIS POINT THAT I REALISED THAT I'D BEEN PLAYED FOR A SUCKER... ALL THE WAY DOWN THE LINE...
I ALSO REALISED THAT I HAD AN HOUR AND TEN MINUTES TO RETURN TO THE ENCLAVE BEFORE THE 'ASTRA KHAN' BOARDED...
SO I DIDN'T HAVE ANY TIME TO WASTE ON CONVERSATION...
WOK!
HE WOULD ONLY HAVE SAID 'NO' ANYWAY...
BUT I NEEDED THAT GLIDER OF HIS...
ONLY FIFTEEN MINUTES BY THE TIME I GOT BACK TO GOOD OL' BULTOG...
IF I CAN CATCH AN UPDRAUGHT, THIS THING WILL TAKE ME ALL THE WAY BACK TO THE GALACTIC ENCLAVE ... IN ABOUT THREE MINUTES FLAT...

YOU SEE, I'D WASTED ALL THAT TIME IN THE FOREST, AND MY MAN HAD NEVER LEFT THE ENCLAVE IN THE FIRST PLACE...
BALFO! STAND WHERE YOU ARE!
WHAT THE BLUE..?
ASTRA KHAN
HE WASN'T GOING TO LEAVE IT NOW, EITHER...
AAAUGH!
MEL!
MY BIG MISTAKE HAD BEEN ASSUMING THAT BALFO'S GIRL-FRIEND WAS A NATIVE TYRONESE. SHE WASN'T.
SHE WAS LIAISON OFFICETTE PAZZ. AND LORELLA WAS THE 'BLOND GUY' WHO SHOVED ME OFF THE WALKWAY. SHE STARTED THE FOREST FIRE, TOO.
ALL TO KEEP ME OUT OF THE WAY UNTIL THE 'ASTRA KHAN' LANDED, WHILE SHE HAD BALFO HIDDEN AWAY IN HER OWN QUARTERS...
OFFICER, ARREST THAT WOMAN...
PITY ABOUT LORELLA, BUT IT'S A TOUGH UNIVERSE...
I WENT LOOKING FOR LUNCH...
The End

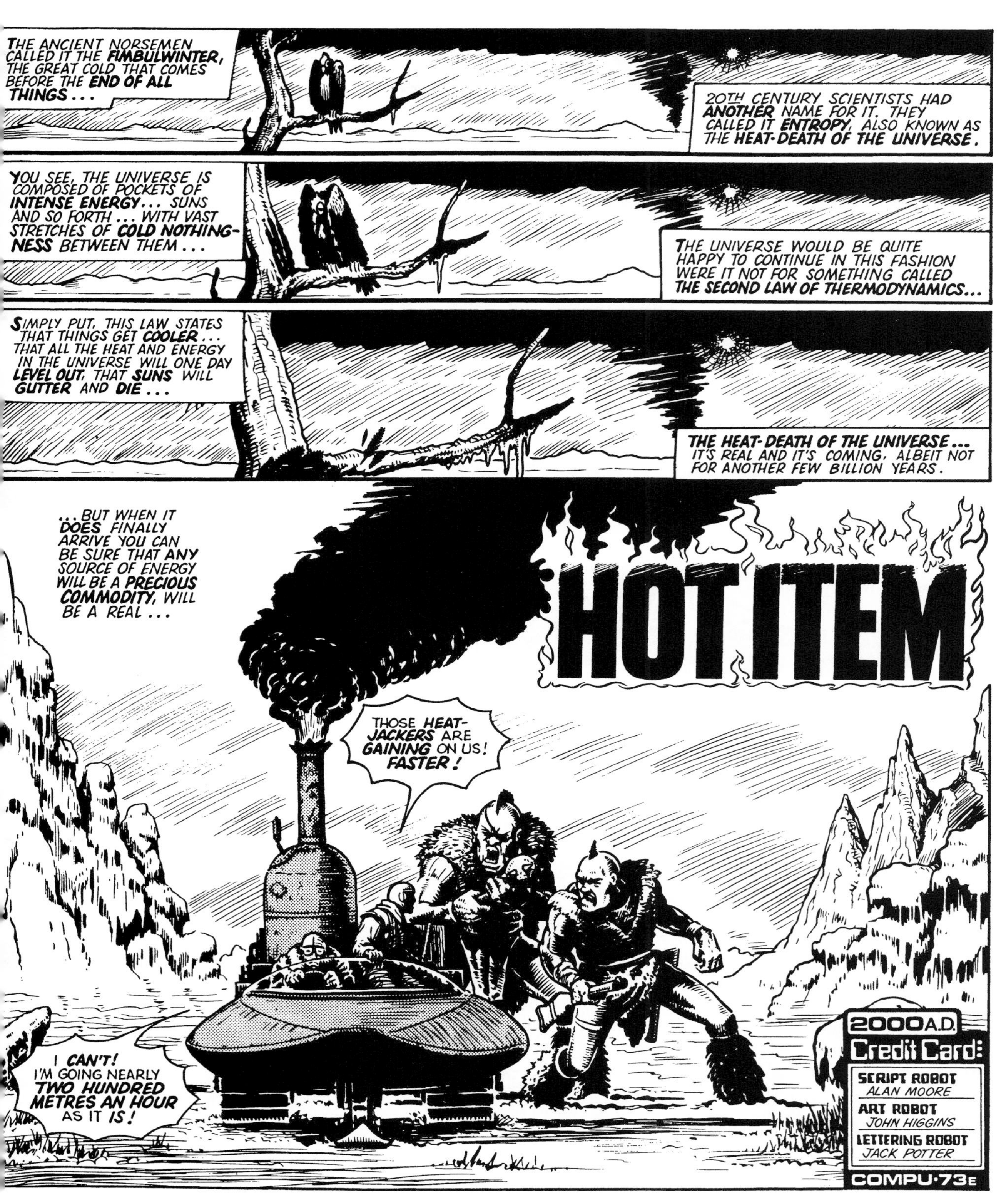
THE ANCIENT NORSEMEN CALLED IT THE FIMBULWINTER, THE GREAT COLD THAT COMES BEFORE THE END OF ALL THINGS...
20TH CENTURY SCIENTISTS HAD ANOTHER NAME FOR IT. THEY CALLED IT ENTROPY, ALSO KNOWN AS THE HEAT-DEATH OF THE UNIVERSE.
YOU SEE, THE UNIVERSE IS COMPOSED OF POCKETS OF INTENSE ENERGY... SUNS AND SO FORTH... WITH VAST STRETCHES OF COLD NOTHINGNESS BETWEEN THEM...
THE UNIVERSE WOULD BE QUITE HAPPY TO CONTINUE IN THIS FASHION WERE IT NOT FOR SOMETHING CALLED THE SECOND LAW OF THERMODYNAMICS...
SIMPLY PUT, THIS LAW STATES THAT THINGS GET COOLER... THAT ALL THE HEAT AND ENERGY IN THE UNIVERSE WILL ONE DAY LEVEL OUT, THAT SUNS WILL GUTTER AND DIE...
THE HEAT-DEATH OF THE UNIVERSE... IT'S REAL AND IT'S COMING, ALBEIT NOT FOR ANOTHER FEW BILLION YEARS.
...BUT WHEN IT DOES FINALLY ARRIVE YOU CAN BE SURE THAT ANY SOURCE OF ENERGY WILL BE A PRECIOUS COMMODITY, WILL BE A REAL...
HOT ITEM
THOSE HEAT-JACKERS ARE GAINING ON US! FASTER!
I CAN'T! I'M GOING NEARLY TWO HUNDRED METRES AN HOUR AS IT IS!
2000 A.D. Credit Card:
SCRIPT ROBOT ALAN MOORE
ART ROBOT JOHN HIGGINS
LETTERING ROBOT JACK POTTER
COMPU-73E

...BUT WE CAN'T LET THEM STEAL OUR ENERGY SUPPLIES! THE VILLAGE NEEDS THEM!
BESIDES, WE'VE TRAVELLED FOR MONTHS TO FIND THEM! WE MUST HAVE COVERED NEARLY TWO KILOMETRES!
TOO LATE! LOOK!
HAR HAR! WE'VE GOT 'EM! LET 'EM HAVE IT, SKRANGLES ME LAD! BOTH BARRELS!
AYE AYE, CAP'N!
BANG
PLUP!
PHUD!
BLISTER ME VITALS! THERE'S NOT ENOUGH KINETIC ENERGY LEFT TO GET THE BULLETS OUT OF THE BARREL! WE'LL HAVE TO JUMP 'EM INSTEAD!
URFF! IT'S NO GOOD! THEY'VE PUT CENTIMETRES BETWEEN US WHILE WE'VE BEEN NATTERING!
DON'T WORRY, CAP'N! I'LL HAVE ME BREATH BACK IN HALF AN HOUR, AND THEN I'LL GET AFTER 'EM!
HALF AN HOUR? DON'T BE DAFT, SKRANGLES! THEY'LL BE METRES AWAY BY THEN!
BESIDES, I CAN'T BE BOTHERED CHASING 'EM ANY MORE. I AIN'T GOT THE ENERGY...
PHEW! THEY'VE GIVEN UP! THE ENERGY SUPPLIES ARE SAFE!
DON'T BANK ON IT! WE'VE GOT ANOTHER THREE OR FOUR HUNDRED METRES TO GO BEFORE WE REACH THE VILLAGE!
ANYTHING COULD HAPPEN!

INDEED IT COULD, FOR THE COLD AND DYING PLANET IS NOT WITHOUT ITS DANGERS. FOR EXAMPLE, THERE ISN'T AS MUCH FRICTION AS THERE USED TO BE..
LOOK OUT! THAT BIG ROCK HAS ROLLED LOOSE! IT'S FALLING!
... ON THE OTHER HAND, THERE ISN'T AS MUCH GRAVITY EITHER...
HURRY UP! ONLY ANOTHER METRE AND WE'LL BE CLEAR!

SLOWLY, THE INTREPID PAIR CONTINUE WITH THEIR LIFE-OR-DEATH JOURNEY, UNTIL..
IT'S GETTING DARKER! THE SUN MUST BE GOING DOWN...
I DOUBT IT. THE SUN'S BEEN IN THE SAME PLACE FOR THE LAST TWELVE HOURS. IT MUST BE GOING OUT!
HMM. YOU'RE RIGHT..
ACTUALLY, IT PROBABLY WENT OUT YEARS AGO AND IT'S TAKEN THIS LONG FOR THE LIGHT TO REACH US..
AYE. THE SPEED OF LIGHT'S NOT WHAT IT WAS, IS IT?

ONWARD THEY GO INTO THE GATHERING DARKNESS, ALONE SAVE FOR THE STEADY TICK OF THEIR METROMETER...
OOWOOOWOOOOO
OR RATHER... ALMOST ALONE...

LOOK! LUMBERING OUT OF THE SHADOWS! WHAT ARE THEY?
IT'S A PACK OF THERMO-LEECHES... THEY MUST HAVE SENSED OUR BODY-HEAT!

THIS IS IT, OLD FRIEND. WE MAY BE DOOMED BUT AT LEAST WE'LL GO DOWN KICKING FEEBLY...
WAIT! LOOK AT THAT!

SOMETHING'S HAPPENING TO THE BIGGEST ONE... IT LOOKS LIKE HE'S STARTING TO MELT!
OF COURSE! HE'S REACHED CRITICAL PHASE... ALL OF HIS VALENCY IS DRAINING AWAY...

VALENCY? WHAT'S THAT?
IT'S THE ELECTRICAL CHARGE THAT HOLDS ATOMS TOGETHER. HIS HAS JUST RUN OUT!

GROOP!
WE'RE IN LUCK! THE OTHER LEECHES ARE STOPPING TO WARM THEMSELVES OVER HIS ESCAPING BODY HEAT! THEY'VE FORGOTTEN ABOUT US! LET'S GO!
WHURR!
MNNUGH!

LATER...
THE VILLAGE! WE'VE MADE IT!

MUCH LATER...
COME ON! LET US IN!
LATER STILL...
PIFCO BE PRAISED! IT'S ERIK AND NOGRED! LONG HAVE WE PRAYED TO THE SACRED ELECTRIC BLANKET FOR YOUR SAFE RETURN.
DO YOU HAVE... THE ENERGY SUPPLIES?

AYE, THAT WE DO! COME, HELP US CARRY THEM TO THE CENTRAL STOCKADE!
WHAT ARE THEY? LUMPS OF ANTHRACITE? SAFETY MATCHES? URANIUM ISOTOPES?

NO, OLD ONE. ERIK AND I HAVE DISCOVERED SOMETHING FAR MORE POWERFUL THAN MERE URANIUM!
WHAT WE HAVE HERE WILL GIVE OUR PEOPLE ALL THE ENERGY THEY NEED FOR YEARS TO COME!
GASP!
AND SO, SEVERAL HOURS LATER, IN THE CENTRAL STOCKADE...
FRIENDS! ERIK AND NOGRED HAVE RETURNED WITH THE ANSWER TO ALL OF OUR ENERGY PROBLEMS!
BUT HOW? DID THEY STUMBLE ACROSS AN ABANDONED POWER STATION?
YES! THAT MUST BE IT! OR AN OIL REFINERY... MAYBE THEY FOUND AN OIL REFINERY!
NOTHING SO CRUDE, MY KINSMEN. WHAT ERIK AND I FOUND WAS...
...A MUSEUM!
A MUSEUM???
AYE! AND WITHIN WE FOUND THE ONE SOURCE OF POWER WHICH NEVER WANES NOR GROWS DIM! BEHOLD, BRETHREN...
..THRILL-POWER UNLEASHED!
THRILL-POWER!
I CAN FEEL ITS WARMTH FROM HERE!
DREDD
ZARJAZ!
...AND THERE WAS GREAT CELEBRATION WHICH WENT ON ALL NIGHT...
...AND THE NIGHT WENT ON FOREVER.
THE END

THE GREAT DETECTIVE CAPER

Hemlock Bones----Who He? Part 1

OUT OF THE SINISTER MIASMA OF A THAMESIDE MURK, NOT A MILLION MILES FROM WAPPING OLD STAIRS— STRIDE TWO FAMILIAR FIGURES...
2000 A.D. Credit Card:
SCRIPT ROBOT JACK ADRIAN
ART ROBOT JOHN HIGGINS
LETTERING ROBOT STEVE POTTER
COMPU·73E

THE GAUNT INDIVIDUAL IN THE INVERNESS CAPE, HIS AQUILINE NOSTRILS QUIVERING WITH THE THRILL OF THE HUNT...
COME, OLD FRIEND— THE GAME'S AFOOT!

THE FAITHFUL COMPANION— STOCKY, PLUCKY. HIS FACE TWITCHING WITH SHOCK AND OUTRAGE...
LOOK— LOOK THERE! MERCIFUL HEAVENS...

THE HAPLESS VICTIM. THE LIGHT OF HOPE DAWNING IN HER EYES AS SHE RECOGNISES HER VALIANT RESCUER...
MY SAVIOUR!

THE GREAT DETECTIVE'S KEEN, PENETRATING EYES SHEAR THROUGH THE DOCKSIDE GLOOM...
DON'T WORRY, MY DEAR...

...AS HE STRIDES FORWARD...
YOUR TROUBLES ARE...

...AND BLUNDERS RIGHT INTO HER!
...OVER— WHOOPS!
EEEGH! Y'GREAT CLUMSY OAF!

CUT!
DAMNIT, GRICE! YOU'VE JUST RUINED ANOTHER TAKE!
DIR

ANOTHER EPISODE OF "HEMLOCK BONES— MASTER-SLEUTH" IS NOT QUITE IN THE CAN...
NOT TO MENTION MY RIBS!

UHH... SORRY. CONTACT LENSES DROPPED OUT AGAIN...

ERNIE GRICE'S FELLOW ACTORS AREN'T SYMPATHETIC...
THAT'S THE FIFTIETH TIME...
IN ONE DAY!
WHY DO WE HAVE TO PUT UP WITH THIS IDIOT?

GAAH! IF IT WASN'T FOR THE FACT THAT HE LOOKS EXACTLY LIKE SHERLOCK HOLMES...
UH-UH, JG— HEMLOCK BONES, REMEMBER? WE CAN'T USE THE NAME SHERLOCK HOLMES IN THE SERIES. COPY-RIGHT PROBLEMS.

OH. RIGHT. WELL, IF IT WASN'T FOR FACT THAT HE LOOKS EXACTLY LIKE HEMLOCK BONES...
I'D FIRE HIM!
EXIT
DONK!

THE 'GREAT DETECTIVE' PLODS HOME TO HIS ONE-ROOM FLAT IN CROUCH END...
CAN'T EVEN AFFORD A TAXI...
J6'S INVOKED SO MANY PENALTY CLAUSES IN MY CONTRACT, I'M ALMOST DOING THE HEMLOCK BONES SERIES FOR FREE!
SOMETIMES I WISH THE EARTH'D JUST OPEN UP AND SWALLOW ME...
SUDDENLY...
UHH? BEAM OF LIGHT... HITTING ME... FROM THE SKY...
GREAT GODFREY! I'M DISAPPEARING!
SECONDS LATER...
IT WORKS— IT WORKS!
THE TTTB WORKS!
TTTB?
TRANS-TEMPORAL-...
...TRACTOR-BEAM!
WITH IT, WE'VE BEEN ABLE TO SHATTER THE DIMENSIONAL BARRIERS...
...TEAR APART THE LAWS OF SPACE AND TIME...
...AND SCOOP UP...
...THE GREATEST DEDUCTIVE GENIUS...
...OF ALL TIME...
...THE MOST BRILLIANT ANALYTICAL MIND...
...IN THE HISTORY OF THE UNIVERSE...
...SHERLOCK HOLMES!

BECAUSE ONLY HE...
...CAN AID US IN OUR HOUR OF NEED!

I'M HEMLOCK BONES! ER... THAT IS TO SAY I'M ERNIE GRICE—AN ACTOR...

HEMLOCK...
...WHO?
NOT...
...SHERLOCK HOLMES?
ERNIE...
...GRICE?!

AN IMPOSTOR!
DO YOU KNOW HOW MUCH THE TTTB COST TO BUILD?

MAKE HIM PAY...
...WITH HIS LIFE!
HURRRRR!
I WANNA NEW CONTRACT!
NEXT PROG: MONSTER MASH?

THE GREAT DETECTIVE CAPER
Hemlock Bones---Who He? Part 2
PLUCKED FROM THE PLANET EARTH BY A TRANS-TEMPORAL-TRACTOR-BEAM AND DEPOSITED ON THE PLANET SQUARL IN THE CHIPPERFIELD SYSTEM, HAM ACTOR ERNIE GRICE, ALIAS HEMLOCK BONES, FACES SOME NOT VERY NICE ALIENS...
YOU'RE NOT...
...SHERLOCK HOLMES?
WELL, ACTUALLY— NO!
YOU SEE, MY REAL NAME'S ERNIE GRICE BUT I PLAY A CHARACTER CALLED HEMLOCK BONES ON THE TELLY BECAUSE ANOTHER COMPANY WAS DOING SHERLOCK HOLMES SO WE COULDN'T...
AT THAT MOMENT—
WANNA KNOW WHAT WE DO TO IMPOSTORS, SQUIRE?
I THINK I CAN GUESS.
S'RIGHT! WE TEARS 'EM LIMB FROM LIMB!
IT'S NOT REALLY SURPRISING THAT IMMINENT DEATH SHARPENS THE MIND WONDERFULLY. NOT TO MENTION THE REFLEXES...
ZZIPP!
WHUMP!
AN UNUSUALLY SMART MOVE ON ERNIE GRICE'S PART...
BUT NATURALLY DOOMED TO FAILURE...
HUU-UUURRFF!
AT THAT MOMENT—A WELCOME INTERRUPTION.
IT'S CLEAR YOU'RE JUST THE MAN FOR THE JOB!
I AM? WHAT JOB? WHO ARE YOU?
I AM HIS SUPERIORSHIP VULGAN-BARFF—LORD-HIGH-MOST-THINGS ON THE PLANET SQUARL!
MOST THINGS? WHO LOOKS AFTER THE REST?
2000 A.D. Credit Card:
SCRIPT ROBOT JACK ADRIAN
ART ROBOT JOHN HIGGINS
LETTERING ROBOT STEVE POTTER
COMPU·73E

AH! THERE'S THE RUB! NORMALLY, THE EMPEROR OF SQUARL...
UNFORTUNATELY, WE HAVE TWO CANDIDATES FOR THE POST.
IDENTICAL TWINS?!
PRECISELY! BUT BY THE HIDEOUSLY ANCIENT LAWS OF SQUARL ONLY ONE MAY RULE— THE ELDEST!
WHAT HAPPENS TO THE YOUNGEST?
HE GETS THE CHOP.
I'M THE ELDEST!
DON'T LISTEN TO HIM —I AM!
HE'S LYING! IT'S ME!
ME, I TELL YOU!
YOU SLIMY SQUIRL-MUNGE!
YOU GREASY GRELL-BROX!
YOU SEE OUR PROBLEM?
BUT SURELY SOMEONE MUST KNOW?
THEIR FAITHFUL OLD NANNY?
ALAS, SPIRITED AWAY BY GYPSIES.
THEIR FAITHFUL OLD RETAINERS?
ALL STRUCK BY LIGHTNING.
THEIR PARENTS?
AN ATTEMPTED COUP. THEY LOST THEIR HEADS— LITERALLY. MOST UNFORTUNATE...

THAT IS WHY WE'VE SPENT TWENTY YEARS COMBING THE FAR-MOST REACHES OF TIME AND SPACE FOR SOMEONE WHO CAN ROOT OUT THE TRUTH!
AND THAT'S YOU! HEMLOCK BONES— THE GREATEST DETECTIVE IN THE HISTORY OF THE UNIVERSE!
BUT I'M NOT...
I KNOW THAT, YOU BLOCKHEAD! THOSE IDIOT SCIENTISTS MADE A COMPLETE MESS-UP WHEN THEY DRAGGED YOU HERE! YOU'LL JUST HAVE TO DO THE BEST YOU CAN...
FOR TIME IS RUNNING OUT FOR THE PLANET SQUARL: WE NEED AN EMPEROR! SOMEONE STRONG... COMMANDING...
SOMEONE TO GUIDE OUR DESTINY ... LEAD US TO OUR RIGHTFUL PLACE IN THE FOREFRONT OF THE CIVILISED GALAXY!
WHILE YOU MAKE UP YOUR MIND, BONES, CONSIDER TWO THINGS.
YES?
THE OFFICIAL EXECUTIONERS.
I'LL DO IT.
THE 'GREAT DETECTIVE' SUBJECTS HIS SUSPECTS TO THE CLOSEST, MOST RIGOROUS INTERROGATION...
ARE YOU THE YOUNGEST?
NO!
WHAT ABOUT YOU?
CERTAINLY NOT!
RIGHT! THAT'S ALL I WANNA KNOW.
RARELY HAVE I BEEN CALLED UPON TO CRACK SO FORMIDABLE A CASE! FROM THE START, I'VE BEEN SURROUNDED BY A TISSUE OF LIES... A VERITABLE WEB OF DECEIT!
THE KIDNAPPING OF THE FAITHFUL OLD NANNY... THE SUDDEN ELECTROCUTION OF THE SERVANTS... THE SLAUGHTER OF THE PARENTS— ALL LEAD ME TO BUT ONE CONCLUSION!
YES?
YES?

NEITHER OF THESE TWO IS THE RIGHTFUL HEIR TO THE THRONE!
EH?
WHAT?
HANS ABOUT!
HERE IS YOUR EMPEROR! ABDUCTED FROM HIS CRADLE, HIS BIRTH-RIGHT FILCHED FROM HIM, FORCED INTO A MENIAL, INFERIOR, SECOND-RATE ROLE IN LIFE... LET'S HEAR IT FOR VULGAN-BARFF!
YAAAYYY!
IT'S A FIX!
A WISE CHOICE, BONES.
NOW CAN I GO HOME?
WELL, WHAT ABOUT A REWARD?
UNFORTUNATELY, DUE TO THE FACT THAT THE TRANS-TEMPORAL-TRACTOR-BEAM CAN ONLY BE USED ONCE— NO.
YOU ALREADY HAVE ONE, BONES... YOUR LIFE.
SO THE 'GREAT DETECTIVE' REVERTS TO A MORE ACCUSTOMED ROLE—
NEVER FEAR, ZNN'LLRR'YH, I'LL— WHOOPS!
MY HERO— NUMBSKULL!
SORRY, CONTACT LENSES SEEM TO HAVE POPPED OUT AGAIN...
WHICH ALL GOES TO SHOW THAT THE MORE THINGS CHANGE, THE MORE THEY REMAIN EXACTLY THE SAME.
The End

HOMER THE BARBARIAN

I WAS RUNNING THIS SWEET RACKET ON THE EDGE OF THE PROMETHEAN MARSHES WITH THE OLD "SWORD-IN-THE STONE" ROUTINE—
ROLL UP! ROLL UP! PULL THE MYSTIC DIRGEBLADE FROM THE STONE, AND YOU GET TO KEEP IT!
2000 A.D. Credit Card:
SCRIPT ROBOT STAVROS
ART ROBOT BELARDINELLI
LETTERING ROBOT PETER KNIGHT
COMPU-73E
ITS MAGIC POWERS WILL MAKE YOU INVULNERABLE- RICH—THE SCOURGE OF YOUR ENEMIES AND THE ENVY OF YOUR FRIENDS! ONLY TEN GROATS A THROW!
HERE- I'LL TRY IT!
ME TOO!
A BAND OF MERCENARIES WAS CAMPED NEARBY, AND BUSINESS WAS BOOMING. THE BARBARIANS ROLLED UP, AND THE GROATS ROLLED IN—
SEBEK'S BONES! I CANNOT BUDGE IT!
AAOOW! ITS MYSTIC MIGHT HATH INJURED MY INNARDS!
LET A REAL MAN TRY!

OF COURSE, IN THIS BUSINESS YOU GET TO EXPECT THE OCCASIONAL TROUBLE-MAKER.
ONE SIDE, CURS!
KARNAK'S KNEES! IT'S HOMER THE BARBARIAN!
MY TURN!
ER... EXCUSE ME. THAT'LL BE TEN GROATS, ER... SIR!
WHAT?
Glurk! F-FREE, SIR! I SAID- IT'S FREE TO YOU!
THANK YOU!
THE BARBARIAN'S MIGHTY SINEWS TENSED-TESTED-TUGGED...
SWEAT POURED FROM HIS BROW LIKE THE BLOOD OF HIS ENEMIES FROM THEIR WOUNDS-
IN SILENT COMBAT, FLESH AND BONE PITTED AGAINST SORCERY AND STONE!

BY AYYA'S ARMPITS! HOMER HAS DONE IT!
HE'S PULLED THE DIRGEBLADE FREE!

HO-YAAAAAAH!
THE BATTLE-URGE IS ON HIM! DEFEND YOURSELVES!

AAAAAH!
THE DIRGEBLADE CUTS OUR WEAPONS LIKE GOAT'S-CURD!

HE'LL SLAY US ALL— AAAAAGH!

THE BLADE FIGHTS WELL ENOUGH!

NOW, CUR— HOW WILL IT MAKE ME RICH?
UHH... TAKE THE SWORD TO A QUIET PLACE. THROW IT HIGH IN THE AIR. WHERE IT POINTS ON LANDING- THERE LIES TREASURE BEYOND BELIEF!

I WILL BE BACK IF IT DOES NOT WORK. DON'T GO AWAY!

AND SO—
SONDAR'S SKULL! THE BLADE TWISTS AND TURNS LIKE IT IS ALIVE!
OH-OH!
AAAAGH!

TOUGH LUCK, HOMER!
PLIK!
PLIK!
LIKE I WAS SAYING. IN MY RACKET YOU GET TO EXPECT A CERTAIN AMOUNT OF TROUBLE-
IT'S NOT SO MUCH THE GORE I MIND...
PLIK!
PLIK!
IT'S THE WALK HOME CARRYING THE GOLD!
WE'RE GOING TO NEED A NEW ROCK, TOO...
The End

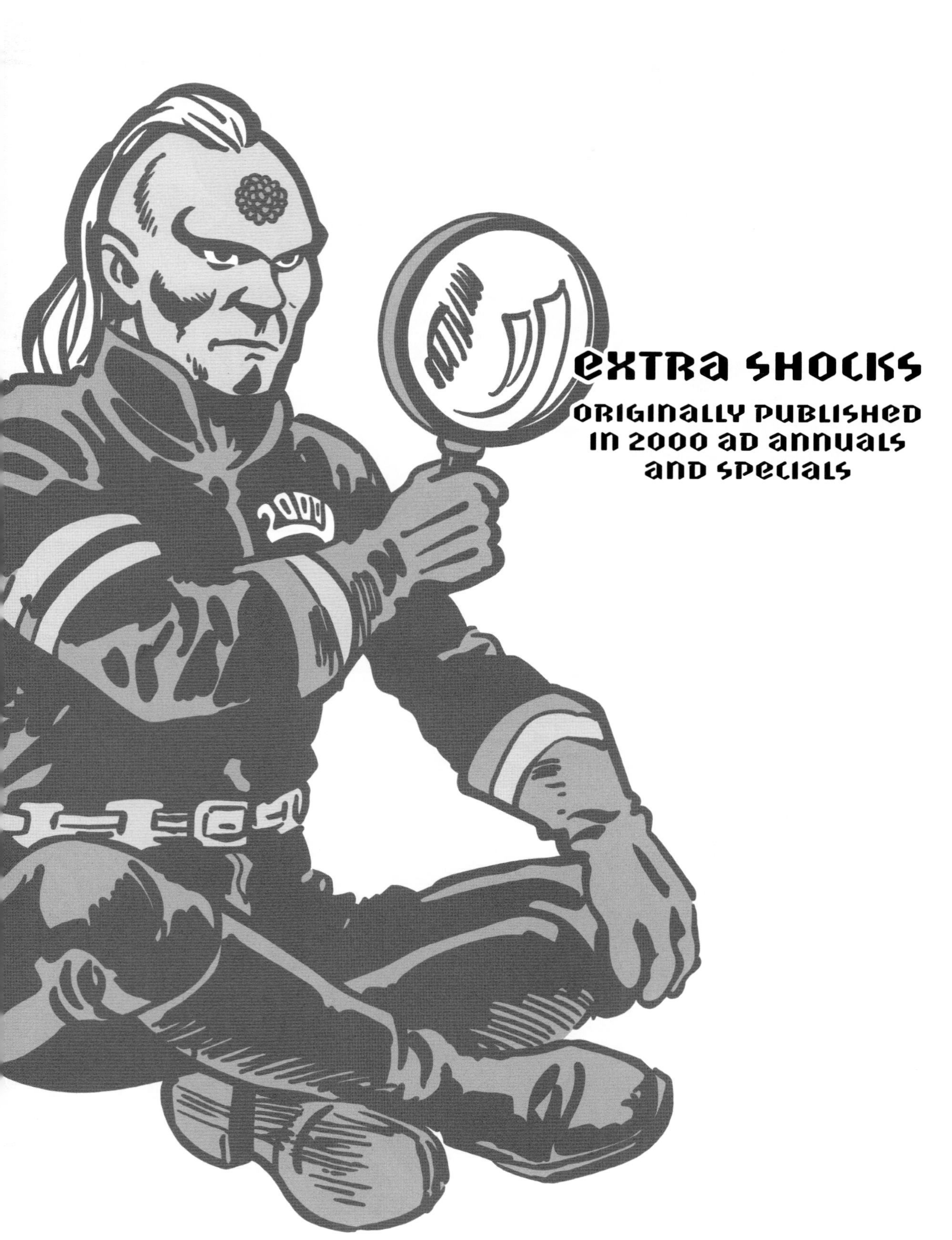

EXTRA SHOCKS

ORIGINALLY PUBLISHED IN 2000 AD ANNUALS AND SPECIALS

BENNY'S TALE
THE BIGGEST TRAFFIC SNARL-UP IN THE HISTORY OF MEGA-CITY ONE HAD TO HAVE A CAUSE! AND THE CAUSE WAS BENNY THE BEAN – THE MOST STUPID CITIZEN IN THE HISTORY OF THE FUTURISTIC MAN-SWARM!
POLICE
GET THAT STUPID CAR MOVIN', YA LUNKHEAD!
DUH... I THINK I'M LOST – AGAIN! HO WELL – I'LL JUST HAVE A NAP AND SEE IF I CAN REMEMBER WHERE I WAS GOING!
EASY MAP
HEY, C'MON – I GOTTA DELIVER THIS 'DROID BY NOON!
HMM – I SEEM TO BE MOVING AGAIN! MAYBE I'M NOT LOST AT ALL! I BETTER GET OUT THE CAR AND SEE...
Tadpole
AY LANE
...WHAT'S GOING ON! AAAWWWK!
GOOD OL' TRAFFIC PATROL! USE THAT ANTIGRAV LIFT – AND GET HIM OUT OF THERE!
HEY! WATCH THE PAINTWORK, BUDDY!
LOOKIT THE IDIOT – HE'S FALLEN OUT!
SCRUUNCH!
DAVID JACKSON

IT'LL COST YA 1,000 CREDS TO GET YOUR CAR BACK, DINGBAT!
I WISH ETHEL COULD HAVE SEEN THAT! SHE'D HAVE DIED LAUGHIN'!
DUH... (CHOKE) I WISH I WASN'T SO STUPID! I CAN NEVER DO ANYTHING RIGHT!
TIRED OF BEING STOOPID?
BEFORE- a brainless slob
AFTER- a mental genius
Hey, Dumbo! MAX ATLAS and the new CRANIO-BULGE MACHINE can change your life!
DUH — THAT SOUNDS LIKE JUST WHAT I NEED! I'LL GO ALONG AND INVETSIG — INSTEVIG — CHECK IT OUT!
IT TOOK BENNY TWO DAYS — BUT AT LAST HE FOUND THE MENTO-GYM!
MAX ATLAS MENTO-GYM
GOOD MORNING, CITIZEN! I MUST SAY YOU'RE A LIKELY-LOOKING CUSTOMER FOR OUR CRANIO-BULGE COURSE! TELL ME — HAVE YOU ALWAYS BEEN STUPID?
DUH? OH YEAH, ALWAYS!
"I REMEMBER WHEN I WAS AT SCHOOL —"
BENNY, WHEN DID THE GLORIOUS THARG ARRIVE ON OUR PLANET?
EH, 1066? NO, THAT WAS THE NEUTRON WAR! OR WAS IT? HOW ABOUT 1914?
"AND WHEN I WENT TO GET A JOB —"
SORRY, CITIZEN BEAN! ALL WE HAVE FOR SOMEONE OF YOUR LACK OF BRAINS IS STAND-IN FOR M.A.C.H. ZERO! AND I'M AFRAID YOU AIN'T GOT THE BUILD FOR IT!
DUH...THANK YOU FOR BEING SO NICE TO ME!

DON'T DESPAIR, MR. B! WHY, SOME OF THESE CLIENTS UNDERGOING TREATMENT WERE *ALMOST AS STUPID AS YOU* ONLY A FEW SHORT WEEKS AGO!
COURSE 4
A FEW SHORT WEEKS, HUH? YOU SURE MUST HAVE A REAL CLEVER MACHINE TO EDDUC—EDUCAT—*TEACH* THEM WITH!

WE HAVE INDEED, MR. B! THIS ELECTRODE GIVES THE CLIENT A CRANIAL SHOCK—AND AT THE SAME TIME *THIS* ELECTRODE FEEDS HIM INFORMATION. THE BRAIN ASSOCIATES THE TWO—AND THE DATA TO BE LEARNED IS *BURNED UNFORGETTABLY* INTO THE MIND!
AH... I SEE!
EH?
THIS SPOOL CONTAINS YOUR *FIRST, FREE LESSON*—"HOW TO HAVE A PHOTOGRAPHIC MEMORY"! THE MACHINE WILL FEED YOU A STREAM OF HIGH-DENSITY DATA... AND YOU CAN SAY *GOODBYE* TO *STUPIDITY*!
HOW CAN I GET A *'PHOTO-MIND'* IF I DON'T EVEN GOT A *CAMERA*?

THIRTY MINUTES LATER, BENNY WAS UNPLUGGED!
WELL, MR. B? WHAT DO YOU THINK?
I THINK I CAN CONSTRUCT ALGORITHMS! I CAN NAME *EVERY PLANET* IN THE KNOWN UNIVERSE! ***I CAN COUNT TO TWENTY!***

IT'S AMAZING—IT REALLY HAS WORKED! I AIN'T GONNA BE STUPID NO MORE! I MUST TAKE THE REST OF THE COURSE—*WHERE DO I SIGN UP*?

WEEK BY WEEK, AS THE COURSE PROGRESSED, LIFE STARTED TO LOOK UP FOR BENNY! FOR INSTANCE, AFTER THE LESSON ON SELF-CONFIDENCE —
OOH! WHAT A BEAUTIFUL CRANIUM!
BENNY, YOUR MENTAL MUSCLES ARE FANTASTIC!
I'M SO POPULAR! AND I OWE IT ALL TO THE MAX ATLAS CRANIO-BULGE!
THE CRANIO-BULGE SESSIONS BECAME THE HIGH POINT OF BENNY'S LIFE!
LESSON 15 TODAY — "SPEAK ANY LANGUAGE INSTANTANEOUSLY"! HOW'S THE HUNT FOR A JOB GOING, BY THE WAY?
GREAT! I START AS A TELEKINETIC THINK-TANK LEADER AS SOON AS THE COURSE IS COMPLETED!
ALL TOO SOON, IT WAS TIME FOR BENNY'S COURSE TO END.
CHING CHING! TIME TO WAKE UP, CLEVER BENNY BEAN!
I FEEL ABSOLUTELY WONDERFUL! TODAY'S MY LAST LESSON AT THE MENTO-GYM, SO I THINK I'LL SKIP MY SYNTHICAFF, CLOCK, AND PERAMBULATE DOWN TO MAX'S!
BUT AS BENNY CROSSED THE ROAD OUTSIDE HIS CON-APT BUILDING —
LOOK OUT! RUNAWAY ROBO-CAR! CLEAR THE STREET!
CLEAR THE STREET? NO NEED FOR THAT! I'M ALMOST A GENIUS — SURELY I CAN HALT A RUNAWAY ROBO-CAR! LET'S SEE NOW...

DO YOUR STUFF, BRAIN! SPEED: 50KPH! TRAJECTORY: 19° OFF MAGNETIC NORTH! EXTRAPOLATION: 78% CHANCE HEROIC SUCCESS IF I LEAP ABOARD TO STOP CAR!
21% CHANCE CAR'S OWNER IS A BEAUTIFUL WOMAN! 40% CHANCE OF RECEIVING A SUBSTANTIAL REWARD! WOW! ALL THESE POSSIBILITIES–AND MY BRAIN IS FIGURING THEM ALL OUT!
BENNY'S BRAIN ACTED LIKE LIGHTNING – BUT UNFORTUNATELY HIS BODY DIDN'T!
HERE'S A NEW CEREBRAL MESSAGE COMING IN! 100% CHANCE – REPEAT 100% CHANCE...
"...OF BEING HIT IF I DON'T GET OUT OF THE WAY!"
AAAAGH!
MEANWHILE, AT THE MENTO-GYM–
HMM, I WONDER WHERE CITIZEN BEAN IS TODAY? IT'S NOT LIKE HIM TO BE LATE! THIS IS HIS LAST LESSON, TOO – 'HOW TO MAKE DECISIONS...FAST!'
AFTER ALL, TOO MANY FACTS CAN BE DOWN-RIGHT DANGEROUS IF YOU DON'T KNOW HOW TO USE THEM!
OR, AS ONE OF MY FATHERS USED TO SAY, A LITTLE LEARNING IS A RISKY THING – BUT A LOT OF LEARNING CAN BE FATAL!

WITH ALL THE **TECHNOLOGY** THE **COPS** HAD GOING FOR THEM IN 2079 A.D. LIFE COULD BE PRETTY TOUGH FOR THE **SMALL-TIME CROOK** IN MEGACITY FOUR! FOR INSTANCE, TAKE THE CASE OF **WILLY THE CEE**—

GOING STRAIGHT

EXIT
WHY SHOULD I HAVE TO GET A JOB AND BUY FOOD? IT'S SO MUCH EASIER TO STEAL IT!

ANYTHING TO DECLARE, CUSTOMER?
MILK
OH, I AIN'T BUYING NOTHING— I WAS JUST BROWSING!

HELP! HELP!

CITY HIVE ROBOCOP

12

SHOP

DROKK IT! ALL THESE PACKETS I STOLE HAVE **ANTI-THEFT VOICETAPES** IN THEM! AND **DOUBLE** DROKK IT— HERE COMES A ROBOCOP!

I'M BEING STOLEN!

STOP THIEF!

FERRER 70

SO WILLY WAS TAKEN TO THE DOWNTOWN COURTS — TO APPEAR BEFORE JUDGE-MACHINE KOX!
JUDGEMACHINE KOX
I FIND YOU GUILTY! YOU HAVE AN APPALLING RECORD OF PETTY CRIME — BUT MY CIRCUITS TELL ME TO GIVE YOU ONE LAST CHANCE!
I PLACE YOU ON 10 YEARS' PROBATION! UNLESS YOU GO STRAIGHT FOR THIS PERIOD YOU WILL BE SENT TO THE TIME STRETCHER PRISON.
I WILL GO STRAIGHT, YOUR MACHINESHIP — I REALLY WILL! P-PLEASE NOT — THE TIME STRETCHER!
WANTED DEAD OR ALIVE THE HUMANANT
WANTED DEAD OR ALIVE THE MAD MELTOBOMBER
HUH! AIN'T NO JUSTICE! POOR OL' WILLY GETS COLLARED FOR STEALING A FEW CANS... BUT THEY CAN'T CATCH THIS "MELTO-BOMBER" LOONEY WHO'S GOING ROUND BLOWING UP PLACES ALL OVER THE CITY IF THEY DON'T PAY HIS EXTORTION MONEY!
WHY DON'T THEY BUILD COURTS CLOSER TO THE SCENE OF THE CRIME? MY FEET ARE KILLING ME — AND I STILL GOT 20 MILES TO WALK! THAT CAR... HMM, I WONDER?
THE KEYS ARE IN THE STARTER! I PROMISED TO GO STRAIGHT — BUT 20 MILES IS TOO MUCH! STEALIN' THIS CAR WILL BE MY VERY LAST JOB!
START!

JUST START THE MOTOR AND—AAAARGH! DROKKIN' ROBOALARM'S GOT ME!
UNKNOWN DRIVER! CONCLUSION: THIEF! ACTIVATE SIREN: EEEEEEEEEEE!
PHEW! LUCKY I MANAGED TO SLIP OUT OF MY OUTSIZE SHOPLIFTING COAT! BUT NOW HERE COMES THE CAR'S OWNER!
HEY YOU—STOP!
COME BACK HERE, THIEF! HELP—SOMEONE CALL A ROBOCOP!
GARBAGE PICK-UP POINT
(PUFF) IF HE CATCHES ME I'LL BE GOING STRAIGHT ALL RIGHT—STRAIGHT TO THE TIME STRETCHER! GOTTA REACH THAT CORNER—
ROBOCOPS! NEVER AROUND WHEN YOU WANT ONE! NOW WHERE'D THAT RATTY THIEF GO? I'LL DIS-INTEGRATE HIM!
WHAT A STINK! YECCH! BUT STILL—I ESCAPED! AND I SURE HAVE LEARNED MY LESSON NOW—'HONEST WILLY', THAT'S ME NOW!

I ONLY GOT 5 CREDITS TO MY NAME– BUT I'M GONNA START MY **NEW, HONEST** LIFE WITH A SLAP-UP SYNTHI-MEAL! AND BOY, DO I NEED IT!
MURPHY'S RESTAURANT
MENU
INSIDE THE RESTAURANT–
YOU GOTTA BE RICH TO EAT HERE! I MEAN, LOOK AT THAT CLASSY GUY CRADLING HIS **BRIEF-CASE!** I BET IT'S FULL OF **MOON-GEMS** OF **CREDITS,** THE WAY HE'S CUDDLING IT!
MURPHY'S MENU
HEY– I CAN'T BELIEVE IT! THAT GUY'S GOING– BUT HE'S **LEFT HIS CASE!** HE MUST HAVE FORGOTTEN IT!
BUT WILLY DIDN'T GET FAR!
I SHOULD BE **HONEST** AND RUN AFTER HIM!
BUT IF I **STEAL** IT, I WON'T NEED A **JOB!**
ROBOCOPS– THEY'RE EVERY-WHERE! MAYBE STEALIN' THIS CASE **AIN'T** SUCH A GOOD IDEA!
I GOTTA BE HONEST– I'M A **LOSER** AT CRIME! BUT I COULD BE A **WINNER** AS AN HONEST CITIZEN!

YEAH, I'LL TAKE THE CASE BACK! I WON'T EVEN LOOK INSIDE IT! MAYBE THE OWNER'LL GIVE ME A REWARD! THERE HE IS NOW—IN THAT VIDBOOTH!
VIDEOFONO
VID
NO TABAC

I WARNED YOU, MURPHY! AND THE MELTO-BOMBER DOESN'T JOKE! YOU WON'T PAY ME EXTORTION MONEY—SO I AUTOMATICALLY DETONATE THE MELTO-BOMB I HID IN YOUR EATERIE!

I'M SQUEEZING THE DESTRUCT TRIGGER NOW! BYEBYE MURPH— AAAARRGH!
HELLO. I'M HONEST CITIZEN WILLY THE CEE AND I FOUND YOUR CASE AND—

AAAAAAA!
SSCCHHLLUURPP!

IT SURE IS TOUGH BEING A PETTY CROOK IN MEGACITY FOUR, EH, EARTHLETS? IF THE ROBOCOPS DON'T GET YOU, THEN YOUR FELLOW-CROOKS WILL!
VIDE
MAYBE WILLY'S DISHONESTY HAD MELTED AWAY— BUT UNFORTUNATELY, SO HAD WILLY!
End

THE MAN WHO SAVED THE WORLD
THE MANIAA WERE DIFFERENT FROM HUMANS IN MANY WAYS — TECHNOLOGICALLY MORE ADVANCED, PHYSICALLY MORE POWERFUL, EMOTIONALLY MORE STABLE. THERE WAS ONE SIMILARITY, THOUGH. LIKE MEN, THEY LOVED TO CONQUER . . .
THERE IT IS, JAEK... THE PLANET EARTH. NOT A PARTICULARLY VALUABLE PRIZE, BUT A PRIZE, NEVERTHELESS.
I WILL WIN IT FOR US, COMMANDER KAEZ, I AM CHAMPION OF ALL THE MANIAA — MORE THAN A MATCH FOR ANYONE IN THIS GALAXY.
BUT EARTHMEN MAY HAVE DIFFERENT CUSTOMS, JAEK.
IF THEY DO NOT SEND A CHAMPION AGAINST ME, EARTH WILL BE DESTROYED FOR ITS COWARDLINESS! IT IS OUR LAW, COMMANDER.
YOUR DESTINATION IS OLYMPIC CITY. THE HOME OF THEIR STRONGEST INHABITANTS. FIND THEIR CHAMPION AND DESTROY HIM!
ACTIVATE THE TRANSPORTER BEAM!
BY THE 22ND CENTURY, OLYMPIC CITY, CALIFORNIA, WAS INDEED THE HOME OF EARTH'S MIGHTIEST ATHLETES. BUT, LIKE ALL CITIES IT HAD ITS SHARE OF, SHALL WE SAY, UNDESIRABLES...
APOLOGIES FOR REQUIRING TO USE FORCE, SIR. BUT I CANNOT ALLOW YOU TO ENTER. IMPROPER DRESS.
MECHANICAL MORON!

BACK TO THE CITY DUMPS — WHERE YOU BELONG!
HECK, EVEN THE KIDS CALL ME NAMES NOW! AND TO THINK I COULD ONCE HAVE BEEN A CHAMPION ATHLETE!
TEARS OF SELF-PITY WELLED INTO FRED PEART'S EYES...
EVER SINCE I BROKE MY LEG TWENTY YEARS AGO, MY LUCK'S GONE FROM BAD TO WORSE!
I'LL GET SOME PEACE AND QUIET HERE IN THIS PARK AND MAYBE A BIT OF SHELTER FROM THE RAIN. HUH! NO JOB, NO MONEY — WHAT A LIFE!
BUT THE NIGHT HELD NEITHER, NOR QUIET... AS PEART SAT TO REST...
GREETINGS, EARTHMAN. I COME IN HOSTILITY!
I KNEW IT! JUST MY LUCK TO RUN INTO SOME KINDA FREAK, EVEN IN HERE.
BEAT IT, FREAK-FACE! THE LAST THING I NEED IS TO GET HASSLED BY A KOOK LIKE YOU!
HE IS STRONG—AND VERY AGGRESSIVE.
I SEEK YOUR CHAMPION, EARTHLING.
I'M MY OWN CHAMPION, BUD. THE WAY I LIVE, YOU GOTTA BE A CHAMPION JUST TO SURVIVE. AND I'M A CHAMPION SURVIVOR!
THEN YOU ARE THE ONE I SEEK.

AN ALIEN GAUNTLET LANDED AT THE TRAMP'S FEET.
I CHALLENGE YOU TO A DUEL, EARTH-CHAMPION... AND THE WINNER TAKES THE WORLD!
AS YOU ARE THE CHALLENGED, YOU MAY CHOOSE WEAPONS. WHAT SHALL IT BE— THE LASER LANCE?
WHAT KINDA STUNT IS THIS? WHERE'D THAT TREE GO?
OR HOW ABOUT A HALLUCINATORY BATTLE OF THE MINDS? WOULD YOU LIKE THAT, EARTH-CHAMPION?
NO! NO! TAKE IT AWAY!
THIS JOKER AIN'T JOKING! I'M GETTING OUTTA HERE!
YOU WISH TO CHALLENGE ME TO A FOOT RACE? I THINK YOU WILL LOSE.
HOW DO I GET OUT OF THIS? CURSE MY STUPID LUCK!
BACK ON THE ALIEN SHIP, THE COMMANDER WAS FEELING QUITE SMUG...
JAEK WILL HAVE LITTLE TROUBLE BESTING THIS CHAMPION—AND UNDER GALACTIC LAW, TO THE WINNER GOES THE WORLD! AYE, WE WILL SOON POSSESS ANOTHER PLANET!

COME, EARTHMAN— YOUR TIME IS RUNNING OUT! IF YOU DO NOT FIGHT ME, WE WILL DESTROY YOUR WHOLE PLANET WITH ONE BLAST FROM OUR SPACECRAFT! *IT IS THE LAW!*

S-SPACECRAFT DESTROY THE PLANET! SO THAT'S IT— THIS CREEP MUST BE AN *ALIEN!*

THERE'S NO WAY I CAN BEAT THIS DUDE ON *HIS* TERMS—OR ON *ANY* TERMS. BUT MAYBE IF FOR ONCE I COULD HAVE A LITTLE *LUCK...*

OKAY, FELLA THIS IS THE WEAPON I CHOOSE. WE'RE GOING TO *CUT CARDS.*

CUT CARDS? BUT WHERE IS THE DANGER, THE GLORY IN THIS? WHAT KIND OF CHAMPION ARE YOU?
YOU SAID IT WAS MY CHOICE—THIS IS THE WEAPON I CHOOSE! COME ON, ARE YOU YELLOW? HIGH CARD WINS—AND ACES IS HIGH.
SINCE THE CHOICE IS YOURS, WE WILL PLAY THIS AND I WILL BEAT YOU.

SO THE DEADBEAT CALLED PEART GAMBLED HIS LUCK—AND HIS WORLD—ON THE TURN OF A CARD!

I'VE WON, I'VE WON! MY LUCK'S CHANGED! I'VE SAVED THE WORLD!
I HAVE BEEN BESTED. I HAVE FAILED IN MY MISSION!

BEAM ME UP! PREPARE TO SET A NEW COURSE FOR ANOTHER SYSTEM.
HAHAHAHA! I'M A WINNER—I WON THE WHOLE PLANET!

PEART'S HYSTERICAL JOY LASTED BUT A FEW MINUTES.
YOUR LUCK AIN'T IN HERE, LAWBREAKER. BURNING PARK BUSHES IS AN OFFENCE – YOU'RE UNDER ARREST.
WHAT-WHAT ARE YOU ROBOCOPS TALKING ABOUT? DON'T YOU UNDERSTAND – I JUST SAVED THE WORLD!

HE SAVED THE WORLD! BOY, THIS GUY'S REALLY LOST HIS MARBLES!
YEAH! I'D BETTER RADIO FOR THE BOYS IN WHITE!

SOON–
WHAT ARE YOU DOING? YOU-YOU GOTTA BELIEVE ME...
YEAH, YEAH, TAKE IT EASY, BUDDY. YOU'RE GOING TO BE ALL RIGHT!

YOU CAN'T DO THIS TO ME! I'M THE MAN WHO SAVED THE WORLD!
POOR GUY. FRED PEART, WASN'T IT?
OLYMPIC CITY HOME FOR THE MENTALLY SICK.
YEAH. SLEEPING ROUGH AND LYING OUT IN THE RAIN ALL NIGHT FINALLY MADE HIM FLIP HIS LID. IN A WAY, I GUESS THAT WAS ALWAYS ON THE CARDS!

THARG'S FUTURE-SHOCKS
DUEL IN THE DUNES

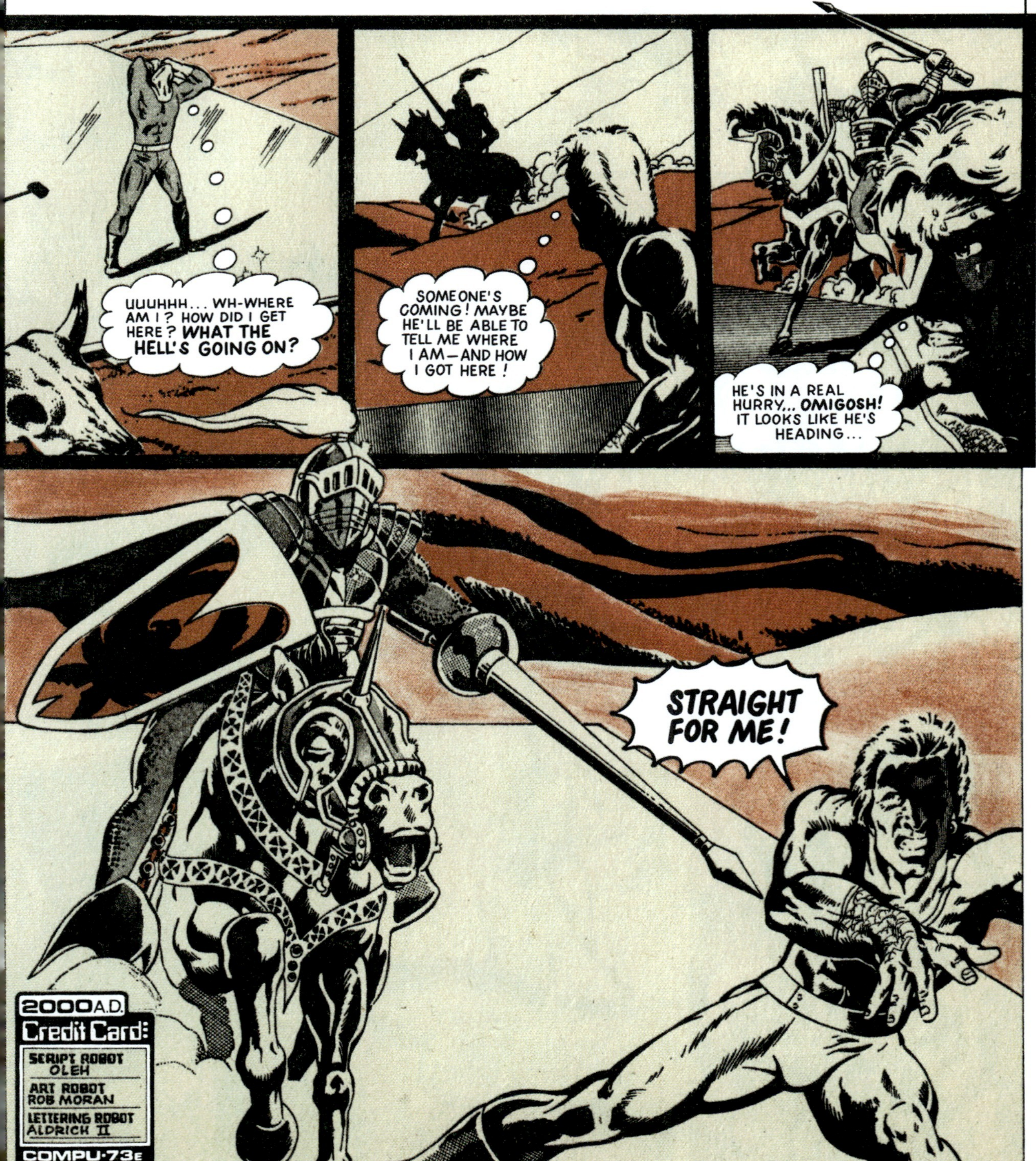

AAARGH! THAT WAS CLOSE!
HOLD IT, BUDDY! I DON'T KNOW WHAT I DID TO UPSET YOU, BUT CAN'T WE TALK THIS OVER FIRST?
UUUGH! I GUESS YOU JUST DON'T WANT TO DISCUSS IT, EH!
HE'S GOING TO CHARGE AGAIN! BUT—WHAT'S THAT? SOMETHING'S ...APPEARED ON THE PLATFORM! IT—IT'S A MACHINE GUN!
AS THE STRANGE KNIGHT CHARGED, KAIN DIVED—
I DONNO HOW IT GOT HERE—BUT I HOPE FOR MY SAKE THAT THE BLAMED THING WORKS!
AIEEEEEE!
PTING! PTING! PTING!
THANK THE STARS! IT'S STOPPED HIM! HE WON'T BE JOUSTING AGAIN!

AS THE MORTALLY WOUNDED KNIGHT DISAPPEARED BEHIND A SAND DUNE—
WHAT DOES IT SAY ON THAT PLAQUE? MAYBE IT'LL HELP ME UNDERSTAND WHAT ON EARTH'S HAPPENING HERE?
..TEN MINUTES WITH WEAPON.......TEN MINUTES WITHOUT..THEN WEAPON RETURNS......
MORAN 77
SUDDENLY...
'TEN MINUTES WITH WEAPON'... WHAT DOES THAT MEAN? WHAT— AARGH!
PREPARE TO MEET THY MAKER!
BUT...
IT- IT'S VANISHED! SO THAT'S WHAT THAT PLAQUE MEANT— AND MY TEN MINUTES MUST BE UP!
ANOTHER ONE! WHEREVER THIS IS IT SURE IS UN-HEALTHY!
I HAVE ASKED THEE FOR NOUGHT, DOOMED ONE!
OKAY—YOU ASKED FOR THIS!
STAND STILL! FACE THY DEATH LIKE A MAN— NOT A LILY-LIVERED COWARD!
GOT TO STALL FOR TIME...
OKAY, OKAY— I MEAN, YEA VERILY! KILL ME IF THOU WISH— BUT FIRST... ER... LET ME MAKE PEACE WITH MY MAKER!
THY WISH IS GRANTED— I WILL STAY MY HAND AWHILE.
I HAVE NOT BEEN A GOOD MAN... YET I HOPETH THAT WHILE I STALLETH FOR TIME, THE OTHER WEAPON MENTIONED BY THE PLAQUE DOTH APPEAR!

AMEN — AND LET'S MOVE!
KNAVE! THOU HAS TRICKED ME! FOR THAT, THOU WILT PERISH SLOWLY!
AGAIN, KAIN DASHED TO THE PODIUM—
HE'S STILL AFTER ME! BUT THE PLAQUE WAS RIGHT—
AND THERE'S MY NEXT WEAPON!
KAIN THREW THE GRENADE...
AIEEEE!
BAAROOOM!
WHEW! WHAT A WAY TO GO! BUT HANG ON — THOSE BITS OF WIRE — THOSE CIRCUITS... IT WASN'T A REAL KNIGHT! IT WAS A ROBOT — A STINKING ANDROID!
I DONNO WHAT'S GOING ON HERE — BUT I'VE HAD ENOUGH! I'M GETTING OUT!
BUT AS KAIN HEADED AWAY FROM THE PLATFORM—
YEEOW! WHAT IN THE NAME OF THANATOS—? IT— IT'S SOME KIND OF INVISIBLE WALL!

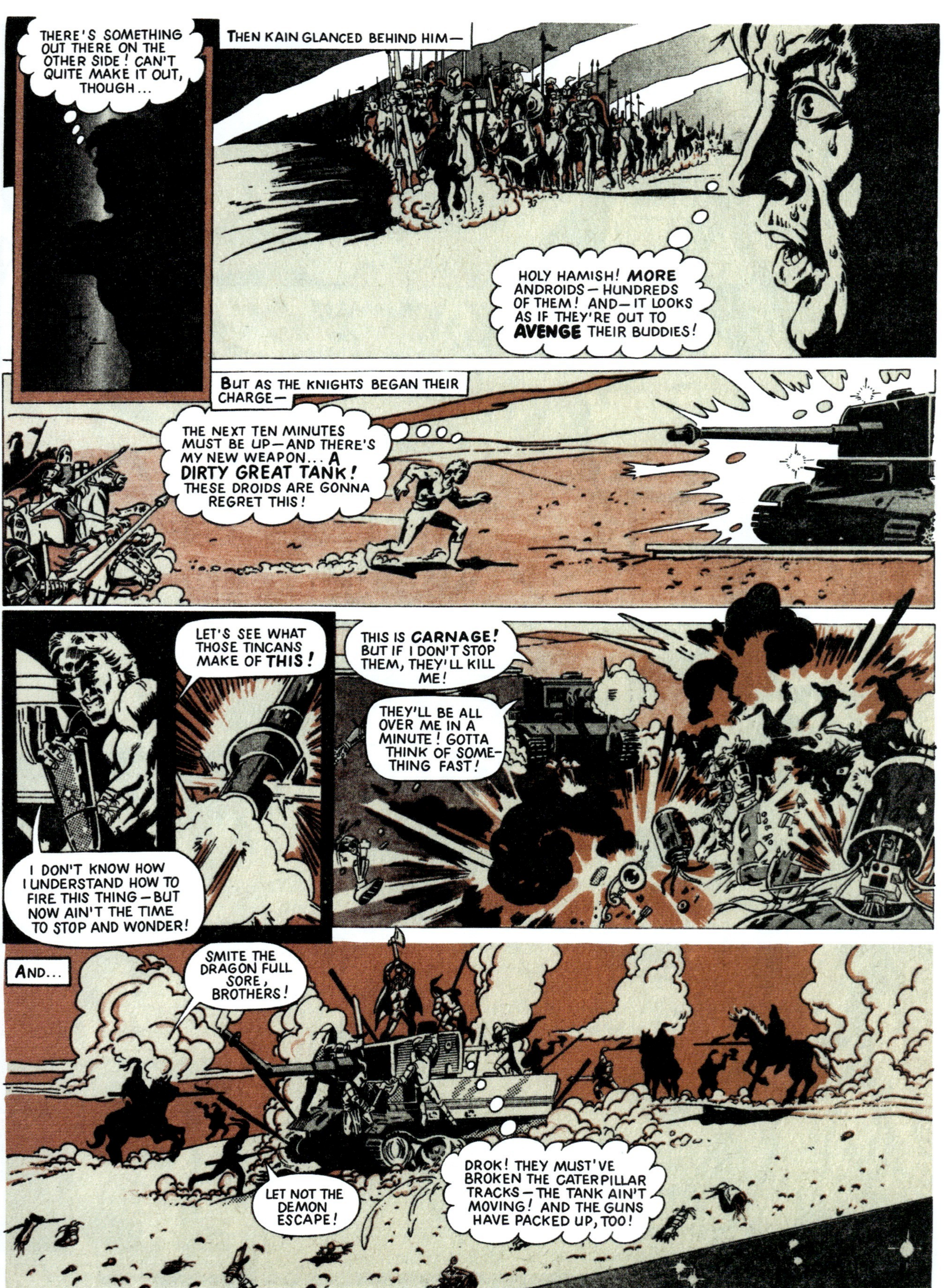
THERE'S SOMETHING OUT THERE ON THE OTHER SIDE! CAN'T QUITE MAKE IT OUT, THOUGH...
THEN KAIN GLANCED BEHIND HIM—
HOLY HAMISH! MORE ANDROIDS—HUNDREDS OF THEM! AND—IT LOOKS AS IF THEY'RE OUT TO AVENGE THEIR BUDDIES!
BUT AS THE KNIGHTS BEGAN THEIR CHARGE—
THE NEXT TEN MINUTES MUST BE UP—AND THERE'S MY NEW WEAPON... A DIRTY GREAT TANK! THESE DROIDS ARE GONNA REGRET THIS!
LET'S SEE WHAT THOSE TINCANS MAKE OF THIS!
I DON'T KNOW HOW I UNDERSTAND HOW TO FIRE THIS THING—BUT NOW AIN'T THE TIME TO STOP AND WONDER!
THIS IS CARNAGE! BUT IF I DON'T STOP THEM, THEY'LL KILL ME!
THEY'LL BE ALL OVER ME IN A MINUTE! GOTTA THINK OF SOMETHING FAST!
AND...
SMITE THE DRAGON FULL SORE, BROTHERS!
LET NOT THE DEMON ESCAPE!
DROK! THEY MUST'VE BROKEN THE CATERPILLAR TRACKS—THE TANK AIN'T MOVING! AND THE GUNS HAVE PACKED UP, TOO!

INSIDE THE TANK, KAIN RACED AGAINST TIME...
OIL
SUPER LUBE
THEY'LL BURST THEIR WAY IN HERE IN A MINUTE! GOTTA WORK FAST—AND PRAY THIS DOES WHAT I WANT IT TO!
SOON...
JUST HOPE I CAN GET CLEAR WITHOUT BEING NOTICED... AND BEFORE THE WHOLE LOT GOES BOOM!
KAABOOOM!
UH... MY HEAD... SOMETHING WRONG... BZZT! BZZ! I FEEL... BZZ! STRANGE!
DONNO WHERE THESE WEIRD ROBOTS CAME FROM— BUT THEY WON'T BOTHER ME AGAIN!
DZZZT! OH. NO! I... I... BZZT! I AM A DROID, TOO—BZZT!
COME ON— DINNER'S READY!
AW, DADDY, YOU ALWAYS WIN WHEN WE PLAY AT ROBO-BATTLE!
NEVER MIND, SON— TOMORROW YOU CAN HAVE 'MAN WITH WEAPONS' AND I'LL TAKE THE 'ANCIENT WARRIORS'!
ROBO-BATTLE
WHAT DID YOU THINK OF THE GAME OF THE FUTURE? IT'S WHAT YOU EARTHLETS CALL 'FANTASTIC'— UNLESS YOU'RE ONE OF THE ROBO-PLAYERS, OF COURSE!
THE END

THE MAN FROM 2000
2000 A.D. Credit Card:
SCRIPT ROBOT OLEH STEPANIUK
ART ROBOT D. HINE
LETTERING ROBOT STEVE POTTER
COMPU-73E
THE YEAR... 1000 B.C. THE PLACE... ANCIENT GREECE!
BYLOR! HE- HE'S VANISHED! WE STAND NO CHANCE AGAINST THESE BANDITS NOW!
THE YEAR... 1 B.C. THE PLACE... ROME!
LANTUS HAS DISAPPEARED! THE DEFENCE WALL IS BROKEN!
THE YEAR... 1000 A.D. THE PLACE... GREENLAND!
KING GRANDVELT— HE'S VANISHED! WE'RE DOOMED! WE CAN NEVER WIN WITHOUT THE KING!
THE YEAR... 2000 A.D. THE PLACE... ALDERSHOT!
WHERE IS THAT TROOPER? I COULD HAVE SWORN HE WAS HERE A MINUTE AGO... THAT'S THE SECOND TIME THIS WEEK HE'S BEEN LATE FOR ROLL-CALL!
ALL FOUR REAPPEARED AT THE SAME TIME, IN THE SAME PLACE— ON BOARD AN ALIEN CRAFT 2000 MILES OUTSIDE EARTH'S ATMOSPHERE!
STOMM! A GREEK, A ROMAN AND A VIKING! WHAT'S GOING ON HERE? WHAT IS THIS PLACE?

IN ANOTHER ROOM ON THE CRAFT, ALIEN EYES WATCHED THE EARTHMEN —
GREEK 2-1
ROMAN 3-1
VIKING 5-1
EURAN 5-4 (FAV)
PLACE YOUR BETS NOW, GAMBLERS! FIND THE WINNER — THE ONE WHO WILL KILL THE OTHERS — AND MAKE YOUR FORTUNE!
THE HUMAN SOLDIERS HAVE ARRIVED!
IN THE CAPTURE CHAMBER, THREE EARTHMEN REACTED PREDICTABLY. BUT —
UH?
BY JUPITER!
WHAT? A MAGIC VALL!
SOME KIND OF FORCE BARRIER CAGING US IN! LOOKS LIKE WE'RE ON SOME KIND OF SPACESHIP... BUT WHY? HOW'D WE GET HERE?
YOU ARE HERE FOR ONE REASON — TO FIGHT! WHEN THE BARRIERS DROP, YOU WILL BATTLE EACH OTHER... TO THE DEATH!
SO THAT'S WHY— WE'RE TO BE SOME KIND OF ALIEN ENTERTAIN-MENT!
I COULD KILL THESE THREE WITH ONE BLAST — BUT I'M DAMNED IF I WILL JUST TO GIVE SOME ALIEN CREEP HIS FUN!
GOTTA FIND A WAY OUT OF HERE... HMM— CAMERAS! SO THEY'RE WATCHING US...
THE FORCEFIELD WAS SWITCHED OFF, AND —
LAST BETS NOW, PLEASE! THEY'RE OFF!
UNNGH!
GOT TO ACT QUICKLY— OR WE'LL ALL BE DEAD MEAT! BLASTER TO STUN!
AAARGH!
THAT'S THOSE TWO TAKEN CARE OF! NOW WHERE'S THE VIK— OH NO!

HAR! NOW VE SEE HOW YOU FIGHT WITHOUT MAGIC METAL!
UUUHH!
STOP! I'M NOT THE ENEMY! WE SHOULD BE FIGHTING THE ALIENS...
THE VIKING SWUNG — BUT THE TROOPER USED HIS SPECIAL UNARMED COMBAT TECHNIQUE —
WODIN CURSE THEE! YOU BLOCK MY BLOW!
OOOOFFFF!
AS THE ROMAN AND GREEK RECOVERED, THE TROOPER SNATCHED UP HIS BLASTER —
OKAY NOW, GUYS. JUST TAKE IT EASY TILL WE GET THIS THING SORTED OUT!
IN THE ALIENS' BETTING OFFICE —
THEY'RE SUPPOSED TO BE FIGHTING!
NO—THE DEATH GAME GOES ON! BUT NOW YOU BET ON THE LAST ONE TO DIE!
HE'S RUINED THE GAME! MY BET'S OFF!
YEAH— GIVE US OUR MONEY BACK!

WE RE-SET THE TIME CONTROLS... AND NOW WE SEND IN...
KREEEAAGH!
...THE MONSTERS FROM 1,000,000 B.C.!
MY DOK! LISTEN — IF WE'RE TO HAVE A CHANCE IN HELL OF BEATING THOSE THINGS, WE'RE GONNA HAVE TO FIGHT TOGETHER!
MY AXE IS WITH YOU!
AYE! AND MY SWORD!
AND MINE!
AS THE HIDEOUS HORDE ATTACKED, THE SOLDIERS RETREATED TO THE CORNER —
SOMEHOW I'VE GOT TO FIND THE ALIENS! BUT I NEED TIME...
RIGHT! YOU TWO — BY MY SIDE! WEDGE YOUR SHIELDS LIKE THIS —
THEN VE HAVE BOTH HANDS FREE! IS GOOD!

THE THREE SOLDIERS FORMED A HUMAN WALL... AND THE MONSTERS STRUCK!
HOPE THEY CAN HOLD THEM BACK FOR LONG ENOUGH! I'LL TAKE OUT THE CAMERA CLUSTER — GIVE THE ALIENS SOMETHING TO WORRY ABOUT!
HAAAR!
GOT THE CAMERAS! NOW IF I CAN JUST FOLLOW THE CONNECTING CABLES...
IN THE ALIENS' VIEWROOM —
THE SCREEN'S DEAD!
THE MAN FROM 2000 HAS RUINED THE WHOLE GAME!
DON'T BE ABSURD! THE HUMANS WILL NOT BEAT THE MONSTERS! THE GAME GOES ON — THE WAGERS STILL STAND!
THE WIRES DISAPPEAR THERE! SO THE ALIENS MUST BE BEHIND THAT WALL!
HURRY, STRANGE ONE! DER BEASTS VILL OVERWHELM US!
I WAS RIGHT — THEY'RE BEHIND HERE OKAY!
GOT IT! I'LL BLAST A HOLE THROUGH TO THE ALIENS — LET THEM FACE THEIR OWN DAMN MONSTERS!
AIEEEE! HE'S FOUND US!
THE MONSTERS — THE MONSTERS WILL GET THROUGH!

OKAY— ONE LAST EFFORT! DRIVE THESE MONSTROSITIES THROUGH TO MEET THEIR MASTERS!
HHAAYYEEE!

GUIDED BY THE BARRIER OF SHIELDS, THE MONSTERS SWARMED THROUGH THE OPENING...
AIEEEE!
QUICKLY— SEND THEM BACK! SEND— ARRGH!
GOT TO RE-SET TIME TRACTOR BEAM...

WITH HIS DYING BREATH, THE ALIEN REVERSED THE CONTROLS... BUT IT WAS TOO LATE! HIS MASTER— AND THEIR CUSTOMERS— WERE DEAD!

THE FOUR SOLDIERS WERE RETURNED TO THEIR OWN TIMES— IN PERFECT CONDITION— AS IF THEY'D ONLY BEEN GONE FOR ONE SECOND! THE EVENT WAS OBLITERATED FROM THEIR MINDS... AS IF IT HAD NEVER HAPPENED!
THE GREEK INSPIRED HIS COMPANIONS WITH SO MUCH DETERMINATION THAT THEY ROUTED THEIR ATTACKERS...

CENTURION LANTUS FILLED THE GAP HE'D LEFT— AND WENT ON TO BECOME THE EMPEROR'S FAVOURITE CENTURION!

KING GRANDVELT TAUGHT HIS MEN HOW TO USE THEIR SHIELDS LIKE ROMANS-
—AND HE NEVER LOST A BATTLE!

AND AS FOR THE MAN FROM 2000 A.D....
SECURITY TROOPER 34839/AX— YOU'RE LATE FOR ROLL-CALL! YOU'RE ON A CHARGE!
B-BUT..? I'VE BEEN HERE ALL THE TIME, SIR!
The End

THARG'S FUTURE-SHOCKS

The Mumps from Beyond the Moon

MANY EARTHLETS HAVE ASKED ME TO PROGRAMME A **FUTURE SHOCK** STORY WITH A **HAPPY ENDING**. SO I, THARG, HAVE LOOKED DEEP INTO THE FUTURE— AND I PRESENT YOU WITH THIS CHEERFUL LITTLE TALE...

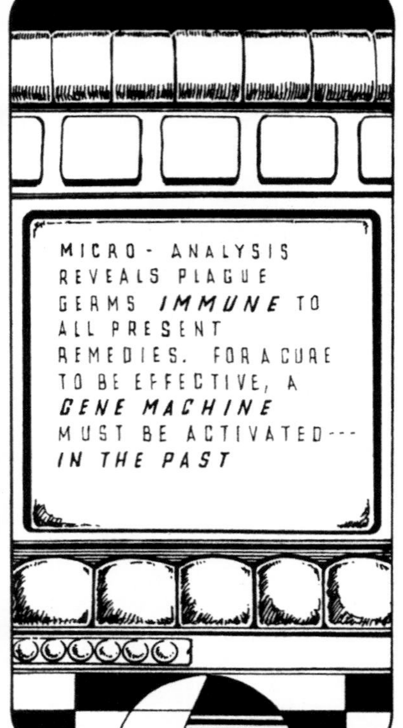

YOU MEAN... TIME TRAVEL? BUT IT'S TOO DANGEROUS! ONE SMALL ERROR IN THE PAST CAN BE MAGNIFIED A BILLION TIMES... UNTIL IT CHANGES THE WHOLE FUTURE!
WE HAVE NO CHOICE! I-I DON'T THINK THE GERM-FREE SUITS ARE GOING TO KEEP US SAFE MUCH LONGER...

CHIEF! YOUR FACE—
YES (GROAN)... UHHH! IT HURTS, BOB! YOU'VE GOT TO DO AS THE COMPUTER SAYS— FOR THE SAKE OF EARTH!

I-I THINK I'LL TAKE THE REST OF THE DAY OFF...
GRUD— I COULD BE NEXT! OKAY, COMPUTER— TELL ME ABOUT THIS CRAZY SCHEME OF YOURS...

YOU WILL TRAVEL BACK IN A TIME-TUBE TO THE YEAR 1980. CONDITIONS THEN ARE PERFECT FOR THE GENE MACHINE TO DO ITS WORK
THE MACHINE WILL STRENGTHEN MAN'S GENES IN THE PAST— WHICH MEANS THAT WE IN THE FUTURE WILL BE CHANGED, TOO. WE'LL BE IMMUNE TO THE PLAGUE!

YOU ARRANGE IT, COMPUTER— AND I'LL GO! I'D AS SOON BE A DEAD HERO IN THE PAST AS FOOD FOR SPACE-BUGS IN THE PRESENT!
C'MON, HUME— YOU'RE NEARLY DEAD ALREADY. GIVE A HARD-WORKIN' DROID A BREAK AND HOP IN THE CREMATION BOX!
G-GET AWAY FROM ME! LEAVE ME ALONE!

WITHIN A MATTER OF HOURS THE TIME-TUBE WAS KITTED OUT... AND BOB WAS ON HIS WAY TO SAVE THE EARTH!
91
90
89
AUTO CALENDAR
2000 A.D.
Credit Card:
SCRIPT ROBOT STACCATO
ART ROBOT ROBIN SMITH
LETTERING ROBOT JACK POTTER
COMPU-73E

AND...
I'VE LANDED RIGHT IN THE HEART OF PRIMITIVE LONDON! HMMM, THE PEOPLE HAVE NOTICED ME... PERHAPS I HAD BETTER MAKE MY CRAFT—
INVISIBLE!
LOOK UP THERE— A UFO!
ARRGH! ALIEN ATTACK!
HUH? WH-WHERE'D IT GO?

WHILE HE WAITED FOR THE COMPUTER TO SET UP A GENE MACHINE, BOB WENT IN SEARCH OF ENTERTAINMENT— 1980 STYLE!
FORBIDDEN PLANE
HMMM... THIS LOOKS PROMISING! MUST HAVE A LOOK...

AN HOUR LATER...
DO BE SURE TO CALL AGAIN, SIR!
WOW! WE DON'T HAVE PUBLICATIONS LIKE THIS IN 2500! THESE COMICS ARE AMAZING!
DEN PL

BACK IN THE TIME-TUBE...
JUDGE DREDD IS FANTASTIC! TOTAL THRILL-POWER!

HAHAHA! THESE DROIDS ARE CRAZY!

WOW! THIS GUY REALLY IS MIGHTY! THESE COMICS ARE SO GOOD, I'VE JUST GOT TO TAKE SOME BACK TO THE FUTURE WITH ME!

EVENTUALLY, EXHAUSTED BY THE UNACCUSTOMED THRILL-POWER, BOB FELL ASLEEP...
ZZZZZ
MODIFICATION IMPUT

SUDDENLY—
ATTENTION! ACTIVATE GENE MACHINE NOW! FEED IN PROGRAMME! FEED IN PROGRAMME!
MODIFICATION IMPUT SLOT
WHAT—? WHASSAT?

ONLY HALF AWAKE, BOB PICKED UP THE FIRST THING TO HAND—
THE GENE MACHINE PROGRAMME? OH... OH YEAH! OF COURSE! I'VE JUST GOT TO FEED IT IN LIKE—
MODIFICATION IMPUT SLOT
DROKK! WHAT IN THE NAME OF TOMORROW AM I DOING?

I'VE GOTTA GET THIS COMIC OUT OF THE MACHINE!
PHEW! GOT IT! WELL... MOST OF IT, ANYWAY!

THAT'S THE CORRECT PROGRAMME IN NOW... I ONLY HOPE THAT SILLY MISTAKE DIDN'T DO THE MACHINE ANY HARM...
GENE MODIFICATION

WELL, EVERYTHING SEEMS TO BE ALL RIGHT... I JUST HOPE THE COMPUTER'S PLAN WORKS!

A MERE HOUR LATER, THE GENE MACHINE'S WORK WAS FINISHED AND BOB WAS HEADING BACK TO HIS OWN TIME—

CALLING BOB! THE GENE MACHINE WORKED—WE'RE WELL AGAIN! OUR NEW GENE PATTERNS CAN'T BE AFFECTED BY THE PLAGUE!
WOW! THAT'S A RELIEF!
2500
YOU'RE A HERO, BOB! HALF OF LONDON'S TURNED OUT TO MEET YOU!

BUT WHEN THE TIME-TUBE LANDED AND BOB STEPPED OUT—
WELCOME BACK BOB!
BORAG THUNGG, BOB!
BOB FAN CLUB
BORAG THUNGG, BOB!
BORAG THUNGG, BOB!
BORAG THUNGG, EARTHLET!
WELL DONE, BOB! YOU SAVED THE WORLD!
IT SEEMS BOB'S SMALL MISTAKE DID HAVE AN EFFECT, AFTER ALL! BUT NEVER MIND— WHO COULD WISH FOR A HAPPIER ENDING THAN SEEING THE WHOLE WORLD TURN INTO THE MIGHTY THARG?
The End

THARG'S FUTURE-SHOCKS

THE LAST OF THE FIRST ONES!

THE CRAFT APPEARED AS IF FROM NOWHERE, SLIPPED EFFORTLESSLY INTO EARTH-ORBIT, AND BEGAN TO BEAM UNINTELLIGIBLE RADIO SIGNALS TOWARDS THE PLANET SURFACE.

INITIAL REACTIONS WERE FUELLED BY PANIC . . .

IT'S A **SOV-BLOK DEATH DEVICE!** HAS TO BE. STAND BY TO LAUNCH 'PAY BACK' MISSILES!

2000 A.D.
Credit Card:

SCRIPT ROBOT
G. P. RICE

ART ROBOT
COLIN WILSON

LETTERING ROBOT
TOM FRAME

COMPU-73E

. . . AND **MUTUAL** DISTRUST.
THE CAPITALIST PIGS HAVE INVADED NEUTRAL SPACE WITH THEIR KILLER SATELLITE. PREPARE **'HARD-VAK' TORPEDOES**...

BUT...
THE MYSTERIOUS VESSEL WAS SECURE BEHIND AN **ENERGY SHIELD**.

EARTH'S LEADERS BEGAN TO SEE REASON...
BUT, DMITRI, IF IT ISN'T **YOURS** AND IT ISN'T **OURS** – WHOSE IS IT? AND WHAT'S THE MEANING OF THIS CRAZY SIGNAL WE'VE BEEN PICKING UP?

WHITNEY

ONE MAN THOUGHT HE KNEW THE ANSWER – NOTED LINGUIST **WEBSTER DUDLEY**.

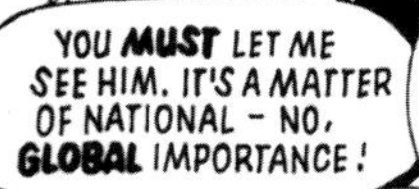

YOU **MUST** LET ME SEE HIM. IT'S A MATTER OF NATIONAL – NO, **GLOBAL** IMPORTANCE!
I DON'T CARE HOW FAMOUS YOU ARE, BUD. YOU DON'T MARCH IN HERE DEMANDING TO SEE THE PRESIDENT!

BAH, CAN'T WASTE TIME ARGUING!

STOP HIM!
KKRAMM!
OH, HELLO WEBSTER. HAVEN'T SEEN YOU IN A DOG'S AGE. CARE TO EXPLAIN WHAT YOU'RE DOING TO CAUSE ALL THIS COMMOTION?

IN THE PRESIDENT'S OFFICE...

I'VE BEEN MONITORING THE SIGNAL. THAT CRAFT IS FROM AN **ALIEN SYSTEM**, MR PRESIDENT – POSITIVE **PROOF** THAT LIFE EXISTS OUTSIDE OUR OWN GALAXY. AND THE ALIENS ARE TRYING TO MAKE **CONTACT**...

SO THE SIGNAL'S NOT JUST NOISE – IT'S ACTUALLY A KIND OF LANGUAGE?

NOT A LANGUAGE OF WORDS, MR PRESIDENT. THE ALIENS USE A SYSTEM OF POLYHARMONIC TONES... SO FAR I'VE BEEN ABLE TO ISOLATE JUST ONE PHRASE; THEY KEEP REPEATING IT, OVER AND OVER...

WELL DON'T KEEP ME IN SUSPENSE, MAN, WHAT IS IT?

"**WE ARE THE FIRST ONES.**" ALL THE TIME THE SAME. "WE ARE THE FIRST ONES."

AND THAT'S WHAT WE'RE GOING TO BE: THE **FIRST** NATION TO CONTACT AN EXTRA-TERRESTIAL LIFE FORM. THINK OF THE GLORY! THE SOV-BLOK WILL GO MAD WITH ENVY!

"WEBSTER – I'M SENDING YOU UP THERE TO TALK TO THOSE CREATURES, WHATEVER THEY ARE. FIND OUT WHAT THEY WANT, THEN SEE IF YOU CAN THEM TO ACCEPT HONORARY U.S. CITIZENSHIP."
THIS SYNTHESIZER PRODUCES TONES SIMILAR TO THOSE USED BY THE ALIENS... THIS ONE MEANS "PEACEFUL GREETINGS", I HOPE...
IT WORKED! THEY'VE OPENED A GAP IN THE ENERGY SHIELD FOR US!
DUDLEY TO CONTROL... I'M ENTERING THE ALIEN VESSEL. THERE ARE FIVE OF THEM. THEY SEEM FRIENDLY, BUT THE SHIP IS DAMAGED AND THE CREATURES LOOK TO BE IN A BAD WAY.
THE LINGUIST SET TO WORK... BUT PROGRESS WAS SLOW.
DUDLEY TO CONTROL... DAY THREE AND THEY'RE STILL AT IT. "WE ARE THE FIRST ONES" THEY KEEP SAYING.
THEY SEEM VERY EXCITED ABOUT THE FACT, BUT IT'S NOT MAKING MY JOB ANY EASIER.
AND THEN...
YOU–MAN... HELP...
YOU – YOU'RE BEGINNING TO UNDERSTAND MY LANGUAGE? I DON'T BELIEVE IT!
BUT THE ALIEN WAS ONLY INTERESTED IN ITS COMRADE...
HIM... DIE... HELP...
THERE'S NOTHING I CAN DO. I'M NOT A DOCTOR, AND I DON'T UNDERSTAND HOW YOUR BODIES WORK!
AND SO...
WHAT DID HE DIE OF?
INJURIES...

LATER... DUDLEY TO CONTROL... THREE MORE OF THE ALIENS HAVE DIED AND THE **LAST** OF THEM LOOKS TO BE ON THE WAY OUT. BUT HE SEEMS DETERMINED TO COMMUNICATE **PROPERLY** BEFORE HE DIES.

YOU JUST MAKE SURE HE **DOES**... OR YOU NEEDN'T BOTHER **COMING BACK**!

FINALLY... FRIEND WEBSTER, MY LIFE DEPARTS. BUT PRAISE THE GODS WE NOW UNDERSTAND EACH OTHER. I AM **THE LAST OF THE FIRST ONES**, WEBSTER, AND THIS IS MY MESSAGE TO YOU...

THE ALIEN DIED AND DUDLEY RETURNED TO EARTH...

HIS NAME WAS KLISS, HIS PEOPLE WERE THE **N'YAN-OLEK**. HE WANTED US TO KNOW THAT WE ARE NOT ALONE IN THE UNIVERSE. THERE ARE **COUNTLESS** CIVILISATIONS OUT THERE...

AMONG THEM ARE THE **DYANS**, THE MOST TECHNOLOGICALLY ADVANCED RACE IN THE UNIVERSE. THE DYANS ATTACKED N'YAN-OLEK, COMPLETELY DESTROYING IT.

KLISS AND HIS FRIENDS WERE THE ONLY SURVIVORS, THOUGH THEY SUSTAINED MORTAL INJURIES.

IT SEEMS THAT DYAN WERE ONCE A PEACEFUL PEOPLE, BUT ARE NOW BENT ON **TOTAL GALACTIC CONQUEST**. NO-ONE CAN STAND IN THEIR WAY!

...AND THAT'S WHAT KLISS HAS BEEN TRYING TO TELL US. **THEY** WERE THE **FIRST ONES** TO FALL TO THE DYAN...

"AND WE'RE NEXT!"

THE END.

THARG'S FUTURE-SHOCKS
FIRST ENCOUNTER
JOIN ME, EARTHLETS, ON THIS HISTORIC OCCASION — AS WE WATCH THE FIRST EVER MANNED EARTH SHIP LAND ON AN INHABITED ALIEN PLANET...
THE INHABITANTS HAVE TURNED OUT TO WELCOME US! LAND ON THAT PATCH OF WASTE-GROUND, PILOT — WE DON'T WANT TO DESTROY ANYTHING...
AND REMEMBER, MEN — DO EXACTLY AS I TELL YOU, THE WHOLE OF EARTH IS WATCHING THIS ON REMOTE-CONTROL VID — I DON'T WANT ANY MUCK-UPS!
UN EARTH
A SHORT WHILE LATER —
I FEEL A RIGHT NERK GRINNING LIKE THIS, SIR.
IT'S NECESSARY, DAVE. — WE MUST SHOW THEM THAT WE'RE FRIENDLY.
WHADDYAKNOW? THEY'RE SMILIN' BACK! WOW! CATCH AN EYEFUL OF THOSE CHOPPERS!
WE COULDN'T HAVE HOPED FOR A BETTER RESPONSE. OKAY — NOW BOW, TO LET THEM KNOW WE RESPECT THEM.
THEY UNDERSTAND US! LOOK — THEY'RE WANTING TO SHAKE HANDS!
PERFECT! THIS IS A GREAT DAY FOR EARTH — A GREAT DAY FOR MAN!
I'M GLAD I GOT GLOVES ON — THEY LOOK REAL SLIMY TO ME!
FASTEN IT, CHARLIE! THIS IS THE PEAK OF ALL MAN'S AMBITIONS — SO KEEP SMILING AND SHAKE HANDS!
THEN EACH ALIEN FIRED A BOLT OF LETHAL ORGANIC ENERGY...
BLASTERS! BUT — EE.EYYAA!
I — I DON'T UNDERSTAND — AAARRGHH!
THE CAPTAIN DIDN'T UNDERSTAND — BUT DO YOU, EARTHLETS? WITH THE AID OF MY SPACE-TIME REVIEWER WE SHALL WATCH THE SCENE AGAIN — AND THIS TIME I, THARG THE LINGUIST, WILL TRANSLATE THE ALIENS' WORDS FOR YOU!

UN EARTH
HERE THEY COME, CHIEF—THE FIRST ALIENS EVER TO VISIT OUR PLANET!
BUT LOOK WHERE THEY'RE LANDING—THEY'RE DESTROYING OUR FOOD-ROCK FIELDS!
A SHORT WHILE LATER—
UGLY CREATURES, AREN'T THEY?
THAT'S ENOUGH, ZXAAX. THIS IS A DELICATE OCCASION —AIEEE! THEY SHOW THEIR TEETH IN THE SIGN OF HATRED!
SNARL BACK AT THEM—SHOW THEM WE'RE NOT AFRAID!
THEY DON'T CARE! SEE—THEY INSULT US! THEY WOULD RATHER LOOK UPON THE GROUND THAN UPON US!
SHOW THEM YOUR FINGER-BLASTERS. THAT'LL MAYBE IMPROVE THEIR MANNERS.
THEY PAY NO HEED! THEIR OWN WEAPONS MUST BE POWERFUL INDEED IF FINGER-BLASTERS DO NOT FRIGHTEN THEM!
IN THE NAME OF NIKKK! THEY'RE AIMING THEIR OWN GUNS AT US!
THEY'RE GOING TO SHOOT! DON'T GIVE THEM THE CHANCE!
EACH ALIEN FIRED A BOLT OF LETHAL ORGANIC ENERGY...
FIRE!
JUST OUR LUCK! WHY COULDN'T OUR FIRST VISITORS FROM OUTER SPACE HAVE BEEN FRIENDLY?
NOW YOU UNDERSTAND WHY THE EARTHMEN WERE ATTACKED, EARTHLETS. THINGS ARE NOT ALWAYS WHAT THEY SEEM, WHETHER ON EARTH OR IN THE DEEP RECESSES OF SPACE. SO, BE ON YOUR GUARD THE NEXT TIME SOMEONE SMILES AT YOU!
SCRIPT: O.A.STEPANIUK. ART: A.CRADDOCK. LETTERING: S.RICHARDS.

THARG'S FUTURE-SHOCKS
"NO MATTER WHAT ELSE MAY CHANGE IN THE FUTURE, ONE THING WILL ALWAYS REMAIN THE SAME... THE HUNGER OF EARTHLET CHILDREN FOR EXCITEMENT!"

THE LAST JUNGLE IN THE WORLD

FAAAN-TAAASTIC! HEROES REALLY WERE HEROES IN THE OLD DAYS, ROB-N!
HUH! TARZAN'S NOTHING SPECIAL! ANY KID OF TODAY COULD MAKE OUT IN THE JUNGLE JUST AS WELL! I BET I COULD!
VICTORIA VID PALACE
OLD MOVIE SPECIAL
TARZAN of the APES

BOASTING'S EASY, BIG-HEAD! I BET YOU A WEEK'S POCKET-CRED THAT YOU COULDN'T DO IT!
WHAT-SURVIVE IN A JUNGLE? OF COURSE I COULD- IF THERE WERE ANY! JUNGLES AND WILD ANIMALS DIED OUT DECADES AGO!

NOT ALL OF THEM! THERE'S STILL ONE PLACE YOU COULD PROVE IT...
SEE: LIONS! APES! RHINOS!
SAVAGE! UNTAMED! DANGEROUS! INSURANCE POLICIES ON SALE HERE
ENTRY AHEAD-5 CREDITS
ONLY REMAINING TRUE JUNGLE- COMPLETE WITH ANIMALS ENTRY CHEAP AT 5 CREDITS
...THE LAST JUNGLE IN THE WORLD!

SO THE BET WAS ON!
RIGHT-YOU'VE GOT TO STAY INSIDE ALL NIGHT! BUT BE CAREFUL, ROB-N... IT COULD BE DANGEROUS!
THERE'S NOTHING IN THERE A 22nd CENTURY KID CAN'T HANDLE! MEET ME HERE IN THE MORNING WITH THE MONEY YOU'LL OWE ME!
LAST TOUR STARTING NOW, CITIZENS! OPEN AGAIN TOMORROW!

SOON-
TIME UP NOW, CITIZENS- SYNTHI-SUNDOWN IN TEN MINUTES!
I LOOK LIKE JUST ANOTHER ROCK UNDER MY ANTI-WEATHER CAPE! EVEN TARZAN COULDN'T HAVE CAMOUFLAGED HIMSELF BETTER!
2000 A.D. Credit Card:
SCRIPT ROBOT STACCATO
ART ROBOT N. NEOCLEOUS
LETTERING ROBOT PETE KNIGHT
COMPU-73E

EVERYONE'S GONE NOW - IT'S JUST ME AND THE JUNGLE! I'LL HEAD UP STREAM - THE WATER WILL HIDE MY TRAIL, LIKE IN THE TARZAN MOVIE!
AIIIEERGGHH! PIRANHA FISH - EATING MY LEGS!

GOT TO BREAK... AUTO-ALARM ON MY... WALLET! SHORT-CIRCUIT ALARM BATTERY IN WATER... STUN PIRANHA!
ZZZZZZT!

THANK GOD - IT WORKED! GOOD JOB DAD GAVE ME THE WALLET FOR MY BIRTHDAY!
... THERE'S SOMETHING STRANGE ABOUT THOSE FISH, THOUGH. I'D LIKE TO SEE ONE CLOSE UP...

THE OTHERS WILL EAT ME ALIVE IF I GO BACK IN THE WATER! BUT I CAN SWING DOWN FROM ONE OF THESE VINES AND SCOOP UP A STUNNED FISH!

BUT-
SSSSSS!
AAUUUHHH! VINE'S REALLY... A PYTHON! S-SQUEEZING ME TO DEATH! GOT TO REACH MY POCKET... ELECTRO-KNIFE!

GOT IT! NO SNAKE'S A MATCH FOR A TITANIUM-COATED BLADE!

ROB-N DROPPED TO THE GROUND...
OOOOFF! I BET EVEN TARZAN COULDN'T HAVE MADE AN ESCAPE LIKE THAT ONE! BUT I HAVEN'T GOT MY FISH YET...

STILL, MAYBE THIS SNAKE WILL TELL ME IF MY SUSPICIONS ARE-WHAT THE-? A LION!
RRROOOWWRR!

ONLY ONE CHANCE-GOT TO ADJUST BEAM OF MY LASER PEN! MAKE IT GIVE A SHORT BURST AT MAXIMUM INTENSITY...

...AND BURN THE BRUTE! GOT IT! BUT IT'S NOT DEAD....

SUDDENLY-
AWWWOOWAAAOOAA!
IT-IT CAN'T BE! TARZAN!

JUNGLE DANGEROUS PLACE! NO GOOD FOR CITY-BOY TO COME HERE! TARZAN SAVE CITY-BOY!
HEY-PUT ME DOWN! WAIT! THAT LION I SHOT-IT WASN'T REAL! IT WAS A ROBOT!

AND THE PIRANHA-AND PYTHON! I KNEW THERE WAS SOMETHING FUNNY ABOUT THEM! THEY WERE ROBOTS, TOO!
WHAT A FRAUD! THE OWNERS RAKE IN A FORTUNE FROM CITIZENS WHO PAY TO SEE REAL LIVE WILD ANIMALS... BUT THE WHOLE PLACE IS ROBOTIC!

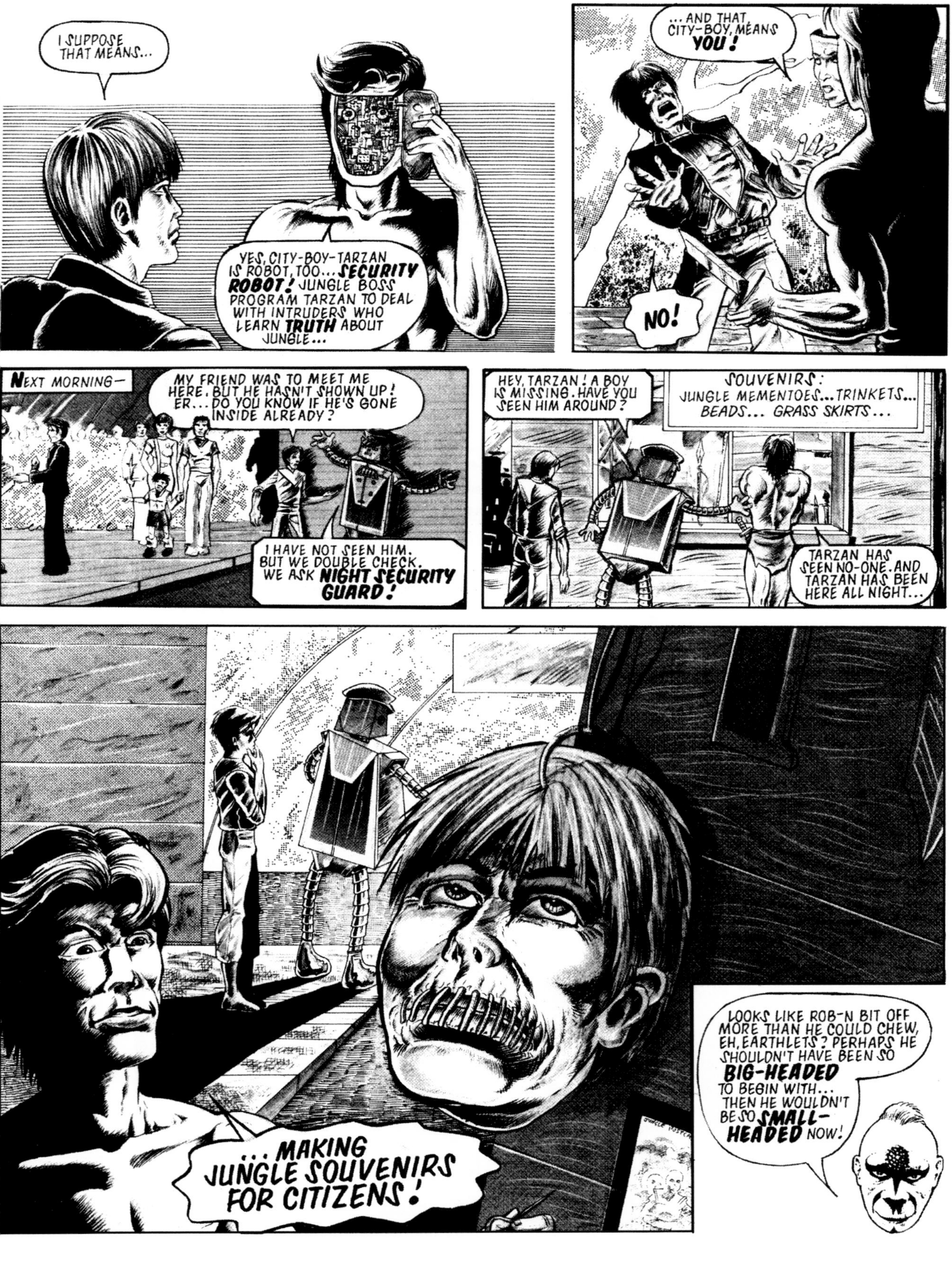

...MAKING JUNGLE SOUVENIRS FOR CITIZENS!

LOOKS LIKE ROB-N BIT OFF MORE THAN HE COULD CHEW, EH, EARTHLETS? PERHAPS HE SHOULDN'T HAVE BEEN SO **BIG-HEADED** TO BEGIN WITH... THEN HE WOULDN'T BE SO **SMALL-HEADED** NOW!

GALACTIC GREETINGS, EARTHLETS! I, THARG, DID NOT MEAN TO INTRUDE UPON STARLORD'S ANNUAL, FOR I KNOW THAT HE HAS MANY EXCELLENT STORIES HIMSELF. STILL, AS I WAS PASSING THROUGH THERE CAN BE NO HARM IN TELLING YOU ONE OF MY FUTURE SHOCK STORIES.
A PRISON CAN BE OF MANY SORTS. IT NEED NOT BE CELL WALLS. OUR MOVEMENT THROUGH SPACE AND TIME IS LIMITED, AND IN A SENSE WE ARE PRISONERS OF THESE RESTRICTIONS. MASTER ESCAPIST, PETE OMEGA, THOUGHT HE COULD BREAK FREE FROM ALL SHACKLES... BUT SEE WHAT HAPPENS TO HIM!
The PRISONER of XENDOR
TOP CRIMINAL PETE OMEGA HAS ESCAPED FROM SPACE-FED JAILS MORE OFTEN THAN I'VE HAD BETELGEUSIAN BEANS! BUT NOW THE FEDS HAVE CAUGHT HIM AGAIN — AND THIS TIME THEY'RE TAKING NO CHANCES!
FREEZIN' HIM IN PLASTEEN AIN'T VERY HUMANE — BUT IT'S THE ONLY WAY WE COULD GET HIM TO JAIL WITHOUT HIM ESCAPIN'!
STILL RECKON IT'LL BE HARD TO KEEP HIM INSIDE!
LEMME OUTTA HERE, YOU DORKS —
I'M SUFFOCATING!

PETE WAS TAKEN STRAIGHT TO THE GOVERNOR'S OFFICE.

WELCOME TO SECURITY BLOCK 'A', OMEGA.
WHAT'S THE BIG IDEA – CASING ME IN PLASTEEN? I CAN HARDLY MOVE IN HERE!
THAT'S THE IDEA, OMEGA! THE GOVERNOR KNOWS YOUR REPUTATION – BUT YOU'RE NOT GOING TO ESCAPE FROM THIS JAIL!

KEEP HIM COVERED, OFFICER! LOOK, OMEGA – EVERY PRISONER'S MOVEMENTS ARE MONITORED ROUND THE CLOCK! WE WATCH EVERYTHING THEY DO ON THESE SCREENS!
I'LL TELL YOU ONE THING – THIS PLACE SURE HAS THE SAME ROTTEN STINK AS EVERY OTHER JAIL I BEEN IN!

"OUTSIDE, WE HAVE GUNS, ROBO-HOUND PATROLS – AND A HIGH-VOLTAGE ELECTRO-MESH DOME!"
"NOT EVEN A BUG COULD GET THROUGH THAT UNDETECTED!"

THERE IS NO ESCAPE FROM HERE, OMEGA! BUT WE DO HAVE A HUMANE WAY OF SHORTENING YOUR STAY WITH US.
TIME CHAIR VIEW PANEL
THE COST OF KEEPING SCUM LIKE YOU IN PRISON IS ASTRONOMICAL, YET WE ARE BOUND TO SEE THAT YOUR SENTENCE IS FULLY SERVED.
WE CAN'T ALTER THE FACT THAT YOU HAVE TO SPEND A CERTAIN NUMBER OF YEARS OF YOUR LIFE IN HERE, BUT WE CAN ALTER THE SPEED AT WHICH THOSE YEARS PASS!
HUHHH? WHAT DO YOU MEAN?

"OBSERVE THE YOUTH SITTING IN *THE TIME CHAIR*. . ."
DO YOU WISH TO PROCEED ?
YEAH, JUST GET IT OVER.
PROPERTY OF PRISON

"...THIS YOUTH COMMITTED GRAND ARSON – HE'S BEEN SENTENCED TO *FIFTY YEARS!* WATCH CLOSELY, OMEGA..."
I'M *GLAD* I CHOSE THE CHAIR – *GLAD!* PRISON LIFE WAS DRIVING ME C–
CCRRRAAZZZyy...

"...HE HAS *AGED FIFTY YEARS IN SECONDS!* ..."
PROPERTY OF PRISON
AM GLOGG... GLAGG! BULUUB...
"...HIS SENTENCE HAS PASSED!"

LATER, IN OMEGA'S CELL...
POOR KID! AND I GOT A *TWO HUNDRED YEARS STRETCH* TO DO – THE TIME CHAIR WOULD ***KILL*** ME! BUT I CAN'T STAY COOPED UP HERE WITH THAT ***JAIL SMELL*** FOR THE REST OF MY DAYS!

I'VE GOT TO GET OUT OF HERE! SOMEHOW, ***I'VE GOT TO GET OUT!***

*BUT AS THE WEEKS PASSED, PETE MADE **NO ATTEMPT** AT ESCAPE...*
SPACE TRAVEL
PROPERTY OF
HE READ A LOT, SAT IN HIS CELL ON HIS OWN A LOT, BUT HE WAS STILL THERE.
ELECTRONICS
PROTON ENGINES

EVEN THE GUARDS WATCHING HIS EVERY MOVE WERE SURPRISED – EVEN DISAPPOINTED –
LOOKS LIKE OMEGA AIN'T *THE GREAT HOUDINI* AFTER ALL! HE JUST SITS READING BOOKS ABOUT ROCKETS ALL DAY.
I RECKON HE'S STARTING TO *CRACK UP* – LIKE THEY ALL DO IN THIS PLACE! I BET YOU TEN CREDITS HE DECIDES TO TAKE ***THE CHAIR!***

AND SOON...
HEE-HEE-HEE-STINKING, SMELLY SWILL!
LOOK AT THE WAY HE'S OGLING THAT SWILL — JUST LIKE A HUNGRY KID! AND WHAT'S WITH THESE *CRUMMY DRAWINGS* ALL OVER THE WALL?
THE BET'S AS GOOD AS WON, MATE — THEY ***ALWAYS*** ASK FOR THE CHAIR WHEN THEY GET AS BAD AS *THIS*!
MOBILE

...A SPACE-TIME CHAIR!

AND I ALSO LEARNED THERE'S A *LIFE-SUPPORTIN'* PLANET CALLED **XENDOR** DUE AT THESE CO-ORDINATES IN *20 YEARS' TIME*– AND **THAT'S** WHERE I'M HEADING!
PROPERTY OF PRISON
SO LONG, DORKS!
IT WAS AS IF SOMEONE HAD **SWITCHED OFF** EARTH IN THE YEAR 2134... AND **SWITCHED ON** THE PLANET XENDOR, 20 YEARS LATER!
OOOFFF! I'M STILL IN ONE PIECE!
PROPERTY OF

THOSE BUILDINGS – THERE'S LIFE HERE, BUT WHAT'S THAT **PUTRID STENCH**?

PETE'S LANDING HAD NOT GONE UNOBSERVED –
THAT SMELL IS **ATROCIOUS**! **A HUNDRED TIMES** WORSE THAN THE JAIL! I'VE GOT TO GET AWAY FROM IT!

⁝COUGH⁝ IS-IS THERE A *SPACEPORT* ROUND HERE, FELLAS? I – *UH* – I GOTTA GET OFF THIS PLANET **REAL FAST**!

WHERE HAVE **YOU** COME FROM, STRANGER? SURELY YOU KNOW **NO ONE EVER LEAVES XENDOR**?

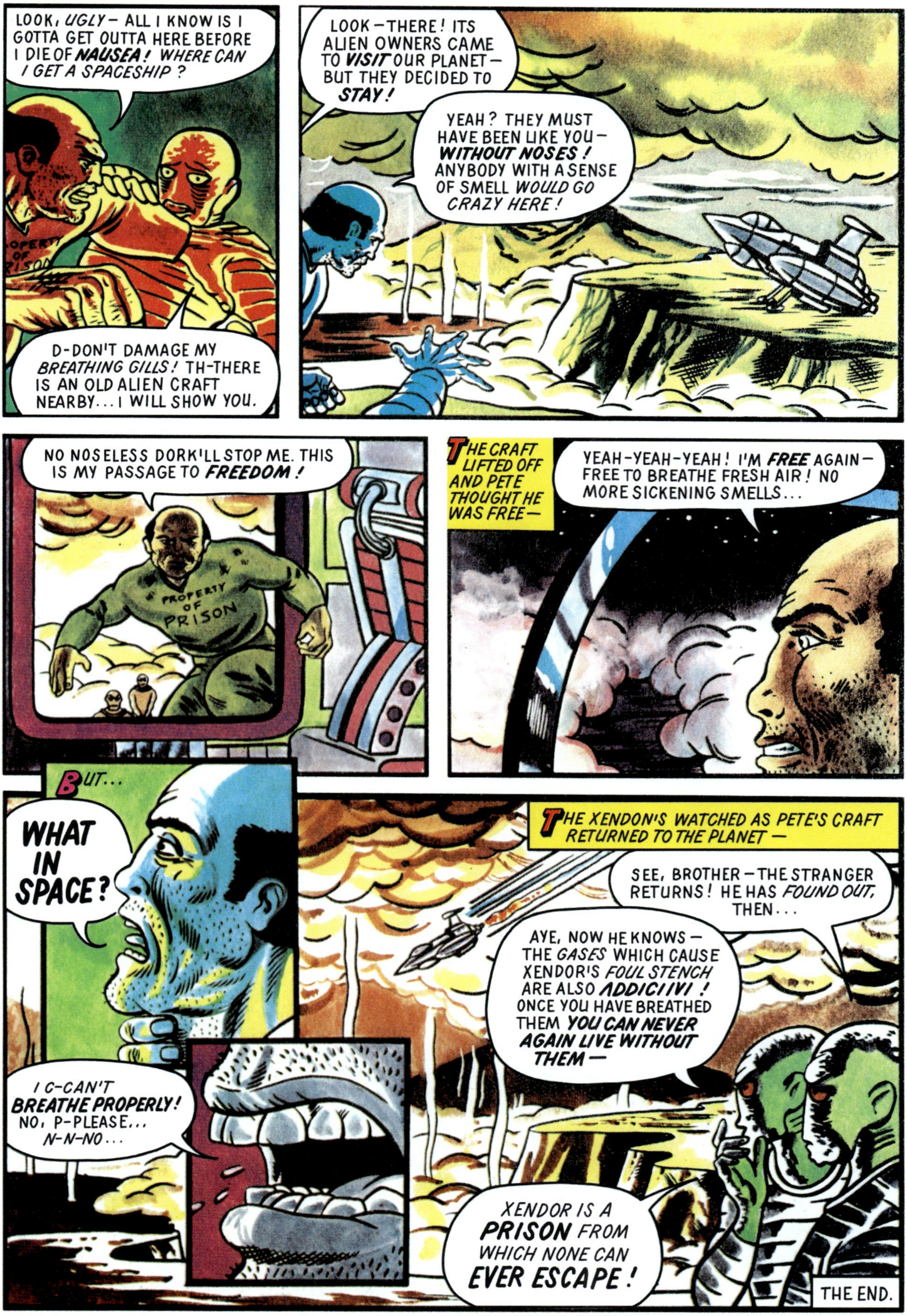

NO NOSELESS DORK'LL STOP ME. THIS IS MY PASSAGE TO FREEDOM!
PROPERTY OF PRISON
THE CRAFT LIFTED OFF AND PETE THOUGHT HE WAS FREE —
YEAH-YEAH-YEAH! I'M FREE AGAIN — FREE TO BREATHE FRESH AIR! NO MORE SICKENING SMELLS...
BUT...
WHAT IN SPACE?
I C-CAN'T BREATHE PROPERLY! NO, P-PLEASE... N-N-NO...
THE XENDON'S WATCHED AS PETE'S CRAFT RETURNED TO THE PLANET —
SEE, BROTHER — THE STRANGER RETURNS! HE HAS FOUND OUT, THEN...
AYE, NOW HE KNOWS — THE GASES WHICH CAUSE XENDOR'S FOUL STENCH ARE ALSO ADDICIIVI! ONCE YOU HAVE BREATHED THEM YOU CAN NEVER AGAIN LIVE WITHOUT THEM —
XENDOR IS A PRISON FROM WHICH NONE CAN EVER ESCAPE!
THE END.

THE EXTERMINATOR
FOR ONE YEAR, THE FREIGHTER "ZARGON" HAD BEEN ON THE PLANET KNOWN AS XK-17. SMALL AND UNINHABITED, ITS ONLY VALUE WAS THE RICH STREAM OF GOLD THAT HAD BEEN FOUND, CLOSE TO ITS EQUATOR. NOW, WITH MILLIONS OF POUNDS OF GOLD ORE ABOARD, FINAL PREPARATIONS WERE BEING MADE FOR TAKE-OFF...
BLAST-OFF IN TEN SECONDS....
NEXT STOP... EARTH!
LEACH
NUMBER FOUR ENGINE IS SLIGHTLY DOWN ON POWER...
THE OTHER THREE HAVE ALREADY CORRECTED. NO PROBLEM!

THAT'S IT, THEN. A SUCCESSFUL TAKE-OFF AFTER A SUCCESSFUL MINING EXPEDITION.

WE WERE THERE FOR A YEAR AND NOTHING NASTY HAPPENED TO US... *YOU'VE* BEEN READING TOO MANY SPACE STORIES!

JUST THINK OF YOUR SHARE OF THE PROFITS FROM THIS TRIP... THAT WILL MAKE XK-17 SEEM REAL FRIENDLY!

MAYBE SO... BUT I'M GLAD TO SEE THE LAST OF XK-17. THERE WAS SOMETHING EVIL ABOUT THAT PLANET...

NO-ONE WOULD HAVE BEEN HAPPY IF THEY COULD HAVE SEEN WHAT THEY HAD TAKEN ABOARD WITH THEIR CARGO OF ORE...

SAMPLE: 7B GGK: 1

FOR A WEEK NOTHING HAPPENED. AND THEN...

THREE DAYS LATER...
AT LEAST WE CAN RELAX NOW, EVEN IF WE ARE SHUT IN THIS OLD TUB FOR A LITTLE LONGER.
I'VE PROGRAMMED THE COMPUTER RIGHT THROUGH TO THE LANDING. THERE'S NO MORE WORK FOR US TO DO AT ALL!

A FEW MORE YEARS AND WE'LL BE REDUNDANT!
...PERHAPS THAT WON'T BE SUCH A BAD THING. I...
HEY! ON THE WALL BEHIND YOU! ***SOMETHING'S MOVING!***

THE SMALL CREATURE WAS TAKEN FROM THE WALL WITH THE AID OF A PAIR OF TWEEZERS.

INCREDIBLE! THAT DIDN'T ORIGINATE ON EARTH! I'VE NEVER SEEN ANYTHING LIKE IT BEFORE!

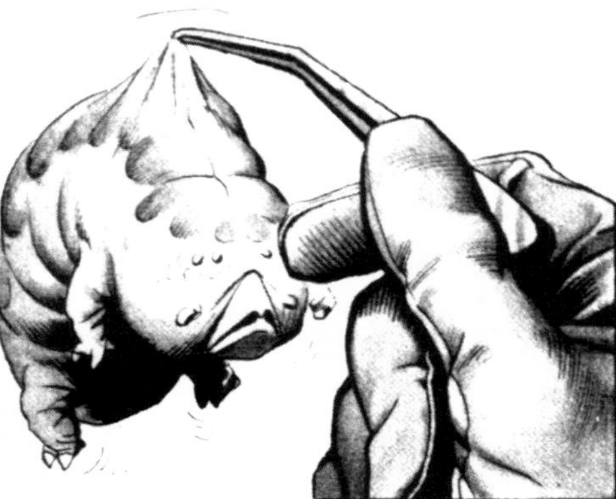

WHERE THE HECK DID THAT COME FROM? THE PLANET WAS SUPPOSED TO BE WITH-OUT ANY LIFE AT ALL...
WE'D BETTER KILL IT...
NO! IT'S TOO SMALL TO DO ANY HARM. LET'S KEEP IT AS A PET, FOR A WHILE AT LEAST.
AND SO...
IT'S A SWEET LITTLE THING! THE SCIENTISTS BACK HOME WILL LOVE FINDING OUT WHAT IT IS AND WHERE IT CAME FROM!
NIGHT, NIGHT, LITTLE CREATURE!
BUT WHILE THE CREW SLEPT, THE ALIEN CREATURE BEGAN TO GROW... AT AN ALARMING RATE!
AND WHEN THE GIRL RETURNED, EIGHT HOURS LATER...
NOW LET'S SEE HOW... UUUURGH! WH-WHAT HAPPENED?
A SOUND MADE HER LOOK UP... AND A CRY OF TERROR FILLED THE ROOM.
AAAARRR
N-NO! N-O-O-O!

IT WAS ALL OVER VERY QUICKLY! ALL THAT WAS LEFT WAS HER BOOT!

ONE MEMBER OF THE CREW DID NOT EVEN KNOW WHAT ATE HIM!

ONLY THE LEADER OFFERED ANY RESISTANCE...

MY BLASTER DOESN'T HAVE ANY EFFECT. K-K-KEEP AWAY!

THE LAST HUMAN DISAPPEARED AS QUICKLY AS THE OTHERS!

EEEAAAH

ONE MONTH LATER, SPACE FREIGHTER "ZARGON" MADE A ROUTINE LANDING ON EARTH...

AND THEN, AS IF IT HAD BEEN WAITING FOR THAT MOMENT...
HUH? L-LOOK AT THE CREW'S QUARTERS... TH-THEY'RE SPLITTING OPEN!

S-SOMETHING'S COMING OUT! LOOK AT THE SIZE OF IT!

IT... IT'S A SPACE MONSTER!
RUN, RUN! IT'LL EAT US ALL!

WITHIN AN HOUR, EMERGENCY MEETINGS WERE BEING HELD...
GENTLEMEN, THE SITUATION IS SERIOUS. ALREADY THAT... THAT CREATURE HAS EATEN SIX TOWNSFOLK. IT'S GOT TO BE STOPPED!
MY TANKS ARE MOVING IN TO BLAST IT RIGHT NOW, MISTER MAYOR!
JETS ARE TAKING OFF...

I DON'T CARE WHAT YOU DO... BUT DESTROY IT. ANY WAY, ANY WHERE! JUST KILL IT!

...JUST KILL IT... UUUAARGH!

THE TANKS WERE FIRST TO OPEN FIRE...
OUR SHELLS ARE HAVING NO EFFECT...

THEN THE JETS WENT IN...
AGAIN, WITHOUT CAUSING ANY DAMAGE...
NEGATIVE DAMAGE DESTRUCTION. RETURNING TO BASE!
THERE IS ONLY ONE THING TO BE DONE... A NUCLEAR EXPLOSION. A DIRECT HIT WITH A MULTI-MEGATON WEAPON WILL DESTROY ANYTHING!
B-BUT WE'LL WRECK HALF THE COUNTRY AT THE SAME TIME! THE FALL-OUT WOULD BE TREMENDOUS...
THERE IS ANOTHER WAY...
...CONSULT THE EXTERMINATOR! HIS RECORD AT TACKLING ALIEN MENACES IS UNBEATABLE. HE'LL KNOW WHAT TO DO! I'LL SEND FOR HIM IMMEDIATELY!
AND SO...
GENTLEMEN, YOU ALMOST LEFT IT TOO LATE! I SHALL RID YOU OF THIS FOUL CREATURE! MY FEE WILL BE TWENTY MILLION CREDITS.

WHAT WILL YOU DO... DYNAMITE IT? ATOMIC BOMB IT?
BURN IT?
FREEZE IT? DROWN IT?
NONE OF THOSE THINGS... I SHALL FEED IT!
FIVE MILES AHEAD OF THIS POINT, I WANT A GREAT WALL OF FOOD SET UP. EMPTY EVERY SUPERSTORE WITHIN TWENTY MILES OF HERE. EVERY FREEZER CENTRE. I WANT THE BIGGEST PILE OF FOOD IN THE HISTORY OF THE WORLD!
THE GOVERNMENT GAVE FULL PRIORITY TO THE ORDER...
MOVE FASTER. THE CREATURE IS ALMOST HERE...
AND SOON...
IT STARTS TO EAT!
SIX HOURS LATER...
MORE FOOD! BRING MORE FOOD!

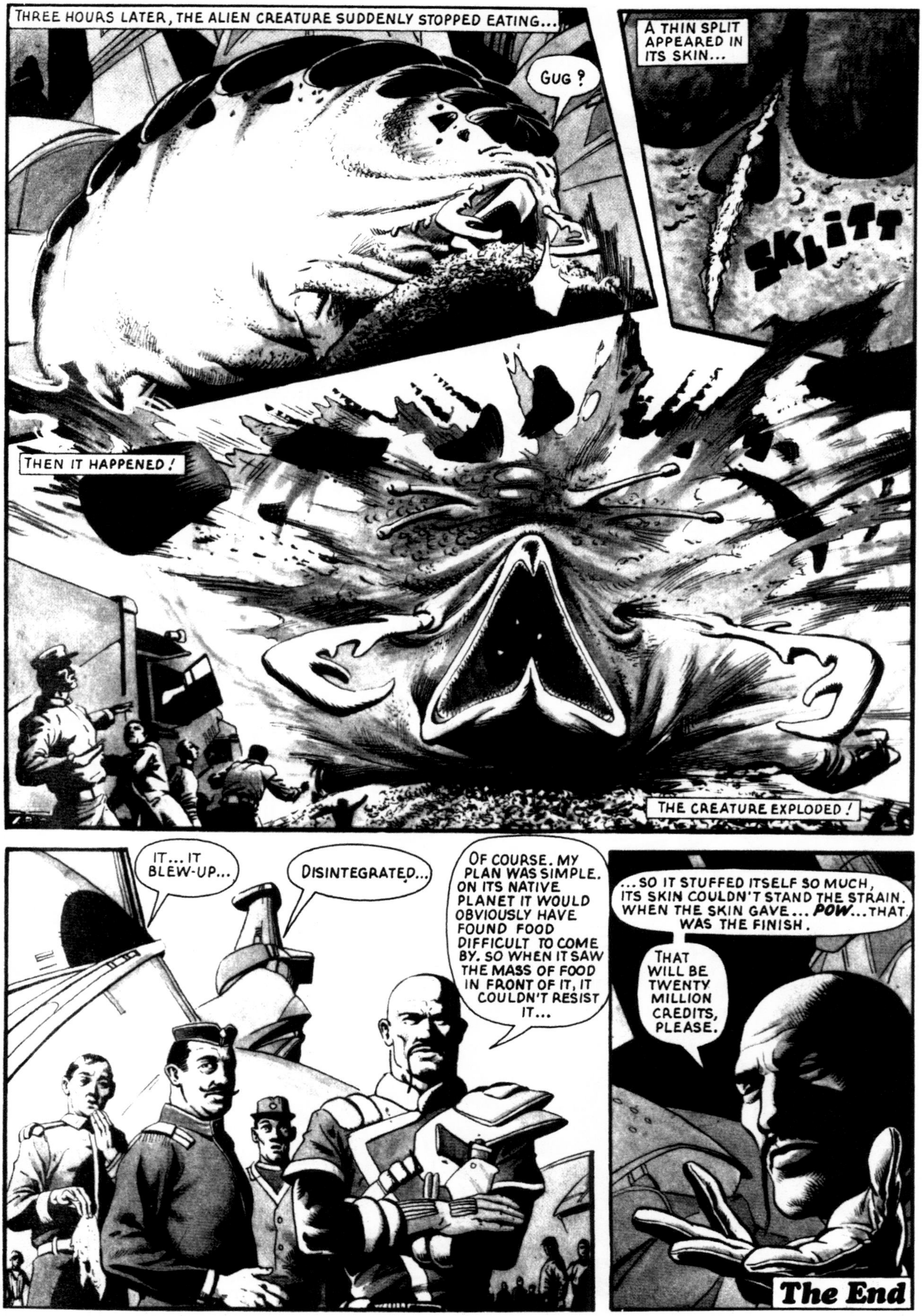

THREE HOURS LATER, THE ALIEN CREATURE SUDDENLY STOPPED EATING...
GUG?
A THIN SPLIT APPEARED IN ITS SKIN...
SKLITT
THEN IT HAPPENED!
THE CREATURE EXPLODED!

3000 AD the traveller
3,000 A.D. THE WORLD IS TORN BY WAR. CHAOS REIGNS – BUT MIDST ALL THE CONFLICT, SOME MEN TRY TO KEEP THEIR NORMAL LIVES TOGETHER. ONE SUCH MAN WE SHALL CALL... THE TRAVELLER...
I TOOK NO CHANCES AS I LEFT THE ROOM. IF ANYONE HAD BEEN WAITING FOR ME OUTSIDE THE DOOR... HE WASN'T WAITING NOW!
THE NEXT PROBLEM WAS GETTING DOWNSTAIRS. I'D BEEN CAUGHT LIKE THIS BEFORE, SO I LOBBED DOWN A COUPLE OF GAS GRENADES, THEN WENT DOWN ON MY BOOT JETS.

BACK OFF, LAUGHING BOY. I'M WARNING YOU...
AAAH!
OKAY, HAVE IT YOUR WAY, PAL!
THAT WAS MY FIRST MISTAKE, AND NEARLY MY LAST. ONE OF THEM HAD BEEN WAITING ON THE GROUND FLOOR AND CAME AT ME WITH A SLIVERING ROD. FOR A SECOND I WONDERED HOW HE'D MISSED THE GAS— THEN HE WAS ON ME...
WITH MY REAR SECURE, I HEADED FOR THE MAIN GATE. I NEVER DID LIKE DOORS, 'COS YOU CAN NEVER TELL WHAT'S LURKING ON THE OTHER SIDE. I DECIDED TO PLAY IT SAFE AND TRY A WINDOW!
I STAYED LOW AS I HIT THE STREET — IT WAS ALWAYS A DANGEROUS POINT. FOR A SECOND ALL WAS QUIET, THEN SUDDENLY...
MINI-NUKES! COMIN' FROM THE ROOF!
I GET MY MULTI-ROLE COMBAT BLASTER FOR ELECTRICAL DISCHARGE.
EAT VOLTS, SCUM! UH! TOO MANY OF 'EM! I GOT TO GET OUT!

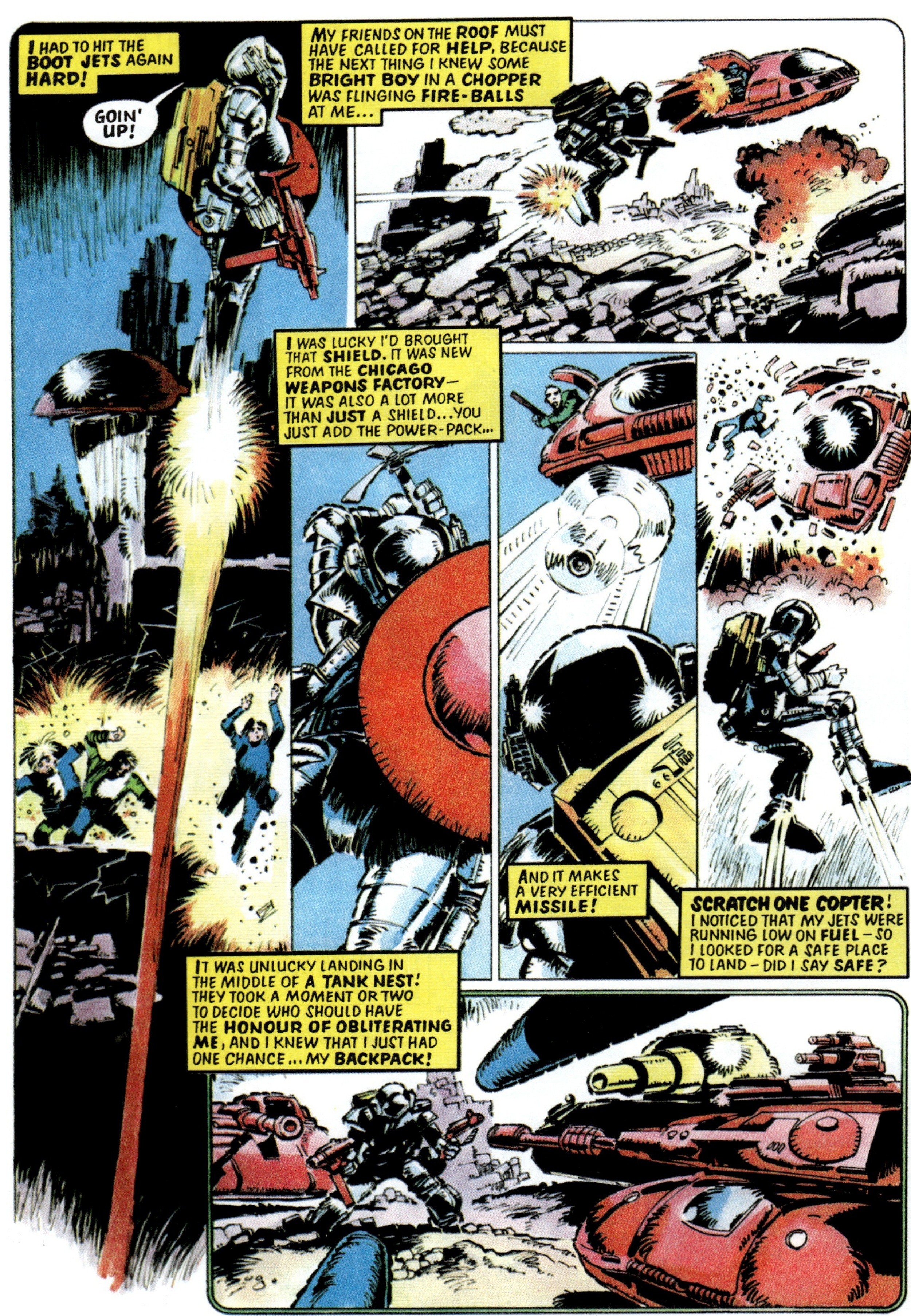
I HAD TO HIT THE BOOT JETS AGAIN HARD!
GOIN' UP!
MY FRIENDS ON THE ROOF MUST HAVE CALLED FOR HELP, BECAUSE THE NEXT THING I KNEW SOME BRIGHT BOY IN A CHOPPER WAS FLINGING FIRE-BALLS AT ME...
I WAS LUCKY I'D BROUGHT THAT SHIELD. IT WAS NEW FROM THE CHICAGO WEAPONS FACTORY– IT WAS ALSO A LOT MORE THAN JUST A SHIELD...YOU JUST ADD THE POWER-PACK...
AND IT MAKES A VERY EFFICIENT MISSILE!
SCRATCH ONE COPTER! I NOTICED THAT MY JETS WERE RUNNING LOW ON FUEL – SO I LOOKED FOR A SAFE PLACE TO LAND – DID I SAY SAFE?
IT WAS UNLUCKY LANDING IN THE MIDDLE OF A TANK NEST! THEY TOOK A MOMENT OR TWO TO DECIDE WHO SHOULD HAVE THE HONOUR OF OBLITERATING ME, AND I KNEW THAT I JUST HAD ONE CHANCE... MY BACKPACK!

THEY TOOK A LITTLE BIT TOO LONG TO MAKE UP THEIR MINDS. AS I CLIMBED UP ONTO MY BACKPACK I THOUGHT OF HOME AND MY LOVED ONES WAITING FOR ME.
THE ONLY THING I DID NOT TELL THEM, AS I HIT THE PACK'S NUCLEAR SPRING-BOARD WAS THAT THERE WAS SOMETHING ELSE IN MY PACK—SOMETHING I HAD TRIGGERED JUST BEFORE I TOOK OFF!
A NUCLEAR BOMB!
THE LAST OF MY FUEL GOT ME BACK TO HOME BASE. I COULD SEE HER STANDING OUTSIDE WAITING FOR ME.
WELL, DARLING, HOW WAS YOUR DAY AT THE OFFICE?
OH, THE ACCOUNTS SECTION IS FINE!
BUT THESE JOURNEYS HOME—THEY'RE GETTING TO BE MURDER...
THE END

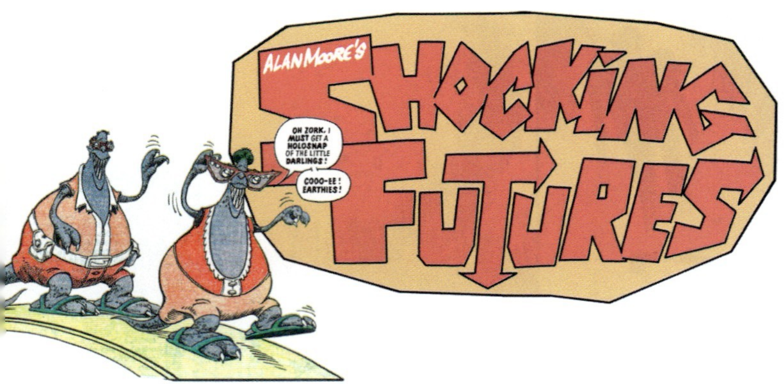

IT'S A FUNNY OLD WORLD. These days, as a colossus bestriding the industry, I can have my work presented in more or less any format I like, see it illuminated by colours plucked fresh and dripping from the opium-racked visions of a Coleridge or De Quincy and have the whole thing printed on paper specially hand-made by a quintet of blind Trappist nuns from Tuscany. This notwithstanding, however, I continue to regard the two years or so that I spent working on stunted little five-page short stories destined to be printed in black and white upon Izal two-ply lavatory paper as one of the most educational and creatively rewarding times of my career thus far.

I realise that, to any upcoming scriptwriter currently wrestling with the often maddening demands of fitting an intergalactic war into thirty panels, this attitude might seem reminiscent of a retired army major waxing nostalgic about the birchings and cold showers of his boyhood, but sometimes there really isn't any gain without pain. Taxing as they are, short stories are still the best place for any aspiring writer to learn his or her craft. The first story any budding scriptwriter wants to produce is a nine-hundred part epic, involving all their favourite characters, which they've been working on in the back of their minds ever since they were twelve. Being told at this point to deliver something four pages long – in which all the characters and situations are introduced, explained and resolved entertainingly – is a face full of cold water which, though it might leave you spluttering and gasping, is vitally necessary to your further development.

Anyway, for what it's worth, collected herein are the stories upon which I cut my white, flashing, perfectly even teeth; with all of the inadequacies, clumsiness and plain wrong-headedness left intact for you to snicker at. Despite their innumerable faults, all the stories here have some reason for their inclusion, however personal or however slight it might be. My attempts to remember what these reasons were are listed below.

GRAWKS BEARING GIFTS was an easy choice. Firstly, it wa the first time (Prog 203) I'd worked with the estimable la Gibson. Secondly, it was the first time I'd managed a stor which conveyed its point about cultural subjugation t my own satisfaction while hopefully remaining amusing Thirdly, it contained a lot of terrible racist slurs directed a Australians. I have no defence for this and, in the traditio of Conservative cabinet ministers when asked why the were card-carrying members of the National Front unti three weeks previously, I put it down to the indiscretion of a reckless youth.

THE ENGLISH PHLONDRUTIAN PHRASEBOOK (Prog 214 came out of fascination with phrase-books and th way they give you often ominous clues to a culture in th phrases they contain. I have a Cajun phrase-book, fc example, in which pages and pages seem to be devoted t the discussion of haemorrhoids. Draw your own conclusions

THE LAST RUMBLE OF THE PLATINUM HORDE (Prog 217) While I'd like to claim that it was a bitter and satirica attack upon the mindless brutalities of war, it was real just plain bloody violent, although John Higgins did sterling job in depicting the lighter side of genocide. Th title, I've since discovered, was partially stolen from Norman Spinrad story which, if you can find it, is muc better than this one.

THEY SWEEP THE SPACEWAYS (Prog 219) was a calculate attempted to incite the working class population of thi country to full scale revolution by rubbing their nose in their joblessness. I'd hoped that, spurred on by th indignity of this obviously bogus job offer, some sort o major insurrection might be in the offing. Sadly, this wa not the case, and indeed many readers even applied fo the job, although they lied about their height. My firs coupling with Gary Leach. Is that the right word?

THE REGRETTABLE RUSE OF ROCKET REDGLARE (Prog 234 was an early example of my pathological tendency toward taking old, well-loved characters and then thoroughl debasing them. Comic fans love this kind of thing, believ me. The name Rocket Redglare was a name I'd use onc before in the *Roscoe Moscow* strip in *Sounds* the musi newspaper, and which I shall probably use again because am rather fond of it. The alliterative title of this and man a subsequent story was a tribute to author J.P. Donleavy Oh all right, I stole this one too.

CAUTIONARY FABLE (Prog 240); this was my first ttempt to establish myself as a Hilaire Belloc for the ighties and bears inclusion for that alone, although I'll lways have a soft spot for the eccentric art job that Paul eary turned in here.

N AMERICAN WEREWOLF IN SPACE (Prog 252). Here o, the story is almost a template example of a 1950's merican S.F./Mystery short, but I just like the bristly-houldered look on Paul's werewolves. It's my book and I an do whatever I like.

VAGES OF SIN (Prog 257) a tour de force by Bryan Talbot, vas intended as a follow up to *They Sweep The Spaceways.* s a catalyst for armed revolt it was equally successful, nd is thus responsible for the peaceful and humanitarian ociety that we enjoy today.

HE WILD FRONTIER (Prog 269) was just one of those tupid things you do when you hear that Dave Gibbons vill be drawing a job, so that you can have a chuckle with im over it the next time you run into him at a comic mart. riginally printed in colour, but no funnier for it.

NE CHRISTMAS DURING ETERNITY (Prog 271) was vritten in response to my coming across a futurological rticle which predicted what life on Earth would be ke after the advent of the immortality pill, with the ubsequent reduction in the number of children and so on. sentimental and yet bleak little yarn, I like to think of it s a sort of cross between Frank Capra and Gary Numan.

SUNBURN (Prog 282) was a 'list' story, in which you just think of an absurd topic or situation and then list as many funny or engaging ideas as you can relate to it. That said, it was probably the best story of its type that I wrote, and I still like the gag about Pallor-Parlours.

BAD TIMING (Prog 291) is distinguishable from the Nick Roeg movie of the same name by the fact that nobody attempts a relationship with a dead person in my story. Another from the same stable as *The Regrettable Ruse of Rocket Redglare* in that it's a brutal cripple-kicking attack on concepts too old and enfeebled to put up a struggle.

THE HYPER HISTORIC HEADBANG (Prog 322) was another 'list' story, magically transformed into something better by the artistry of Alan Davis. If I remember correctly, the groan coming from a member of the decimated audience in the last panel was added editorially to imply that the audience were only stunned rather than dead as I'd originally intended. Turn to the story and fill in this balloon with a black marker pen to enjoy the full and unexpurgated version.

LOBELIA LOAM (Prog 323), following on the heels of the tale of Timothy Tate in *A Cautionary Fable*, was another try at endearing myself to the children's market as a loveable Enid Blyton figure. Where am I going wrong?

EUREKA (Prog 325), finally, ranks amongst the best of the later *Future Shocks* (when, I admit, I was starting to run out of steam) largely by virtue of featuring the most abstract and intangible space monsters to figure in **2000 AD**. Also, it's nice to wrap up this volume with a story where everybody ends up happy and smiling.

In closing, I hope you can find a morsel of enjoyment in some of the stories here. Old and creaking though they might be, I'd like to think that most of them deserve to be wheeled out of the home and into the daylight one last time. Thank you for giving me the opportunity to air my shorts.

ALAN MOORE, September 1986.

ALAN MOORE'S
SHOCKING FUTURES
O'NEILL-

THARG THE WELDER!
THE EDITOR STRIKES BACK!
2000 AD
2000 AD
STAR PIN-UP